ENTICING

Did she move first or did he? Her lips were warm, full, moist. She tasted of wine. She placed her hands on his chest and kneaded his skin like a kitten kneads a soft blanket.

He whispered against her mouth, "We shouldn't be doing this." Then he thrust his hands into her hair and held her head while he ran his tongue over hers—again and again.

Each squeeze of his fingers in her silky mane released the scent of flowers—foreign, seductive, enticing flowers.

She ran her hands up and down his chest and made a throaty sound. It jerked him out of the moment.

"Ardra. Damn." He gently set her aside. Her lips were puffy, her eyes dazed. "We *can't* do this."

Then she smiled and touched her fingertips to her mouth. "Do not fret, Lien. It will not happen again."

ANN LAWRENCE

VIRTUAL WARRIOR

LOVE SPELL   *Love Spell*   NEW YORK CITY

To my husband.

LOVE SPELL®

July 2002

Published by

Dorchester Publishing Co., Inc.
276 Fifth Avenue
New York, NY 10001

ISBN 0-505-52492-9

The name "Love Spell" and its logo are trademarks of Dorchester Publishing Co., Inc.

Printed in the United States of America.

Visit us on the web at www.dorchesterpub.com.

VIRTUAL WARRIOR

What shall be the maiden's fate?
Who shall be the maiden's mate?

The Lay of the Last Minstrel
Sir Walter Scott (1805)

Chapter One

Stars moved through a midnight sky. Planets converged, bowed to one another, and continued on in their timeless journey. A small green figure resembling a zucchini with arms and legs appeared. A red question mark bobbed over its head.

Neil Scott watched the creature as it hopped about his computer screen, indicating stars and planets with a pointed finger. Across the bottom of the screen facts about each heavenly body appeared and disappeared.

He punched in another search request, then paused, hands poised over the keyboard. He heard only the rain's gentle beat against the roof and the sounds of the computer processing his request.

The office of Virtual Heaven, his video game shop on the boardwalk in Ocean City, New Jersey, was chilly and dark except for the glow from his computer. The clock on the monitor said 7:12 p.m.

"What are you doing here so late?" he asked without looking up.

"Damn. How'd you know it was me?" asked Gwen Marlowe, his partner in the shop. "I was really quiet."

1

Ann Lawrence

Neil swiveled around to face her. She was a black silhouette against the shop lights behind her. "You smell like roses."

She shook her head, flipped the wall switch, flooding the small space with a stark glare. "What are you doing here, Neil? I saw your car out back, but no lights. I figured you were in here—" She frowned. "What's this? *Astronomaniacs?* Isn't that a computer program for kids?"

Neil shrugged. He pulled off his tie and looped it about the neck of the desk lamp, a habit he knew Gwen hated. "The program may be for kids, but it's easy to understand—"

"This is a list of lunar conjunctions." She shoved him over and leaned in to peer at the screen. Her short blond hair was damp from the misty rain outside. She still had on the neat black suit she'd worn to his mother's funeral that afternoon.

"So what?" And so much for distracting her with the tie. He quit the program, rose, and strolled out of the office. Gwen trailed him into the main room of the shop, weaving between aisles of computer and video games.

"So, why would you be interested in conjunctions? Lunar conjunctions in particular?"

"It was stellar conjunctions, and why not?" Neil sealed *Astronomaniacs* in plastic and then tossed it into the used program bin. "Why aren't you home with your husband?"

"Oh, I was, but this is the night my sister tutors Vad. I got tired of hearing Vad's dissertation on why he'll never use Algebra down at the restaurant. If he spent as much time doing the problems as complaining . . . oh, you don't need to hear this. Let's just say he never bickers over his history lessons."

Neil kept her diverted. "So who's baby-sitting little Natalie?"

"When I left, she was in her usual position, curled up in Vad's lap. She's cutting her three-year-old molars, and only Daddy will satisfy her." Gwen tapped Neil's shoulder.

2

"You're not really interested in Vad's education or Natalie's teeth, so what's going on?"

Neil could not help glancing at the poster behind Gwen. It advertised the latest and hottest of virtual reality games—*Tolemac Wars III*. She whirled around, then back to him. "Oh, no. You can't be . . . you wouldn't . . . you aren't thinking about going into the game, are you?"

Gwen reminded him of a wet hen ready to chase a misbehaving rooster. He cleared up the service counter to avoid eye contact. "Why not? You did. Or so you say."

He could almost hear her grit her teeth. "You don't understand. I've told you this before; it's a barbaric world, complete with slavery."

"So I'd have to make sure I went as something other than a slave." Lying across the end of the service counter was the jacket of his suit, a brand-new suit purchased for today's funeral. He never planned to put it on again.

Gwen shook her head. "Please. Don't make me crazy."

"Then butt out." Neil pulled a small box labeled "Salt Water Taffy" from beneath his jacket and shook it. "This is all that's left of my mom's jewelry. Did you know she got rid of the stuff my dad gave her? I never understood that."

"I know you're probably sick of sympathy, but I'm so sorry about your mom. She seemed to be getting it together there for a while."

He nodded and flipped open the box lid. "Yeah. I did a great job, didn't I? Really took care of her."

Without a word, Gwen wrapped her arms about him and gave him a big hug. He stood still for about ten seconds, then broke away.

She frowned at him. "You can't blame yourself for what happened. You quit a fantastic job in New York for her. You put your life on hold to help her."

"Yeah. Much good it did." Suddenly his head ached. "Why don't you go rescue your sister before Vad reverts to warrior mode and trashes his math books?"

3

Ann Lawrence

"Neil. You have to stop beating yourself up. You weren't driving the car, she was."

"Yeah," he said. It was all he seemed able to say today. *Yeah, my mom drove her car into a bridge abutment. Yeah, second time for that trick. Yeah, she's dead this time.*

Gwen examined the collection of jewelry and then slowly arranged all that remained of Neil's mother's life in a neat row. Except for two items, what remained was costly and mostly bought in moments of depression—something to cheer herself up, she'd said.

"This is pretty," Gwen said. She held up a small chain with a cross on it.

"Take it for Natalie," Neil said, glad of the change of subject. "Mom really liked her."

"Thank you." Gwen carefully wiped a tear from her cheek. "What's this?" She held up a glistening object about the size of Natalie's thumbnail—a tiny red rose. "Is this glass?" she asked.

He nodded and took it from her. "My grandfather worked at the glassworks in Millville. He made these earrings for my grandmother. There should be another somewhere." He plucked it from a tangle of necklaces. "I guess I should keep them together." He stirred the pile with his finger until he found a simple chain. He threaded it through the earring shanks and gave the pair to Gwen. "Would you like them?"

"They're lovely, but I couldn't possibly take them. If your grandfather made them, you might want to give them to your own daughter one day." She put all the jewelry into the box.

"No, thanks. The last thing I want is kids. No offense to Natalie, she's a doll, but kids are a huge responsibility. The last thing I want is responsibility—of any sort."

"Neil! You can't think like that." Gwen slapped his hand.

4

He walked over to the game poster. "So what do you think of this newest *Tolemac Wars* game? Really a departure from the norm, isn't it?" *Damn*. He'd brought the conversation right back to where he didn't want to be.

Gwen stood in front of the *Tolemac Wars* poster and tapped her bottom lip with a manicured fingertip. "I can't decide if I like it. I'm used to a warrior as the feature character . . . and this time it's a woman—"

"What about the Unknown? He's a man."

"Yes, but he's so . . . spooky. If you choose to play the Unknown Warrior, you're inside his head when you're playing, you see what he sees, move with him and so on, just like when you choose to be one of the other characters, but you never really know whose side he's on. He's . . ."

Neil couldn't help smiling. "Unknown?"

Gwen didn't smile back. "I don't like him. He could so easily be on the side of evil."

"Sometimes it's good to be bad." He wagged his eyebrows.

"I know you don't really believe that."

"It's a game, Gwen. Check the stats on this game and you'll find that the Unknown is the most selected character to play, and let me tell you, the dozens of *men* who line up to play him are not interested in Refrigerator Girl."

Gwen giggled. "Is that what you call her?"

Unlike the earlier versions of *Tolemac Wars*, which attracted flocks of women because they featured a really ripped guy, this game poster portrayed a woman. She guarded the ice for the Selaw.

The ice was the source of all the hostilities between Tolemac and the Selaw and hence the reason for the many outbreaks of war that kept the game series going.

Everyone wanted the ice and what might lie beyond it—lands with fantastic weapons and great riches.

Gwen claimed she'd described Refrigerator Girl for the game's creator, and Neil knew she was quite proud of that accomplishment. Gwen also claimed that the woman she'd

helped create for the game really existed. The idea was tantalizing.

Neil leaned his back on the counter and folded his arms over his chest. "She looks as cold as her product. And too skinny."

"Yeah, she's a bit thin. I'd kill to be that thin again."

"Again?" Neil stared at Gwen's waistline.

"Shut up." Gwen fisted her hands on her hips. "She's beautiful, though, isn't she? And in real life, not a bit icy."

"In 'real' life. O-o-okay," he said with a grin.

"Yes. In *real* life."

Neil held his hands out palm up. "Okay, she's real and beautiful. Just in a boring way. Sorry."

"I suppose you like your women with . . . ?" She held her hands in front of her chest.

"With a big rack? Sure. I'm as shallow as the next man."

"I don't get why men are so attracted to big breasts."

He shrugged and walked away from the counter to stare out the shop window. Only a few lone souls walked along the Ocean City boardwalk on this misty evening in November. Rain dripped down the large display window, distorting the view, but Neil had it memorized. No matter where he went, he could close his eyes and see the Atlantic Ocean in all its many guises and smell the scents that were only found near the shore.

The wooden boardwalk extended beyond his vision. He could not see the nearby lights of Atlantic City to the north.

It would be 8:03 in another twenty-two minutes. "Why don't you go, Gwen? I'll set everything up for tomorrow and lock up."

"You wouldn't really try to enter the game, would you?"

He saw her anxious face reflected in the shop window. He shrugged. "Maybe one day. Don't worry, I'll leave you the store in case I don't return."

"Stop it, Neil." She grabbed his arm.

He turned to face her. "*You* did it. Or so you claim."

"Accidentally. If you went in, it would be for all the wrong reasons."

His hands felt sweaty. She was going to screw it all up. He forced his face to relax into a smile. "I just need a vacation. Maybe I'll go to Tolemac or maybe . . . Tahoe. Why don't you let me decide what to do with my life?"

She worried it like a dog with a bone. "If you went into the game, I might never know what happened to you!"

"I'll send you a message no matter where I go. Surfing in Maui, rafting on the Colorado, questing in Tolemac. Satisfied? Now let it go, Gwen."

"Yes, but what if something happened, you got sick or hurt or lost or . . ." She counted out the possible perils to his life on her fingers.

"Or killed in a car wreck on the parkway? Anything could happen anywhere, any day." He slapped her purse into her outstretched hands and had to physically restrain himself from checking his watch.

"You're coming home with me. Right now. You need company. I'll make some coffee, and you can explain to my dear husband how you use Algebra in your daily life. Come on."

Neil gave Gwen a hug, then quickly released her. "Forgive me, Gwen. I didn't mean to upset you. I'm just feeling a bit maudlin tonight. Please, just ignore me and go home." When she hesitated, he forced another smile he didn't feel. "Anyway . . . I couldn't lie to your husband. I never use Algebra." Her shoulders relaxed, and he pointed at the shore outside the window. "We're going to have more beach erosion if this storm escalates. If the roads flood, you'll be stuck here all night."

And I'll miss the conjunction.

Then she sighed and nodded. "Okay. But don't stay here too long. Go home. Maybe call that girl who came to the funeral. Eve, right?"

"Yeah. Eve." He'd never call Eve. When he'd needed her most, she'd left him. She couldn't understand how he

7

could trade a place on Wall Street for a place on the Ocean City boardwalk, hadn't really understood the responsibility he felt for his mother. Eve, too, had said he wasn't responsible for her. But both Gwen and Eve were wrong. He had been responsible. And he'd failed the miserable assignment.

He accompanied Gwen to her car and watched her drive off. When her taillights disappeared around the corner, he grabbed his suit jacket and the jewelry box, then ran quickly upstairs to the apartment above the shop. Only thirteen minutes remained.

The apartment was deserted, used only for storage these days. He dumped the contents of a carton labeled *Costumes/Tolemac Wars Ball* out onto a bare mattress and rooted through the costumes.

He rejected the warrior stuff because the leather jerkins left the arms bare. Although he worked out and ran every day, warriors needed arm rings, and those he didn't have. Finally, he found what he was looking for, a linen shirt and a long scarlet robe, heavily embroidered with gold. It was a generic costume denoting a man of wealth, possibly a merchant or craftsman.

"Let's see if you can figure out where I've gone, Gwen," he said aloud as he carefully placed the empty carton so its label faced the door.

In a few moments, Neil had stripped to his shorts. He continued his one-sided conversation. "You'll probably be a bit pissed with me in the morning, but I figure tonight's the night. As they say, it's written in the heavens—virtual heavens, that is."

He slipped the linen tunic over his head. It fell to midcalf and seemed odd with his boxers but would conceal the tattoo on his arm. Next he belted the long scarlet and gold robe about his middle with an old leather belt studded with silver conchas. It was Southwestern, not virtual reality, but so what?

His old hiking boots which he pulled over some ski socks didn't go with the rich robe, but he'd buy more appropriate footgear when he got there.

There. An almost euphoric sensation coursed through him. *There* no one knew him, and no one depended on him.

He poured the box of jewelry into a soft leather pouch which he suspended from his belt. "Sorry for lying, Gwen. Except for the glass earrings, this stuff is all destined for barter. I figure real gold and silver are going to be just as useful a commodity in Tolemac as they are in the good old U S of A."

In case Gwen missed the costume hint, he arranged his suit on the bed with one arm pointing to the window. He took a final look at himself in the mirrored closet doors. His hair was too short, but hair grew. There was nothing he could do about the hole in his earlobe—or his tattoo. He checked his watch. Time to go.

With a deep breath, he headed back down to the shop and into the booth housing the *Tolemac Wars* virtual reality game. It was four free-standing matte black walls surrounding an inner room, also with black walls. The inner room had a wide screen for spectators who wished to watch a player's progress throughout the game. Players wore headsets and lived the experience. It was expensive, heady, and very addictive.

He started the game and consulted his watch. With satisfaction, he heard the nearby crack of thunder. The storm was escalating right on schedule.

As the game warmed up, he felt sweat prickling his neck and back. Despite his subtle and not so subtle questioning, Gwen had only vaguely explained how she'd come and gone from the virtual reality game. Conjunctions were important to the process. So were the designs of the ancient Celts—and a power boost.

The stars were in alignment. Almost. The Celtic design he'd taken care of at Sid's Family Tattoos (Walk-ins Welcome) on the night Eve deserted him.

9

Ann Lawrence

The power, whatever it was, must come from someone or something greater than himself. He didn't *really* believe in any of it, but he didn't believe in anything in his life in Ocean City either.

The hum of the game filled the room. The words *Tolemac Wars III* flashed on the huge white screen before him, filling the purple Tolemac sky like angry clouds. The O in Tolemac was the flaming scarlet sun of the virtual reality world. He felt as if he stood on a mountain, a distant row of jagged peaks straight ahead. They were aglow in a wash of violet, crimson, and gold.

The title turned and twisted, blowing in the wind across the screen over a landscape of mountain meadows and towering pines. As the words twisted, the sun faded and vanished, the O becoming the turquoise of a Tolemac moon. The sky deepened to indigo.

A woman in green appeared by a stand of pines. She was sweetly pretty, reed thin, gliding with elegant grace toward him along the meadow. An uptight librarian dressed for story hour. "Prissy," he said to the screen. "Go tend your ice."

The woman conjured a fire in her hands. She turned in a circle, casting small flames from her fingers. A ring of candles sprang up, surrounding her. The flames lit her face, touched her blond hair with gold. Neil waited for what he knew came next.

She vanished.

The *Tolemac Wars* title shredded apart, leaving only the turquoise moon behind.

Neil took off his wristwatch and set it on the control panel where he could see its face. When he looked up again, three other moons were rising slowly through a sky now filled with stars.

The view shifted, spun, turned.

Terrain sped before him on the screen, taking him deep into a landscape of forest, an ancient night-filled forest, so dense it looked like a maze. Finally, the dizzy kaleidoscope

10

of movement halted and he was back on the mountain meadow, now bathed in the luminous greenish blue of the four moons.

Tapping a few keys with practiced ease, he chose the character he wished to play. *The Unknown*. A man with no face, owing allegiance to no one, taking part in the Tolemac wars if he wanted, fighting for good or for evil if he wished. He could go either way. His choice. Not someone else's.

Thunder reverberated overhead, and Neil smiled his satisfaction.

His watch said 8:03. Lifting the headset, he put it on.

He pressed *play*.

Chapter Two

Ardra separated herself from her escort with orders that the men make camp at the base of Hart Fell before full dark descended, and then walked swiftly through the trees. Above lay the hut of Nilrem, the wiseman. At the sunrising on the morrow, she would seek what wisdom he could offer in her quest. She held little hope of much more than kind words and expressions of sympathy.

Honor and duty required her to make the journey.

She had a long night of waiting ahead. As she moved to higher ground, she quickened her steps. She did not want her party to know she was about to indulge in an ancient ritual, a ritual of the old gods, one practiced by old women.

Her serving women might nod in understanding, but they would also be quick to deny any belief in the ritual. Men would smile and nudge one another with their elbows. But at this time when she most needed help, she would appeal to any god—ancient or otherwise. The folly of her superstitious belief might result in ridicule and contempt, but follow the old way she must.

The ground beneath her feet was cushioned with pine needles, a handful of which she put in her waist pouch

along with her flint and eight small candles. The occasional tiny woodland flower gleamed white in the gathering dusk, filling the air with a soft, hopeful fragrance. She gathered dry twigs as she walked along. A snap made her pause. She listened but heard nothing more. No animals stirred. With a shrug, she moved on.

She came out onto a high meadow, her arms full of dry twigs and branches. Despite the windy conditions, she gathered rocks and built a fire, using the dry pine needles as tinder. It was a small fire, stubborn to light. The eight candles she set out within the ring of stones were even more troublesome.

Fearful the flames might die in the capricious breezes before the sun set, but doing as tradition bade, she rose with a handful of dirt and faced the red orb. It sat on top of a distant mountain. It appeared impaled on the peak, its glow like blood oozing down the steep slopes. She shivered. With great impatience, she waited, eyes on the horizon.

Despite the sun's gleam, the sky was an angry purple, the air heavy with expectation. Low murmurs of thunder came across the far plains. Flickers of lightning traced paths between mountaintops.

When the perfect moment came—the moment when the sun was just ready to set—she held her dirt-filled fist over the struggling flames and slowly sifted the dust from her palm. The fire died. Next, she walked around the ring of stones eight times. With each round, she sifted dirt, extinguishing one candle in each circuit.

Breath tight in her chest, she then turned her face to the heavens and awaited the coming of the conjunction—the first in fifty such conjunctions—when all four moons would rise together. The ancients had believed it was an augury—of what, she knew not.

They came. The first of the four moons, blue-green, smaller than the sun, but magnificent in color, cast a green glow into the heavens to mingle its cool color with the purple and red.

The rest of the moons rose. Legend said they were sisters, holding hands to kneel before their mother, the sun. They brought a blessing, some ancient prophesies said; a warning, said others. Some feared seeing both the sun and the moons at the same time, in such a precise row. Others marveled. Ardra felt only empty.

It was time to complete the ritual. She knelt, struck her flint, and nurtured a new spark in a handful of dry needles and shredded cloth, blew into the embers her wishes—prayed to the ancient gods just as women had done since the beginning of time.

When the small coal was glowing, she scooped it up and lifted it reverently to the orbs, then cast it onto the kindling as legend demanded. She held her breath, leaned forward, willed the flames to survive. The small fire crackled, took, ate the twigs, fought the errant gusts of wind. Now she must light the candles anew.

A sound behind her made her look up.

Three men stood there. Dirty men. *Outcasts*.

Her throat dried. With unsteady legs, she rose. The men held rough sticks loosely in their filthy fists. She stumbled back, putting the fire between her and them. They came at her slowly, their intent gazes skimming up and down her like touches.

One grinned. His tongue licked along his lower lip. The gesture sent a flood of fear through her.

She glanced over her shoulder, to the trees and the way down to her guards.

The outcasts leaped over her fire.

She whirled around, but a man blocked her way.

A man afire.

She screamed. He stood bathed in the last of the sunlight, rooted in flames of red and gold, his eyes black holes in his white face.

She danced to the left, stumbled on her hem, went down on one knee. The outcasts fell upon her from behind. Pain flashed through her shoulder from the harsh blow of a stick.

14

They tore at her jewels. One grasped her hem and tossed it up.

The flaming man swayed and shimmered.

She fought grasping hands, kicking, clawing with her nails, wordlessly begging the stranger for help.

The red and gold man staggered forward, clasped his hands together, and smashed them down against the filthy head of the outcast now questing beneath her skirts.

With a howl of anger, the outcast turned to the man. Another outcast, his feral smile a gap-toothed sneer, raised his stick and signaled his friends.

In an instant the outcasts had abandoned her and swarmed the man. Suddenly free, Ardra scrabbled backwards on her hands, then with a sob forced herself to stand up and run.

The trees seemed so far away, her feet like iron weights. Breath on fire in her chest, she hurled herself into the shelter of the pines and scrambled up the trunk of a tree.

The vision of the red and gold man still danced in her mind's eye. The sense that he had been conjured from the air made her tremble. Nay, her eyes had deceived her. It was just his scarlet and gold robes aflame in the remaining glow of light that had made it seem so.

As she gripped the rough bark and pressed her head to her hands, she could not forget his sudden appearance. He had come just at the conjunction to save her. How she wished for some means to fight the outcasts as he had fought for her.

Help. She must find help. Her heart pounded, her breath seared her chest. Her men were at the foot of the mountain. But she must pass the outcasts to reach them. Only Nilrem was near, and he was but an old man.

From her perch she could see nothing . . . but she could hear. She wanted to press her hands to her ears and block out the terrible noises, but doing so would deny the man who, bare-handed, had come to her rescue.

15

She must find a way to help him. Cautiously she slipped from the tree branches and crept to the edge of her shelter. The outcasts were like scavengers on prey. They had stripped the man and left him sprawled on the ground, his arms and legs outflung as if beseeching the orbs overhead for mercy. Was he dead? Her eyes filled.

The three filthy men crouched with their backs to their victim, arguing over his robes, his belt, and his pouch.

One of the men cried out. He shook his hand, flinging something away as if it burned his fingers. The others peered at the object, then also backed away, their arms filled with the man's clothing. They darted into the trees with their booty and disappeared.

Her first instinct was to go to the man. But she forced herself to pause. Perhaps 'twas just a ruse by the outcasts to draw her out. When the crash of their progress down the mountain grew faint, she tiptoed from the shelter of the trees.

They had left their victim no dignity in death. Drawing off her cloak, she knelt to cover him, tears rising in her eyes. "If I had been a man, I would have killed at least one of them." With a hesitant hand, she touched his chest.

His heart beat strongly beneath her palm. He rolled his bloody head from side to side and groaned.

"By the gods, you are alive."

There was hope.

She cast her cloak aside to examine him. How terrible it would be if the man bled to death while she fetched help.

His hair was not bloody. His face was, but 'twas not blood that made his hair so dark. She wondered at the deep brown color, but could waste no time on the matter.

Quickly, fearful the outcasts might return, she examined the rest of him. He was young, his battered body as strong as a warrior's. None of his wounds looked mortal.

With a whispered prayer of gratitude to the gods, she stood up and gave him a final look. Blood ran down his

inner thigh, a thigh hard with muscle. His stomach was ridged with muscle as well.

Then her glance fell on his right arm. She reached out to assure herself that what she saw was real. Aye, 'twas the flesh of a strong man but painted with a serpent. It coiled three times about his arm. She rubbed the tips of her fingers over the paint, then sat back to think. "This is a terrible omen," she whispered.

Gently she draped her cloak across the man's body. He was taller than the common man, though not as tall as some of her guards. If she covered his feet, her cloak would come only to the middle of his chest. She tugged the cloak up far enough to conceal the symbol on his arm, leaving his feet exposed.

His eyes flickered open. "What happened?" he asked. He licked his lips.

Ardra stood and backed away. He tracked her movements and lifted a hand.

Nilrem, she thought. *I must fetch Nilrem. He will know what to make of this man and the strange symbol painted on his arm.*

Something glinted in the dirt. A broken chain. She bent and retrieved it. The outcasts had thrown it away, fearful of it for some reason.

Then she understood. Dangling from the chain was . . . nay, it was impossible. It looked like glass, but glass could not be shaped in such a manner. The flames of her meager fire flared a moment, illuminating the small object. A rose. The personal emblem of Tolemac's high councilor.

There in the dirt was another rose. She threaded it on the broken chain and knotted it. Two perfect red roses created of an impossible material.

She folded her hand into a tight fist about the token and forced herself to go for help, when in truth she wished to abandon her savior to the cold night.

17

Chapter Three

Ardra set off up the mountain to Nilrem. 'Twas said the old man's wisdom included healing. The wind whipped her skirt about her legs and stung her cheeks.

Ardra found the wiseman sitting outside his hut, eyes raised to the conjunction. His long gray beard reached his knees.

She thought of the man naked in the cold, bleeding, and took a deep, steadying breath. Sense had replaced fear on her run to the wiseman. Whether the stranger served the high councilor or not, she owed him her life. "Nilrem. Please. You must help me."

The old man started. "Ardra of the Fortress of Ravens! What are you doing so far from home?"

"Please, my reason for coming must wait. I need your help. A man is hurt . . . quite badly."

"Hurt?" The old man staggered to his feet. "How so? Fallen from a horse?"

"Nay." She shook her head and swallowed. "Beaten. By outcasts. Come."

The old man lifted a woolly brow but asked no more questions. He retrieved a satchel from his hut and gestured

18

with his walking stick that she precede him.

Overhead, the spill of light from the rising turquoise orbs lit their way to the mountain meadow. She glanced over her shoulder every few moments to make sure the wiseman was still behind her.

She moved cautiously, ever mindful of the possible return of the outcasts. Without being told, the old man did likewise.

The man was not where she'd left him.

Then she saw him, lying by the fire near the candles she had never relit. "Nilrem, he's moved."

For a moment, she only stared. The man had pushed off her cloak. She had seen enough of men to know that many women would appreciate this one. His body was strong, his muscles honed by war or hard labor. His face was comely too, but she had known comely men before—and been betrayed by one as well.

The glass roses bit into her palm and reminded her that this man was not some innocent victim. "Look," she whispered, indicating the man's painted arm when Nilrem panted up beside her.

Nilrem handed her his staff and knelt. He paid no heed to the mark on the man's arm, but instead ran practiced fingers over the stranger's brow and jaw, probed his skull. "You say outcasts did this?"

"Or rebels."

"Filthy creatures. He is more likely to die of their vermin than of his injuries." Nilrem searched his satchel. He drew out a twist of linen and a tiny flagon stoppered with wood. "I see the candles here. You were practicing the ancient way?"

Ardra nodded. "I would prefer that you not tell anyone. I never completed the ritual."

She held the man's head while Nilrem waved the flagon beneath the man's nose. With a groan and cough, he opened his eyes and began to flail his arms. Nilrem, in a move surprisingly agile for one of his age, leaped to safety.

19

Ardra scooted away, but when the man's energy expended itself and he fell back with a groan, she edged closer to get a better look at his face. His eyes remained open this time. Their color tempted her nearer. She had not seen eyes so dark before, as dark as the hair on his head.

"Who are you?" Nilrem asked. "From whence do you come?" The man said nothing, just stared wildly about.

Ardra knelt by the fire. "He spoke before. Just briefly." She put a hand on the man's bare shoulder. His skin was as cold as the rising wind. "Who are you? What do you want here?" she asked.

"He does not seem to hear us. Build up the fire, Ardra, whilst I determine his injuries." Ardra did as bade while Nilrem began to examine the man in earnest.

"Are you able to sit up?" Nilrem asked, and she could not resist a peek to see if he responded. His bare back was inches from her, a strong expanse of brown skin . . . skin that knew the sun. The valley of his spine was lined with hard muscle and descended to . . . Only warriors looked so very . . . able.

"Thank you," the man said to Nilrem in a hoarse voice. The sound reverberated low in her belly. A splendid voice. Then she looked at the coiled art upon his arm. A serpent. A mark of evil. Shame that she had stared overlong at the naked man made her shift her attention away.

Her fire, lit for ceremonial reasons and badly done at that, flamed as if she had built it with care and fed it with fatted pine cones. It was strange, and somehow as unsettling as the man's sudden appearance at the conjunction. She glanced overhead. The sun had disappeared beneath the horizon.

"Ardra—" Nilrem held out her cloak—"I have several robes I keep for pilgrims that may be of use to this young man. Fetch one. Your cloak will be little protection, I think, when the winds rise." The winds had risen already. Trees around them lifted their boughs in nightly exaltation. Nil-

rem followed her glance. "Aye. It will grow colder every hour. With our help I believe this man may walk, and once settled in my hut, answer your questions."

Ardra ran up the mountain. The old man's hut needed a good cleaning. It smelled of spoiled apples and clothing not washed often enough. On a hook she found several long robes of undyed wool. She snatched one up.

In a trice, she was back with the wiseman. "Here," she whispered. "Clothe him if you must, but we should take him to my men. I would feel better with their protection."

Nilrem lifted one woolly eyebrow.

"He wears a mark of evil," she explained.

"Then let us take him down the mountain, Mistress Ardra. I'll not tend him 'til you decide I should."

"Look." She held out her hand to Nilrem, the two roses sparkling in the firelight. "Why would this man bear the high councilor's personal emblem?"

"Even more reason to let him lie right here." But Nilrem made no move to let the man fall back to the ground.

Blood stained the ground where the man had lain—in several places. She saw again in her mind's eye how he had come to her defense, an unarmed man against three. "Nay. Deny him no care." With a sigh she handed Nilrem the roses.

Nilrem held out his walking stick, but it was quickly plain that although the man's eyes might be open, he had no awareness of where he was. She hurried forward and with Nilrem managed to get the stranger to his feet. Strong he might be, and certainly the arm beneath her hand was as hard as the weapon master's hammer, yet he stared through her unseeingly, moved only when prodded, took no steps on his own. They stumbled along like a three-legged mule.

"How much did I drink?" Neil sat up and rubbed his head, then groaned. His jaw hurt, his nose hurt, in fact, everything hurt. With a glance he took in the hut made of mud

21

and sticks. Sky showed through a gaping hole in the roof. "Where's the little pig? And how fast can I move to the brick house?"

An old man snickered, then bent over him. "Ah. You recover quickly. It is a good sign."

The room spun a moment. Neil swallowed his nausea. When his stomach settled, he gazed around. Beyond the skinny, mad Santa who smelled like he'd been wearing his costume since last Christmas, there were two very intimidating Tolemac warriors. He didn't need the game booklet to identify them. They wore black leather breeches, high boots, and white tunics heavily embroidered in black and gold. They could be Swedish ski champions from the last Olympics if you traded their swords for ski poles.

He'd done it. Gone into the game. Then a tendril of memory curled from beneath the pain in his head. A woman on her knees, a filthy man tearing at her skirt. The memory slipped away. Where had the thought come from?

"Where're my shorts? And where am I?"

The old man grinned and slapped his knees. The sound hurt Neil's ears. "You are at the base of Hart Fell, and I am Nilrem, a simple wiseman."

Nilrem was in the game manual, but little used. Game warriors didn't ask for advice. They acted. A wave of pain flooded Neil's head like ten toothaches hammering at one time. He managed a glance to the roof. "Is this your place?"

"Nay," Nilrem said. " 'Tis a shepherd's hut, no longer used. And who are you?" The man had a smoker's rough voice.

Neil had thought long and hard about his name in this new world. Had, in fact, thought long and hard about coming here and all the questions he would need to answer. He had entered the game to escape everything he was in Ocean City. Everything he hadn't been. Everything he'd screwed up. Without hesitation he christened himself anew. "I am Lien."

"Leeee-en? What manner of name is this?"

"An ancient one from my land. It means good fortune." He'd also learned you needed every break you could get just to survive—in any world.

Nilrem rose and studied him. The scrutiny was at odds with the amused smile twitching the old man's lips. "I am most honored to meet you, Leeee-en. Now, off with that robe and let me better tend your wounds."

"There's a rule where I come from. Keep your robe on in front of an audience. And where're my clothes?"

The two guards left without argument when Nilrem requested it. Neil pulled the robe over his head. "I feel as if I've been beaten with a stick."

"You were—several. I most humbly offer my apologies for such behavior. The men who accosted you were most likely outcasts. They live by thievery. As for your belongings, this is all we could save." The old man held up his hand.

Neil stared at the glass earrings and a broken chain. His hand shook a bit as he took them from the old man's dirty palm. "This is all . . . I mean . . . are you saying everything I had is gone?" What the hell was he to do now? He stared down at the jewelry; a sick dread churned in his stomach. So much for good fortune.

Nilrem nodded. " 'Tis all that remains. Those were cast off by the robbers."

He was truly screwed. "You said 'we.' Who's we?"

"Ah, that would be Ardra. She says you saved her life."

"Ardra." He whispered her name. The woman Gwen had suggested for *Tolemac Wars III*. Refrigerator Girl.

So, it had been Ardra on her knees. "Is she all right?"

Nilrem brought a bowl with a gray gloppy substance in it to Neil's side. "She is shaken, but thanks to you, unharmed." The old man took up a small stick and began to spread the goo on Neil's bruises and wounds. The gray paste was cool, then in a few moments, began to feel warm,

23

like Ben-Gay. The bandages the wiseman wrapped about his leg were white and clean.

"Do you know Mistress Ardra?" the wiseman asked.

"I don't. It's just an unusual name."

"Leee-en isn't?"

Neil pushed the old man's hand away and stood. The room spun and turned; the bile rose in his throat. He gripped the old man's shoulder. "No. It's common as dirt where I come from."

"Mistress Ardra will need to stitch you up. Two of your wounds are too deep for the herbal to heal on their own. Should they fester—"

"Stitch me up? Fester?" Neil said softly. One cut was on his inner arm, from his elbow to his wrist. It was already swelling. The other was on his shoulder, near his collarbone.

"When you have covered yourself, I shall call her."

Neil hastily sat down and drew several of the bed furs over his lower body. He felt vulnerable without his shorts, and his head was still spinning. Everything from stepping into the game booth until he woke here in the hut was fuzzy and vague.

He remembered the attack on Ardra. Maybe. He remembered a fire. The flare of flames. An electrical odor. Pain. A burning pain—as if someone had put his head in a waffle iron.

The door opened and in stepped a woman. Ardra. Her green gown and hooded cloak were embroidered in gold and purple. She dropped into a deep curtsey directed at Nilrem. Her eyes never turned to where he sat.

"Mistress Ardra, 'tis necessary you stitch this man's wounds. I have no talent with the needle."

As he spoke, the old man tapped Neil firmly on the shoulder. Each touch caused pain to shoot down his arm.

"Stitch? I cannot—" She stepped back a pace.

"Aye. You can. Just think of it as two pieces of cloth, a simple joining. If you can render such decorations as are

24

on your cloak, you can do this simple chore."

Nilrem took her hand and drew her forward to stand before Neil, urging her onto a low stool by his bed, which was no more than a pile of clean straw.

She lifted her gaze and met his.

Neil swallowed. The game creator hadn't captured her at all. Oh, the basics, yeah—the oval face, the patrician cheekbones, the sensuous lips—but not the eyes. They were unlike any he'd ever seen—golden eyes, glowing in the firelight as brilliantly as polished amber.

Her hands were cool when she touched his arm to assess the wound. "They were merciless," she said, almost in a whisper.

"Did they hurt *you?*" he asked.

She leaped up. "Your—your voice. I have heard only one other speak as you do."

He didn't answer.

"Nilrem." She turned to the old man. "Whence came he?"

Neil had an answer ready. "I'm from beyond the ice fields."

"Ardra," Nilrem said sharply. "He needs tending."

Ardra hesitated but a moment, then obeyed. With a sharp intake of breath, she bent her head, and Neil felt as if she had dismissed him from her consciousness. She opened her pack and drew out a fabric pouch tied with ribbon. She unwrapped the bundle to reveal needles and thread wrapped on small smooth sticks. The needles looked less than sharp. *Don't be a wimp, Neil,* he told himself.

No, he must think of himself as Lien. He was a different man here. *Lien the pauper.* What a nightmare.

She swallowed and looked up at him, inspecting him like a piece of furniture she had to refinish. Then she spoke, and the quiver in her voice told him she was not distant, just very nervous. "Forgive me. You came to my aid, and now I must come to yours."

25

"Thank you."

"Your thanks are not necessary." She looked at him, and the color of her eyes reminded him of old-fashioned fall chrysanthemums.

"Why weren't those guards with you when you were attacked?"

"I—I was gathering firewood."

The old man made a snorting sound, then rubbed his nose on his sleeve. The young woman impaled the wiseman with a haughty stare. Here was one thing the game creator had captured perfectly—she was as cold as the ice she guarded. "You helped me and I am grateful," she continued, bringing her attention back to his wound.

She clasped her hands about his forearm and pressed the edges of the wound together. He nearly levitated off the pallet. He jerked his arm away.

"This may hurt badly." She poked his wound again.

"Wait!" He covered her hand with his. "I think I want it washed first. With really hot water. And do you have any alcohol?"

Ardra and Nilrem merely glanced at each other and shook their heads.

"Alcohol? You know . . . wine? Ale? Something like that?"

"Ah. The man wishes to be drunk! A wonderful idea. He will feel less pain that way." Nilrem cackled in amusement. He was gone but a moment before returning with what looked like a wineskin from the hippie era. Lien tugged off a wooden stopper and sniffed the inside. It was wine.

Ardra pursed her mouth, and he realized she did not approve of the idea of his getting drunk. After she bathed the wound in very hot water, she cried out when he doused it with wine. He clenched his fist against the hot flare of pain as the red fluid coursed along the deep cut.

"Now you can stitch it." He rested his arm on his lap and fisted his hand.

26

She patted the wound dry with a clean cloth and began. It hurt like the devil, and he had to bite his lip to keep from swearing. Bad as it was, it was pretty tame stuff compared to the jackhammer in his head.

"Can't you go any faster?" he gritted out when she had neatly gathered together about half the wound. Cold sweat broke out on his brow.

"I have never done such work. Perhaps I am going too fast." She jerked the thread tight and tied a knot. When she looked up, he saw something in her gaze that told him she was angry. It took several moments for her to thread her needle again. His arm throbbed from shoulder to wrist.

"Never mind," he muttered as she slowly began on the second half of the wound. He wanted to vomit. He took a deep breath. She wore an exotic scent he imagined didn't exist in Ocean City . . . or anywhere else in the U S of A.

"Now your . . . chest." She leaned forward to inspect the wound. She bit her lip . . . her very full lip. Wherever had he gotten the idea she was prissy?

His head filled with a vague buzz. He slipped backwards and groaned.

"Oh! Nilrem!" Her hand was cool on his brow. "He is soaked in sweat!"

Nilrem pushed her gentle hand away and replaced it with his scratchy claw. "He is not feverish. 'Tis just that he is not so brave."

Lien closed his eyes and groaned. The food he had eaten after the funeral threatened to erupt from his lips. Somehow, the meal and the funeral seemed a world and a millennium away.

The rustle of Ardra's skirt told him she was near. She placed a damp, cool cloth over his eyes.

"Foolish is more accurate," she said. "He came after the outcasts with naught but his bare hands."

Lien knew when he was being insulted. "I can sit up now." He pushed her hand away.

"Nay. Remain as you are." She touched his shoulder.

27

It was easier to do as she said. He fell back against the bedding.

Without being told, she bathed his chest wound in very hot water, repeatedly, then doused it well with wine as he had done. He felt the warm liquid soak the cloth beneath his body.

"Waste of good wine. Give me that, child." Nilrem took the wineskin and poured a hefty draught into a wooden cup. He slurped it down, smacking his lips and then wiping his mouth on his sleeve. "I think our Lien needs to explain this curious mark on his arm."

Lien feigned sleep. Each stitch turned his stomach. As Ardra sewed up his shoulder wound, she and Nilrem whispered about him.

"A snake is a mark of evil," Ardra whispered.

"Aye. But it coils thrice about his arm and in the very place a warrior wears his arm rings," Nilrem whispered back. "Perhaps he is a warrior from . . . his place."

"In scarlet and gold robes?" Her fingers drifted from his shoulder to his upper arm. They did not touch his tattoo, but he could almost feel a static charge as he pictured her fingertips hovering over the design.

Her breath whispered soft as a summer breeze across his shoulder. "And look . . . the snake markings are not scales. They are one of the old designs . . . the weave of eternal goodness found on the cauldrons of the ancient priests."

"Most curious," Nilrem said softly. "So, he wears a mark of evil, yet it is richly decorated by ancient markings of goodness. Hmmm. And what of this?"

Lien couldn't resist. He peeked. There dangling from the broken chain, inches away from his nose, were the two glass rose earrings.

"They're mine." He reached out with his good hand. Pain rocketed through his shoulder as he strained to reach the jewelry.

Nilrem held it just out of his reach and stepped away.

Lien threw back the blankets and side-stepped Ardra to reach the old man. He snatched the chain from Nilrem's hand, then dropped it over his head and turned back to Ardra. "Now. Finish the job," he said.

Ardra just stared at him, mouth open. He felt his cheeks flush hot as he realized just how naked he was. Forcing himself to move at a normal pace, he walked past her to the straw, sat down, and drew a blanket over his lap.

This time, she kept her eyes downcast as she stitched.

"Of what significance is the jewelry, young man?" Nilrem took another deep drink of his wine.

"The earrings belonged to my mother."

"But they are glass. No one may make such a thing here," Ardra said.

"They were not made *here*." *And damn it*, he decided, *I'm not saying another word.*

When Ardra had finished her work, she coated each wound with the gray paste, then tore strips of clean cloth and bound both his arm and shoulder.

"Thank you, Mistress Ardra," he managed.

For the first time, she smiled. Only a small smile, which died quickly as she caught sight of his tattoo.

"Have you no such marks as these here?" he asked.

Nilrem answered for her. "Once, when men ran about in nothing but furs, they marked themselves on their faces, chests, and so forth, but not in such an artful manner . . . and not in such a place. The place of arm rings."

"There are no arm rings beyond the ice fields," Lien said simply. "Do you have something I could wear?"

Nilrem handed him what looked like a monk's robe. It was thick and scratchy. So much for sartorial splendor.

He glanced at Ardra. In a swirl of skirts she was gone.

Nilrem offered him a strip of rough leather to loop about his waist with the words, "I have asked Ardra's men to collect a few pairs of boots for you."

"Her men?" Lien imagined a small army of warriors, garbed in leather, armed with sharp swords. Great. He

tugged at the robe, which reached only to his calves.

"Oh, aye. Did you think a woman would travel about unprotected?"

"No," Lien said slowly. "I didn't know she was traveling anywhere."

Nilrem burst into a delighted laugh complete with knee slapping. When he calmed himself, he finally spoke. "You did not suppose her to reside with me?"

Lien shrugged. "If I can just have those boots, I'll be on my way."

"Your way? And which is your way?"

Before Lien could answer, Ardra entered the hut. Behind her were three large men. Blond, hard-looking men. The cold air went straight up his robe. He was nearly naked, barefoot, and outnumbered.

"Come. Come." Nilrem waved them all in. The hut became immediately crowded. Maybe it was the pain in his head, but the boots the warriors dumped at his feet looked enormous—as did their swords.

When her guards retired to the outside—gone but close enough that Lien could hear the murmur of their voices— Nilrem asked Ardra, "What brings you here to me, Mistress Ardra of the Fortress?"

Ardra turned her wide tawny eyes not to Nilrem but to him. She slid her hands into her sleeves and looked, not hesitant, but wary. Lien concentrated on the boots lying at his feet, tried to appear uninterested. Maybe he'd hear something useful before setting out on his own. It had been his plan to check out the local politics before settling in any one location.

Nilrem nodded in Lien's direction. "You must speak before this young man. He is not fit to stand outside awaiting our pleasure."

Good; the more feeble they thought him, the less of a threat Ardra might see in him.

She nodded as if coming to a decision. "I fear I must speak if he is not able to . . . go."

Her hair was loose about her shoulders. The fire's glow cast a soft sheen on the ripples. He shook his head. What the heck was wrong with him? It was just hair.

She pitched her voice low, and he pretended to be intently interested in the boots he was trying on. He tried not to appear to be eavesdropping.

"Tol is grievously ill," she whispered.

"What may I do?" Nilrem patted her knee gently. "I have several potions that will ease his pain."

Ardra squeezed the gnarled hand on her knee. She nodded, and for a moment her head bowed. "I accept with my deepest thanks. The healer has been unable to give him ease."

"Done." Nilrem rose. He opened a wooden cask and withdrew a stoppered stone bottle. He tapped a small pile of yellow powder into a square of cloth and folded it as if it held gold dust. "Here." He handed the parcel to Ardra. "Four grains only in clear water as he needs it. Allow him to decide when he needs more. Twice as much . . . is fatal."

Ardra opened her cloak, and Lien saw an embroidered gown in a deep green. He thought she could be Robin Hood's mate, all garbed in shades of green as she was. She tucked the package into a leather purse hanging from a belt at her waist.

"It is not just for Tol's ease I have come. He sent me with grave news to impart."

Lien settled on one pair of boots and realized he had no socks. There seemed to be nothing resembling socks here. With a sigh, he wrapped some strips of fabric about his feet and became aware that Ardra was watching him most intently.

The boots were stiff brown leather, without the distinction of being a left or a right, but fit him well enough with the cloth wrappings. He imagined that if he walked far, he'd have horrendous blisters. Where was Dr. Scholls when you needed him?

As he contemplated the sorry and not very clean robe he was wearing, Nilrem and Ardra continued their hushed conversation, but she kept glancing at him, worry etched on her face. Lien decided to fake sleep. He groaned as he tried to shift his feet onto the pallet. The heavy boots defeated him. He settled for falling diagonally across the straw mattress and watching through half-closed eyes.

"What other matter brings you here?" Nilrem asked Ardra.

"Samoht is camped on the border. Did you know?" Ardra leaned forward and knotted her hands into tightly clenched fists.

Nilrem followed her gaze but shrugged. "Is he? Alone?"

"Nay! He comes with an army." She began to pace and wring her hands. "Oh, 'tis said he comes to await the birth of his first child." Her tone was sneering. "His Selaw mate was not good enough to dwell in his Tolemac palace. Nay, she must be returned to her mother in Selaw once she was breeding. He treated her like a mare, taken to stud. I despise the man!"

Lien wanted to rub his aching temples, but bruises prevented him—and would alert her that he was awake.

She planted herself before him. "I know you are listening."

He opened his eyes. She was very close and practically quivering with emotion. "Is Samoht your master?" she spat out. "You bear his symbol. He comes to take my lands, my fortress. Some say he covets me as well." Her head bowed. No color rose on her cheeks, but he sensed she was deeply mortified. Then he saw a single tear run down her cheek. "He could not even wait for Tol's death to come."

"Samoht? Tol?" Lien struggled up on his elbow. What had he landed in?

Nilrem took a deep breath and answered for her. "Tol is Ardra's lifemate. He is ill."

Nilrem's tone said it all. Tol's illness was terminal, Lien interpreted. "Can't you heal him?"

Nilrem caught his eye and gave one quick shake of his head. If Ardra caught the gesture, she did not react. "What else may I do for you?" Nilrem took Ardra's hand and gently rubbed it between his. "I am at your service."

She looked up. As Lien watched, she visibly gathered herself and took a deep breath. "I cannot lose the fortress, Nilrem. I cannot."

"Tradition will not allow you to rule, my child." He patted her hand. Lien winced at the patronizing gesture.

"Tradition!" Staring up at her hurt his neck. "This is tradition." Her long, elegant finger pointed at him. "A rose passed from one man to another. Secret symbols to tell one man that another is on his side. Well, I will not be deceived by it. Men may rule by might, but a woman may do just as well with her wits."

"Whoa," Lien said. "These roses are just jewelry. Nothing more. I've never met this Samoht."

Her mouth opened, then closed. "One may serve a master even if one is too lowly to be permitted into his presence."

"Perhaps he tells the truth, my child." Nilrem hooked his hands together on his belly. "After all, we know little of the lands beyond the ice fields. Roses may have other meanings there."

Lien mirrored the old man's stance, linking his fingers and leaning back. It hurt his arm like hell, but he didn't shift position. "Yeah. I'm from way over there. Where I'm from, roses are just a flower you give a girlfriend."

"Girlfriend? You mean lover? One may not have a girl as a friend. This is nonsense you spin to distract me." Ardra lifted her nose into the air. "You bear the rose emblem. It is enough for me."

"Enough for what?" Lien asked mildly.

"Enough to believe in your treachery. Deceit. Licentiousness!"

"Licentiousness? What a great word. I always wanted

33

some of that." Suddenly his brain wasn't working so well. Ardra grew large, then small, shrinking and growing again like Alice in Wonderland. He fainted.

"I like him," Nilrem said as he hefted Lien's booted feet onto the pallet and settled his head on a folded length of cloth. "He can find amusement even when he is in great pain. Lift his robe; he is bleeding somewhere." Nilrem pointed to a few spots of red.

Ardra sighed and tried for dispassion as she drew the young man's robe up his legs, stopping with discretion at his groin. "Does this man walk about naked? His legs are as brown as a field worker's." The thought caused an uncomfortable sensation in her belly. She ignored it.

"Here, Nilrem, this wound needs stitching."

Blood soaked one of the cloths Nilrem had bound about the man's thigh. Together, they removed the strips of cloth. She touched the needle to his skin, and his thigh muscle jumped. He clamped a hand over hers and sat up, eyes wild and wide awake.

Nilrem put a hand on the man's shoulder. "She is helping you. Now sit back."

The man held his hand over the robe bunched in his lap and watched her work.

"Why is your skin so brown in places, pale in others?" she asked. The wound was in the paler area of skin. He had dark hair on his thighs the same color as on his head. Never before had she seen such a color on a person.

"I like the sun," he said, then moaned at the tug of the thread on the wound.

When she knotted the final stitch, he slumped to the side in another faint.

It unnerved her to touch a man so intimately, a man not her mate, so she tugged his robe down over his legs.

"He has the body of a warrior," Nilrem said, poking the man's belly. "Look at his arms and thighs."

"As I said, Nilrem, he is a treacherous deceiver. He is

one of Samoht's guard, most likely, posing as a merchant or some such. It was most unwise of us to talk before him."

"Nay. He has ancient symbols of goodness on his arm. Surely, Samoht would not allow such pagan markings on his guard. And where are his arm rings? Nay. I think he is what he claims, a simple man from beyond the ice fields—one who saved your life, do not forget."

"With that mark on his arm, he cannot be so simple." Ardra knelt at the man's side. "Have you ever seen hair so dark? It reminds me of the rich brown dye my women make from winter thistle."

"And that only grows in the rock crevasses out on the ice fields, does it not?"

She rubbed her fingers in the soft hair of Lien's head. "Has he dyed his hair?"

Nilrem snorted. "Even that on his body?"

"Why would one do that? Who is he, Nilrem? He appeared from nowhere—"

"And saved your life."

Nilrem could say what he wanted, but Lien would not bewitch her. She knew evil when she saw it, and evil was in the mark on this man's arm and in the red of the roses. She drew off the braided leather belt she wore looped three times about her waist.

"This man could overpower many of my men." She slid the soft leather belt through her fingers. "I have learned many skills from Tol. He taught me to rule, allowed me to take the reins of leadership, but this skill I learned from my women." As Nilrem sputtered a protest, she trussed the man, hand and foot.

Chapter Four

Lien winced as the cart in which he lay bounced over another bump in the road, although calling this washboard nightmare a road was a joke. It was nothing more than a dirt path skirting the base of Hart Fell. Off in the distance lay a barren plain filled with rock and sand in ever-changing patterns of red, like the desert of Monument Valley in Arizona.

He focused his gaze on the lavender sky overhead. If his hands had not been bound, he'd pinch himself. From the incredible sky to the intriguing woman riding directly behind him, it was all just a bit unbelievable. Even the air smelled different.

He'd done it. Gone into the game. His calculations, only half believed, had been right. He had given himself a new name, and with it, a new identity. Okay, so he wasn't the prosperous merchant he'd planned; he was a poor merchant. Still, he had only himself to feed. He had no responsibilities, no one depending on him.

An unaccustomed feeling coursed through him. A feeling of complete freedom.

His euphoria lasted until the next big bounce of the cart. At that moment, with his hands bound painfully behind him, freedom was just a concept.

He shifted and groaned. He immediately felt Ardra's amber eyes on him. He glowered at her. She bit her lip and glanced away.

His arms and legs had gone to sleep. When they stopped, he'd be a complete cripple. He winced as he imagined being lifted from the cart to take a leak. His hands would be so useless he'd need someone to hold Mr. Happy.

How could he convince Ardra he was harmless? Maybe glaring wasn't such a great idea. He'd try a little honey instead. But first he needed to bring her close enough for conversation.

He groaned aloud and bit on his lip. Through half-closed eyes he saw her maneuver her horse closer to the cart.

"You are in pain?" she asked.

Lien groaned louder as a wheel jounced into another rut. "A bit. I can't feel my hands," he said between gasps.

She trotted forward, and he heard her order the driver to halt.

Within moments she'd climbed lithely into the back of the cart to where he lay amid her bundles and boxes.

"Sit forward," she ordered as if he were one of her minions.

To his intense embarrassment, he found he really couldn't move.

Ardra knelt cautiously by his side. "I want to check your dressings. Nilrem," she called to the wiseman, beckoning him near. "We must see to his wounds."

Nilrem was assisted into the back of the cart by two of Ardra's behemoth warriors. Lien tried not to blush as the two men stripped his robes off him, then dumped him on the floorboards of the wagon. He lay there like a trussed chicken on the lumpy mess of his wool robes.

"This is a pretty shabby way to treat someone who saved your life," he said to Ardra while Nilrem draped a fur over

37

his hips. "If these ropes were any tighter, I figure I'd lose the use of my arms. How do merchants without arms earn their living here?"

Her eyes widened, and she darted a look at Nilrem. He shrugged.

"Is this how you folks in Tolemac reward people?" he asked again. "By crippling them?"

She lifted a hand, and he fell silent. "I am sorry for your discomfort, but I do not know whom you serve. Until I do, I must be cautious. And I am Selaw, not Tolemac."

"Selaw. Tolemac. You seem one and the same to me."

Her head whipped up. Her eyes narrowed. He watched her fight for control, the muscles of her throat working. So, this woman didn't much care for such a comparison. Good. He'd found a small chink in her armor.

Up close her skin was flawless. If he embraced her, would she be warm and willing or as cold as the ice on which she lived? Her hands certainly weren't cold when she undid his dressings.

He blinked in disbelief. The wound in his shoulder looked as if it were a week old. It was pink and healthy, the skin smooth about the stitches which she gently picked out with the tip of her razor-edged dagger.

When she went to work on the stitches in his thigh, he saw that that wound too looked nearly healed. "You only keep stitches in for a few hours?" he asked through gritted teeth as her dagger worked its way up his thigh.

She lifted her gaze from her work to his face. Her eyes were not completely gold . . . or cold. They had flecks of deep amber and were rimmed with a darker, warmer shade.

"If I left them longer, the skin would heal over them," she said matter-of-factly. She sheathed her dagger and then bound his wounds with clean cloths she dug from a leather pack by his feet.

"I think we should untie his hands, else you cannot tend his arm wound." Nilrem took the pack of cloth from Ardra

and sat on it. Lien noticed that although the wiseman didn't smell great, his sandaled feet were clean, and so were his fingernails.

Nilrem gripped Ardra's wrist. "Your men surround us, and I warrant this one cannot move a muscle after lying so long in this manner. Release him and treat the wound. As a healer, I humbly ask it of you."

Lien felt hypnotized by Ardra as she studied his face. He tried to look harmless.

She drew her blade. "Roll over."

He couldn't obey. He was truly paralyzed. With a disconcerted look on her face, she and Nilrem turned him on his side, whereupon she slashed his bindings.

When they drew his arms forward, he could not stifle a real groan. Gently they placed his arms on the fur that covered his lap. Then Ardra bent over his wounded arm. She made a small hissing sound as she removed the bandage. This wound was still raw and ugly.

"Binding his arms has hindered the healing," Nilrem said. He mixed more of the gray paste and Ardra smoothed it on, not with a stick this time but with her fingertips.

Her hands were warm. The muscles in his arm began to jump. She moved around until she could kneel comfortably, her thigh against his; then she began to gently chafe the circulation back into his hands. It was painful and arousing at the same time. He tried to concentrate on her and not the burning pins and needles in his fingers and palms, or the warmth of her leg against his.

Ardra shook her head over his condition. It sent her hair sliding across her shoulder to cascade down her arms. Interspersed in the mass of gold were tiny braids. Each was tied at the tip with gold thread and amber beads.

"I am sorry for this. I did not think 'twould hinder the healing." The thumbs she dug so enthusiastically into his palms each bore a silver ring with different knotwork patterns.

39

Ann Lawrence

Her clothing was soft green wool. Encircling her waist was a length of common rope, and he realized she'd sacrificed her belt to bind him. She really must be afraid of him. In his world he figured she'd be one of those idle, rich woman with plenty of time for her wardrobe and two-martini lunches.

Of course, women in his world didn't carry knives. The hilt of Ardra's dagger was silver and heavily engraved. The markings were similar to the knotwork he'd had tattooed on his snake instead of scales. The *Shield* the pattern was called. Small amber cabochons studded the blade's hilt and adorned the leather sheath that dangled loosely from the rope belt.

If his arms weren't lying in his lap like a pair of dead mackerels, he'd snatch the knife, hold it to her throat, and make an escape.

Sure. Where would he run? Besides, he could never hold a knife on a woman. He shifted uncomfortably on the lumpy wool robe and then groaned as arrows of pain shot up his arms.

"Lie still, young Lien. Else you will open your wound." Nilrem patted his arm. "See, Mistress Ardra, I am touching this painted snake and it hasn't bitten me," he said and cackled.

Ardra remained on her knees, massaging Lien's hands. As the pain waned, arousal surged through him. He jerked his hands away. "Enough. I'm fine."

"As you please." She rose and lifted a hand in the direction of her men. Immediately, a guard separated himself from the orderly rank and rode up to her. He dismounted and helped her from the cart like a loyal subject assisting a queen.

Then the man took something from his saddle. When he turned, Lien saw what it was. More rope.

But Ardra surprised him. "Ollach, clothe him and leave his hands free. He can go nowhere hobbled in such a manner."

40

The guard did not argue. He assisted Nilrem to his horse, then jumped back into the cart and cast the fur aside. Lien immediately felt heat on his face. The man took so long to shake out the woolen robe, Lien snatched it and shrugged into it himself, despite the screaming pain in his shoulders.

When the soldier had resumed his position behind the cart, Lien finally looked up at Ardra. He wished she'd ride at the fore of her men. Her presence was unsettling, and he didn't know why. He'd seen better-looking women, and her frosty manner didn't exactly endear her to him. He liked his women smiling and . . . with a bit more meat on their bones.

He flexed his hands and rotated his wrists and shoulders to ease the stiffness. He couldn't believe how the wounds on his shoulder and thigh had healed. What was in the gray powder? He'd love to take some back with him.

That thought led to the idea of going home. Every mile from the mountain might mean less chance of getting home. Of course, there was nothing at home anyway. Instead of dread over his position, he felt the return of the heady euphoria. Maybe there was something in the atmosphere.

"Hey, Nilrem. Where're we going?"

The old man grimaced as his horse trotted up to the cart's side. "We are searching for Ralen, brother to Ardra's lifemate."

Lien rotated his shoulders. "Why's she looking for this Ralen?"

The old man shot a quick glance at Ardra, but her attention was occupied by the guard who rode at her side. The man seemed to be a personal bodyguard. He was a typical Tolemac warrior—tall, blond, blue-eyed.

"Tol will die anon." Nilrem spoke in a tone barely above a whisper. Lien had to strain to hear him.

"But 'tis expected in one so old. He is close to three

41

score and ten conjunctions. He will be sadly missed by men of reason, but we all must die in our time."

So Mistress Ardra was a trophy wife. Or, from what he knew of the game, simply a pawn, given in marriage wherever it was politically expedient at the moment. He wondered who would get her next.

"Mistress Ardra hopes Ralen will prevent the usurpation of her lands upon Tol's death."

"She wants to lifemate with Ralen?" He used the game term for marriage.

"Nay. If I know Ardra, it is not a mate she seeks, merely a staunch supporter. As Tol's brother, Ralen's wishes will be considered over others' in the fate of her people. Ardra's son is not yet old enough to rule, you see, and a guardian must be chosen. Many will vie for the honor."

So, she had a son. "Who's after the chiefdom?" As he asked the question, he found he knew the answer from the game—the head councilor of Tolemac, of course.

"Samoht, the Tolemac high councilor." Nilrem echoed his thoughts. "Samoht and his army are camped on Ardra's border. She fears he will take her fortress upon Tol's death. You have heard of the Fortress of Ravens, have you not?"

"Yes. It controls the mining of the ice." Lien was not about to say *how* he knew about it. If not for the outbreaks of tension over the ice and who controlled it, there would be no war between Tolemac and the Selaw. And there would be no game.

That thought made him examine the men riding near the cart. These soldiers were playing no game; the swords and knives they carried were all too real. Now that he was broke, the primary defense he'd planned on—bribing himself out of trouble—was no longer an option. He needed a weapon. But not a sword. He wouldn't know how to use it effectively.

Lien noticed a walking staff stuck in the straps holding Nilrem's saddlebags. A strong stick might be helpful.

Once upon a time, before his Johns Hopkins lacrosse

coach had converted him to the attack position, he'd played defense. Although he had starred in the attack position, he had always been a defenseman in his heart.

Maybe he could talk Nilrem into getting him a stick.

And he'd need one just to walk if they kept him tied up this way. His best defense might be the appearance of weakness. Then the ice princess might take pity on him.

"Look, do you think you could get Ardra—"

"Mistress Ardra," Nilrem corrected.

"—Mistress Ardra to untie me? I'm just a harmless merchant, and I can't even feel my feet anymore. How am I supposed to take a leak?"

Nilrem scratched his chin. "Take a leek? I do not believe you will have an opportunity to eat leeks. The cook has few greens—"

"Not that kind of leak. I meant urinate. And I'm going to need a stop really soon. If you don't untie my feet, someone's going to have to carry me behind a tree. Think of how humiliating that will be. What do you say?"

"I like that . . . take a leak. I am seeing a cask of wine with a stream . . . heh-heh. I would imagine such a turn of phrase will delight Mistress Ardra's men." Nilrem grinned.

Then, gratefully, Lien watched Nilrem turn his horse toward Ardra. They took part in a spirited discussion that ended with the same soldier climbing into the cart again and freeing his feet.

Lien stretched his numb legs. At least he wasn't going to have to crawl behind a bush somewhere. After a few minutes, the wiseman pulled alongside again.

"How are your legs?" he asked. "Tolerable now for taking a leak?" The old man cackled, and Lien saw Ardra frown.

Ardra forced her attention to her men. They were ranged on either side of her entourage. No outcasts, no rebels, would think of attacking them. Try as she might, she could not keep her eyes from the merchant.

The vision of him ablaze in the setting sun, his hands raised to deliver the blow that saved her, kept coming into her mind's eye. Why could she not douse the flame of this vision?

Did his appearance at the time of the most rare of conjunctions augur good or ill?

If good, she had mistreated him, according to Nilrem. The thought preyed on her mind, but no less than the knowledge of Samoht's presence on her border.

A shiver ran down her spine. No matter what Nilrem said about Lien's decorated arm, he carried red roses. Until he proved otherwise, she would treat him as if he were Samoht's man.

Moments later, her company set up camp. She paced as fires were built and meat roasted. The delay in returning to Tol chafed her badly. Her guards helped Lien from the cart, and he swayed a moment before straightening. His walk was halting and he stumbled a bit as he disappeared with the other men behind a wall of brush.

She pushed her concern aside. He might truly be a serpent in her nest.

"Mistress Ardra," Nilrem called. He led a grimy man forward. "This messenger is looking for you."

"Ah, you have found us. What news?" Her heart began to pound in her chest. Did Tol still live?

"Tol has ordered himself taken to Samoht's camp. He has called for the high eight to be assembled."

She whipped around to conceal her grief. To have done so, Tol must know he had few sunrisings left of life. Tears welled in her eyes—hot, useless tears. She took a long, shuddering breath and then faced the messenger. "Is Tol strong enough to make it to Samoht's camp?"

The man bowed. "It is not for me to say."

"What of Ralen, Tol's brother?" Nilrem asked. "Has any word of him been circulating?"

"Oh, aye. Samoht sent him on a mission."

"Where?" If she knew where Ralen had gone, she could plot a course to intercept him. A warrior of Ralen's level would meet directly with Samoht to make his reports.

"I know not where, only for what purpose. Ralen was sent to find the Goddess of Darkness."

The Goddess.

A sudden haze clouded Ardra's vision. Her hands went cold, her body hot. She swayed and put out her hand. It was clasped by a warm, strong one. For a moment, she allowed herself to lean on Ollach's strength. Sickness swept into her belly, but she fought it, forcing herself to straighten and hold her head up.

"Thank you," she said and turned to Ollach. It was not he who held her hand. It was Lien. She jerked her hand away. He merely arched a dark brow and walked off. His gait was halting as he moved toward the cook's campfire. He dragged his injured leg.

When he was out of hearing range, she turned to the messenger. "Please. What need has Samoht of the Goddess?" Just saying her name was difficult.

Nilrem placed a comforting hand on her arm. Did the old man know the Goddess was responsible for Ardra's mother's death?

The messenger shrugged. "Samoht does not explain himself to Selaw folk, mistress."

She nodded. "But you know the gossip. It is why I pay you."

"This needs a bit of extra, mistress. We are talking of the Goddess of Darkness." There was a tiny thread of fear in the man's voice.

"Aye. You shall have three pieces of gold."

"Tolemac coin, mistress." His words told her all she needed to know about the state of the Selaw treasury.

"Tolemac coin it is. Now, what need has Samoht of the Goddess?"

" 'Tis rumored—" the man shuffled close—"that the

45

Goddess has stolen a treasure from the vaults under Tolemac."

"How could she?" Ardra scoffed. "The vaults are impregnable."

Nilrem squeezed her arm. "Let the man speak. What treasure?"

The man grinned. "Why, one o' yours, Nilrem. The Vial of Seduction."

"By the saints!" Nilrem's fingers tensed into a claw about her arm. "This is a disaster. In the wrong hands . . ."

Ardra nodded. "From one catastrophe to another. First Tol, now this. With the vial, the Goddess will seduce someone powerful and take him as consort."

"We must take comfort in the knowledge that only an honorable person may use the treasures. It is part of their mystery. A dishonorable person will not be able to use the potion to seduce—"

"The Goddess will find a way around the mystery."

Ardra jerked from Nilrem's grasp. "Oh, I see how this will go. The Goddess will be all-powerful on the east. Samoht on the west. And I and my hapless people must bow down to them both."

"Now, Ardra. Mayhap Ralen has found the Goddess and taken back the vial."

"Dream, Nilrem, if you must. When the vial was deposited in the Tolemac vaults, it was with the provision that the full council and only the *full* council would decide its use. This bodes ill for all people."

"We must find Ralen, mistress, if you want a strong warrior to command in Tol's place."

With bitter anger, she whipped around to face Nilrem. Several of her men and Lien had drawn near. "Aye. We will hunt for Ralen. Let us find a *man* to hold my fortress."

Then she decided on a course most men would fear even to consider. "We must save time. We will go by way of the Tangled Wood."

"Ardra. Is that wise? You know the dangers of such an action." Nilrem danced from one foot to the other like a small, frightened child.

"I know the dangers well. But if Ralen seeks the Goddess, he must traverse these woods as well. I will not miss Ralen or fail to see Tol one more time for fear of some woman. It is your sort—men—who continually tell me women are harmless. What need have I to fear a woman then? And perhaps you will think twice before concocting such *treasures* next time."

Nilrem leaned on his staff, looking twice his years. Ardra regretted her hard words, but they were all she seemed to have since this final illness of Tol's. "There will be ample light to ride during the night now the four moons are in alignment."

Ardra strode quickly through the camp to see her horse saddled. Another shiver, more from fear than cold, swept through her. Only well-armed warriors ventured near the Wood. She would not be less than they in daring. She must show her mettle now more than ever.

When night fell, the turquoise moons mocked her. They cast a soft gleam across the distant Scorched Plain and touched the trees with a haze of silvery blue. The land changed drastically with each mile crossed. It altered from cursed barren rock to wind-blasted pine, to thicker stands of hardy fir. And finally, on the edge of the Tangled Wood, to great stands of timber.

"Mistress Ardra." Ollach drew up. "Do you think this wise?"

She jerked her reins and pulled her mare to a halt. "You question my decision?"

"The men are uneasy."

"Then they will grow even more uneasy. I want to cut more time from our journey by going through the forest, not around it."

"Mistress!"

47

"Tol fails as we argue the issue. Samoht awaits us at the border." She made her tone as hard and cold as the ice and stone on which the Fortress of Ravens was built. She must be as strong.

Ollach took a deep breath and touched his brow, then bowed. "If that be your wish, mistress."

It must be. The fortress and all who dwell there depend on me.

Lien figured that if he could get out of his bindings with a few pathetic groans, he could get out of his scratchy robe too. He contemplated the many men who rode in Ardra's force. There were a few women, servants by the look of them, among the entourage, but mostly Ardra rode in singular female splendor, a green and gold jewel surrounded by a company of men in black and white.

He had finagled a horse by convincing Ardra that Nilrem needed the cart far more than he. Granted, she'd made sure his hands were bound, albeit loosely, before allowing him to swap places with the old man. Now Nilrem lay spread-eagled on the many packs, snoring.

Lien thanked heaven that his best friend in college had owned a horse farm in Maryland, so he could now ride with reasonable skill.

It was drafty wearing a long robe with no underwear. In fact, it was damned uncomfortable. He examined the men to see what kind of clothes he wanted. He settled on a compromise between what he'd like and what he could reasonably gain. With a little kick of his heels, he maneuvered his fat mare close to the wiseman.

"Nilrem." He spoke softly so Ardra and her companion, Ollach, couldn't hear him. "I need to get out of this robe."

"You disturb my meditation."

You mean napping. "Sorry. It's just that I'm used to a bit more luxury."

"Deprivation is good for the soul." Nilrem sat up and stretched. "What had you in mind?"

Lien glanced about. "Well, I think I'd like a pair of those black leather pants."

"Soft as butter, I would imagine. Warrior garb. Not possible."

"But if I wore them under this robe, wouldn't that be okay? It's not as if I'm trying to be a warrior."

Nilrem lifted his beard and used it like a napkin to stifle a cough. Or laugh. "Forgive me, son, you are about as far from a warrior as a man can be. You are a slave, I imagine, who has stolen his merchant master's robes and run away. Not that I care."

Lien had to bite his tongue to keep from snapping the old man's head off.

Nilrem continued. "You cannot put warrior gear under a pilgrim's robes."

"Then maybe I could wear the pants with one of those tunic things." Lien lifted his bound hands and indicated a portly man with white hair who bounced along behind a pair of warriors.

"Oh, the cook? Hmmm . . . what is wrong with the rest of his garb?" Nilrem lolled back in the cart, ankles crossed and hands stacked under his head.

"Lacks dignity." The cook wore what looked like tights under his tunic. Lien knew that if he wore tights he'd feel like a damned fool but the tunic, which reached to midthigh, looked soft and well made.

Nilrem opened one eye and began to laugh, then choked the sound off, looking beyond Lien's shoulder.

Lien turned. "Mistress Ardra." He made an awkward bow.

"I have heard what you said, Lien. You wish for different garb. Why?"

"I'm a merchant and used to better than this. The robe chafes the skin in some rather awkward places." Why lie?

Her eyes dropped to his lap, then darted quickly to his face. "I see. We would not want you uncomfortable." He heard the sarcasm in her voice.

49

"No, you don't want me too uncomfortable. If I can't ride, I'll slow you down, won't I?"

"I shall merely have you tied in the cart again."

"Mistress," Nilrem protested. "There is not room for two. I cannot possibly ride."

She stifled a sigh, and Lien tried to keep his smile behind his teeth.

"I see. You, Lien, cannot ride in pilgrim garb, and you, Nilrem, cannot ride at all. Perhaps I should just leave you behind, merchant." She wheeled away and took her place with Ollach.

Ouch.

They all rode in silence until the next stop. The cook prepared a hasty meal of cold meat and a tough-looking bread that was actually quite tasty. Lien had to eat with his hands bound. He had almost passed the meat by until he saw the cook take it from a barrel where it had been packed in ice and sawdust. The meat was cold and delicious, tasting like a cross between chicken and ostrich . . . not that he'd ever actually eaten ostrich.

After the meal, Ollach dumped a pile of clothing at his feet. Lien picked up the clothes, thanked the man, then looked about for Ardra. Should he go and thank her? He decided not to. She seemed unapproachable, a green and gold wraith in a pool of moonlight.

He looked up into the alien sky. There were billions of stars visible, but none of them took on the pattern of constellations he recognized. More evidence that he was in another world.

One of the warriors led him a few paces behind a tree and untied his hands. Lien pulled on the soft, worn pants, bemoaning his lack of underwear, and laced them up the front. They fit reasonably well.

The tunic, long-sleeved and made of linen, was soft and smooth. It had a design of amber and black embroidery at the wrists and hem reminiscent of ravens in flight. Once

he pulled the tunic over his head, he felt like a Russian Cossack from the steppes.

When he mounted the horse, it was with a lot more dignity than when he'd dismounted. No one had bound his hands. Ardra rode at his side for a bit. Before she opened her mouth, he knew what she would ask.

"If you are not one of Samoht's men, how come you to have the roses?"

"Look, Mistress Ardra—" he touched the chain beneath his tunic—"where I'm from, the roses are jewelry, like the rings on your fingers. In fact, these are meant to be worn on the ears. They're earrings." Her gaze shifted to his ear, and he knew she'd noticed the hole there. "These earrings are sacred to me. They were made by one of my ancestors for my mother's mother." He indicated the relationships as one would in the *Tolemac Wars* game, invoking religion with the word "sacred," hoping to defuse the political nature of the rose for her.

"I see." She was silent for a moment. "What were you doing on Nilrem's mountain?"

He'd figured out a story to explain his appearance on the mountain. After all, a merchant or craftsman belonged in the capital, not on some empty mountain. "I was seeking wisdom as most others who journey there do. I was a warrior, but gave it up." He ignored her small snort of derision and tried to sound solemn. "I became a merchant when I tired of bloodshed, trading on the many rewards I earned in my warrior days. But I also thought I ought to make a pilgrimage of redemption. I made a vow never to raise a sword or dagger against another being." That took care of his lack of sword skills.

She examined him, her gaze sweeping over him from head to foot. "You were making a pilgrimage of redemption?"

"Aye. To atone for some of my exploits."

"You have no arm rings. You are not a warrior." She tossed her head.

51

The action did something to his insides. "Where I'm from, we've stopped wearing arm rings. We get tattoos instead." At her blank look, he explained. "A tattoo is a marking on the skin that's permanent. You did notice that the snake coils three times around my arm?" Thank God for that little coincidence. "And the scale pattern is in the pattern of the Shield."

"You can be naught but a slave without arm rings."

"Maybe here, but not in Ocean City."

"Ocean City . . . your place? I knew someone from Ocean City once."

She said no more, and he decided he wasn't going to mention Vad or Gwen until he found out how they stood in the memory of this world.

"My men are troubled by the question of your status. They do not know how to treat a man who has no arm rings."

"So I'll pick up a few somewhere." What would her reaction be to that crime of crimes?

Ardra's eyes grew wide. She touched a gloved hand to her breast. "And have your belly slit and your entrails roasted while you still live? How can you make such a jest? To steal arm rings . . . to wear ones you have not earned . . . the penalty is appalling."

"Arm rings or no arm rings, I'm a retired warrior who became a merchant and is on a pilgrimage. Nothing more." He tugged on his reins and let his horse drop to the rear of the company.

Ardra thought about Lien's tale. She knew of two people who had come from across the ice fields. One good. One evil. Both had disappeared. What manner of man was this one?

Her memory of the attack told her that Lien had appeared as if from the very air. But perhaps it was only her fear that had made it appear so.

It was a mistake to think a comely man was honest and

good. Samoht, the high councilor, was quite beautiful, but all knew he could be ugly in word and deed.

Lien was alluring, perhaps dangerously so. His voice was seductive, his tale amusing. Yet he must be a man who had committed grave deeds to undertake a pilgrimage to Nilrem's mountain.

She was grateful that Lien was a pilgrim. The rest of his status, whether runaway slave or wealthy merchant, mattered little.

Lien, the pilgrim, could be set from her mind. Ollach could worry about him, not she. After all, what good did it do her to think of this man?

Certain women might be thrilled to find a runaway slave. 'Twas thought they made excellent bed partners. A runaway slave would be desperate to please or he might find himself sold in the common marketplace or, worse, returned to an angry master.

An uncanny heat curled in her belly, but she ignored it. She was not interested in bed play. It pleased the man well, but the woman little.

Nilrem called to Lien and pointed toward the thick line of trees ahead. Lien was unlike any of the fair-haired warriors who rode at her side. He was lean and well browned as if he walked about naked in the sun. The image brought a return of the quick, hot heat in her loins.

She imagined that Lien had charmed more than his share of woman to bed play in the past, but what had she to fear of him this day? If Lien was truly a pilgrim as he said, he had no need of women—nor desire for them, either.

Pilgrims were celibate.

Chapter Five

Lien complimented himself on his pilgrim tale. It muddied the water about his status. In the game, pilgrims were protected, no matter what their original occupation. It was considered bad luck to kill a pilgrim. That thought warmed his innards.

Of course, he imagined that slaves weren't permitted to be pilgrims, but if he said he wasn't a slave enough times, maybe Ardra would eventually believe it.

He didn't really believe much in omens or such, but it did seem more than a coincidence that he had entered the game at the very moment when Ardra needed help. Somehow he thought it might be bad luck to just walk away from her . . . at least for a while.

He didn't much care for the mood of her men, though. Once they set foot on the barely perceptible path into the forest, they began murmuring amongst themselves when Ardra was out of earshot.

Nilrem called a halt to the party at dawn. Deep in the woods, the blood-red sun announced its presence with a strange light as if the trees were on fire. Nilrem stood up

in his cart and gestured for all to gather about him.

"I have made an important decision," the wiseman began. "Mistress Ardra, I ask that your party leave me behind." He touched the staff on which he leaned. "This cart cannot keep pace with the rest of you. Neither can I ride a horse for many miles. Therefore, I suggest you leave me with a man or two as guards and proceed at full speed."

Ardra bit her lip. "Will Tol not need you?"

Nilrem climbed awkwardly from his cart. He hugged her. "I fear Tol will have no need of either healer or wiseman."

Lien watched her. Her eyes glittered a moment, but then she donned a cold manner.

"It will be as you suggest." She turned toward her men and indicated two, then spoke to Lien. "And you, pilgrim. You came to seek the wiseman, so it seems most fitting you tend him."

Before he could open his mouth, Nilrem spoke. "I fear, mistress, you must take Lien with you. He saved you at the precise moment the conjunction began. You must agree 'tis an omen."

She fisted her hands on her hips. "I do not agree. He is useless to me. He does not ride well; he might be a runaway slave. He is—"

"Take him. I see it in the stars." Nilrem spoke softly, and Ardra's men murmured and glanced from one to another.

Lien grinned. Not because he wanted to be in Ardra's party over Nilrem's, but because he could almost see steam coming out of Ardra's ears. "I know when I'm not wanted. I'll be happy to stay with Nilrem."

Ollach stepped forward. "Mistress, we have entered a place of magic. I must caution going against the wiseman's words."

Nilrem nodded. "Mistress Ardra, you must take Lien with you. I feel it in my old bones. He is needed in some way."

55

Ann Lawrence

Lien looked at the old man but could detect no humor in his face. In fact, as Nilrem leaned toward Ardra, he seemed to be urging her to obey him with every fiber of his body.

Ardra dropped into a deep curtsey. What did the old-fashioned gesture mean? Capitulation? A nod to something greater than herself? A belief in magic?

While Ardra's men distributed the wagon's provisions among their saddles, Nilrem stumped over to him. "Listen to me, young Lien. This is the Goddess of Darkness's domain. Tread lightly here, I warn you."

"Look, what possible good can I be to Ardra? As she said, I don't ride that well, and my vow says I can't pick up a sword, so why not let me stay with you?"

"She will take you through the forest and to the border between Selaw and Tolemac. From such a location you can make your choice, go in any direction. But you may also prove of some use. Have you no sense of responsibility to this woman whose life you saved?"

"No. None. Don't put that on me." He hadn't been able to preserve his mother's life despite the marvels of modern science and psychology; how could he do any better in a primitive world of weapons and superstition? "I saved her; I'm done with her."

"Then simply take advantage of these many men who may protect you on your journey. Remember, your status is in doubt. Ardra owes you her life. She will not take such a debt lightly."

Lien looked around. Nilrem would have three warriors and the cart. Ardra had about a dozen retainers. Some were servants, but most were men with swords. If he stayed with Ardra, he'd get the nickel tour for free, food and lodging included. "Okay. I'll stay with Ardra." Once made, the decision felt right.

"Remember one other thing, young man. Once you have claimed the debt she owes you, 'tis claimed. You cannot

call on her twice. So pick your time wisely." Nilrem bowed
and Lien returned it.

He assisted the old man into the cart. For the first few
miles, the old man and his party kept pace, but gradually
they fell behind. Twice Ardra lifted her hand, and twice
her men picked up their pace, wending deeper into the
forest.

The Tangled Wood was unlike anything Lien had ever
seen. Giant trees towered overhead, their huge branches
forming a canopy that blocked out the light in many places.
The roots, as thick as his arms, erupted from the trunks,
then twisted on each other before disappearing into the
earth. Despite the lack of light, vines intertwined with the
roots, some with white flowers shaped like teacups. The
effect was a sea of vines around the base of each tree. It
was difficult to tell where one tree began and another
ended.

"Have you ever been here before?" Lien asked Ollach.

"Nay. 'Tis an evil place. This path we ride is said to
have been hewed from the forest in the ancient time. No
one remembers who performed thc task. 'Tis said to be a
road of magic, trod by the Goddess and her minions."

"Jolly."

Ardra's entourage made too much noise for Lien to catch
sight of animals or birds. He saw only the pale shadows of
deer that looked as white as snow.

The deeper they went, the darker the forest grew. After
a few hours, Ardra ordered torches lit, and although Lien
guessed it was about mid-afternoon, they needed the glow
of the smoking flames to see where they were going.

Every now and then they would burst into a clearing.
The sky overhead, a dazzling bowl of amethyst, might tell
everyone else it was still day, but it told Lien he was definitely not in his own world.

His sense of euphoria lasted until his rear began to ache.
He was grateful when Ardra called a halt. Her men took
advantage of the short stop to take naps. Twelve hours of

solid sleep wouldn't have been enough for Lien.

"I should have stayed with Nilrem," he said to Ardra when she stopped at his side.

She sank down in a pool of green skirts and took his arm. Her fingers were gentle as she untied the bandages and inspected her work. For the first time, she smiled. Lien found himself staring.

"Why?" she prompted. "Why should you have stayed with Nilrem?"

"I think I left my ass a few miles back."

She laughed. It was a low, throaty sound. "You cannot have been a warrior if you do not know you ride a horse, not an ass."

"No. Ass." Lien rubbed his backside. "Where I come from, this part of the body is sometimes referred to as an ass."

She ducked her head and inspected her work. "I see. Forgive my ignorance of your ways."

He placed his hand over hers. "No. Forgive me for my impolite behavior. My mother would be appalled." Then he remembered that his mother wasn't around to care about anything. In fact, hadn't cared much about him or herself for a long time.

Ardra took his hand. "You look troubled. Is something wrong?"

"Nothing's wrong. I'm impressed with that gray goop, whatever it is."

"You are troubled by thoughts of your mother, are you not? Is she ill?"

He stood up and rolled his sleeve down. "My mother's dead."

Ardra rose and stood before him. "I sense 'tis a recent thing, her passing. If so, you will understand my need to get to Tol."

"Sure, I understand. I just don't understand the rest of all this." He swept a hand out to her men. "How can Ralen help you?"

"He has influence. I did not finish with your arm. Hold it out, pilgrim."

"What of your own influence?" Lien did as she asked. She wrapped his arm in fresh bandages and tied it snugly.

"A woman has no influence in Tolemac and little in Selaw. I had only the influence Tol allowed me. With his passing . . ."

"You love him?" Lien felt it important to know if he was lusting after a grieving widow, or a soon-to-be grieving widow.

Whoa. Where had that thought come from?

"I love him." She said it with great heat, then turned and watched her men. "He is like no other man I have ever met. He is my teacher, and I his student. He taught me to understand my people, to listen to their needs, and find a way to alleviate their suffering."

"I gather he's older than you." He watched emotions play over her face.

"He is my mentor. The father of my dear son. I will never replace him. Never."

"Then we'd better get to him quickly."

A shadow dropped over her face. It took him a moment to realize it was a net. Without thought, he reached out and scooped her up, net and all. In two strides he was off the road. Trapped in the net, she screamed. He hissed at her to be silent.

Nets dropped all around them, engulfing the warriors, tangling horses, smothering torches. Men garbed in rags dropped on the hapless travelers, flailing clubs and shouting. Lien remained miraculously free.

He glanced about at the writhing mass of nets and men to be sure he was unobserved, then slipped into a gap in a tangle of tree roots. He pushed deep into a cave of greenery. Ardra squirmed in his arms.

"Ardra. Stop it." She lay instantly still. He tried to find the edges of the net and failed. He could feel the rapid

59

panting of her breath on his face. "I need your dagger to cut you free," he whispered at her ear.

She wriggled in his arms; then something poked him in the stomach. He worked his fingers into the netting and pulled out her knife. Carefully so as not to cut her, he sawed the strands of the net apart. It was made of the vines that entangled the tree roots. They were tough but finally parted, and he helped her struggle free of their grip. Then, to help conceal her further, he pulled her hood up and over her hair.

He held up a finger for her to be silent. "Keep your head down. I'm going to see what I can do."

He crawled out of the roots. He couldn't fight the men from the trees, not with one tiny dagger. He duckwalked to the closest warrior and cut him free. It was Ollach. With a finger to his lips, Lien pointed left, then right to indicate the direction each should take.

All around Lien, men were shouting, horses thrashing, and women screaming. He slid along the ground, cutting the mesh and freeing warriors. Each man drew his sword and began to slash and cut at their ragged enemies, who had only clubs for weapons. In moments, it was all over. The men from the trees swarmed up the trunks and with shrieks and howls abandoned the fight.

Ardra's men sheathed their swords, cut the remaining prisoners free, then began to inspect the wounded.

Lien crawled into Ardra's shelter, offered her his hand, and tugged her from her hiding place. She walked slowly around the camp, speaking to each person and making use of her pouch of gray goo where needed. Lien walked behind her and watched.

The cook had a goose-egg on his forehead. His fat face gleamed with sweat, and he trembled. "Mistress, we must move on." The man's eyes swept the lush canopy over their heads.

"Aye, we will do so." She patted his shoulder. "After Ollach and his men bury the dead. Luckily, none of them are ours."

Lien took her arm and helped her up. She did not remove it as they continued the inspection of her men. When they were ready to mount their horses, he looped his fingers together and she placed her boot in his palm, one hand on his shoulder.

"Lien," she said before he boosted her into the saddle. "Again, I owe you my life." The hood slid off her head. She looked disheveled and weary.

"I guess I'm not so completely useless, and you have a leaf in your hair."

"I will not forget your help." She lifted her hands, and ran them through her hair, and plucked out the leaf. For a moment, she sat there, the leaf between her fingers. "This is a rare find." Then she extended it to him. "Keep it. For luck."

The leaf was thick and glossy, shaped like a spade in a deck of cards. It was odd. He saw no other trees nearby that had leaves shaped in the same way. He shrugged and tucked it into his tunic.

"Against your wound," she said. "It comes from the Tree of Valor. 'Tis said the old ones used it to heal."

"Old ones?"

"Aye. The old ones who once inhabited the forest. They disappeared hundreds of conjunctions ago. Many say because they feared the goddess."

His horse was led forward by Ollach, and Lien knew he was going to have to mount up, sore ass or not. "So this goddess is immortal?" *Right. And fairies sing.*

"Nay, Lien. Each goddess trains her firstborn daughter to carry on her evil."

Ardra posted two warriors, one in front and one behind, to keep an exclusive watch overhead as they traveled on. Would it be enough? What else might befall them? Luckily no one of theirs had been killed.

Lien rode at her side, and it somehow seemed right to do so. She now owed him twice for her life.

"If there's a daughter goddess, there must be a god somewhere."

Ardra glanced at him. Curious marks were blooming across his cheek. A puffiness distorted the fine line of his jaw. "A consort. Goddesses take consorts. It is said that one may know him because he will be wearing the goddess's Black Eye."

"Black eye?"

She saw him shift in the saddle. He appeared most uncomfortable, yet did not complain. She recalled the blows he had sustained on her behalf. Why had she not allowed him to remain behind?

"Hello, Ardra? Black eye?" He did something with his fingers and a sharp sound was produced.

"How did you do that?" she asked.

He looked down at his fingers and then up at her. "I just snapped my fingers, nothing much." He did it several times.

"Show me," she said. " 'Tis marvelous."

He demonstrated, and she tried repeatedly. Although she succeeded in reproducing the sound, it did not match the sharpness of his. Perhaps it was the stronger male hand that made the difference. Thoughts of his hands and how they had held her hard against him as they hid in the tree roots brought a sheen of sweat to her palms.

"Ardra, now that you've unlocked that little secret, what's the black eye?"

She snapped her fingers and laughed, then sobered. "Oh, the Black Eye is a jewel. Unlike the amber and turquoise which are healing and sacred, the Black Eye is considered cursed. Only the consort may wear it with impunity. Only one such stone has ever been found in the many mines of the chiefdoms."

She noticed her men watching her and realized she had given Lien far too much of her attention. "I must move forward."

Lien nodded and muttered something under his breath when she lifted her hand for more speed. She overtook the few men who separated her from the forward guard.

"Push the men faster, Ollach," she ordered. "I do not wish to meet with another disaster. Those men who attacked us—do you think they were outcasts?"

Ollach shrugged. "Most likely, mistress. If they had been sent by the goddess, they would not have been so easily routed. We could have used some archers."

"Aye. 'Tis a pity Samoht would not allow us any."

"Forgive me, mistress, but is it wise to talk to the pilgrim?" Ollach asked.

"You forget your place," she said.

She wheeled her mount and moved back to a center position next to the pilgrim to show Ollach he could not dictate her actions. "Lien, I must thank you for saving my life again."

"No problem." His answer was curt.

"You are in pain?"

"I have pains on my pains. How much farther do you think we need to go?"

"If Ollach is correct in his estimations, we will leave the forest at the next sunrising."

"And what time is it now?" He raised his gaze to the canopy overhead. For a brief moment, in the dark shadows of the trees and torchlight, he looked like one of the ancient ones carved in ice rock. A wave of dizziness came over her.

"I do not know," she managed. But she did know. The sunrising would not be for a long time. The distance to the Selaw border was long also. Tol might be dead ere they reached it. The wave of dizziness receded as she pushed her horse to greater speed. Once Tol was gone, these warriors would melt away from her as the ice did when brought to the fire, for they were Tol's men, Tolemac warriors, as Ralen was. They would feel no obligation to serve her unless Samoht so ordered it.

63

She remembered well Samoht's arrogant face as he had bade her to his bed on his last visit to the fortress. Though she had never mentioned the incident, Tol had known. He had sensed the truth and been angered enough to draw his men about her whenever Samoht visited.

A shout jerked her attention to the lead warrior. A party approached them. She felt suddenly cold. They were Tolemac warriors. Had they news of Tol?

When the party drew near, she saw that unlike her own men, these warriors were well prepared for the forest trek. There were archers with bows ready, and the group was twice as large as hers. At the head of the phalanx rode a man she would know anywhere, anytime.

'Twas Ralen. Each time she saw him, she thought of how Tol must have looked in his youth—tall, imposing, full of life and vigor. Ralen had the same shade of hair as her son. It reminded her of honey streaked with ribbons of gold. And like her son, Ralen had Tol's eyes too. They were so pale a blue, they looked almost silver, but Ralen's were often narrowed with displeasure. Ralen was not a joyful man.

Ollach helped her dismount, and she went down on one knee to the warrior. "Ralen. I bid you peace."

"Mistress Ardra. Might I be so bold as to ask why you are in this bedeviled forest?"

"I was seeking you."

Ralen dismounted and gestured for his men to circle their party. "There has been an influx of rebels in these woods. It is not safe for a woman—"

"The goddess would disagree with you."

Ralen nodded. "Aye, but you are not she. Is my brother mad, that he sends his mate to risk her life?"

"Nay; he is near death."

Ralen looked down. He whispered something she assumed was a prayer for his brother's soul. When he looked up, his expression was grim. "So, now we know 'tis not the birth of his heir that brings Samoht to the border."

"Aye. May I speak with you in private?"

Ralen nodded and took her arm. He moved with her to the edge of the party, but not so far as to leave them unguarded. His grip was not gentle. It was the hold of a man who wished to demonstrate that he was in control and she but a nuisance.

"What is it you wish to—" He abruptly turned toward Lien. "By the moons, who is that?"

"A pilgrim who saved my life."

"He is not a pilgrim. Not garbed in such a manner. I have never seen hair so dark." Ralen strode past her as if she were invisible.

She wanted to scream in frustration. "Ralen. He can wait."

Ralen paused. He turned back and sketched a quick bow. "Aye, mistress, forgive me."

" 'Tis said you seek the Goddess of Darkness."

"I have just come from her domain. Samoht suspected her of a serious theft."

"Aye, the Vial of Seduction."

"You are well informed." Ralen shrugged his shoulders. "It was a useless effort. If the woman has the vial, it is hidden so that mortal man cannot find it."

"You spoke to her?" Ardra watched him carefully. Had the woman bewitched Ralen?

"Aye. The goddess is naught but another comely woman who works her wiles on old men. Her consort must be Tol's age."

Two of Ralen's warriors who stood nearby snickered.

Ralen shot them a hard look, and they moved away. "Forgive me. I did not mean to imply—"

"There is nothing to forgive." Ardra cut him short.

"As I was saying, if the goddess wants the vial in order to lure a younger man than her current consort, she has not used it yet."

Ardra knotted her fingers together to conceal her agitation. "And has she a daughter?"

65

"None that I saw. Perhaps that is the cause of the rumors. The vial is missing, the goddess's consort is old, and she has no daughter; thus she must have stolen it to find a more potent man."

An awkward silence fell between them. Ralen cleared his throat. "Now, you had something of import to tell me?"

"Tol suffers much. The healer has tried everything, and Tol hoped Nilrem might know of some potion she did not. 'Tis how I come to be here. It was the wiseman who thought we should find you, that you should be with Tol now.

"I know Tol hopes you will stand in his place as a voice of reason when"—she had to look up to stem the tears—"when he passes. If you do not, I have no one. The Fortress of Ravens will be Samoht's unless I fight, and without a warrior of your stature, I have little hope of holding out against him."

"I cannot fight Samoht. I am his lieutenant, and Tol knows that." Ralen took a step toward her, but not near enough to show he held any interest in her troubles. Pain burst within her. Her search had been for naught.

"Tol understands that you cannot stand against the high councilor, but someone must sit in Tol's place at the council table and represent his chiefdom, and mine."

"I am not a councilor, nor do I wish to serve as such."

He was as cold as ice. "Tol believed it was time you took his seat."

Ralen shrugged. "I could never be content in a councilor's chair. I much prefer the saddle. Tol presumes too much."

She must beg. She drew in a deep breath and fisted her hands so she would not weep and prove that women were weak and hapless beings. "I humbly beseech you to reconsider. It is not necessary, according to Tol, that you relinquish your warrior status to sit in his place while he yet lives. He said if he is too ill to take his seat, you may do so at his bidding."

"I will think about it." With a sharp, dismissive gesture, Ralen walked away.

She would not humiliate herself by running after him. He gave orders for his men to mount up and join her party. She heard him direct his men to the Selaw border. So, she would have some time with him and might convince him yet.

Then Ralen strode to where Lien was checking his horse's girth.

"Who are you?" Ralen asked without any of the customary polite greetings one made to a stranger.

"Who are you?" Lien asked in turn.

Ardra shook her head slightly at his curt response and tried to send him a silent message that Ralen was not to be trifled with.

Ralen ignored the question. "What are you doing with Mistress Ardra?"

Lien gave her a barely perceptible nod, then spoke with more civility. "Mistress Ardra and I met by accident while she was gathering wood. Three outcasts attacked her, and I happened to be handy." He mounted his horse, and Ardra suspected he did so to set himself above Ralen, who stood a hand taller than he.

"He saved my life, Ralen," she said. "I am giving him safe conduct."

The look Ralen shot her spoke his distrust of her and Lien. "You have never gathered wood in your life."

She clenched her jaw. "I have learned much at Tol's knee, the least of which is that one must sometimes take care of oneself."

"So—" Ralen looked up at Lien, who in turn merely arched a dark brow. "You saved Ardra's life? You expect my brother will reward you?"

Before Lien could reply, she jumped in. "Nay. He asks nothing. You do not understand. Lien saved my life, and in doing so, lost all he had to my attackers. I have furnished him with clothing and a horse. It is the least I can do. I

am also granting him safe conduct. You would do at least as much for one who saved your life."

Ralen placed a hand on Lien's bridle. "Hear this, pilgrim. Whatever debt Ardra owed you, it is now paid. Do you understand? When we reach the border, I want you gone."

Ardra gasped. "Ralen. I will decide when my debts are paid."

Lien jerked his horse away from Ralen's grip and moved into the line of men heading off through the forest.

"If I stand in Tol's place, I will decide." Ralen took his reins from one of his men. "Now mount up and let us make all speed to the border. I have a report for Samoht that cannot wait." He led his horse away.

She silently cursed his broad back.

When they'd gone a few leagues, and Ralen was well occupied at the head of the party, she drew her horse next to Lien's.

"I hope you will accept my word that I do not consider my debt to you discharged. Food and clothing are not an equal measure for a life," she said.

He smiled. It was a lopsided smile as his cheek had puffed up in a most alarming way.

"Don't worry about it. I didn't rescue you for a reward. I take it that's Ralen."

"Aye. He is Tol's brother. Does your face hurt a great deal? I have never seen such injuries. It is as if an invisible brush has touched you with color."

He touched his cheek. "Yeah. It's just a bruise. It'll go away without any help."

"We are not so afflicted when injured." She wanted to skim her finger over the mark but dared not be so familiar. Still, the urge was there and it made her uncomfortable. She cleared her throat.

"So why is Ralen so hostile? I thought you were going to hook up with him and stand against this Samoht."

"It seems Tol is wrong about Ralen. He did think Ralen would welcome this chance to take a council seat."

"It goes to his brother if Tol—"

"—dies. Nay. Council seats are chosen. But if Tol recommended Ralen, a man of such high birth and respect would almost surely be granted the honor. There is no one who might vie for the position against him and win."

"No ambitious person waiting in the wings?"

"In the wings? You have such odd turns of phrase. But I think I take your meaning. Nay. There is no one save Samoht who covets Tol's chiefdom, and, thank the gods, Samoht may not represent more than one chiefdom at the council table. He is the high councilor and rules Tolemac itself."

"I see. So, there are a bunch of chiefdoms ruled by councilors and they all get together and sit around and decide what's best for the people in general?"

"Aye." He was so easy to talk to. There had been one other like him . . . but nay, she would not think of the past and what could not be undone. "As Selaw folk, we have no seat on the council. We are not worthy."

"Are you saying that when this council meets, the Selaw aren't represented?"

"Nay. We are outside the eight chiefdoms. We have, through all the ages of the ice, stood alone."

"Then what do you need Ralen for?"

"In an effort to avert war, I was given to Tol. As my mate, he controls all that is mine—the fortress is key to the power of the Selaw. Through Tol, we Selaw had a voice on the council. He spoke for us and kept the other councilors in check."

Lien scratched his chin. She noticed that, although Ollach and Ralen, who had not shaved in many days, had but a soft glimmer of golden hair upon their cheeks, Lien's beard was dark, clearly defining the shape of his jaw.

"Why didn't Tol just turn the fortress over to Tolemac?"

Ann Lawrence

"Is that what you would do? Of course—you are a man. Tol is different. He understood . . . understands what the Selaw people need. It is not subjugation to Tolemac."

"Whoa. I understand. Don't get in a lather."

"I am not a horse." She twisted her reins in gloved hands.

"I was not saying you were. It's just an expression, not much different from saying, 'By Nilrem's beard.' I was saying I did not want you to get upset."

"Forgive me. You are so strange."

"Thanks." He smiled again, then winced.

"When next we stop, you must allow me to tend your face."

"I think one of the tree people clunked me with something."

No sooner had he spoken than their horses emerged from the trees and the parties halted.

Ralen rode back to her side. "Come forward, mistress. See what you ask." He then cantered back to the fore of their party.

Ardra looked at Lien. "Will you come too?" she asked. She did not know why it was important to her that he remain nearby.

"Sure. Lead on." He swept out his hand to gesture her forward.

It was such a startling thing for a man to tell a woman to lead, she almost fell off her horse. Head up, she nodded and maneuvered around him. He fell in behind her.

They reached the front of Ralen's party, which had spread out in a single line. The forest ended at a steep cliff top. Below was a rocky plain cut by a broad river. The plain stretched for many miles, and even here, sheltered at the edge of the forest, one could feel the change in the temperature. The wind was sharper, the chill cutting through her cloak. On the horizon a white streak was visible: the ice fields. And nearer, on the opposite side of the river, lay her land and her people.

Between her and the river, scattered like gems on a gold-smith's table, were the tents of Samoht.

"So many," she whispered.

"Aye," Ralen said. "Look and understand what you wish to stand against. And know you ask the impossible."

Chapter Six

Lien repeated every prayer he knew as their party negotiated a narrow path from the cliff to the rocky plain below.
Most of the time, he couldn't see the path beneath his
horse's hooves. He thought it might be easier to walk a
skyscraper ledge.

Sweat slicked his skin beneath the tunic. So he wasn't
real happy with heights, so he wasn't happy with windy,
narrow paths on high cliffs. So what? So he didn't even
ride the Ferris wheel on the boardwalk and had not taken
the mule ride at the Grand Canyon despite Eve's ribbing.
So maybe this was the day he'd die.

So who would care? He closed his eyes and let the horse
do the work. He hoped the horse didn't have a death wish.

Cold wind whipped Ardra's skirts against her horse's
flanks with dull snaps, but he was hot, almost burning in
the rising, blood-red Tolemac sun. He thought he might
pass out.

Gwen would never know what had happened to him.

"Lien," Ardra called out. She had twisted around in her
saddle. "You cannot allow your mount to wander. He

72

nipped my mare." She snapped her fingers at him.

He managed a grin. So it wasn't her skirt he'd been hearing. "Sure. No problem. I'll watch death rise up to meet me. Sure. I'll let this hapless nag drag me off the edge of nowhere," he muttered. "Damn, teach a woman a skill and see how she abuses it."

His head hurt just one degree more than the rest of his body, which was one giant ache. His horse nipped Ardra's again. She snapped her fingers at him.

His horse bucked. For one dizzy moment he hung half off his saddle over the world below. The next moment, the horse had settled down. Ardra scowled another warning. He wanted to lift his hand and give her a wave to let her know that everything was okay, but he found he could no more let go of the reins than he could open his mouth.

When the path widened, he took a deep breath. His throat hurt. *Shit*, he thought. *I'm sick, and no antibiotics in sight.*

That thought occupied him until his horse reached level ground.

"Thank you, God," he whispered.

The party picked up its pace and galloped toward a city of tents clustered on the edge of the river. The pace did nothing for his insides, his wounds, or his bruises.

Samoht's army was massive. It took about an hour to work their way through the formidable force that Samoht had brought to the Selaw border. Lien figured Ardra's fortress was toast.

As they passed he noticed the wary looks directed his way. He would need to make himself as unobtrusive as possible and hope he wasn't challenged.

Ollach helped Ardra dismount. Ralen hustled her toward a long tent that was the color of the lavender sky and decorated with painted symbols of the sun and moon. The other tents were also of fanciful colors with birds and animals painted on them, but only on this one were celestial

73

bodies depicted. The tent was surrounded by a small army of blond, blue-eyed warriors.

Lien dismounted and drifted along with Ardra's men as if he were part of the action. There was no way he was going to freeze out in the wind. His nice, comfy tunic now felt grossly inadequate, damp as it was and clinging to his skin. He'd have to wheedle a cloak out of Ollach.

Although the guards stared at his hair, when they noted his tunic they let him pass along with the rest of Ardra's men.

Inside the tent, it was as quiet as a tomb and as hot as a sauna. Braziers glowed in every corner. Everyone's attention centered on a dais and the old man reclining there. His bed, a sort of padded chaise longue, was covered in furs and heavy gold cloth, making the man appear to be some illustrious sultan. This must be Tol.

So he had made it to the border before he died. Ardra knelt at his side.

An elderly woman stood beside the councilor. Despite her long white hair and a face pleated in wrinkles, she was an arresting woman, tall and stately, dressed in ivory and gold.

Tol might once have been a heavyset man, but today, so close to death, he was skeletal, his robes hanging like a pile of old drapes about his body. He had a mane of white hair and very pale blue eyes. He might be brother to Ralen, but whereas Ralen looked anywhere from thirty to forty, Tol looked near eighty.

Ralen knelt beside Ardra, and the rest of the party stood respectfully aside near the entranceway.

"Tol, I bid you peace," Ardra said.

Tol placed a trembling hand on her head and stroked her hair. "I knew you would return in time."

Ardra drew a small fabric packet from her purse and handed it to the woman. "Four grains only."

The woman bowed to Ardra. Tol beckoned the old woman near. She leaned close to him, listened, and nodded gravely.

With a low bow to Ardra, the woman stepped to a long table situated behind Tol's couch. There she opened the packet, fussed about for a moment, then poured what looked like wine into an ornate silver goblet set with turquoise. It was she, not Ardra, who supported Tol's hand as he drank.

Everyone held his breath as Tol settled back onto the couch and gasped for air. Several moments passed in silence.

Finally, Tol spoke. "Ralen," he said. "Can you fetch a holy man or a wiseman? I wish to speak to Ardra on matters of grave importance."

"Nilrem could not keep pace with us, Brother. He will be here in perhaps a sunrising or two."

Tol smiled and shook his head. "I have not the luxury to wait that long. Nay, is there no other who might stand in his place?"

"We have no such person in our company," Ralen said.

The woman at Tol's side pressed her hands tightly together and bowed her head. Lien assumed that Tol wanted the Tolemac version of last rites.

Ardra rose and took the woman's hand. "Deleh, do not despair. We have a pilgrim. Will that not do?"

The woman and Tol exchanged a glance, then a nod, but Ralen protested. "Nay. He is not a pilgrim. Ardra, what ails you?"

Ralen jumped up and marched to where Lien stood. He prodded him in the chest. "This man has no means of proving who he is or whence he comes. When have you ever seen hair of such a color? Or eyes, for that matter?"

The old woman floated gracefully in Lien's direction. She gave him a close inspection, then issued a soft command. Everyone save Tol, Lien, Ardra, and Ralen left the tent. The woman bowed respectfully and asked, "Are you a pilgrim?"

He could not lie to a woman with such an intense stare. In fact, she reminded him of a nun who used to scare the

living daylights out of him in elementary school. "I was traveling to Nilrem for some wisdom. If that makes me a pilgrim, I'm a pilgrim."

"From where?" Tol asked in a breathy voice.

Ardra went to Tol and placed a hand on his shoulder. "He is from beyond the ice fields. Just as the conjunction began, I was attacked by three outcasts. Lien saved my life."

"Ollach saw him disrobe; he wears a sign of evil." Ralen crossed his arms on his chest as if that ended the discussion. "And who can cross the ice fields? 'Tis nonsense."

"Show me," the old woman said to Lien.

Well, heck, Lien thought. *Everybody else has seen me naked, why not Mother Superior?* He pulled his tunic off.

With no sign of fear, the woman brought her fingers close to his tattoo but didn't actually touch him. She counted the snake's coils and then bent closer to inspect the knotwork.

"The serpent bears the Shield pattern, Tol."

"Come closer," Tol whispered, and Ardra stepped aside, her hand still on Tol's shoulder. Lien bent to one knee by the old man, and as Tol inspected the tattoo, Lien found he could not look away from Ardra.

She was staring at him too, her gaze moving back and forth from his arm to the roses on his mother's chain. She frowned, reached out, and touched the design. When her fingertips touched his tattoo, a hot pulse swirled around the coils, like blood pounding in his veins during sex. Where had that thought come from?

Tol jerked and his breath hissed.

"Tol?" Ardra slid her hand away from the tattoo. The heat disappeared, and Lien and Tol exchanged a glance.

"Closer," Tol said, lifting his hand. "Ardra?" She entwined her fingers with his. "Touch the snake," Tol directed.

Ralen shifted impatiently from one foot to the other.

"Nay," Ardra whispered, but she did as Tol bade, barely touching her cool fingertips to the tattoo.

Lien was ready this time. He forced himself to be as cool and distant as she was. But the heat still surged, the pulse rioting around his arm to shoot up his shoulder and into his head. Tol moaned and jerked, pulling his hand from Ardra's. The sensation instantly disappeared.

Ralen jumped forward and thrust himself between Lien and Tol. "Stop this!"

But Tol shook him off. "Nay. Leave the pilgrim here. He will do. He will do."

Ralen opened his mouth, but Tol forestalled him. "Say nothing. I have no time. By our father's heart, be still."

The Mother Superior stepped in, ending the exchange. She handed Lien his tunic and then took Tol's hand. Ardra knelt again at her lifemate's side, her back to Lien and Ralen.

Lien pulled the tunic quickly over his head and remained a respectful distance from the old man. Tol looked too frail to survive another hour.

Ardra's back was stiff, her hair in a loose mane. The tiny amber beads shimmered in the torchlight, set to trembling by some strong emotion, Lien suspected.

"What do I do?" Lien asked no one in particular.

"Kneel here and bear witness to all we say," the old woman whispered. Ralen made a noise in his throat and wandered over to a brazier. He lifted a set of tongs hanging beneath the iron bowl and began to stir the coals. His actions spoke of his contempt for the proceedings.

"I have little time," Tol began.

"Do not say that. Wait to see if Nilrem's powder eases your pain," Ardra said.

"Deleh?" Tol looked up and smiled at the old woman.

"I gave him all of it," Deleh said. "It is what he wished."

Ardra's mouth opened, but no words came out. She bent her head, and Lien saw a tear roll down her cheek. "How could you? What of our son?"

Whether she spoke to the woman or Tol, Lien didn't know.

"It is of him I think as I lie here," Tol said. "It is his hard life I regret." He put out his hand, and Ardra gripped it in both of hers. "I should never have presumed to add such a burden to your young life either. Had the boy Tolemac bones and not just the eyes, he might have faired well. 'Twas folly for me to think that through our son I could change the story of time."

"Samoht's child will also be of mixed blood."

"He cares little for the child save as a pawn to move on the board of power. He will hold the child as ransom for his mother's good behavior. Watch that Samoht does not do the same with our son. Is he hidden?"

"He is in the labyrinth beneath the fortress. No one will find him there."

Tol nodded and closed his eyes. No one spoke for about five minutes. The old woman wiped Tol's brow with a cool cloth.

He roused himself. "There is no place in our world for a child of mixed birth. He will suffer all his days, a man different from all others."

"Our son need not fear if the fortress is strong enough. I will gather the men and beseech them to—"

"Ardra, Ardra. You dream, and I, to my shame, have allowed you to hope. No man will follow a woman. When I am gone, Samoht will send his warriors to guard the fortress in our son's name, but in truth, it will not be so. Samoht will take the fortress, and to stand against him will mean death."

"I will not give up the fortress. It belongs to my people. Samoht sees all the Selaw as inferior. He will treat us little better than slaves—your son included! I beg of you to speak the words that will help me stand against him."

Lien could feel the energy she poured into the simple entreaty.

Tol shook his head. "I will say the words, but you must accept what you cannot change." The old man beckoned to Lien. He moved closer, his hip touching Ardra's.

"Young man, you stand as witness to my words. Although I think 'tis folly, I beg of you to bear witness to Samoht of what I will now say. Ralen might be suspected of conniving with Ardra to gain power. Come back, Ralen. Set aside your ire and come here."

They all gathered about Tol. The old man's voice now held a tremor and was as soft as a whisper. "It is my wish that Ardra take control of the fortress. It is my wish that she, and she alone, rule it for our son until he is of age."

Tol coughed and reached out blindly with his free hand. The old woman took it and motioned Lien and Ralen out of the tent.

The two men left the tent together, but Ralen split off immediately and strode away. Men and women lingered in silence around the tent. They surely knew that Tol was nearing his end.

Lien wanted to wait for Ardra. He saw a low stool near a fire that no one seemed interested in. He wrapped his arms around his middle to keep from shivering and waited.

After a short while, Ardra came out of the tent and walked toward the river. Lien jumped to his feet and hurried after her, touching her shoulder. "Don't you want to stay with him?" Lien asked.

"Tol?" She looked back at the tent and shook her head. "Nay. He wants this time with Deleh."

"Who is she? Some religious person?" He kept pace with her as she walked through the clusters of tents.

"She is his concubine."

Lien stopped in his tracks. "Wait a minute. Concubine?"

"Aye. She has been so since he first lifemated in his youth."

"Let me get this straight. That woman is a . . . never mind. Aren't you jealous?"

"Of Deleh? Nay. She is like a mother to me. Have you no concubines in Ocean City?"

He was at a loss how to respond. "Explain the relationship a little better and maybe I can give you an answer."

79

She walked to the river's edge. It was a formidable body of water, but the tents were at a ford. It looked as if it were filled with ink. Where it rippled over stone, it frothed with shades of lavender and gray. In places, the water looked about two feet deep. Shallow enough for an invasion.

"If a man has sufficient worth, and wishes it, he has concubines for his pleasure. 'Tis simple."

"And you don't mind?"

"Mind?"

"Object?"

She drew her hood up, and he could no longer see her face. "A woman may not object to her mate's choices in such a matter."

"I don't think you'd find it that way in Ocean City. I don't know too many women who'd allow their . . . mates to sleep with other women." They negotiated the low riverbank and stood at the water's edge.

Ardra appeared to stare at the distant ice on the horizon. "I imagine Deleh sleeps in the women's quarters, Lien."

"That's not what I meant." He picked up a flat stone and skipped it across the water. "The women of my place would not take kindly to their mates making love to other women. We're kind of a one-woman, one-man-at-a-time society."

She handed him another stone, then glanced quickly back at Tol's tent. "Deleh came to the fortress with Tol and has been with us ever since. If a man wishes to copulate, his concubine must be there. Would you teach me the trick with the stones?"

Lien couldn't see her face as she searched for more flat stones by her feet. Her voice held no inflection.

"Sure." He showed her how to hold the rock between her thumb and index finger and how to flick her wrist. She got it on the first try. "The object is to see how many times you can make the stone skip. So, let me get this straight, the men of Tolemac only copulate with their concubines?" he asked. What did he care about Tolemac sex lives? Why

was he asking? They could screw their horses, for all he cared.

Her head jerked up. She stared at him as if he were stupid. "What folly you speak. If they wish a child to inherit their wealth and family name, they must seek congress with their mate. Deleh attended our son's birth."

"I see."

"I sense you disapprove. Do not men seek pleasure where you come from?"

"Sure. All the time." He thought about how to answer her. "But where I'm from, if two people are mated, they seek pleasure from each other . . . only. It's part of the vows they make to each other. Some folks stray, but I figure most people try to be faithful."

"I cannot imagine a desire for such an arrangement." She scrambled up the bank and disappeared into the night.

Lien woke in confusion. Where was he? What time was it? Then he remembered. Ollach had come to him at the river to say Ardra had found him a bed. Not in the women's quarters, darn it, but comfy just the same.

The tent in which he lay was smaller than Tol's but every bit as luxurious. He was on a couch, covered with furs, fully dressed. The air was cold. A curious swooshing noise made him sit up. The sound came again, and he saw it came from Ollach, who sat on a stool nearby and swept a whetstone along the blade of a sword.

"Where is everybody?" he asked.

Ollach looked up. "They still attend Tol as he slips from this life to the next."

"I see." Lien stood up, his muscles tight and sore. He went through the stretching routine he'd always used before lacrosse games. He knew Ollach was staring at him; the whetstone no longer hummed on the steel blade.

Lien knew he definitely needed a weapon to defend himself.

The tent, like Tol's, was the color of the lavender sky. By the light of a few wicks floating in oil, he could see that the ceiling was painted with puffy white clouds and strange blue hawklike birds. "Whose tent is this?"

"Whose tent it is need not concern you. Now you are awake, so I will go."

"Hey, before you go, do you think you might be able to find me a walking stick or something to lean on? I'm really sore. I feel like I can hardly walk."

The noise Ollach made in his throat as he left the tent told Lien he was now considered a weak, pathetic being. Perfect. If opponents underestimated him, he might have a chance in this world of swords.

Ollach returned in a few moments, a long staff in his hand. "This belonged to some beggar who died." He tossed it to Lien. Lien deliberately fumbled it and groaned as he bent over to pick it up. With a cluck of his tongue, Ollach left the tent.

Lien weighed the staff in his hand. It was poorly balanced and riddled with tiny holes, maybe from insects, but it would do. He held it in both hands, horizontally, and poked the air. He grinned. "Once a defenseman, always a defenseman."

His stomach growled. He examined the tent and found a tray of food under a linen cloth. There was bread and a bland, white cheese. He ate it all and hoped it wasn't supposed to be Ollach's dinner too. There was only a pitcher of water to drink, and as he gulped it down, he imagined invisible microbes percolating through his gut. At least his throat no longer hurt. Maybe the soreness had been from the screams he'd been holding in as they rode down the cliff.

He threw himself back on the bed and contemplated the puffy clouds overhead. When Tol died, Samoht would move his army across the river to wherever his wife lay in childbirth. Once the child was born, Lien figured Samoht would turn his army loose on Ardra's fortress.

Lien rose and lighted a couple of thick candles from one of the wicks floating in oil. He roamed the tent, drank more water, and examined the decorative knotwork carved into the tables and chairs and woven into the ivory cloth on the table. He paced, lifted the tent flap, and looked at the moons, which were now down quite a bit. He must have slept a few hours anyway.

When he turned, something glinted in the light. It was a pin in the bedding. Then he realized he'd been sleeping under a heavy cloak. The hooded cape, black as night and lined with fur, had only a pin to clasp it. The pin, of silver and amber, looked like a museum piece and was heavy in his palm.

He slung the cloak over his shoulders. It took him about five minutes to fasten it securely enough so that the pin didn't pop open when he moved.

"First chance I get, I'm inventing buttons," he muttered.

He gripped his stick, took a deep breath, and left the security of the tent.

Outside, he stared up at the incredible moons. They were no longer in a neat straight line. They were separating. The small orbs glowed turquoise as if lighted from within. He saw no craters and wondered if they were gaseous in nature; that might account for their incredible luminosity. A pang of homesickness for the Earth's dull old moon with its lumpy surface lasted about ten seconds, swept away by a gust of icy wind. It whistled around the tents and the men huddled at nearby fires.

Lien quickly realized he should have his cloak pinned at the shoulder, not directly in front, to allow the hand holding the stick to be more or less unencumbered. He shifted the cloak before lifting the deep hood.

Tol's tent was easy to find. The crowd that stood outside had grown considerably. Lien wormed his way through the throng and lifted the flap. No one stopped him, which he attributed to the cloak. It was finer than most of the ones worn by the people he passed.

Tol still reclined on his couch, but his eyes were closed, his breathing labored, his skin snow white. Ardra, Ralen, and Deleh knelt by Tol, their heads bowed.

A lean, handsome man stood behind Ardra. Despite his comely features, he reminded Lien of a hawk waiting to strike.

The man did not kneel, nor did he wear the tunics and leather of the warriors. Instead he wore a long robe the same color as the moons, trimmed with rich silver embroidery. It must be Samoht, the high councilor.

The scene before Lien reminded him of the deathbed vigil he'd held for his mother. Only it had just been him and the priest there. No crowds had awaited the news of one lonely alcoholic's passing.

He knew the drill. The breaths would grow farther apart. They'd all find themselves staring at Tol's chest to see if he took another breath . . . and one time he wouldn't.

Lien left.

For two hours he wandered the shore of the river and contemplated his options. He felt restless. His ass ached, but not his head.

He wondered if Ardra had been lonely during her time with Tol, a woman outside the affections of a couple together for decades. Had Deleh and Tol had any children of their own? And what did Ardra's son look like, that everyone had only to see him to know he was of mixed birth?

What came next? War over Ardra's fortress? Or a simple directive that she stand aside, accompanied by nothing more than her anger and humiliation?

As the moons crawled across the bowl of indigo sky, he made a decision. He would wait here until Nilrem's party made it into camp. Nilrem might have some advice for him.

But that might take a few days. What if everyone moved away for the birth of Samoht's child? It was ironic that as one important political figure died, a political pawn was being born. And how long till that happy event? How

would Nilrem find him, or he Nilrem if they moved? And would the hulking warriors who guarded the tents and sat around the fires leave him alone during the wait?

The last thing Lien wanted to do was get involved in Ardra's troubles. He'd come into the game to get away from his own troubles. He didn't need to adopt someone else's. And what about his long-range plans? Where did he want to go? His first intention had been to try to reach the Tolemac capital and barter the jewelry he'd brought into local coin, then just travel around for the hell of it.

Lien heard a drum begin to pound in a low, steady beat. A murmur rose from the crowd around Tol's tent. Lien knew that Ardra's lifemate was dead.

Chapter Seven

Tol lay covered by a rich cloth decorated with turquoise and gold knotwork embroidery. Some of the symbols were those of the Shield found on Lien's arm.

Inside, Ardra felt empty. Tol's wisdom and patience were irreplaceable. How empty and afraid she felt without the shelter of his power. She was also angry. Tol had taken all of Nilrem's potion and left her without his support. Nay, left their son without his support. Why had he not seen to the fortress's rule before ending his life?

"Tol will be sorely missed," Samoht said.

Ardra suspected that Samoht cared less for the passing of an ancient warrior than for the opportunity to lay his hand on her.

"You will join me in my quarters," Samoht said. "We need to speak of your keeping now that Tol is dead."

"I do not need a keeper," she said, but to his back, for he had walked away. She closed her eyes and touched her breast, then opened them and touched Tol on the forehead. "I wish you peace," she said.

Reluctantly she followed Samoht. As they passed through the camp, she felt someone watching her. It was

a strange sensation, almost a touch on her skin, as if she had walked into the gossamer strands of a web and it trailed behind her as she moved.

She glanced around and saw Lien.

The black cloak made him almost invisible in the darkness, but it was as if something connected her to him. Why had she ordered Ollach to give Lien the rich garment? What had happened to her fear of the pilgrim?

Without seeing it happen, she knew he followed. She clasped her hands together within the confines of her cloak. "Samoht, I wish some witnesses to our conversation."

Samoht whipped around. "You question my integrity, mistress?" For a moment, his handsome features looked as hard as stone.

"I question everything."

"Whom do you wish? Ralen?"

"Aye, and Lien."

"Leen? Who is he?"

"Leee-*en* is how he pronounces his name. He is a pilgrim who saved my life and also served as Listener to Tol's last words."

Samoht glared at her, and she feared he would refuse her. "Summon them."

"I'm here," Lien said, not ten steps behind her.

Ardra exhaled with relief, not aware she had been holding her breath. "Thank you. Could you fetch Ralen?"

"Sure. I'll find him."

Ardra watched Lien hurry away. He held a tall walking staff in his hand. What need had he of such a thing? Had he been injured anew? Nay, he moved with the grace of a dark cat. She thought of the gulap who roamed Nilrem's mountain. Huge black cats they were, uncanny beasts, wild and untamed. They took the white hart with one blow of a huge paw, tore out its heart with their long fangs. Heat pulsed in her middle.

Samoht interrupted her thoughts. "The pilgrim's speech is beyond strange," he said. "Whence comes he?"

"He is from beyond the ice fields." She watched Samoht's eyes widen, then narrow.

"You said he saved your life?" His attention shifted from her face to Lien.

"Aye. I sought Nilrem that he might concoct something to ease Tol's pain. I was set upon by outcasts. Lien rescued me."

"How many of your men did you lose?"

"None. I was alone."

Lien and Ralen approached, and they all followed Samoht to his tent. It was easy to pick it out from the rest; it flew a most distinctive banner—a red rose on a field of black. His personal guard, black-garbed men, each had a rose stitched over his breast.

There was nothing in the men's greetings to indicate that Samoht knew Lien. Still, Lien's roses might still mean he was Samoht's man—but one too unimportant for him to know personally.

Samoht held the tent flap open for Ardra and followed her in.

Inside the tent, a long table was filled with rolls of documents and a map lay stretched out, anchored by Samoht's seals of office.

Reclining on his bed couch was Einalem, Samoht's sister. She had hair so blond it would appear white in moonlight. Like her brother, she was comely. Even her gown, a silver material that gave a faint hiss as she rose, was a mirror image of Samoht's, trimmed in the sacred color of turquoise, the embroidery thick at the hem and sleeves. Clasped around her waist was a chain of silver links studded with turquoise. Bartered, it would feed many Selaw families.

Ardra dropped into a curtsey to Samoht's sister. Einalem kissed each of Ardra's cheeks. "I am sorely grieved I could not ease Tol's suffering."

"You are known as the best healer in Tolemac. If you could not save him, then 'twas his time to go."

"Aye. He had reached a great age."

Samoht nodded. "He was a fine councilor, and his advice will be sorely missed."

Ardra knew that Samoht had rarely taken Tol's advice, but she nodded assent.

The tent flap was lifted by one of Samoht's guards. Ralen and Lien entered.

Einalem paused in her graceful turn and stared.

Samoht followed her gaze and frowned.

Ardra put out a hand to Lien, and after a moment's hesitation, he took it. She drew him forward. "This is Lien, the pilgrim who saved my life on Nilrem's mountain. He then saved my life in the Tangled Wood—"

Einalem interrupted her. "You ventured into the wood? Were you not afraid?"

"I was well guarded," Ardra said.

"You were attacked," Ralen said. "You had not one archer with you."

"Folly," Samoht said.

Ardra wished to kick Ralen in the leg. How dare he imply she was not capable of fending for herself? "I requested archers, Samoht, as you will recall. You deemed it unnecessary."

"I did not think you would be in a cursed place," Samoht said. "Now let us all be seated and discuss Ardra's keeping."

The more he said it, the more it would be believed that she needed a keeper. "I will sit, but I will not need a keeper."

Samoht waved her words aside with a long, elegant hand. "Sit. Sit. Einalem, send for meat and wine."

As Einalem moved past the men, she paused a bare moment near Lien, and Ardra watched the woman slide her glance up and down him. Anger flared through Ardra. Nay, not anger—'twas jealousy. *Jealousy?* It could not be. Jealousy was a shameful emotion.

89

They took seats on low benches, Lien beside her and Ralen alone. Samoht took the only chair, an ornately carved thing which she knew served as a symbol of his authority when the council gathered in remote locations.

Einalem returned with several servants bearing covered trays. The cold had tightened her nipples, and it did not escape Ardra that both Ralen and Lien looked at her breasts. Were men all alike no matter whence they came? Was it naught but a pretty face and large breasts that drew them?

Einalem draped herself on Samoht's bed couch. Ralen and she chatted a moment while the servant set up a jointed table in the center of their small group. How dare Ralen smile and whisper with Samoht's sister?

Anger, hot and raw, filled Ardra. Then she reminded herself of one of Tol's many lessons: Never let an opponent see you angry. She wiped her face clear of emotion. She accepted neither food nor drink. Her hands might shake and betray her emotions.

"Now," Samoht said once the servants were gone. "Tol summoned the high eight here to the Selaw border while I await my child's birth. I fear the journey shortened Tol's life, however. I imagine he wished to ask the council that you"—he indicated Ralen with the point of a small dagger he was using to pare an apple—"take his seat until a more permanent representative could be found."

Ralen accepted a goblet of wine poured by Einalem. "I have no wish to sit on the council, although I am honored to take my brother's place in the short term."

So, Ralen had given a bit, Ardra thought.

"Agreed. I shall put it forward on the morrow after we have honored Tol." They sat in silence, eating their apples and cheese, slicing meat and drinking wine as if her life and that of her people did not hang in the balance.

"Now, as to the fortress, Ardra." Samoht leaned forward and patted her knee. "You need not be concerned about its care. I will send my men to see to it."

"I ask that you do not. I have ample men of my own."

Everyone stared at her. Lien drank from his cup, unmoved by her incredible statement.

"You know that cannot be. Your men will not heed you."

"My men will not wish to heed a Tolemac warrior."

"I will send my personal guard, then. They represent me, not Tolemac as such." Samoht smiled. No warmth was evident in his cold eyes.

"I thank you, but still I must refuse the offer. I ask only that Tol's guard escort me home. I will release them to you at that time."

Einalem laughed. It was a musical sound. "Oh, Ardra, you are mad."

"Hush," Samoht said. He leaned forward to Ardra again. "Do I understand you correctly? You wish no army, no warriors, to help you hold the fortress?"

"You understand."

"What do you think? Is she mad?" Samoht appealed to Ralen.

"Tol wished Ardra to rule the fortress," Ralen said. Ardra silently blessed him that he had not belittled Tol's last request.

"What?" Samoht stood up. He fisted his hands on his hips.

Anger whipped visibly through his body, and Ardra knew why Tol had counseled her not to let her anger show. She now knew the extent of Samoht's desire for the fortress.

"What sickness possessed Tol's mind that he would wish such a thing? He was not of sound mind. Support me in this, Einalem."

Lien forestalled Einalem. "I witnessed Tol's final words. He stated that Ardra should rule. He might have been weak, but he was clear and decisive. I can quote him if you like." To Ardra's delight, he did not await permission. "Tol said, and I quote, 'It is my wish that Ardra take con-

91

trol of the fortress. It is my wish that she, and she alone, rule it for our son until he is of age.' "

Einalem stared at Lien. "You are bold," she said.

Lien shrugged. "I assume my purpose is to be a witness to Tol's last words. He said Ardra should rule."

Ralen cleared his throat. "It is as the pilgrim says, Samoht. Tol was not in any state of madness, and I will not allow you to besmirch his memory with such an idea."

"Einalem?" Samoht threw himself back into his chair.

"What, Brother? I was occupied in my tent, treating a cook's burn. I did not attend Tol's final moments. Since I was not there, I cannot speak to his final state of mind."

Ardra said to Samoht, "Did you not bring each councilor to Tol's side as he arrived so that he might make the customary greeting? 'Tis tradition that you do so, is it not?"

"Aye." Samoht's frown deepened. He knew what she implied by her words. Each time a councilor greeted another of higher station, ancient words were spoken. It was a long and tedious set of speeches when one man was near death. If Tol was capable of remembering his part and greeting each man without prompting from either Deleh or the high councilor, Samoht could not charge that Tol was not of sound mind. That was the purpose of the greeting.

"Let me understand," Ralen said. "We have here a vacant council seat. Someone must wish to sit in it, and that person must be deemed worthy. I certainly have no wish to serve, but will sit in the seat as Tol's brother until another is chosen. Second"—he nodded at Ardra—"we have the issue of the Fortress of Ravens and who will see to its care and that of Tol's son."

"Aye, this would not be an issue if your father had not been treacherous," Samoht said. He stabbed his finger in Ardra's direction. "Your father should have been brought here and punished for his crimes."

"My father banished himself on the ice. He is dead."

"He almost destroyed the treaty between our people. I should have sent an army then and taken control of the ice

mines once and for all. Instead, Tol pitied you and took you as his mate."

"Tol served the Selaw well," Ardra said.

"No one questions that, but it is imperative that a proper authority take Tol's place. Your father escaped onto the ice, something you allowed and did nothing to stop. For all we know, your father could be mounting an offensive to take back the fortress now that Tol is dead."

"No one survives the ice," Ralen said.

"No one?" Samoht said. "Lien. Are you not from beyond the ice fields? Tell us. If no one survives the ice, how did you come to be here?"

Lien tried to keep his tone mild and unassuming. "Actually, I have no idea. I do not remember much of the journey once I reached the ice. I had a raging fever—caught a chill, I guess. In fact, when I found myself on Nilrem's mountain, I thought I was dead. Of course"—he looked at Ardra—"the minute I saw the men attacking Ardra, I knew I was alive."

"He cannot remember." Samoht threw up his hands. "We should put him to the question."

"Nay." Ardra shot to her feet. "I will not tolerate the torture of a pilgrim. Ralen, surely you will not countenance such a thing."

Torture?

Ralen opened his mouth, but before he could speak, Einalem did. "Ardra, take your seat. Brother, we have no need to examine this man. He has naught to do with our business. Now, Ardra, you say Tol wished you to rule in his place?"

Lien saw a hard glance exchanged between Einalem and Samoht, but didn't know enough about them and Tolemac politics to interpret the look.

Ardra remained standing. "Tol made his wishes clear. He said he wished me to hold the fortress. Ralen and Lien have confirmed it."

93

"Never. I will not allow it," Samoht said. "You have shown no ability to handle authority. You went into the Tangled Wood without archers, and let us not forget the circumstances that necessitated this pilgrim saving your life."

"I requested archers and was denied," Ardra said calmly.

Samoht smiled. "And what woman of sense goes onto Nilrem's mountain alone? I assume you were alone, as you lost no warriors when you were attacked."

Lien watched Ardra. She licked her lips and finally spoke. "I considered it a pilgrimage of sorts. One cannot approach the wiseman with a troop of men. It takes from the sacred—"

"You are making excuses for foolishness. A foolish woman may not rule," Samoht said.

Einalem smiled. "Please, Samoht, Ardra, stop this. You will only anger each other and nothing will be accomplished. Might I suggest a compromise?"

She patted Samoht's knee as the councilor had done to Ardra. Lien figured the patronizing gesture pleased him no more than it had Ardra.

"What compromise could possibly—" Samoht began.

"—please you, Brother?" Einalem laughed. Her full breasts quivered against her silky gown.

"I too suspect that little will please you, Samoht," Ralen said. "Ardra is right. Tol's wishes were clear, but I cannot agree with them. It is foolish to allow a woman too much—"

"Whoa," Lien said. "Let's just hear the compromise."

"Thank you, pilgrim," Einalem said.

She leaned forward so that more of her cleavage became visible, and took a drink from her silver goblet. Her eyes locked on his over the rim. The goblet was so encrusted with turquoise, he wondered how she could lift it. When she set it down, she licked her moist, full lips.

"What I propose is simple," Einalem said, rising. "Ardra must prove herself before witnesses."

"Prove myself?" Ardra sat down with a thump next to Lien on the bench. He stifled an impulse to wrap a comforting arm around her.

"How?" Ralen and Samoht asked at the same time.

Einalem stretched, and Lien thought of a cat well satisfied with herself. "Set Ardra a task to perform. If she succeeds, she will have her way—control of the fortress. If not, she will kneel before you, Samoht, and all the council. She will accept whomever you designate as the protector of the Fortress of Ravens. In fact"—she smiled—"she will mate again where you bid. Now, I have much to do. If you will excuse me?"

"Of course." Samoht rose and bowed to Einalem, who swept from the tent. "My sister's plan is magnificent," he said when she was gone. "What say you, Ardra?"

Samoht had agreed too fast. Lien knew that some form of this agreement had been hashed out between brother and sister even before Tol's death.

"What can I say—"

"Wait, Ardra," Lien interrupted. "Don't agree until you hear what the task is."

She took a deep breath and nodded her thanks to him. "Aye. First I must know how you wish me to prove myself."

Samoht linked his fingers together. He watched Ardra from beneath his straight brows. "You may have heard we had a theft from the vaults beneath Tolemac?"

Ardra nodded. "The Vial of Seduction."

"In the wrong hands," Samoht continued, "this potion could be ill used. An unscrupulous woman might use it against a man of worth, a councilor even. It is said the Goddess of Darkness has the vial. Find it. Return it to me."

"An unscrupulous person cannot use the potion," Ardra said.

Lien perked up. This was news.

"However," Samoht said. "If the goddess finds an honorable person capable of administering the potion, it may bode ill for us all. Will you seek the Vial of Seduction or not?"

Ralen held up his hand. "Wait, we have been over this before, Samoht, and you have my report. I have already met with the goddess. She made no attempt to block my search of her fortress. The tales of her are greatly exaggerated. There are no serpents guarding the place. She made no attempts to bewitch me. In fact, the woman could not have been more cordial."

"She is evil," Ardra said.

Lien touched her arm. She quivered with some emotion held in check with great effort.

Samoht dismissed her words with a quick flick of his hand. "We know 'tis said she is responsible for your mother's death, Ardra, but nothing was ever proved."

"Regardless," Ralen continued. "I see little need to seek the potion with the goddess. If she has it, we will never find it. No surprise visit will reveal it, nor any amount of persuasion. I was as thorough as possible with her."

Samoht nodded. "I like it." He spoke as if Ralen had said nothing. "Should Ardra find and return the potion, she will have proved herself worthy. A marvelous plan."

One of the Red Rose warriors entered the tent. He was dusty and carried a leather pouch.

"Ah, you come from Boda?" Samoht asked.

"She is his Selaw mate," Ardra whispered at Lien's ear.

The messenger handed Samoht a rolled document, then hurried away. Samoht unrolled the lengthy parchment, scanned it, then frowned. He turned to Ardra. "I wish you to take up the challenge. If you do not, we will proceed as I decree."

Before anyone could make a further objection, Ardra bowed. "I accept the challenge."

Chapter Eight

Samoht dismissed everyone except Ardra. Although Ralen didn't seem concerned that Ardra was alone in Samoht's tent, Lien felt uneasy.

Ardra had been too quick to accept Samoht's challenge. Lien wished she had waited. The whole thing looked suspect to him.

He hobbled along with his stick in case anyone was watching. Where should he go? He headed for the tent with the puffy clouds. It was dimly lighted by a wick floating in oil.

A pitcher of hot water sat in a brazier. The soap and towels on the table were a subtle hint that someone ought to wash up.

Lien stripped off his tunic. As he unwrapped the bandages on his arm and shoulder, he marveled at the fresh, healed skin. He carefully tucked the leaf Ardra had given him into his boot.

Before the water could cool, he scrubbed the travel dust from his skin. He plunged his tunic into the water as well, soaped it several times, and wrung it out.

Outside, he draped the linen shirt over one of the ropes that held down the tent. He stared toward Samoht's tent. What was going on in there?

It was too cold to remain outside half dressed, so he fetched the fur-lined cloak. It must be about three o'clock in the morning, he guessed.

He wondered about Ardra's decision. It wouldn't have been his. She might rush toward responsibility, but he, personally, would run in the opposite direction, kid or no kid.

Samoht's tent flap opened, and Ardra shot out like a bullet fired from a gun. After several steps, she slowed to a walk, her chin up, her shoulders back. She came directly toward him.

He slipped into the tent to wait for her. She threw the flap back but didn't see him. She went to the table, planted her hands on the cloth, and bowed her head. Her shoulders shook. The back of her gown was half unlaced.

It was too late to disappear, and disrespectful to hide his presence. "Ardra," he said softly.

She whipped around. "Lien." Her face shone with tears.

In the next second, she was in his arms. She burrowed inside his cloak, her wet face hot on his chest. He closed his arms around her and held his breath. Her body trembled against him.

"What happened?" He tipped her face up. "Tell me."

She shook her head. He slid his hands down to her shoulders and walked her backwards to the couch, then sat her on the edge.

"He attacked you, didn't he?" He didn't wait for an answer, charging out of the tent.

She ran after him through the camp, grabbing for his cloak. "Do not, Lien, I beg of you, please."

Something in her voice made him stop. He rounded on her. She looked up at him and shook her head. "Please. Not here," she whispered. She tugged gently on his cloak. "I beg of you."

He jerked his cloak from her grasp and turned back to her tent. Once inside, he threw off the cloak and pointed his finger at her. "Don't ever beg."

She stared at him, eyes wide.

"Forget the roses and my tattoo for a moment and trust me. What happened?"

"He tried to kiss me." She didn't meet his eyes.

"Fine, let's assume he only kissed you. Then why the tears? And who unlaced your dress? How can you let that slime get away with—"

"Stop. Let me explain." She stood up straight, her chin in the air. "Samoht tried to embrace me, aye, I will not deny that. But to have you storm in on him and take up my battle will not do me any good. He will see me as weak, hiding behind a man's strength."

"So nothing happens to the bastard?" He shook his head.

"I will take care of him in my time, in my way."

Lien cupped her face in his hands. "Did he hurt you?"

She looked away, and he knew she was going to lie. "Only my dignity."

He skimmed his thumbs over her cheeks, dry now. "Ardra, you can't let men maul you and get away with it."

Did she move first or did he? Her lips were warm, full, moist. She tasted of wine. She placed her hands on his chest and kneaded his skin like a kitten kneads a soft blanket.

He whispered against her mouth, "We shouldn't be doing this." Then he thrust his hands into her hair and held her head while he ran his tongue over hers—again and again.

Each squeeze of his fingers in her silky mane released the scent of flowers—foreign, seductive, enticing flowers.

She ran her hands up and down his chest and made a throaty sound. It jerked him out of the moment.

"Ardra. Damn." He gently set her aside. Her lips were puffy, her eyes dazed. "We *can't* do this."

Then she smiled and touched her fingertips to her mouth. "Do not fret, Lien. It will not happen again."

"What are you smiling about?"

"Oh, 'tis just that I have discovered why he did it." She walked briskly to the table, peered into the pitcher, frowned, and rounded on Lien. "You used my water?"

"Yeah. Sorry. What do you mean, you discovered why he did it? Who? Discovered what?"

"You look tired." Ardra tipped her head back and examined him. He rubbed his chest, and her eyes followed his hand. He dropped it to his side.

"You didn't answer my question. Stop staring at me."

She lifted the pitcher and held it tightly against her chest. "Forgive me, Lien. I will answer your question. I smiled because I learned something from you I never knew . . . that a kiss can be sweet." She ducked her head. "And I imagine there is little sweetness in Samoht's life."

Lien lifted her chin on the edge of his hand. "Ardra. You need to understand something. A kiss between two people who want to kiss is far different from a kiss between two people when one is unwilling. What Samoht did was wrong."

"I have found that men believe it their right to copulate whenever it suits them."

"Look, Ardra, I can't speak for Tolemac men, but where I come from, sex is consensual or it's a crime."

"Sex? Crime?" She tipped her head.

"Sex—copulation. Crime—offense for which you get punished publicly."

"Oh." She sighed over the empty pitcher. "Can we speak of this at another time? I am sure that Samoht is plotting something as we speak, and I need my sleep."

If she wanted to change the subject, who was he to persist? "I think Einalem's compromise sounded a bit—"

"Preplanned? Most likely. If I die as a result of my quest, Samoht will claim guardianship of my son and the fortress."

"You don't seem too concerned," Lien said.

"Perhaps I am too tired to feel concern."

He took the pitcher from her and placed it on the table. When he turned around, she was curled on the couch. "You look too young to rule a fortress." Before he could clamp his tongue on the words, they were out of his mouth.

She was off the bed in an instant. She shook her finger in his face. "How dare you! I have commanded men far better than you for the last three conjunctions. I have decided the fate of hundreds of miners, seen to their families, buried their dead. And I can take care of myself. Samoht will not sit well in the saddle for several days." She snapped her fingers in his face.

Lien wrapped his fingers around her wrist and smiled. "So, you put a knee in Samoht's gonads, did you?" He bent his head and kissed her fingers.

"Gonads?"

"I think you know what I mean."

She smiled back. "It was not my knee. I used the end of a candle stand. It was made of iron."

He kissed her fingers again. "Good girl."

Her hand flexed, but she didn't pull away. "Do not call me girl. Can we do it again?"

"What?"

"Kiss." She slid her other hand around the nape of his neck.

She had a child but seemed as innocent as a virgin. "You do know that kisses lead to other things."

Her hand fell from his neck, and she tucked it behind her back.

Lien went outside for his tunic. It was only partially dry from the whipping wind, but he needed the protection from her heated gaze.

She raked him critically after he'd belted the tunic in place. "Who washed it for you?"

"I did it myself. Just call me laundry man."

"Men do not do laundry." She clapped her hands over her face and laughed.

Her laughter had a manic quality that told him she was way past exhausted. "Look, you need your sleep."

She knelt on the couch, tucking her skirts around her feet. "Aye, but you must leave. It would not do for anyone to think we were copulating here."

"Now you're worried. Sure, Ardra. Just use me and toss me aside," he said, but he smiled to let her know he was kidding.

She snapped her fingers. "Tell Ollach I need fresh water."

He decided there was nothing behind her kiss except a need to wipe out the one that Samoht had forced upon her.

She snapped her fingers again. "Lien, are you listening? Please tell Ollach I need fresh water."

"I forgot to tell you something about finger snapping. Where I come from, it means you want to have sex—you know, copulate." Her eyes widened. "If you snap them like this"—he snapped his fingers twice, quickly—"it means you want the man right *now*."

Her mouth formed an O. Lien snatched up his cloak and left the tent. He figured she'd never snap her fingers at him again.

Sleep eluded Ardra. The taste and feel of Lien's mouth ensured that she might not sleep for many moonrisings. Nay, it was not his mouth, although it was a lovely mouth. It was his dark eyes . . . the way they had slowly closed, his black lashes settling on his cheeks. Should she have closed her eyes too? She knew nothing of kissing.

Kissing led to other things.

Tol had not kissed, and Samoht's kiss was rough and wet. Lien's were like wine—intoxicating.

Where did Lien sleep? Was he cold?

Nay, his skin was very warm, as if he had a brazier and coals inside him. She imagined what it would be like to lie

with him, skin to skin, and look at him from head to toe. A pulsing sensation in her belly made her shift uncomfortably on the bed couch. She already knew what he looked like head to toe.

She must forget him. He was a pilgrim, and she had tempted him from his vow of celibacy. 'Twas a shameful thing.

Despite his vows, he had kissed her back and wanted her. "By Nilrem's knees," she swore, and clapped her hands over her eyes to block the memory of Lien's desire from her mind. It was not so easily banished.

"He did desire me," she whispered. She knew it just as she had known that Samoht wanted to copulate with her. Deleh had told her that men were easily understood. If they put their hips against you and they were hard, they wanted you. If not, they didn't.

She tossed off the furs and coverlet and allowed the chilly air to bathe her sweaty skin. How could she have such thoughts when she must see Tol on his final journey?

"Oh, Tol, I shall miss you sorely." Tears spilled down her cheeks. She must shed them here, else Samoht or Ralen might think her a weakling. She thought of Deleh. Tol had been Deleh's life. Little good fortune came to concubines of her age. The fortress could remain her home, but even though she had never complained, Ardra knew that Deleh hated the ice.

"I wish I might have known such a love as theirs." More tears ran down Ardra's face, but as she dashed them away, she acknowledged they were for herself, not Tol.

Ardra closed her eyes again. The sight of Lien lying naked on Nilrem's mountain came to her mind again. She flipped her pillow over and buried her face in its cool surface. How terrible to imagine a man as he lay helpless with blood on his skin.

But she could not help it. Liquid heat coursed through Ardra's body. Would this strange sensation never stop?

* * *

"Ardra, are you awake?" The small girl who stood at the tent flap held a pitcher nearly as large as she.

Ardra leaped from the bed. "Come in." She took the pitcher from the girl. "Have you heard any news?"

"Just that they will see Tol off today. Deleh is not well. Brokenhearted, she is."

Ardra washed and dressed quickly. She suffered the girl's attentions to her hair so that she might honor Tol, but as soon as the comb was set aside, Ardra dashed off to find Deleh.

Deleh sat by Tol's side and looked up when Ardra entered Tol's tent. Ardra knew at once that Deleh had been there all night in honor of her dead lover.

"Should I leave?" Ardra asked.

"Nay, come forward." Deleh fussed with Tol's drape.

Ardra hugged Deleh and then knelt for a moment at Tol's side. "He lived a good life, did he not?"

"Oh, aye. He worried so about the boy and you. He wished he could have done more for you."

"He gave me more than I could have ever dreamed. He gave me strength. Now I have come to ask you to walk at my side today."

"At your side?" Deleh held her hand to her breast. "Samoht will be very angry."

"But he will say nothing. I suspect he may even excuse himself from the procession."

Lien rolled over and groaned. Ollach and Ralen snored a curiously in-sync chorus on two comfortable-looking chaise lounges. He, on the other hand, had only a fur between himself and the cold dirt floor of Ralen's tent.

Ollach, Lien assumed, was ostensibly a bodyguard so that Lien wouldn't murder Ralen in his sleep.

He murdered his lumpy pillow instead and rolled onto his back. This tent was an unadorned, no-nonsense affair like its owner.

Sleep eluded him. His thoughts arrowed straight to Ardra. Her innocence intrigued him. Of course, her lifemate had a concubine, so he imagined that Ardra was often left out in the cold. He stifled a laugh. Refrigerator Girl was out in the cold.

Actually, he wasn't going to be able to call her Refrigerator Girl anymore. She was a warm, seductive woman.

He let his imagination wander. In his mind's eye, Ardra smiled as he helped her out of her gown. She stretched out on his fur-lined cloak. Her perky breasts stood at attention, and so did Mr. Happy. Her amber eyes opened wide when he finally entered her.

Rewind. No condoms.

If he slept with her, he'd be responsible for her. He was suddenly grateful she'd turned shy on him.

Chapter Nine

Lien hated funerals, and Tol's took the cake. It was the funeral of all funerals. The man was carried out onto the plain in a long procession by six Tolemac warriors. Despite the cold, Ralen, who followed the pallbearers, wore a white sleeveless tunic. The man was pretty ripped, and his warrior arm rings reminded Lien that men without them had no status in Ralen's world.

Ardra and Deleh walked side by side behind Ralen. Ardra wore a loose lavender robe. It looked like a ceremonial thing. Her hair had been braided into a crown around her head, and she looked regal and humble at the same time.

Deleh wore the same thing she'd worn while looking after Tol the day before. In contrast to Ardra, the old woman was a wrinkled mess. She wept the whole way, her head bowed.

When they were at some distance from the camp, they stopped and Tol's body was placed on a wooden platform. The pallbearers lighted torches and handed them to Ralen and Ardra, who requested one for Deleh. Lien was close enough to hear Ralen refuse and Ardra insist. Finally,

Ralen acquiesced. *Good girl*, Lien thought; *show them who's boss*. A third torch was given to Deleh.

Moments later, Lien gasped as Tol went up in a whoosh of flame. Cremation—in the open. Lien felt sick as the smoke and scent of death reached him.

They all knelt and bent their heads. As time dragged on, Lien felt the pain of the kneeling position in his spine. He found he could forget the sight of Tol's burning body if he stared at Ardra. He realized there was a pattern woven into her loose robe. Each time she shifted, the flames caught the design of swirling lines twisting on themselves. More symbolic knotwork.

The pyre died away until all that remained was a pile of ashes. The procession returned to the camp. Ralen went to Samoht's tent, probably to find out why the high councilor hadn't attended the funeral. Lien hoped Samoht's balls were the size of grapefruit.

Ardra went directly to her puffy-cloud home away from home. He followed her. She was incredibly beautiful. He imagined her in ancient times walking down the nave of a massive Gothic cathedral to be crowned at the side of some worthy king.

He, on the other hand, could play the part of court jester at the party afterward. He too was a wrinkled mess. His beard itched, and he wondered how Ralen and Ollach shaved. How did he ask without looking like a complete idiot?

He rapped his knuckles on one of the tent poles, and Ardra called out for him to enter. She stood at the table washing her hands. "Ah, Lien. I am so glad to see you."

She had dropped the lavender robe over the bed. Under it she must have had on this other dress, because there was no way she could have changed so quickly. The dress looked like a long gold column covered by a tight ivory jumper that laced at the sides. Little chunks of amber were stitched down the front of the jumper thing.

Ann Lawrence

He frowned. Maybe she was a Marie Antoinette, feasting while her people starved. "If the Selaw are poor, why don't you sell a few of those amber stones on your dress and distribute the proceeds?"

Ardra's hand went to her breast. She touched the stones stitched into an intricate pattern there. "Do you think me so unfeeling of my people that I would harm them to my benefit? The stone is sacred, but not valuable."

She wiped her hands on a towel, and he saw that her amber eyes were shot with red. He imagined she had done her grieving in private.

"I'm sorry. I guess that was pretty stupid of me."

"Aye," she said, so softly he could barely hear her.

He shrugged out of his cloak and tossed it over a bench, then touched her shoulder. "It was bad timing, too."

She turned and leaned into him, her forehead on his chest. If he put his arms around her, he'd pick her up and take her to bed. The urge was visceral and intense.

Instead he stood there, his arms at his sides. After a few moments, she stepped back and looked up at him. There was something more than a little spellbinding about her sad eyes, innocent and weary at the same time.

"I'm sorry about Tol," he said. It was one of the empty things he'd heard a hundred times at his mother's funeral. It did nothing for the pain, but he now understood why people said it. You had to say something.

"Thank you." She touched his bruised cheek. "This looks better today. Why do you not shave so I can see if it is clean?"

He shrugged. What should he say? *Without my electric razor I'm lost?*

She put her own interpretation on his silence. "Forgive me. Of course, everything you had was stolen. Sit. I will shave you. It is a small service in exchange for all you have done for me."

"Uh, you don't have to do that." Actually, it sounded great to him. Like going to a barber, and he wouldn't have

108

to spy on Ollach and Ralen, or flub the effort in front of them.

"Sit, Lien. You protest too much over trivialities. Do unto others as you would have them do unto you."

"We have the same expression where I come from," he said.

She pulled the heavy water pitcher from the brazier and poured some water into a basin that appeared to be made of marble. Next, she opened a wooden box and withdrew a rolled bundle and what turned out to be a cake of soap wrapped in cloth. She flipped the rolled bundle open and displayed a collection of blades—sharp ones.

"Ah . . . that is, maybe I'll grow a beard. Nilrem has a beard—"

She smiled. "Are you afraid? You need not be. I may not be a personal slave, but I shaved Tol all the time. Now sit."

He sat on a bench. His heart raced like an Indy car.

She stood between his thighs. One of his pistons misfired. Then she lifted his chin with the tip of one finger and ran her thumb back and forth along his jawline. His engine flat-out stalled.

"Does this hurt?" she asked, lingering on the bruise.

"No. Yes. Maybe."

With a slight smile, she lathered her hands, smoothing soap on her palms and then on his face. He recognized the scent of the soap as the one he'd smelled in her hair. When she put a blade against his cheek, he closed his eyes and tried not to tense up.

Her legs were warm against the insides of his. Each time she stroked the knife along his cheek, her breath whispered along his freshly shaved skin.

"Breathe," she said. "I will not hurt you."

Finally, she was done. She stepped from between his thighs to wet a cloth and wipe his face. She held the warm cloth to his cheeks and examined his bruise.

"This is healing nicely on its own, but I think 'twould serve well to keep your face shaved."

She bent and kissed his mouth. He wrapped her up and pulled her into his lap. He lifted his hips and pressed against her.

She moaned. An instant later, he held a wild creature. She raked her fingers into his hair. Her mouth moved on his—lips, tongue, breath—in a maelstrom of sensation.

Her laces defied him, but finally parted. He pulled the jumper thing aside and cupped her breast. It was small, firm, warm through the linen. He clasped her nipple in his fingertips and tugged. She jerked in his arms, and the sounds she made in her throat were low, guttural—feral. They inflamed him.

A braid uncoiled and slithered across his hand. He took the silky gold rope, pulled her head back, and put his mouth on the long, slim column of her throat.

Her pulse throbbed beneath his lips. He dropped her hair and took the sweet mound of her breast into his hand again. She pushed against his palm. Hard metal grazed his knuckles as he caressed her. Armrings. Encircling her upper arm. He held a woman of status, one far above him in her world.

She kneaded his hip and he forgot why it mattered. Her fingers were so close. His heart began to thud in his chest. He wanted her hand on his erection.

He dropped his hand over hers. "Ardra," he said softly.

She opened her eyes. They were hazy, lost. Then they widened.

"Nay." She pulled out of his embrace. "Oh, forgive me. I am not wanton, truly I am not. I just . . . forgive me."

He got up and embraced her from behind. She froze the instant his body touched hers. "Yes, I want you." He kissed her neck. A small quiver went through her, but she was tense in his arms.

If he let go, she'd walk away. He needed her to walk away.

He opened his arms. She took a step and fumbled with her jumper thing, pulling the laces tight.

"What's going on here?" he asked.

She shook her head and another braid fell down. With a small sound of dismay, she tried to put them up but made a mess of it.

"I just want to understand what message I'm getting here," he said.

"What message?" She touched her breast. His insides danced.

"If you hadn't called a halt just now, we'd have ended up over there—" He jerked his thumb at the chaise. "In about ten minutes, you and I would have been buck naked and screwing our brains out." He cupped her face. "Is that what you want?"

Her eyes widened, and she drew back. She picked up a comb and ran it through her hair working out the remnants of her plaits. He gave her time to think. *He* needed time to think. She tied her hair at her nape with something that looked like gold cord.

"I like your kisses," she said, "but I have never wanted what follows."

And that did it for him. Maybe not physically, but it did it for the rest of him. What kind of lifemating had she had, to not want what followed kissing? He scooped up his cloak.

"I do not know why I kissed you, Lien." Her eyes were wide, and she tipped her head and drew the ponytail over her shoulder, then twisted her fingers in the ends.

"You're mourning Tol. Maybe you just wanted comfort."

"That must be it. I wanted comfort." She took the rope of hair in her two hands and stroked it over and over.

Blood surged through his veins.

"Kisses lead to other places, Ardra. I don't want you making love to me just because you feel bad. The only thing you're going to feel afterward is regret. Let's not go there again."

Ann Lawrence

"Agreed." Her abrupt acquiescence suited him but also disappointed him.

"Ardra, just out of curiosity, how do you prevent pregnancy here?"

The soft, vulnerable look on her face disappeared.

"Why? Are you concerned that your fine Ocean City blood might be tainted by association with a Selaw woman? That I might bear a mixed child and shame you?"

"Absolutely not. That's not what I meant. I was just curious, nothing more."

She threw open her coffer and tossed in her comb. "All know that a child born of a slave and a free woman is a slave. I would not subject a child to such a life. If I wanted to lie with a man, especially one with such a questionable status as yours, I would take the proper herbs."

Her chin was up in the air, her hands on her hips, but her eyes were huge and glittery.

"You haven't a clue. You may know that some herbs or whatever exist, but I'll wager my left hand you've never taken them."

She hissed through her teeth. "Are you calling me a liar?"

"No. I'm saying I've kissed enough women to know you haven't kissed many men—"

"Out." She pointed at the tent flap. "Out."

He ran his hands over his hair. "Okay. Fine."

Ardra turned her back on him, wiped off the knife blade she'd used to shave him, and began to wrap up her bundle of blades. He was glad she wasn't pitching them at him.

Time to escape. He pulled up the tent flap.

"Lien. Wait." She held the basin of shaving water in the circle of her arms and walked slowly toward him, her hips swaying.

If she wanted another kiss, she wasn't getting it.

"Please find Ollach and tell him I want Tol's men ready to leave at the sunrising. Tell him I want him to stand guard outside my tent after the scattering of Tol's ashes so

112

I may rest undisturbed." She thrust the basin into his arms. "Please dispose of this."

Ardra led the Procession of the Ashes out of camp when night fell. No moons guided them tonight, and a misty rain fell. It caused the torches to smoke as Tol's mourners wound their way across the level ground toward the mountains.

Finally they halted. Ralen handed her the stone jar containing Tol's ashes and then led the rest of the procession back to Samoht's camp.

Tradition required that she do this alone, but Deleh stood with her. When the many torches were out of sight, Ardra took a deep breath.

Despite Deleh's presence, Ardra had never felt so alone as she did standing on this silent, wet plain. Her thin mourning robe offered no protection from the rain.

She opened the jar. "Hold my hand," she said to Deleh.

They walked in a circle eight times, eyes closed, scattering the ashes, chanting the ancient words that would accompany Tol's soul to the next life.

It should be just Deleh here. The love between her and Tol was so strong, death could not end it.

Finally the jar was empty. Now they must find their way back to camp.

"Which way?" Deleh asked. Her thin hand trembled.

"Away from the mountains." Ardra frowned. The light rain had become a downpour. It pelted her shoulders and turned the rough ground muddy. Were they facing in the right direction?

She put her arm around Deleh's shoulders and directed her to stand still. Where were the mountains? Why could she not see torches?

She listened for the river, but heard only the hiss of rain.

"We are lost, Ardra, are we not?" Deleh whispered. " 'Tis Samoht's wish that we perish."

"Stop it," Ardra said, but she shivered.

113

"Why are there no guards to make sure we find our way back? All know that to walk in circles with one's eyes closed makes one dizzy and disoriented. We will perish." The old woman began to weep.

Ardra held Deleh in her arms. "I will find the way back. Trust me."

Deleh sniffed. "I do not weep for myself. In truth, I can think of nothing but joining Tol. I have prayed that it will not be long. But you—you are so young. Your son needs you. And I know that Samoht would relish your death. 'Twould mean he could take the fortress and the boy without bloodshed or dishonor to Tol's name. If we die, Samoht solves two problems at once. I am a useless old woman, and you are too much trouble."

"I will not believe Samoht so base as to allow two women to perish in such a way." But doubts niggled at her composure.

She took Deleh's hand and tugged her forward. "I will find our way back. We shall walk until we find the river, then follow it."

Inside, she was sick with dread.

A shadow stepped in front of her. Deleh screamed.

"Lien!" Ardra clamped down on her joy. She forced herself to walk past him. It would not do to let him think she had been lost. As he walked at her side, she noticed he did not depend on his walking staff. His stride was fluid, easy.

"Camp's the other way," he said and pointed off to her right.

"Of course," she said, veering in that direction, dragging Deleh behind her.

"I figured you must be lost, you were gone so long."

She could not see his face in the heavy rain, but heard no mockery in his tone. "I again must thank you for your care."

"No problem. I aim to serve. I heard voices, and that told me where to find you. Where is everyone anyway?"

A most apt question. Where were the guards to guide her home?

Lien pulled off his cloak and draped it over Deleh's shoulders. He pulled the hood up, tucking it close about the old woman's chin.

In silence, he led them back to the camp. Even when they were right upon the tents, the camp was nearly invisible in the heavy rain. Ardra went directly to Tol's tent. Lien left them at the entrance.

No guards stood outside, and the itch of unease she'd felt became a certainty of some evil. Was Deleh right? Were there no guards because Samoht had expected them to perish on the plain?

Ardra helped the old woman into a warm woolen gown, stirred the braziers, and heated a warm drink for her. Then she pulled off her own soaked clothing and donned one of Deleh's loose robes.

"You waste time," Deleh said. "Go to the young man. He must need his cloak." She crawled onto Tol's bed couch and pulled a heavy fur over her legs. "Lien was uncommonly kind. Not even Tol would have given his cloak to a slave."

"He is surely in Ollach's tent by now."

"I will wager my silver hair beads for a scented candle that he is outside as we speak," Deleh said.

"I have no need of your hair beads. He is not so much a fool that he would stand in the rain."

"My bath oil for a scented candle."

"Ah, now that is worth the wager." Ardra peeked outside. At first she did not see him; then a glimmer of white caught her eye. Was it a guard making his rounds? Nay, 'twas Lien sheltering against the side of a tent, the white his tunic.

"I owe you a scented candle. Now I must go," she said to Deleh, picking up Lien's wet cloak. "Rest and stay warm."

"Thank him, Ardra, but be wary."

115

"What does that mean?" Deleh often tried to mother her.

"It means Lien is a most intriguing man, but I wonder if he was born with such dark hair or if some evil curse changed him. If he was cursed . . . you may fall under ill luck in his company."

"I mean only to return his cloak."

"Ardra—" Deleh held out her hand. When Ardra took it, the old woman squeezed it. "I know Tol taught you much that a woman should not know. I could never agree with such nonsense. Do not allow his teachings to bring you harm. Accept the mate that Samoht will surely choose for you, and raise more babies. Forget the fortress."

"It is not the fortress, but the people within its walls I worry about, my son included. Now rest. When the sun rises, I will speak to Samoht and Einalem about a place for you."

"Old slaves have no place when their master dies." A single tear ran down Deleh's cheek.

"Do not speak so. I swear I will see to your care. Now please, sleep." She kissed Deleh's brow and drew the fur up to her chin. Deleh closed her eyes and sighed.

Ardra took up Lien's cloak again and went out into the night. Where were the guards? Who neglected his duties so that her tent and Tol's went unprotected?

She crossed the muddy expanse of ground to where Lien stood. She handed him the cloak. "I must thank you for your kindness to Deleh."

"No problem. Anyone would have done the same."

"Nay, not here. Could I impose upon you yet again to fetch Ollach? Please ask him to stand guard outside my tent." She curtseyed and walked away. She did not look back.

She banished thoughts of what Lien would do about his wet clothes, or how he would get them dry. She would *not* think of him pulling the wet tunic over his head, or drawing the black leather breeches down his hips.

*   *   *

Einalem watched Ardra speak with the dark one, then watched him stand in the rain until she disappeared into her tent. He pulled the cloak over his shoulders and went to the tent Ralen shared with Ollach. A few moments later, Ollach left the tent and stood guard before Ardra's. The dark one did not reappear.

The thought of him, so exotic, so completely different from the other men, stirred her desires for a moment, but she thrust them aside. He would serve for a bed game or two, but that was not what she wanted. She skirted a muddy puddle and summoned one of Samoht's guards.

"My brother wishes to speak with Ralen. Could you fetch him here?" The man bowed, and she pressed a coin into his palm. Now the man would say 'twas the high councilor who wanted Ralen, not she. Gossip could be so troublesome.

While she waited she would tend to other matters. And she knew Ralen would keep her waiting. His need to defy her in small ways was part of his allure.

She opened a large coffer filled with the impedimenta of her craft. She drew one unexceptional stone bottle from a row of others much like it and tapped a bit of dusty powder onto a linen square. After filling a goblet with a fine wine she kept warm in a brazier, she poured the powder into it.

Lest the wine's taste be ruined, she dropped dried fruit peel into the goblet. She placed it close to the brazier and then wandered around the tent, plumping pillows, lighting a wick in a dish of scented oil. Idly she considered a drop of hypnoflora between her breasts, but discarded the idea. Languid compliance was not what she wished from Ralen.

She heard the murmur of voices outside. Ralen entered the tent and shook the water from his cloak before draping it across a bench.

"I should complain to Samoht that you keep me waiting," Einalem said.

117

"But you will not," Ralen said. He pulled off his tunic and took care to lay it out neatly.

Einalem licked her lips. "Any punishment to you would punish me as well." She ran her hands up his chest and pulled his head close. "Have I told you how the sight of you makes me wet with desire?"

He kissed her. "Many times, but I never tire of hearing it."

She could not prevent a shiver.

"You are cold," he said and lifted her into his arms. He placed her on the bed couch. When he opened her robe, he smiled. "There are other things I rarely tire of as well."

His mouth was hot on her breast. She pushed him away. "I want to watch you disrobe."

He grinned and raked his thick, blond hair off his face. "Whatever pleases you pleases me."

Quickly he tugged off his boots. But when he stood before her, it was with agonizing slowness that he unlaced his leather breeches and peeled them off his hips.

"I see you are very pleased," she whispered and reached out for him.

"Do not be greedy, Einalem," he said, evading her grasp. "A woman should be more circumspect in her desires."

"I have never learned the skill." She climbed onto her knees and put out her arms. He stepped into her embrace. His body was roped with muscle, his skin cool from the night air. A small groan of desire escaped him as she rubbed her breasts against him.

"Now." She urged him down over her. "It must be now or I shall perish of the need of you."

He granted her request. As he filled her, she stifled a cry, arching into his hard rhythm and biting his lips.

You will be mine, she chanted silently as the power of his thrusts overwhelmed her. *You will be mine,* she thought with triumph as he moaned through his climax.

He rolled off her and lay on his back, sweat glistening on his skin. She rose and walked to the table. She brought a basin and linen towel to the bedside, then went back for the goblet of wine, which she set near to hand.

"Allow me to bathe you," she said.

"You would make an excellent slave," he said as she propped the pillows behind him and then knelt at his side.

She smiled and said nothing. *It would be he who was enslaved after he drank of the wine.* "It is quite a pleasurable task, Ralen. You have the finest body of any man I have ever bedded."

Ralen encircled her wrist and tugged her close. "I saw you watching the pilgrim. Has he been in your bed yet?"

She pulled against his hard grip. "Are you jealous?"

"Answer the question."

"Nay, although I must admit that he is most alluring."

His fingers tightened. "Just remember, Einalem, if you share another man's bed, you will not share mine."

His pale blue eyes were almost silver in the candlelight. They were as cold as Ardra's ice.

"I too will not share." She bent her head and gently bit the back of his hand. He eased his hold. She tongued the spot.

When she raised her head, some of the chill had left his gaze.

"Now that we have established what selfish beings we are, is that wine for me?" he asked.

"Ah. Forgive me." She lifted the goblet. "This is a special blend I have mixed just for you. 'Tis said if a man drinks of it in a certain way, his manhood will rise five times in one night."

"Only five times?" He grinned.

Slowly she straddled his hips. She pressed the goblet against her breasts. "I will warm it a bit for you."

His icy eyes widened, his manhood stirred against her warmth.

119

She took a sip of the wine and allowed the taste to suffuse her mouth; then she leaned forward. Her breasts grazed his chest; she nestled down on the heat of him.

He pulled her mouth to his, and she trickled the wine over his tongue. She swirled her tongue over his, sharing the wine, the infusion of herbs, the ancient rite.

"Again," he whispered. He clasped her buttocks in his palms and shifted her against his hardness. She drained the wine and then sealed her mouth on his. He participated this time as he must, rolling his tongue on hers, sealing his fate.

Chapter Ten

The sun rose, a dazzling red jewel in the sky. Hope filled Ardra's breast as she stepped from her tent. Such a clear and lovely day must bode well.

She yawned. Her sleep had been restless, filled with dream kisses, and the most embarrassing realization that it was she who did all the kissing whilst the man, a shadowy person who held no place in her memory except as warm lips, insisted she stop.

Then she frowned. She saw no warriors readying their horses for a journey into the Tangled Wood. Ollach was gone.

She hurried to Samoht's tent. He stood by his table, a map spread before him. Einalem reclined on his bed couch. Did the woman have no duties? Was no one ailing this morn?

But alarm filled her when she saw the other men who sat on benches along the wall. The Tolemac high councilors. Ralen was not among them.

Other than a solemn greeting, Samoht ignored her. She walked down the row of men, curtseying low to each so

they could touch her on the head. Each murmured some condolence on Tol's passing. No one met her eyes.

Samoht continued his disregard of her presence. Was he angry with her for shoving the candle stand into his manhood? Why should she care? 'Twas he who had behaved badly. She had but defended herself. 'Twas he who had tried to put his hands beneath her skirt.

He rolled a map, tied it up. "What may I do for you, Ardra?" he finally asked, his arms crossed on his chest.

"I seek Tol's men," Ardra said. "I want to leave immediately."

"They will not go."

"What do you mean?" Ardra stared at his handsome face and saw a glimmer of satisfaction there. A councilor behind her whispered to another.

Einalem answered. "They will not serve you. They did so only by Tol's order, and now Tol is dead."

Ardra ignored her and directed her words to Samoht. After all, he held the power, not Einalem. "And you will not order them to serve me, will you?"

If she challenged him, would one of the other councilors champion her cause?

"I will not." He inclined his head to the councilors. "We decided that Tol's men should serve Ralen until another councilor can be chosen in his place. At that time, Ralen will transfer his authority."

A mad desire to push Samoht onto his table of maps swept over her. She controlled it and spoke with all the dignity she could gather. "I see. You have set me a task that requires me to go into a cursed wood after a woman who is evil, and now you tell me I must do it alone. *You* would not do it alone."

As a Selaw woman, she was not permitted to directly address the council and influence them, but they must know what Samoht was doing to her.

She gathered her wits. "It seems to me, Most Esteemed High Councilor, that you do not really wish to regain the vial."

"Nonsense. The vial is of great importance. And your task remains the same. If you wish to rule, you must find it," Samoht said. "I do not believe we need detain these worthy men any longer. They traveled far to honor Tol and must return to the capital."

The other councilors rose like sheep and filed out. Ardra dropped a curtsey to each one, though they did not bow or acknowledge her. The exchange humiliated her.

Her head pounded with both anger and fatigue. When the councilors were gone, she said, "You never set the task with any intention of fairness. You are a dishonorable man, Samoht, and I will not hesitate to say so to whomever will listen."

"Watch your tongue, Ardra." He uncrossed his arms, and she thought he might strike her.

Ralen entered the tent and paused, glancing from Ardra to Samoht. "What is wrong here?"

Ardra rounded on him. "You ask what is wrong? Surely you are a part of it?"

"What are you talking about?" Ralen asked.

Einalem stepped between Ardra and Ralen. She placed her hand on Ralen's chest. "Ardra is angry that Tol's men will not ride with her."

Ardra watched Ralen's face and felt a small measure of relief that he appeared confused. He sidestepped past Einalem. "Why not?"

Samoht shrugged. "It is the council's decision. Ollach said his men fear the Wood. They also think it humiliating to be commanded by a woman. This last is reason enough for the council."

"Ollach is my man now; I will speak to him," Ralen said. "Ardra cannot seek the goddess alone. If you want the Vial of Seduction found, how can one woman alone accomplish it? 'Tis folly, Samoht."

"I imagine Samoht has no intention that I succeed," Ardra said. "I believe he intended that I should perish on the plain after scattering Tol's ashes."

"How dare you accuse my brother—" Einalem began, but Ralen ended it.

"Be silent. I will escort Ardra. Tol's men will follow me."

Einalem gasped. "Surely you do not mean to leave already? You have just arrived."

"I agree," Samoht said. "What nonsense. I cannot spare you to such a task."

"Yet it makes good sense that I do so. I claim my right to mourn my brother. Besides, I know the way. I have met the goddess and found her quite amiable. Now I must speak to Ollach and ready our party. Ardra—one packhorse, no more." Ralen left the tent.

Samoht glared after him, then turned to Ardra. "I grant you only the eight days of mourning for your quest. At the end of that time, you must either produce the vial or accept whatever measures I deem appropriate for the well-being of your people."

"Samoht, Einalem." Ardra bowed to them each in turn and hurried after Ralen before they could stop her. She ran up behind him and took his arm. "Ralen. I must thank you."

He glowered down at her. "Do not thank me. This mission is a waste of time and supplies, and I did not volunteer in order to aid you. I did it out of respect for Tol. He would never have countenanced such treatment of his lifemate. He too would not care to have his son under Samoht's thumb. I merely want to do as he might."

Then his frown softened. "Why did you say Samoht wished you to perish when you scattered Tol's ashes? What happened?"

Ardra told him as they searched for Ollach. "Visibility was down to a stone's throw after you left. Would you not have posted guards along the way back to camp so a mourner could find her way home? Samoht did not. He knew I would have naught but my mourning robe—no mantle, no hood to protect me in the storm."

"Samoht is cunning, but I will not believe I serve a man so treacherous. I am sure 'twas an oversight, but I will speak to him myself on the matter."

"What will that serve? He will only deny it."

"Still, I will speak to him. Now I must prepare my men. See to your own." He strode away.

Ralen was a cold contrast to Lien's warmth. Ralen, she suspected, would not give his cloak to a slave.

A commotion drew Ardra's eyes. "Nilrem!" She lifted her hem, dashed between two tents, and leaped across a muddy puddle. She curtseyed to the wiseman when he had climbed down from his cart.

"Ah, Ardra. I see I am too late." Nilrem took her hand and kissed the back of it.

She touched her hair, long, loose, and unadorned. It was a sign of mourning, as was the lack of thumb rings on her hands. "Aye. You are too late. We will speak of it another time. Now I need your advice."

"I must pay my respects to Samoht first, my child. Await me in your tent. We will talk, I promise you."

As Ardra headed for her tent, she wondered what tale Samoht and Einalem would weave for the wiseman. How she wished to be invisible and listen to their conversation.

She swallowed hard and looked out over the plain to the smudge of white on the horizon. Home had never seemed so far away or so enticing. She had but eight days, an impossibly short time.

Lien leaned on his stick and watched Ralen give orders. The guy was really efficient. Everyone jumped when he spoke, even Ollach, who had groused all morning about dying in a cursed place. Lien gathered that Tol's men expected to be swarmed by serpents when they reached the goddess's fortress; none wanted to linger in agony as the venom ate through their bodies.

Lien wasn't so enamored of snakes himself. He had one on his arm only because his teammates had dubbed him

125

"the snake" after a lacrosse game in which he'd "snaked" his way between two All-American defensemen and scored to win the championship.

That night, he'd gotten drunk at a frat party, then gone with a bunch of the guys to a tattoo parlor. Afterward, Eve had reamed him out big time. Not for the tattoo, which he suspected turned her on, but for the drinking. That was before he had really accepted the fact that his mother was an alcoholic. It was before his dad had died of cancer and taken all his mother's reason for being with him.

Lien moved toward a string of horses, saddlebags over their rumps. He'd heard Nilrem was in camp. He'd like to see the old bugger and get some advice on where to go next.

Nilrem was with Ollach. The old man was directing the warrior in a pedantic tone that made Lien smile.

"Nilrem," Lien said. "How're you doing?"

"Ah, pilgrim. I am well, although I much regret I could not be here to celebrate Tol's passing. He was a good man."

"Can I talk to you a minute?" Lien asked the wiseman.

"Are you ailing? You lean most heavily on that stick. Is it a potion you need? Stitching?" Nilrem took his arm.

"We'll talk about me another time," Lien said, evading the issue of his health. "I just need advice."

Lien figured they looked like two old geezers stumping along with their sticks. He led Nilrem away from Ralen's men to the outskirts of camp. The old man leaned against some rocks. Overhead, a blood-red sun burned in an alien purple sky.

Lien took a deep breath. "Look. I'm not from around here. I don't have any clothes. I don't have anything to barter for my keep, either. What do you suggest I do?"

Nilrem hummed and chewed his lower lip. "Has Ardra repaid you for saving her life?"

"Forget Ardra. I don't want to involve her in my problems."

"You cannot prevent it. It is not possible to ignore the entwining of your lives. You sought my wisdom at the exact moment Ardra needed you. My advice is to hitch your cart to her star."

Nilrem cackled a moment, and Lien frowned. Something bothered him, but he couldn't quite put his finger on what it was.

"I don't think Ardra wants me anywhere around her."

"Oh? She is coming. I shall ask her."

"No, don't," Lien began, but he was too late. Nilrem waved his arm like a windmill. Ardra could not help seeing him.

She hurried over and curtseyed to the old man. Lien loved the gesture. It was somehow delightful, this old-fashioned mark of respect.

"The high councilor told me of the challenge he has set you, Ardra," Nilrem said. "I think it madness. Eight days only! But I understand why you feel the need to acquiesce to his demands."

"I am sure he wishes me dead," she said.

Lien frowned. Her words were less angry than resigned, and yet she was determined to go. He admired her courage. If it were his choice, he'd be on the first wagon train back to the fortress.

"Then you must heed me," Nilrem said.

Ardra bowed her head. "What should I do?"

"Take Lien with you. Do not let him out of your sight."

"Whoa!—" Lien began.

"I will not take him," Ardra said. Her chin went straight into the air.

Nilrem put a hand out and she took it. "I understand your anger and disappointment. But one may not ignore the augury of the gods. You were practicing the old ways when Lien saved your life. You owe him, and until you pay, your life is tied to his."

"Don't I have a say in this?" Lien asked.

"Nay. You do not. When Ardra has saved your life, you may part company with her."

Good thing Nilrem didn't know he'd saved her life twice more—once in the forest and once on the plain. Hell, if he went by Nilrem's advice, he was stuck with Ardra forever.

"I will not take him." Ardra dropped Nilrem's hand and jammed her hands on her hips. "I will not."

"You will take him for protection," Nilrem said. "It is imperative, for you see, you must also take Samoht."

Ardra concealed her anger as they climbed the steep path up the cliff to the edge of the Tangled Wood. Samoht and Einalem led the party. If their horses moved any slower, they would go backwards. Their pace must be calculated to prevent her from accomplishing her task. At this rate, it would take eight days just to reach the summit.

The moment they reached the summit she would ask Ralen to lead. He too had but eight days and might understand her urgency.

Nilrem also held the party back. He was a terrible rider. Luckily, Lien's riding skills seemed to have improved. Although, curiously, when she looked back at him on the treacherous trail, his skin had lost much of its color.

Samoht had loaded the party with every possible impediment: the wiseman, his sister, her three personal slaves, and four packhorses. Not to mention the full complement of Red Rose Warriors. At least the party also included Ralen's archers.

Ardra gritted her teeth to keep from screaming aloud.

When they reached the scrubby trees that marked the beginning of the great forest, she kicked her horse to a canter to pull even with Ralen.

He frowned at her as if she were a troublesome child. So be it, trouble she would be.

"What is it, Ardra?" he asked.

"We move too slowly. Can you not take the lead and quicken our pace?" She tipped her head in Samoht's di-

rection. He was chatting with his sister, pointing out trees, indicating a bird's nest.

"First, why is he on this venture?" Ralen asked. "What happened?"

"Nilrem said that Einalem expressed a desire to meet the goddess. She claimed that as a healer, she might learn much from someone who is touted in story and song as a great herbalist—albeit an evil one. Samoht decided to accompany Einalem to keep her safe."

"Do you think Einalem has something else on her mind?" Ralen asked.

"I think Einalem and the Goddess of Darkness might be too much evil in one forest," she said.

"Einalem is not evil, merely concerned with little beyond herself. She can be quite good company if she wishes."

"I see." She sighed. "Is that why Samoht did not object to your leading this party? He did not want to displease Einalem?"

Ralen did not answer.

"Do you think we could make greater speed? Does your influence extend to taking control of our pace?"

She could not help a bit of emphasis on "influence" so that he might know she understood the nature of his relationship with the high councilor's sister.

"Resume your place in line, and I will see to the pace."

Ralen was as good as his word. He wove his way through the long, meandering party and placed himself between Samoht and Einalem. After a bit of conversation, Ralen edged his mount ahead. Einalem pulled forward to speak to him as if attached to the tail of his horse with a bit of thread. When Ralen picked up his pace, Einalem did too.

Ardra thought she should remember this method. He had accomplished his goal through manipulation, not confrontation.

The Tangled Wood grew cooler as they moved deeper into the goddess's domain. Soon Ardra would meet the woman who was responsible for her mother's death. The

129

thought knotted her insides and caused her hands to sweat in their leather gloves.

With a glance over her shoulder, she checked to see where Lien rode and saw him between Nilrem and Deleh. Lien scratched at his neck and had a most disagreeable scowl on his face. The shadow of his beard was back.

She must tell Nilrem how she had tempted Lien from his vows. What penance should she serve for such a deed? Nilrem would know what a priest would say. Henceforth she intended to call Lien "pilgrim" as Nilrem did. That would remind her of his celibacy.

Deleh looked frightened, peering up at the great arms of the trees overhead. Whenever a blue-hawk cawed, she gasped. Lien reassured her each time. 'Twas folly for Deleh to come, but she had been too frightened to remain behind with Samoht's army. Luckily, her riding skills put Nilrem's to shame.

Ardra caught Lien's eye and glanced quickly away, but he pulled from his position and rode up to her side. "Deleh's a bit unnerved, I think."

"Again you are kind, pilgrim."

He shrugged.

"Deleh has never been into the Wood."

"You have?" He scratched his neck.

"Only the one time with you. What is wrong?"

"I think I must have done a lousy—"

"Lice! You have lice?"

"No. No. I don't have lice. No, where I come from, 'lousy' also means bad. I think I did a *bad* job rinsing out this tunic. The soap's irritating my skin." He smiled.

What straight white teeth he had. What had become of her resolve? It would not do to think of his teeth . . . or mouth . . . or lips.

"I shall have Ollach find you a new tunic." She glanced around. Only Deleh seemed to be paying them any attention. "May I ask you a question? One that you may refuse to answer if it offends you."

"Ask away. If you get too personal, I'll plead the fifth."

His grin annoyed her. "You are unlike any pilgrim I have ever met. Pilgrims should be solemn, reverent, not . . . gleeful."

His smile widened.

"You are so hard to understand. You sprinkle your speech with words I do not understand. You speak too quickly, you slur your words together—"

"Whoa. I'm sorry. Now, is that the question? Why is my speech so bad?" His grin grew even wider.

"Nay. I wanted to know why you are so kind to Deleh. She is naught but a slave. How do your actions serve you?"

"She's an old woman. Why wouldn't I treat her kindly? Why does it have to serve me in some way?" He frowned, and she was sorry for the loss of his smile.

"Because you are a man. And it is my experience that men do only what serves them best."

He examined her as if inspecting her for lice. It was a hard look. Cold and hard. "Well, Ardra, I'm not like other men," he finally said.

With a kick of his heels, he cantered up to the fore of the company, nearer to Ollach than was seemly for a pilgrim. No one challenged Lien. He seemed to have an invisible aura that made the other men wary.

"True," Ardra whispered. "You are unlike any other man."

The company halted to rest the horses. Lien watched the subtle way Einalem slipped into the woods after Ralen. To avoid the couple, he walked upstream, following Ollach's directions. Ollach said he'd seen a track along the stream bed. Ollach thought if Lien followed it, he might find a quiet pool for bathing.

Samoht insisted they camp long enough to make a hot meal, so while Ardra steamed over the delay, Lien intended to find the pool. He needed a bath—badly. His arms and neck itched like crazy.

The stream looked ice cold and deep, a river of grape drink. The bank was steep and thick with roots. The trees by the stream all reminded him of giant mangroves.

Flowers, similar to the ones entwining the tree roots along the forest road, knotted themselves around the roots here. These flowers, however, were tiny, the size of his thumbnail, and profuse, their peppery perfume filling the air. He saw signs of deer hooves on the footpath, but no snaky, slithery marks.

An awking sound drew his attention. On a nearby branch, a sleek blue bird sat and watched him, following his movements with an unblinking stare. It opened its mouth, and the awking sound came again. The unearthly creature reminded him of a turkey buzzard.

"Hi there," he said softly to the hawk. "Keep an eye out for snakes, okay?" The bird lifted its wings and rose, soaring silently and skillfully between the branches, and disappeared.

Another sound, one he recognized more readily, came from his left. He had no wish to watch Ralen screw Einalem, so he veered to the right and made a circle around them to come back to the trail.

Ollach was right on. The path led to a break between the trees. The break didn't exactly lead to a pool but to a narrow section of the stream where several trees had fallen and formed a bridge. It was not quite a dam—no water flowed over it, but the fallen trees did serve to slow the current.

After stripping, he took a cautious step out on the tree trunk, bounced a bit, and found it fairly solid. He walked to the center of the stream and lowered himself into the waist-deep water. The bottom was sandy and fairly smooth. His skin looked a sickly lavender in the water's reflection.

"Gee, I hope I'm not this color when I get out."

The water brought instant relief to his itching. He examined his arms and legs. His wounds from the outcasts

were almost gone, but a rash of tiny red dots encircled his wrists, and he imagined it was the same around his neck, just in the spots where his tunic was snug against his skin.

Because Nilrem had suggested it, Lien scrubbed the rash with mud from the riverbank, then took a more conventional bath with some soap Ollach had given him. The water wasn't any colder than the ocean in midsummer, so he swam in a lazy crawl for a bit, reluctant to leave its soothing relief.

He dunked and came up, shaking water from his hair. There on the bank stood Einalem. She perched on the fallen tree between him and his clothes, smiling like a Cheshire cat. Her dress, a clingy thing, was the intense blue of her eyes. And mighty nice eyes they were when they weren't examining him like a raptor after a rodent— as they were now.

He resisted an urge to cross his hands over his groin.

"Nilrem informs me you suffer from a rash. May I see it? I am a healer, considered gifted by many."

He waded to where she sat. Although her blond hair was in a neat braid over one shoulder, not an errant strand in sight, and her dress fairly wrinkle-free, she had a just-been-satisfied look about her that told him old Ralen had been a naughty boy . . . or a very good boy, depending on your point of view.

He extended his arm. "I think the rash is from my tunic. I don't think I rinsed all the soap out when I washed it."

She took his arm and stroked her fingers over the red dots. "Why did you not command a slave or Ardra to do your wash?"

He realized the grape-ade water wasn't quite as opaque as he'd thought, but Einalem seemed intent on her skin inspection.

"I like to do things for myself," he said, and when she released his arm, he took a step into deeper water.

Einalem pursed her lips. "I have seen many rashes, but none such as this." She leaned forward, peering at his

throat. "Come closer; I want to see your neck."

She toppled into the stream. He watched her flounder about for a moment, then rise to stand upright, spluttering and spitting water.

No one could fake such surprise. He laughed. She darted a sharp look at him, then began to giggle too. The light sound wiped away much of her haughty veneer.

Her dress was just about transparent against her breasts as she waded toward him. Her nipples were large and distended. Mr. Happy was in heaven.

"I might as well make the most of this opportunity and look at your neck," she said.

When she touched his skin, her fingers were cold. She stroked along the rash where it encircled his throat, then drew her hand along his shoulder to his arm, but did not touch his tattoo. "This is a most fascinating thing, this mark. How is it done?"

"Needles and some dye stuff."

"I could please you well," she whispered. Her hand disappeared under the water.

"No, thank you." He protected Mr. Happy and waded toward the bank. "Not to offend you, but aren't you involved with Ralen?"

"And?" She lifted her arms and fussed with her hair as she waded toward him. Her dress hugged her body. "And?" she whispered again.

"Uh. Pilgrims don't like trouble." What if he offended her? Did she have enough influence to foul him up somehow? Leave him behind on the trail, possibly? She was Samoht's sister, after all.

He dove beneath the surface and swam underwater a few yards before coming up in a pool of shadow where the water was much colder. She was a nice, safe distance away.

"I forgot you were a pilgrim." Einalem paused, looked up at the bank, and dropped her arms.

"What are you doing?" Ardra asked, appearing suddenly from the trees.

"I fell in the stream; is that not amusing?" Einalem put out her hand. Ardra grasped it and helped Einalem climb up the bank.

From Lien's position, Einalem's dress looked like a second skin; she might as well have been naked.

"Are you hurt?" Ardra asked. "Shall I fetch you a dry robe?"

"I am not hurt, am I, Lien?" Einalem said his name in a low, sultry voice, turning to him.

Ardra turned as well. She looked at him, then at Einalem. She curtseyed. "Forgive me for intruding." In the next moment, she was gone, lost in the greenery.

Damn.

"What ails her?" Einalem turned and gave Lien the full show.

"I imagine she thinks we're doing something we shouldn't," he muttered. *Damn and damn and damn.*

Einalem wrung out the rope of her hair. "All I have done is fall in the stream."

How he wished the woman in the water with him were Ardra. What would it be like to have her legs wrapped around his waist while the strange water swirled around them?

Einalem plucked at her wet gown. "I will find a soothing oil for your rash. Visit me when next we halt our party, and I will rub it on for you."

I bet you will. "What about that gray stuff? Nilrem probably has some with him. He put it on this wound here"—he pointed to his arm—"and there's hardly a mark left."

"It has little effect on rashes."

She picked up the clean tunic Ollach had found for him, slipped it over her head, and walked off toward camp.

He flung himself onto his back and floated with the current.

Damn. Now he'd need to get Ardra alone and explain that nothing was going on. "Whoa," he said aloud. "Why?

135

Ardra's nothing but a sweet woman who's horny but doesn't know it. Or is it me who's horny?"

When he climbed out of the stream, he let the air dry him for a minute, more than a little annoyed that he had to put on his old tunic.

Ardra would not have taken his tunic. She was one of the least selfish people he could think of. Everything she did was calculated to serve her people. Was that what made her so interesting?

The red dots began to flare up now that he was out of the soothing water. He reached for his pants.

A woman stepped from the shadows, coming from the direction of the camp. At first glance he thought it was Einalem, but a second told him it was a stranger.

Well, hell, would wonders never cease? Another blonde. She stopped in her tracks and stared. Her gaze ran up and down him. His rash tingled as though tiny insects were having a feast.

He held his pants in front of his crotch.

She didn't say a word, but turned and vanished back into the foliage, directly into the tangled tree roots.

He waited a few moments before tugging the pants over his damp skin. As he laced them up, he froze.

Dangling in front of him, right where the woman had stood, was a black snake. As thick around as his arm, it was at least six feet long.

He held his breath. The snake's head lifted. It tested the air with its red tongue.

Slowly Lien dropped his hands to his sides. A glance told him he had nowhere to go except the stream. Common sense told him the snake would get him before he hit the water.

Lien pointed at the snake. "Be gone."

The snake undulated in the air, head poised to strike. Lien held his place.

A ripple washed down the snake's body. The snake dropped like a stone and slithered through the grass—

straight at him. And past him. It shot into the water.

Heart racing, mouth dry, Lien watched the snake zigzag downstream.

"Well, I'll be damned." His hands shook a bit as he tied his laces and pulled his tunic over his head. He jerked on his boots, snatched up his walking stick, and hurried back to camp.

Ardra sat on her horse, ready to go.

"Sorry to hold you up," he said. "But I ran into a huge snake back there."

"What color?"

"Black."

"The black ones are lethal." With a brisk nod, she turned her horse and joined Ralen at the front of the company.

Ollach gave him a leg up, then thrust his long sword into a saddle sheath. "I hear Einalem came back all wet and wearing that tunic I gave you," he said.

"She fell in the stream." Lien took up his reins.

"Watch yourself. There are those who might use your behavior against you."

"Why? She fell in the stream. I didn't invite her company, and nothing happened. How could someone use that against me?"

Ollach raised an eyebrow. "Are you mad? You have no arm rings. If you did not claim the pilgrim status, you would be condemned as a runaway slave. There are those who would not hesitate to use any excuse to challenge you, but most are wary of harming a celibate man. 'Tis bad luck."

"Celibate?"

"Aye. To forgo the pleasures of the flesh is an esteemed choice, so it protects you—now. But if you prove lecherous, many will believe you hide behind the vows for other reasons, such as eluding your master's grasp. Then they will act—for the reward if nothing else. And surely you know

137

that slaves without masters are fair game for those who wish to make a quick fortune."

So he was thought celibate. Well, hell. Was that what held Ardra back? She thought he was celibate? And how did that make him look? He was supposed to be a man of principle and at the first opportunity he'd forgotten his vows. She must think he was the biggest hypocrite in Tolemac.

It didn't matter. In fact, it helped. He might feel obligated to watch Ardra's back, but as long as he didn't sleep with her, he could leave her at the first opportunity.

Lien was damned tired of riding. What was a fun activity when visiting friends in Maryland was just hard work after five or so hours. And now that it was night, the outriders carried smoking torches that stung his eyes.

It also annoyed him that Ardra had resisted his efforts at conversation. She must think he'd hooked up with Einalem.

"Deleh?" Lien guided his mount closer to the old woman.

She nodded.

"Tell me what you know of pilgrims hereabouts."

"Pilgrims? They are usually traveling to Nilrem's mountain or perhaps the capital to see the priests. I have known pilgrims to go both places for different matters."

"And once they reach the capital?"

"They seek some penance or wisdom. If they get it, they return home. Some pilgrims never find what they seek and so wander all their days. 'Tis an excuse to avoid gainful employment, if you ask me. 'Tis laziness. I hope you are not one of those."

"Uh. Definitely not. I've always been gainfully employed. Anything else you can tell me?"

"If you are a pilgrim, you should know." Her eyes narrowed.

"I'm from across the ice fields. I'm just comparing customs."

"Ah. Well." She pursed her lips. "Pilgrims are ofttimes lazy souls, as I said. Lazy or not, they all eschew the pleasures of the bed. Some might also refuse wine or meat until their penance is done. It depends, I suppose, on what it is a pilgrim seeks, what deeds they feel they must atone for."

Damn.

Chapter Eleven

"How much longer?" Ardra asked Ralen.

"It depends on whether you wish to arrive in the light or the dark," he said. "I could call a halt now, set camp, and then we would arrive at the goddess's fortress before the midday meal."

"And the other alternative?"

"Ride through the night and arrive while the orbs are overhead. It matters not to me."

"We have wasted three days on this journey. I do not want to waste a moment more," she said.

"Then we will ride on."

Ardra watched the sky each time a break in the tree canopy appeared. When she finally saw the orbs directly overhead, the Tangled Wood thinned.

Not much later they burst from the forest, and there at the foot of a low hill sat a lake. Wisps of fog rose from its surface.

Energy surged through her. Was there something in the heavy aroma of the flowers, so thick in the tree roots here, or was it the anticipation of meeting the goddess that banished her fatigue?

Beyond the mist-shrouded lake, on a rise, the orbs silvered the vine-covered walls of an ancient fortress. A tall tower hinted at a substantial dwelling within.

"How appropriate that we should arrive in darkness to meet the goddess," she said to Ralen.

"I found her most amiable," Ralen said. He reached over and touched her hand.

"I am afraid," she said, then wanted to bite her tongue that she had revealed a weakness to this man who served Samoht. "Oh, what am I saying? 'Tis just the tales one is told, nothing more."

"Aye, just the murmuring of old women to frighten children."

"What frightens children?" Lien asked.

"Ask Einalem, pilgrim," Ardra said, and regretted it the moment he hauled on his reins and dropped behind to do just that. What had possessed her to betray her jealousy in such a manner?

"How will we cross the lake?" she asked Ralen to cover her confusion.

"We do not need to cross. It is a pretty thing, not a defense. We have but to ride around it. An hour or so more. In fact, I wager we will be met and escorted."

Ralen pointed to the gleam of torches on the high tower of the fortress. "The lookouts will inform her we have arrived. She will send out riders."

"What are her defenses if not this lake?"

"Naught but a long view and strong walls," he said.

"And superstition," Ardra added.

They rode along the lake's shore in silence. Ralen's men rode with confidence, but his archers were wary, bows ready.

Servants and slaves who had wandered a bit from the close ranks maintained by the warriors drew in, Lien and Nilrem among them. Was it deliberate that the pilgrim who had avoided her for many hours now drew near? She re-

membered Nilrem's admonishment that Lien must make
this journey to protect her.

Would she need protection?

"Look," Lien said. He pointed to a black hole appearing
in the solid wall of the fortress. From it poured a procession
of mounted men with torches.

Ralen said, "She is prompt in opening her gates. It appears we will be welcomed and given a bed for what remains of the night." He issued quick orders that everyone
was to keep his sword sheathed.

Ardra felt a shiver of dread. She must not look for re-
assurance from Ralen or Lien. Whatever happened here
must be accomplished by herself. Samoht must be satisfied
it was she, and no other, who gained the vial, or he would
take her fortress and her son's future.

The two parties met. Ralen explained who they were,
and the men from the fortress, garbed in a deep green that
shimmered in the orb-glow, dismounted and bowed to
Samoht and Einalem. Ralen did not introduce Ardra,
though she held as much status in Selaw as Einalem in
Tolemac.

They followed the men, who held their torches high.
When they passed over an ancient drawbridge, Ardra
stared around in awe. Behind the dark, vine-covered walls,
all was light and beauty.

On the inside, the vines were more delicate, lacy even.
Their white flowers gave off a subtle perfume.

"Ardra," Deleh said. "Where have we smelled this
scent?"

"In the perfume we give to maidens on their tenth conjunction."

"A strange flower for the goddess to cultivate here," Deleh said and shivered. "I want my bed, Ardra."

"Soon, Deleh, soon."

The courtyard in which we dismounted, and where
they left all but a few of their men, was covered in a weath-
ered mosaic. Ardra had seen such tiled pictures in the Tol-

emac capital. This one was a simple design of vines that led the eye to the great hall and the stone steps leading to white double doors.

"Some place," Lien said. He traced the tip of his stick along the ancient tiles. "It seems the vines and flowers have been around a long time." His avid examination of the fortress reminded her of a child's simple pleasure in something new.

"Evil. It is all evil." Deleh hooked her arm in Lien's.

Ardra knew she must show neither Lien's awe nor Deleh's fear. "It is a fortress much like any other."

"I bow to your assessment." Lien smiled; then his eyes shifted. "Well, I'll be."

"You will be what?" Ardra asked, and then saw where his gaze had settled.

The double doors had opened. On the top step stood a tiny woman. *The goddess*.

Her blond hair, a streaky mixture of gold and the pure white of the flowers, rippled down her back nearly to the floor. It might have been night, but she was garbed as one should to greet a high councilor. Her draped gown, the same shimmery green as her guards' tunics, opened in a V to reveal a heavy gold chain. Nestled between her ample breasts was a large dull stone.

The Black Eye.

The goddess walked down the steps and dropped into a deep curtsey before Samoht. She looked younger than Einalem. Too young for her evil reputation.

Ralen introduced her. "Samoht, Esteemed High Councilor of the Eight Chiefdoms, may I present Cidre, Goddess of the Tangled Wood."

"I am honored to share my home with you," the goddess said.

Lien whispered to Ardra, "What did Ralen call her? *Kid* what?"

"Cid-re. It means bright and beautiful."

Ann Lawrence

Lien thought there was a bit of jealousy in Ardra's voice. "No kidding," he quipped.

"Nay, Lien. Cid-*re*." She enunciated the name for him, and he remembered that a beautiful woman usually had no sense of humor when it came to another beautiful woman.

"Before you go in there, I have to tell you something." He took Ardra's arm.

"It must wait." She pulled away and stepped forward to be presented, her heart in her throat.

Ralen introduced Einalem. The goddess curtseyed again, less deeply, then held out her hand to the warrior.

"Welcome, Ralen. To what do I owe this visit so hard upon your last?"

Ralen took the goddess's hand; it looked like a small child's in his. "I am afraid we have not yet done with our quest for the Vial of Seduction."

The goddess frowned. "You have searched here, Ralen. There is nothing to find."

"We understand that," Samoht said. "It is our hope that you may help us in some other way."

"You have a wiseman in your party—can he not help you? Nilrem, is it not?" She did not bow to Nilrem or curtsey as she had to the Tolemac high councilor and his sister.

Nilrem leaned on his stick and sucked on his lower lip. He looked as stupid as a stone. "Eh? Did someone say my name?"

"Forget him," Samoht said. "We bow to what you know from the ancient times as a wise woman. It is for knowledge we have come."

The goddess touched the black stone on her chest. "There are those who fear my knowledge."

All around her, the slaves and servants of Samoht's party stepped back and huddled together.

The goddess smiled and held out her hands, palms up. The wide sleeves of her robe fell back along plump, soft arms. "Come, do not be afraid. I know the tales you spin

144

in Tolemac about me. You call me the Goddess of Darkness. Here I am but Cidre of the Tangled Wood, the daughter of a wise woman. There is nothing to fear. I am no more cursed than this old wise *man*," she said, with a finger pointed at Nilrem.

She shrugged when no one moved closer to her. "I much enjoy the tales. It suits me well to encourage them. It keeps away the rebels and outcasts who might take it upon themselves to raid a small fortress such as this. Come, Samoht, I bid you welcome."

Samoht rapped out an order and the men hastened to their tasks. The goddess linked her arm through his and they walked into the fortress. Einalem and Ralen followed. Ardra stood alone by her horse, unacknowledged and unsure how to proceed.

Lien took her elbow. "Get in there."

"Aye," Nilrem took her other elbow. "Samoht appears to be helping you in your task, and that concerns me."

"Yeah," Lien said. "I don't like it either. He's made it seem like he's the one on the mission, not you."

They flanked her to the doors, then gave her a little push ahead of them. The guards flung wide the double doors.

"Wow," Lien said.

Ardra did not know the word but understood the sentiment. The doors opened on a dazzling white interior. She stared along with the others, save Ralen who had seen it all before.

At one end of the lofty hall someone had used a mighty tree to support the roof. Then Ardra realized it was not a support but a live tree, its tangled roots bursting from the floor, its thick branches vanishing through the roof.

"Where do you think the tree ends? It does not protrude from the roof. We would have seen it from across the lake." Nilrem scratched his head.

Lien shrugged. "Who knows?"

How the tree lived Ardra did not know, for the center of the trunk had been hollowed out and lined with stone to

hold huge logs. The fire burned with an intensity that caused everyone to shed his cloak. But it was not for the soothing warmth, Ardra suspected, that the men collected about the hearth.

Nay, some canny artist had carved the roots into naked women, their sexuality emphasized to the point of mockery.

The effect was of women dancing about the base of the tree whose heart burned, impervious to the flames.

A blue-hawk's caw drew her eyes to a lofty branch.

"A predator bird in a predatory woman's lair," Lien said under his breath.

"I see you are admiring my hearth," the goddess said, for the first time directing her remarks to Ardra. "The tree is said to be as old as time."

Close up, the goddess was even more beautiful than from a distance. Her skin glowed with youth, and her eyes, Tolemac blue, gleamed with a hint of amusement.

Ardra realized it was not possible for this goddess to have caused her mother's death. Cidre appeared even younger than Einalem. It must have been Cidre's mother instead. Did the woman yet live? Was she here, perhaps above stairs?

"It is a great feat of building to make the hall around a tree this size," Lien said. He bowed to the goddess.

" 'Twas built to honor the first goddess and her mating ceremony," Cidre said.

"Mating ceremony?" Lien inspected the dancing women, then shrugged. "If you say so."

"Who are you, may I ask?" The goddess smiled at him.

Ardra felt a surge of jealousy, but it was not the tearing kind she had felt when she had seen him so close to Einalem in the stream.

"I am Lien, a pilgrim. I met up with Nilrem and he invited me along."

"May I see your stick?" She put out her hands. When Lien passed it to her, she closed her fingers about his and

they stood there a moment, the stick clasped between them. "I am mistaken. I thought the stick might be made of sacred oak."

A ripple of unease ran through Ardra to see Lien's sun-darkened hands covered by the goddess's milk-white ones.

"I sense great turbulence in you," the goddess said before releasing the stick.

Ardra said, "Is it not the nature of the pilgrim to be in turmoil? Else why would he need to make a pilgrimage?"

"Well put," Lien said.

The goddess acknowledged Ardra's words with a nod. "Come, see the tree up close."

Ardra tried not to let her revulsion show when Cidre took her arm. Cidre might not be the woman who had caused her mother's death, but she practiced the same arts that had.

The goddess led Ardra to the tree, where Samoht and Einalem were admiring the artwork. Each life-size carving represented the female dancers who entertained the male before a mating ceremony. They served to arouse the man so that he might be ready for his lifemate.

Samoht murmured something to Ralen, then stroked the thigh of one of the figures. Ralen smiled and glanced at Einalem, who kissed the air in his direction.

Ardra knew well what a mating ceremony was and had no wish to see it immortalized in wood or stone or any other material.

She removed her arm from the goddess's grasp when the woman fell into conversation with Samoht. Ardra went to the foot of a mundane staircase built from common wood by a less imaginative carpenter. Lien joined her.

"Have you noticed anyone missing?" he asked her.

"Nay." She scanned the crowd. "Who?"

"Cidre's consort. Where do you think he is?"

"Abed? He is said to be old. And what of Cidre's mother? Where is she?"

"I didn't know her mother would be here," Lien said.

147

The goddess gave a flurry of orders, and before Ardra knew it, everyone had quarters for the night, hot water for bathing, as well as bread and wine to stave off hunger until morning.

Ardra was given a large chamber, the first indication the goddess knew she was more than a serving woman in Samoht's party.

Ardra bathed away the tension and dirt of travel, then pulled a loose woolen robe over her head. She knelt on the bed to comb out her hair. Come the sunrising, should she ask for a private meeting with the goddess to discuss the Vial of Seduction?

Deleh wandered around the chamber, wringing her hands. "Tol would not have accepted such a room for me. I cannot sleep here. It is too cold. There is no window. I cannot see the sky."

"Deleh. Settle. We must get some sleep. The goddess plans for us to dine at first light. I have no wish to be stupid with fatigue—"

She was interrupted by a light rap on the door. Deleh opened it a crack, then stepped aside to admit the caller.

"What are you doing here?" Ardra asked Lien.

"Where are you sleeping?" Deleh interrupted. "Have you a window or view of the sky?"

Lien smiled and swept a hand out to the door. "I have a small room down the hall, but it does have a window, or a big slit of some kind. Maybe for archers."

"An arrow loop," Ardra supplied.

"Would you like to trade?" Lien asked Deleh. He leaned on his stick and grinned.

"You cannot sleep here," Deleh said, her hand to her throat, eyes wide.

"No. But I can sleep on the floor outside Ardra's door, like a guard."

Ardra sighed. "Go, Deleh. Go, but bring Lien's belongings here. I will find him other quarters."

Deleh did as bade, scuttling off with her things, then dropping Lien's pack into his arms before dancing away again, muttering about seeing the heavens.

"She should have remained back at the border," Ardra said.

"Look, I meant it when I said I'd sleep outside your door. Nilrem seems to think I should protect you. I'm just not sure how I'm going to be very effective against someone with a sword, but I'm willing to give it a try."

"I thank you, Lien."

"Before I sack out, can I talk to you? It really can't wait." He leaned in the doorway, half in, half out of the chamber.

"Aye, come in."

"Do you want me to leave the door open?" Lien asked. "In case anyone passes by?"

Ardra pressed a finger to her lips. They listened a moment. No voices were heard, no laughing, no men hauling their belongings to chambers. The thick wood doors muffled any sounds.

"I believe the household has settled," she said.

"What about sentries? Guards?" He had his head turned to the open door as he spoke.

The light from the hall torch outlined his jaw, shadowed again with his beard. How the look of him drew her. Even so, she might have been able to resist his physical allure, but his kindness, represented by the pack in his arms, ensnared her.

"Guards will make their rounds," she said. "If you feel more comfortable with the door open, then leave it so."

"I'm thinking about you. What would make *you* comfortable?"

"Close the door."

When he had done so, he set his pack down. She kept her feet curled beneath her, else she might be tempted to . . . do what? "You needed to speak to me?"

"Yeah, but what I have to say sounds like madness."

"And visiting the Goddess of Darkness does not? Say what you need to say."

Lien propped his stick against the wall. "I saw Cidre in the woods when I was bathing."

"Cidre?"

"I saw the goddess in the forest."

"Not possible."

"Agreed, on the face of it. But I know what I saw. I was dressing, and a woman stepped out of the foliage. She just looked at me for a moment, then left, not on the path, but through the trees again—almost parted the roots as if they were nothing but cobwebs."

Ardra examined his face. "You are not playing a game with me, are you?"

He paced the chamber. "I'm not playing a game."

"Then it was magic. But I do not believe in magic."

"Neither do I. So, let's say it wasn't magic and Cidre was really there. When I asked Ralen if he saw any sign of other travelers, he said nothing recent."

"You think Cidre is in league with Ralen?"

"I don't know. The man's an experienced warrior. Wouldn't he be able to tell old tracks from new ones?"

"He would."

"And right before I went into the water, there was this huge blue bird, and did you notice? There's one in the tree here."

"The blue-hawk. They are not so rare. Sit, Lien. Your pacing is distracting. You may not need that stick, but surely you can use some rest?"

"I'm too hyped up to rest." He lifted the pitcher of wine and frowned. "Did you drink any of this yet?"

"Deleh availed herself of it, but I have not had time. A pilgrim interrupted me."

He smiled, and something turned in her belly. But as she watched, the smile became a frown. "Back in a moment," he said.

He was as good as his word. But his frown had become
a scowl.

"Deleh is fast asleep. A bomb wouldn't wake her."

"A bomb? What is a bomb?"

"A bomb is a weapon in Ocean City. It makes a lot of
noise."

Ardra jumped up and headed for the door. "Is she ill, do
you think?"

"Wait. I don't think she's sick; I think there was something in the wine. It's way too quiet here."

"You think the goddess put everyone to sleep?"

He nodded. "Don't drink it." He took her hand. "And
one more thing: When I saw Cidre, she was coming from
the direction of camp. I thought it was Einalem at first."

Ardra stood there, separated from him by the length of
their arms. "Einalem is very beautiful."

"She's a raptor."

"You found her beautiful."

"How do you know?"

"I am not blind."

"Ardra, men react to naked women. It's a fact of life,
but not very meaningful. Einalem may be beautiful, but
she's also cold and calculating. She scares the living daylights out of me."

A laugh bubbled in Ardra's throat. She put her fingertips
over her lips to hold it in. "I do not believe you."

"Okay. I lied. Her brother scares me."

"Samoht scares me too," she whispered and placed a
hand on Lien's chest. "The thought that the goddess put
everyone to sleep scares me."

"I'll be right outside in the hall."

"Stay here." The words were out of her mouth before
she could stop herself.

He looked down at her hand, then up at her face. "There
was nothing going on between Einalem and me."

The fortress was silent around them. She felt hidden
from the world. From its censure. From its rules.

Ann Lawrence

"What's going on between you and me?" He kissed her forehead.

"Nothing, Lien. You are a pilgrim." His lips were so warm, so soothing.

"Yeah. I'm supposed to be celibate. In Ocean City it doesn't work like that."

"Here it does."

"Here in general, or just here in your room?"

A tremor swept through her. She must choose. Now was the time. Treat him as a pilgrim, or treat him as a simple man.

"I am very confused," she finally managed.

"I'm not. I want you in my bed, but you only want a kiss."

"I know what follows the kiss, Lien. It is a man's business."

Lien held her by the shoulders. "Do you think Einalem would spend so much time in Ralen's drawers if she didn't get something out of it?"

"You are speaking your Ocean City language again, but you are wrong. Very wrong. You believe Einalem enjoys Ralen's lovemaking, and I believe she merely wishes him for a lifemate. He may rival Samoht one day in power, and Einalem knows that. She revels in power. That is all she seeks from Ralen."

His hands kneaded her shoulders, and she wanted nothing more than to move closer.

"Ardra," he said and bent his head. "I wish you'd let me show you how wrong you are."

His mouth moved over her lips to her cheek, her temple, her ear. His breath was warm on her throat. His fingers entwined with hers.

"You wanted to leave us," she said when he touched his palm to her breast.

He dropped his hand and shook his head. "Look, Ardra, you made it clear you didn't need me." He picked up his cloak. "Maybe I'd better sleep outside."

He would leave if she did not stop him.

"What is it Einalem gets from Ralen?"

The cloak slid from his fingers. "Why don't I show you?"

He reached her in two steps and wrapped her in his arms. They stumbled backward to the bed couch, and she felt as if all the air had been snatched from the room.

"Wait." He pulled away.

She almost cried aloud at the loss of his warmth. He jammed a chair beneath the latch and placed his stick on the floor beside the couch. Still her protector.

"You are beautiful," he murmured and pulled his tunic over his head, then dropped it on the floor.

On his chest rested the gold chain. And the red roses. Samoht's emblem.

"What's wrong?" he asked.

"You wear the red roses."

"Back to that?" He wrapped his hand around the chain.

"Inside, I know you are not Samoht's man. It is just hard to ignore something I have been raised to fear."

Lien turned around and pulled the chain over his head. "That's the first time you've admitted I'm not Samoht's man." He knelt by his pack and stuffed the chain inside. "It's all I have from my family. I'll leave the roses off, but I won't part with them. Think of them as I think of your arm rings."

She rubbed her upper arm as she went to his side. It was easy to forget the mark of her status. When she looked into Lien's pack, she saw only his spare tunic. He truly had nothing.

She pulled out the chain. The roses glinted in the meager light of her single candle. "Wear them."

He took the chain from her and slipped it over his head. When he embraced her, she spread her hands across his chest and touched the roses. They were naught but cold glass—a marvel, but not sinister. She had nothing to fear from them.

Or him.

He had done naught but defend her. Three times.

His nipples pebbled when she rubbed them with the flat of her thumbs.

"Are you sure you want to do this?" he asked.

She looked up at him. "I am not sure what it is we will do."

"Kiss. Touch. Nothing you're uncomfortable with."

They returned to the narrow couch and lay down. Nose to nose. Chest to chest. He ran his fingers through her hair, combed it back, and studied her face.

"You have black and gold in your eyes, Lien," she said.

"And you have gold and gold and gold in yours," he said, then kissed her.

He tasted forbidden. She could not prevent a small moan when his tongue entered her mouth. She arched against him. His body was ready for lovemaking.

"Is this meaningful, Lien?" she asked, pressing against the hard ridge that lay along his belly.

"Very. God, Ardra, yes. It's meaningful."

"I am . . . frightened . . . nay, not frightened. I do not know what I am. I want to touch you, and I want to run away."

He was hungry. She recognized that. She knew the feel of an aroused man.

"I'll look after you," he said and ran his hand over her breasts. Again and again.

Each pass of his hand raised a need she could not express to him. "I want . . . I do not know . . ."

"Shhh," he whispered. "You'll understand. Later."

He slid down and pressed his lips to her breast. His mouth, hot, eager on her, made her insides ache.

A quick, sharp jolt from her breast to her groin startled her. A liquid heat followed it.

It took one heartbeat to decide she wanted to do as he had. She must taste him.

The moment she ran her tongue across his nipple, he arched and shifted his hips on her. Ready? Nay, she had

deceived herself before. Now—*now* he was ready.

He put his hands on her head, and every breath he took was harsh and loud in the silence of the room.

"Ardra?" he whispered. His hands cupped her face; his thumbs skimmed her lips. "This is the time when you can say stop . . . if you wish to."

"I do not wish to stop, Lien."

He ran his hands down her body, over every curve to her ankles. Then he ran his hands up her legs, her gown going with it.

He bared her to the waist and leaned down to kiss her hip and then her thigh, the inside of her knee.

"More?" he asked, moving up her body to claim her lips again.

She could only nod, lost in the depth of his eyes, now black in the faltering light. He placed her hand on his waist.

Together they fumbled his laces open. She spread his breeches and skimmed her fingers along the smooth pale skin of his belly. She tasted him from his throat to his waist.

He drew her gown up as she tugged his breeches down. She got caught up in her gown, and tore at it. Then she was free and he was too.

They lay again, face to face. His chest heaved with each breath he took.

He skimmed his thumb over her nipple again and again. It maddened her, and she slapped her palm over his hand to still the motion. A small smile curved his lips but disappeared when she bit on his lower lip.

Another jolt of something both painful and pleasurable twisted her insides. She gasped, and did it again, took his lower lip between her teeth and bit down.

He groaned. His fingers clenched on her shoulders.

She sat up, nearly tossing him onto the floor. She threw her legs over the side of the bed couch and wrapped her arms around her middle.

"Forgive me," she said. "I did not mean to hurt you."

He sat behind her, putting his legs on each side of hers. His arms hugged her like a warm cloak. Her feet looked so small flanked by his large ones on the cold wood floor.

His whole body embraced her, the hard length of his manhood nestled against her back. He held her so snugly she could not fail to feel every inch of him.

"Do I act like I'm in pain?" He kissed her neck. "I'm sorry for scaring you. It wasn't pain I was feeling, it was great pleasure."

She leaned her head back and arched into his warm palms when he cupped her breasts. "Have you a brazier in your chest?"

"Why? Am I hot?"

"Very." The word was hard to say, for he had slid his hands down her. His fingertips stroked closer and closer, urging her to something she did not understand. She spread her hands over his hard thighs and hung on. "What of you?"

"Just forget about me," he said. "Close your eyes." His lips roamed her shoulder. "Forget about me."

Impossible.

She leaned back on him, let her heart jump and thud. Let his touch bewitch her.

Unbidden, she spread her thighs wider for him. She closed her eyes and gripped his left hand. His right hand roamed. He stroked, caressed. Invaded.

Strange sounds came from her throat, sounds she could not stay, sounds of madness.

She pushed against his fingers. Sought something elusive.

And found it. Suddenly. A tide of sensation flooded her. It swamped her body from his fingertips to her breasts, feet, hands.

She gulped air again and again to keep from screaming.

Then it ended. In waves of tiny spasms.

"Ardra?" He wrapped his arms tightly about her. "Are you all right?"

How to answer? Should she lie? Should she tell the truth? The truth would enslave her.

"I understand now." She stood up. Her legs trembled; her body ached. Her gown seemed so far away, discarded by him.

He reached for her, but she evaded his grasp, sweeping up her gown and pulling it over her head. She went to the table and snatched up some bread. Her hands shook so hard she could barely get it to her mouth. It was dry, but she forced herself to eat it.

The room tipped.

"Ardra?"

She turned around. He was standing. A black line of hair on his belly drew her eyes straight to his hard manhood.

Then she saw the snake about his arm. It had writhed as if alive when he had caressed her. *Or had it?*

Where had that thought come from?

She took a step and offered the bread. "Are you hungry?"

"Not for bread." He held out his hand to her. The snake on his arm shifted.

She stumbled to the table and lifted the goblet.

"No. Don't drink the wine."

He took the goblet away. When he touched her, her fear fled and it seemed all nonsense, all some strange trick of the light. She skimmed her fingers over the snake. A pulse ran through her fingers—an echo of the pleasure he had given her.

"Come to my bed, Lien." She tugged on his arm, then stumbled on the hem of her gown.

"Steady," he said, guiding her back to the bed.

She lay down on her side, and when he settled beside her, she burrowed against his heat. "What comes next?" She yawned.

"Nothing, Ardra. Just rest." He kissed her forehead. "I guess the drugs were in the bread, not the wine. How do you feel?"

Ann Lawrence

"Who are you?" she managed.

He kissed her mouth. "Your faithful guard dog."

"Nay. You wear the snake. And the roses—" She wanted to say more, but he slipped from her embrace and picked up his tunic.

His manhood still jutted from the dark hair at his groin.

She wanted to call him back, invite him inside her, know all the secrets hidden by the mating ceremony. A surge of liquid heat made her shiver. The words would not come. Her lips felt thick, her tongue slow.

Her eyelids grew heavy, and he faded. She tried one last time to call to him, but he made no answer.

Lien tiptoed from the chamber and set out to explore the fortress. All of Ralen's men were fast asleep. It was Sleeping Beauty's castle. Nothing stirred.

Why had they all been put to sleep? What was Cidre hiding that an unexpected visit might interrupt?

He investigated a whispering sound. The source was a young woman who walked toward Cidre. They stood in the entrance to a stairwell leading down into the bowels of the fortress.

"Ywri! There you are," Cidre said to the girl. "I have looked everywhere for you." Her voice rose. "How many times must I tell you, strangers are dangerous?" She gripped the girl's wrist and dragged her to the hall. "Look. Dangerous men, fortunately asleep. You know what may happen with men."

Lien held his breath and willed himself part of the stone wall as the two women neared his hiding place by the stairs.

The hearth lighted the young woman's face, and Lien understood the goddess's concern. From where he stood, he could see that the girl was a beauty. He could also see the vacant look on her face, the puzzlement in the angle of her head.

"I will try," she said to Cidre. "Is not my gown pretty?"

158

Cidre sighed. "Aye, but you are not to show yourself until these men leave. Do you understand, Ywri? Do you?"

The young woman nodded, but she was peering around at the sleeping warriors and Lien suspected she did not.

"Thank the gods I found you before one of them did."

Lien waited until Cidre had led the girl away to the lower levels of the fortress. He considered exploring further but didn't want to risk tripping over one of Cidre's guards.

Although he thought it extreme, he understood why Cidre had put them to sleep. Perhaps some warrior had threatened the girl in the past. It showed a concern he had difficulty reconciling with the evil reputation she had.

Chapter Twelve

The sunrising announced itself outside, though Ardra saw none of it. She knew only that it was a new day when Deleh burst into the room. A slave girl brought buckets of hot water and clean linens. Deleh and she shared the water; then Deleh washed Ardra's hair.

"You must appear at your best, Ardra, else Cidre will treat you badly."

"Or Einalem will," Ardra muttered. Deleh combed her hair loose about her shoulders.

Next, Ardra stepped into a gown of soft ivory linen. Over that she wore a long-sleeved amber tunic, tied with turquoise thread. She slipped a silver chain over her head. From it dangled a disk of silver with a chunk of amber at its center. Etched around the amber was the path of the labyrinth beneath her fortress. No one seeing the lines would guess 'twas anything more than a knotwork design from the ancient days. No one would know it was the key to the maze's many twists and turns.

The pendant was a symbol of her power in Selaw just as the Black Eye was Cidre's in the Tangled Wood.

Thoughts of another chain, another symbol, entered her head. Roses, red roses, sliding across Lien's dark chest as he moved toward her . . .

"Hurry, hurry. Everyone is waiting," Deleh nagged.

Lien will be waiting.

She shooed Deleh away and sat on the edge of the bed. She stroked the covers and furs. Had she really sat just here and let Lien bring her pleasure?

She now understood what Einalem received from Ralen. Physical pleasure did exist. Not in a mating ritual, but in private, between one man and one woman when no one watched.

And why had Lien not stayed the night with her? Where was he? Had he slept outside the door? Or here in her arms, leaving with the first light?

She remembered his words about the bread. It was gone, taken by the slave girl with the water.

Did Lien despise her for leaving him unsatisfied? Think her useless? Or was he grateful that his pilgrim vows had remained intact? Or somewhat intact.

A sudden sensation coursed through her. A small reminder of the greater sensation, the twisting, ripping pleasure of a climax.

She jumped to her feet, her palms sweaty. She wiped them down her thighs.

Shoulders back and chin up, she left her chamber.

The morning meal had been set out in the great hall. It was filled with light from the dazzling white walls and tall windows that were inset near the ceiling. A long table on a dais, draped in white, now stood before the hearth.

Samoht, Einalem, and Ralen descended the stairs together. Where was Lien?

Deleh tugged on Ardra's sleeve. "Whose bed did Einalem share last night? 'Tis said she loves her brother more than is natural."

Ardra's breath hissed in. "I have told you not to speak such tales. It is kitchen talk."

161

Lien and Nilrem walked down the steps behind the goddess, who was dressed in a gown the same color as the one she'd worn the night before. The sleeves of this gown were tighter, however, the neckline higher, the Black Eye no longer about her neck.

Although Lien used his stick, he moved as fluidly as a cat. She now knew he faked the need for it, but did not blame him.

Were they not all hiding something?

Was she herself not hiding her fear and loathing of the goddess?

"How shall we address you?" Samoht asked.

"Why, simply as Cidre. We need not be formal, need we, Ralen? We became good friends on your last visit, did we not?"

Cidre sat at the head of the table and waved everyone close. "Come, sit on my left, Samoht, and Ralen, on my right."

Einalem sat beside her brother, and Ardra walked around the table to Ralen's side. She did not wish to align herself with Samoht or miss some silent exchange between him and the goddess.

Lien sat with Nilrem—far away. The sight of his sun-darkened hand on the snowy cloth made her insides heat. He had magic hands. But she did not believe in magic.

"Where is your consort?" Ralen asked of their hostess.

"Venrali? He is indisposed, but I am sure you will meet him soon."

"Can I be of some service to him? I am a healer," Einalem said.

Cidre waved a negligent hand. "Oh, he suffers only the pangs of age. He needs no healers."

Servants handed around platters of warm bread, bowls of sliced apples, and pitchers of sweet wine.

Cidre sipped her wine from a goblet decorated with etchings of vines and flowers. Her guests' cups were plain wood. The goddess saw to their every need, even noticing when

Lien refused the wine and ordering spring water fetched for him.

Was the food tainted with some potion? Ardra wondered. Was it safe to eat? Only Lien and she picked at their food, while the rest ate heartily.

"Are you Ardra of the Fortress of Ravens?" Cidre asked while the slaves served the next course of fish and river snails.

Ardra inclined her head. "I am."

"I am honored to meet you. I have heard much of you and your work with the Selaw miners. Your efforts have eased the hardships of many who cut the ice."

"So has the fine price the Tolemac treaties have placed on the ice," Samoht said.

Ardra acknowledged his words with a nod. "I do not wish to take credit where it is not earned."

A child of no more than six conjunctions edged down the steps. Her hair was wrapped in a yellow cloth to match her gown. She curled on a cushion in the corner.

"What a sweet child. Is she your daughter?" Einalem asked.

"I have no children," Cidre said. "Nay, a slave's child. She fancies a place here."

"Children serve here?" Ardra frowned.

"If it suits me. Here is her father now."

A man not quite as tall as Lien or Ralen, nor as handsome as Samoht, carried in a huge meat tray. He set it before Samoht and offered him a carving knife.

Ralen smiled. "Cidre's kitchens are magnificent."

"Pork?" Einalem said, looking at the meat.

"It is the wild sow, slaughtered when she is in heat. One cannot surpass it for taste," Cidre said.

"You do us great honor, then," Ralen said.

Cidre turned to Ardra. "The sow is my totem spirit."

The food stuck in Ardra's throat. How was she to go about finding the Vial of Seduction in such a huge place? It could be hidden in some knothole in the tree hearth or

163

behind a stone in Cidre's bedchamber. Failure seemed inevitable.

The meal ended and everyone rose. Ardra took her courage in hand. "Might I speak with you in private, Cidre?"

"Of course you may. You need a potion, do you not?"

When everyone fell silent, Cidre laughed. It was an amused, seductive laugh. "Not *that* potion. Rather, one for a womanly ill we all must tolerate from time to time. Come, follow me."

Heat filled Ardra at the personal remark, but she fought a retort. She must get close to the goddess.

As they passed the men and Einalem, Cidre stopped before Lien. "I must say, I have never met a man with hair so dark."

She touched her hand to his cheek, then his lips, then the center of his chest.

Lien merely sat there, one dark brow arched in question.

Ardra felt the molten flames of envy.

"You are strong," the goddess said. "Not just of body, but of soul. You defend. It is your nature, is it not?"

"I'm just a humble pilgrim," Lien said and bowed.

"Come, do not be too humble, else you will disappoint me."

Cidre turned away, and Ardra followed her to a small chamber in the lower levels of the fortress. The herbarium was a simple, whitewashed room, fragrant with hanging bunches of herbs and simmering pots of oil, lighted by ranks of candelabra fitted with thick candles.

On one wall was a painted wheel. It was intersected by lines marking the holy days and festivals.

There was a painted wheel much like it in Ardra's fortress, in the kitchens.

"Fear not, Ardra. Sit—" Cidre indicated a chair. "I am a simple healer, nothing more. Now, might I have your hand?"

Ardra placed her hand in the goddess's and wiped her mind as clean as possible. She sensed that the goddess used her touch to delve into a person's thoughts.

"You are mourning, are you not?"

"That is easy to divine. I wear no ornaments in my hair or rings on my hands."

"I too wear no ornaments in my hair or on my hands, but I am not in mourning."

"Then someone has told you my lifemate recently died."

Cidre smiled and leaned back in her chair, releasing Ardra's hand. "You are correct. I heard it from one of my slaves as I saw to our meal. Let us not mince words. Samoht may say he is consulting me about the potion, but he believes I have it. You are his instrument, am I right?"

"He has charged me to find the vial."

"You will not find it here. You are foolish even to try."

"I have but my eight days of mourning to find the potion; then I must submit to Samoht's wishes in regard to my fortress. Would you want someone to claim this fortress? Would you not make the effort regardless of how futile?"

Cidre took several dishes from a shelf. She spooned some of the contents of each into a bowl, ground them with a pestle, then tipped them into the center of a square of linen. She folded the linen into a triangle and fit it into the neck of a stone bottle. Next, she shook the cloth and withdrew it.

Last, she put a wooden stopper on the bottle. She held it out. "Lie to Samoht. Hand him this and say 'tis the potion. Tell him I wish to keep the vial itself as it is far too lovely to part with."

"Why are you doing this?"

A candle on Cidre's table smoked, filling the chamber with a spicy scent.

"I am not a thief. It insults me to be visited in this manner and suspected. Samoht may have me taken to the capital and put to the question. It is how my mother died, you know."

Ardra took a deep breath. "Nay, I did not." The questioning was much like a Selaw testing. She had witnessed one and had no wish to see another.

165

"The last high councilor had my mother questioned over a boy's disappearance. He was only a slave, but the councilor had some mad notion that my mother might have ensorcelled the child and done some wickedness—sacrificed him even. By the gods, men are so stupid. A goddess practices herbal healing, nothing more."

"And your mother died during her questioning?"

"Nay. She was questioned and found to know nothing. But the child's mother got wind that she was to be released and lay in wait for her. She stabbed my mother eight times, one thrust for each year of her child's life. If the high councilor had not believed the tales of old women and slaves, she would be alive today."

"He did not stab her."

"He put her in harm's way. One cannot change the turning wheel of fate." Cidre indicated the circle painted on her wall.

Ardra stared at the wheel. Cidre's mother had changed the wheel of fate for a small child years ago—her fate.

"You are remembering how we are connected, are you not, Ardra of the Fortress?"

"I know of no connection between us." Her heart began to beat hard.

"Was your mother not cursed by your father's concubine? Did the woman not curse your mother by calling on the Goddess of Darkness to avenge her for your mother's unholy treatment of her? Did your mother not fall ill and die soon after?"

"My mother, wrongly, had my father's concubine tested. The woman's wounds festered, and aye, she did curse my mother on her deathbed. And aye, my mother sickened and died soon after."

Cidre stood up and pressed the bottle into Ardra's hand. "But you believe your mother died because the concubine called on the goddess. It is what many believe. Let me tell you the truth.

"Your mother died because her own evil permeated her body, causing her to sicken. It had naught to do with *my* mother. The Goddess of Darkness is a legend. A tale to frighten children and silly women such as yourself. My mother was also named Cidre. She was Cidre, Goddess of the *Tangled Wood*, nothing more."

Ardra set the bottle of powder on Cidre's table. "Samoht will not believe this is the potion. He will not believe you gave it up so easily."

"Then you are doomed to failure."

Ardra turned to go.

"Oh, and Ardra. Is it not also said in the legends that the goddess birthed a beautiful daughter and an ugly son? I have no brother, just as I have no children."

"Lien? Where are you?" Ardra hurried toward him, weaving through the hall, peeking in corners, opening doors. She was all dressed up. He liked the way she looked, but much preferred her as she had been in his arms. Softer, unsure of herself, ready to explore.

The woman approaching him had a determined frown on her face. Much like the one Eve wore when she wanted to manage his life.

"Right here, Ardra." He shifted his shoulders against the swollen nipple of a dancing mantel figure.

"What are you doing?" she asked. "I have looked everywhere for you."

"I'm just admiring the artwork." He resisted the urge to tell her the dancing babes made great scratching posts. It also sounded insane to say that he thought Cidre had somehow caused his itchy rash.

"May we walk?" She gestured to the door, and he checked out her nails. Too short to be useful. He cast a longing look back over his shoulder at the dancing women. His glance also made a quick check for Samoht and his men. They were still at the table, talking and laughing.

"Why are men so fascinated by large breasts?"

"I have no idea. Ask Nilrem, he's the wiseman."

A guard opened the double doors for them, and Lien noticed more of Samoht's men and Ralen's wandering about the courtyard eyeing the goddess's guards. They all wore expressions that said they'd draw swords in an instant and start a miniwar if anyone farted wrong.

Lien's stick seemed inadequately light and brittle.

No one challenged them when they passed over the drawbridge and wandered down to the lake. It had a pebble shore, so he skipped stones while Ardra paced.

He decided she was either regretting the sex or just overly shy.

Finally, she came to stand near him. "The goddess gave me a potion to turn over to Samoht."

So much for male intuition. "I gather it's not the right one."

"You gather rightly. She mixed it up from stores on her shelves. What am I to do?"

"Search?" He groaned and raked his fingernails on his wrist.

"What are you doing?"

"Shh. Lower your voice. I think the goddess must be around. Close, in fact."

"How do you know?" she asked in softer tones.

"Well, I'm beginning to think this rash wasn't caused by my tunic. The itching ebbs and flows. It's at its worst when Cidre's around. And it's pretty bad right now."

"A woman cannot give a man a rash."

"Why not? She can give him a headache." Ardra didn't laugh. "Never mind. Look, I didn't get the rash until I entered the Wood, and when she touched me, the red dots—" he pulled up his sleeve and showed her the rash— "prickled hot."

Ardra leaned very close. He felt her breath on his skin. Was it his imagination that the terrible itch subsided in just that spot? Wishful thinking, probably.

"You must be sensitive to all this lush foliage. Did bathing help you?"

"A little bit. And Einalem gave me an oil to rub on it this morning."

"I'm sure she did."

He decided to push her buttons a bit more. "She wanted to rub it on for me, but I said you'd be pissed."

"Pissed?" She frowned. "Piss is urine."

"In Ocean City it also means angry."

She tossed her head. The hair thing really did it for him.

"I am not angry," she said. "I am merely disappointed that she would try to tempt a pilgrim."

Lien hid a smile. "How soon you forget your own tempting kisses."

"Oh." She touched her breast and licked her lips.

The gesture caused an immediate reaction in him. He wanted to carry her to a soft patch of grass and finish what they'd started. "Look, Ardra, this is where we have the morning-after talk. We get all our regrets out in the open."

"Do you have regrets, Lien?"

"I'm sorry you fell asleep."

Her eyes were dark amber, wide, unsure. "Forgive me for eating the bread. I know you must think me a fool."

"You didn't know the bread was drugged."

"I stopped you before I ate the bread."

He nodded. "Yeah, you did. Why?"

"I have never felt that way before. It was a small madness."

"It wasn't regret?"

She shook her head. Her hair slid across her breasts and shoulders. He remembered what it felt like against his chest.

"I have only one regret."

His heart began to thud. "And that is?"

"You found no happiness."

"Happiness? Oh, I was very happy." *And Mr. Happy is getting damned elated talking about it.* "It was probably

169

for the best; I was feeling a bit out of control. I don't need to leave any little Liens around when I go."

She suddenly moved off a few feet.

"Look, you have more important things to think about than my happiness," he said. "How can I help you?"

She opened her mouth, then closed it and extended her hand. A flat stone lay on her palm. "If this were the potion, where would you hide it?"

"In with a bunch of other pebbles."

"Aye." She threw the pebble into the lake. "I think I need to inspect Cidre's herbarium with someone who knows potions. She has so much there, I fear the vial could be in plain sight and I would not know it. Do you think Nilrem would help me?"

"You'd have to be sure Cidre wasn't around. And that sounds mighty dangerous."

He took her hand. A warmth suffused his skin, and the itching at his wrist eased. Was it wishful thinking again, or something more? He certainly couldn't remember thinking about his rash while caressing her.

"Ardra, there are just some things that are life truths. One is, don't spit into the wind. Going into Cidre's herbarium while she's loose in the fortress is asking for trouble."

Several of Ralen's men walked over the drawbridge and stood there chatting, looking in their direction.

"A cloud crossed your brow just now. What is it?" she asked.

"I'm thinking of something Ollach told me. I cannot appear intimate with you in front of these men."

Ardra's hand slid from his. It was a loss. Damned celibacy.

"Come, Lien, we must have help. Let us consult Nilrem."

It was the first time she had made it a "we" venture. He wasn't sure he wanted that much involvement.

"Look. I don't think there's anything you can do during the day. How about after everyone's in bed, in the middle of the night? Take a really long nap during the day, then let's hook up . . . er, get together and search, just the two of us."

"Why did you hesitate just now?"

He wasn't about to tell her that "hookup" referred to casual sex. He told her a partial truth. "Oh, I was just wondering how I would know when 'later' was. In Ocean City, we have timepieces to mark the hours."

"We have the same. Come, I will show you."

They walked up to the fortress and over the drawbridge. The men loitering at the massive gate nodded to Ardra in a rude, perfunctory manner. She returned their nods in the same elegant way she always did. He was completely ignored.

Her spine straightened even more after the snub. She was positively sailing across the courtyard.

"Ardra. Slow down. Why were those men rude to you?"

"It has been so since Ralen took control. They defer to him, but I no longer have their allegiance."

He would talk to Ralen. If he didn't, he might end up shoving his stick down one of the warriors' throats, and that would not do.

"Why is there only one kind of flower here?" she asked.

"Hmm. I hadn't noticed." She was right. Large or small, the flowers were the same. So were the vines, whether the lacy ones on the inside walls or the thick ones on the outside.

Everything here was so different from . . . home. Even something as simple as a shadow held different shades of color. The lavender sky over the lake was now streaked with green and gray. It looked angry and powerful at the same time.

In the courtyard, Ardra led him to a simple sundial surrounded by tiles.

171

"Uh. Yeah. I know how this works. But won't we be in the dark?"

She laughed and had a coughing fit.

He pounded her back. "You don't laugh very often, do you?"

Ardra ducked her head. "I have no time for laughter."

The urge to embrace her was almost overwhelming. He shook it off. "Speaking of time . . ." He tapped the sundial with his stick.

"When it is dark we consult the stars. Or we know the time by the sound and rhythm of the fortress. You lie awake and listen. Guards make their appointed rounds. Cocks crow. You listen to the night sounds."

Like the sounds of lovemaking. Like Ardra's sharp little gasps and stifled moans. He needed some distance. "Why don't we make use of the daylight hours to consult Nilrem? I don't even know what this vial is supposed to look like. Once we talk to him, we should rest. We can't stay awake all day and then expect to be up all night."

They walked into the hall. Nilrem was stretched out on his back on a bench, fast asleep. When Lien shook him by the shoulder, the wiseman awoke quickly.

"Eh. Pilgrim. Ardra. What may I do for you?"

A burst of laughter drew their attention to where Samoht, Einalem, and Ralen still sat at the long table with Cidre, who had returned from her herbarium.

"How can they sit there doing nothing?" Ardra asked.

Nilrem answered her. "They have no cares. It is only you who has a care."

"That's not quite true," Lien said. "I assume this Vial of Seduction means something to Tolemac or it wouldn't have been locked away in a vault. Let's get outside."

He led them into the courtyard and crouched down by the sundial. The day was marked off in the same twelve-hour increments as at home. "Ardra has only so much time

to find the vial. If she fails, Samoht wins her fortress. But that doesn't solve his problem. The Vial of Seduction will still be missing. If I read him right, he's going to drag his feet and hamper your quest until the eight days are over. Then—"

Nilrem finished for him. "Then his men will draw their swords, as will Ralen's, and they will take this fortress down, stone by stone."

"Is that what you think too, Lien?" Ardra asked.

"Pretty much. Can't you feel the tension among the men? They're only kept in line by Samoht's orders, I'll bet. Cidre doesn't have that many guards. She's pretty unprotected, if you ask me."

"I had not expected violence," Ardra said.

"Well, think about it." He stood up. "So, Nilrem, what does a Vial of Seduction look like anyway?"

"It is most unexceptional in appearance. A thick brown bottle, made of a soft stone, not glass as some vials are. The potion, which some consider a spice, looks a bit like dirt."

Lien took Nilrem's arm. "Come on, Ardra, let's walk. I want to check out the territory. And isn't that a little door over there? Let's see where it leads."

"Excellent proposal, pilgrim. We also do not want to draw too much attention to ourselves. We look like we are having a meeting."

Ardra walked a bit ahead of them. They left the fortress through the small door. It opened into an orchard redolent with the scent of apples. Lien picked one up from the ground. It was smaller than those he was used to, and when he bit into it, less juicy. But it was still an apple. He never thought he'd admit it, being a pizza and burger kind of guy, but he missed the green stuff.

Nilrem also picked up an apple and munched away, talking of the weather. Lien dodged apple spit as he talked.

Ann Lawrence

Ardra finally halted by a carved wooden seat. Nilrem sank down on it and scratched his belly. She was seething with something, Lien could tell. It soon popped out.

"Nilrem. How dare you create these . . . these treasures. If you had not concocted this potion, none of this would be happening. My son would be safe." Tears glittered in her eyes.

Lien wanted to take her in his arms, but he could see a woman picking apples a few rows of trees away.

"I did not concoct the treasures, Ardra. I *found* them. Each one comes from one of the eight chiefdoms. They are ancient treasures, created in ancient days."

"Ancient! That is just a way of making something seem sacred to fools. Well, I am not a fool. It is evil to seduce someone against his or her will. Evil."

Nilrem patted the wooden bench beside him. "Sit, Ardra. I will tell you a story."

"Nay. I have no time for stories." She looked off to the horizon, and Lien knew she was thinking of home and her child.

"This one you will."

Ardra perched on the edge of the bench.

"When I was a youth, I traveled about the chiefdoms, always wandering. Each chiefdom had its fantastic tales of treasures and mysteries. But each treasure also caused great grief—"

"And continues to do so."

"Aye." He patted her hand. "So I collected them and buried them. But eventually they were returned to the council, and I thought it right and proper at the time. I still do. Who was I to bury them? Who was I to take them in the first place? I felt comfortable that they were in the Tolemac vaults, heavily guarded."

Lien watched the slow progress of the young woman who wandered through the orchard. "See that girl there?" They

174

turned. The girl seemed to inspect each individual apple before plucking it from a tree. Was she really so fussy or was she watching them? "I think Cidre put us to sleep to protect her. She was being reprimanded that night for wandering off. Cidre seemed to be very concerned our men not see her."

As if to confirm what he'd said, a boy ran through the trees, took the young girl by the arm and tugged her away to the fortress door.

"She is lovely," Nilrem said.

Ardra tapped her foot impatiently on the ground. "Lien. Nilrem. You must concentrate on the vial. Cidre may find a way to use it. She may trick some honorable person. At least we know Samoht will not be able to use the potion if we find it."

"Yeah, explain to me how that works." Lien sat on the ground and stretched out his legs. He craved a long run on a hot beach.

"One of the reasons the treasures cause so much trouble is they can only be used by an honorable person. In the case of the Vial of Seduction, I suspect honor also implies a state of innocence."

"You're saying that even if Samoht gets the potion, he knows he can't use it. He'll just have to lock it up again."

"Aye, but I believe the council will look most favorably upon their leader if he returns the treasure himself."

Lien said, "And who will know if he used just a bit of the powder before returning it to Tolemac."

Nilrem nodded. "But unless he can find a way around the honor bit, he is stuck."

Ardra began to laugh. She rocked back and forth.

"What's so funny?" Lien asked.

Nilrem lifted a shaggy gray brow.

"Do you not see?" Ardra asked. "I have been wondering who stole the treasure from the vaults. It had to be someone who had access. A councilor only. One of the very men who challenged me to find it.

175

"And I assumed the man sold it to the goddess to make a comfortable life for himself. Now I learn the potion must be administered by an honorable person, perhaps an innocent one as well." She wiped her eyes with the backs of her hands. "Here we sit in the orchard of the goddess, the most dishonorable woman alive. Why would she want the potion? She, of all people, could never use it."

Lien frowned. "Unless she has discovered a way around the honor bit."

Nilrem sighed. "I pray you are wrong, pilgrim. This was the one treasure I worried about most if it fell into the hands of the wrong person."

"Great." Lien shook his head. "Okay. Here's another wrinkle. Let's say some councilor saw a way to get some power if he could seduce a woman or even a man. He stole the vial, but couldn't figure out how to use it, 'cause just by stealing it he proved he's dishonorable. Right so far?"

Ardra and Nilrem nodded.

"So the councilor trades or sells the potion to the goddess for a quick buck—"

"A councilor would not sell a treasure for a buck. Not even the white hart," Ardra said.

"Okay, Ardra. The councilor sells it to the goddess for some gold. She wants it because she's learned a way around the honor thing. Maybe she could get a child to give it to someone—"

"A child? Not a seduction potion. What man would take a love potion from a child? Nilrem." Ardra turned to the old man. "We must inspect Cidre's herbarium. Will you take me through it?"

"Me?" The old man drew back. "I have no wish to tempt evil. You will have to find another way to search her space."

"You disappoint me," Ardra said.

"What I want to know is why the goddess wants the potion?" Lien asked, hoping to ease the tension between

the two. He'd persuade the old man sometime when Ardra wasn't around. "What is Cidre missing in her life?"

Nilrem rose to his feet. "That I am happy to answer. Cidre is young and beautiful; she has no daughter. Her consort is old. I will wager she has chosen another. And he is unwilling."

Chapter Thirteen

"Who's that?" Lien stood up and pointed through the apple trees toward the lake.

"Travelers? Your eyes are better than mine, young Lien," Nilrem said.

"Maybe. Men. Walking."

"Let us see," Nilrem said.

As Lien and Ardra followed in Nilrem's wake, Lien thought the wiseman pretty chipper for an old guy.

On the path that edged the lake, a small party of men could be seen. Swirls of dust wreathed their feet.

Lien shaded his eyes to see better and thought of another thing he missed—sunglasses. The group became visible as five men. They wore long robes like Nilrem's, but unlike the wiseman, they were young and healthy-looking.

"Interesting," Nilrem said. "We travel to a fortress that I imagine receives few visitors, and now we find more on our tail."

They returned to the hall, and Nilrem informed Cidre she had guests. It was an unnecessary announcement, as guards were rushing across the courtyard to greet the party.

Ralen rose and walked to Ollach. "Remain with Ardra."

Ollach stood behind her, one hand on his sword hilt, the other on a rather long dagger in his belt. Lien felt a bit useless but hung around anyway.

The visitors were deemed harmless, Lien supposed, because they were escorted to where Cidre sat. She had moved to a chair between two guards, tall men that Lien had to look at twice to be sure they weren't twins. Frick and Frack, he had dubbed them.

The visitors turned out to be pilgrims. Lien swallowed a chuckle.

"I bid you welcome," Cidre said. She did not rise or do the curtsey thing.

The pilgrims all bowed to her. They wore long, scratchy robes similar to the one Lien had first worn.

The leader was tall and reed-thin, with a pointy chin. His friends were also thin, except for one short man, the shortest Lien had seen so far in Tolemac. The other three pilgrims were so nondescript that he would not be able to pick them out in a crowd later, he thought.

"We wish to trespass on your hospitality. Our supplies are low, and it is our hope you might spare us some apples from your orchard," the leader said.

Cidre smiled. "You may pick all you can carry." She signaled to the child in yellow. "Tell the kitchen to give these pilgrims some of our fresh bread." She addressed the pilgrims again. "My fortress is known for its bread," she said.

Watch out for the surprise ingredient, Lien wanted to say.

"You are too kind." The pilgrims all bowed an excessive six or seven times. Maybe they'd heard the evil-goddess rumors on their travels.

"We have a pilgrim with us," Samoht said, and everyone looked in Lien's direction.

Damn.

The five men pivoted with the rest and peered about the hall.

"Lien, come forward," Samoht said.

Lien couldn't refuse, though he hated to leave Ardra's side. He worked his way to the fore of the crowd and bowed to the visitors.

The pilgrims looked him over as if it were he who smelled like a stable, not them.

"You are garbed as a warrior. Lien, is it?" the tall one said. His nose was as pointed as his chin.

Lien nodded. He thought he should say as little as possible.

Nilrem poked his own sharp nose into the conversation. He tapped his stick on the ground for attention. "Lien was set upon by outcasts and nearly killed. His robes were stolen."

Yeah, my wealthy non-pilgrim robes, damn it.

"Ah," the leader said, and his cronies nodded in unison. "Then you are in luck. Iak, have I not an extra robe in my satchel?"

"Why, of course!" One of the nondescript three rooted in a pack and drew out a robe that looked none too clean.

Samoht hooked it from the man's fist. "This is most kind of you. Here, Lien, put this on that you might be once again recognized by all as a pilgrim."

Go to hell, Lien thought, but he took the robe. It was heavier than the one Nilrem had given him and had a deep hood. It was still a rough garment.

"I have a most wonderful thought," Samoht said. "Why do you not join these men and continue your pilgrimage?"

Lien felt all eyes on him. He could feel Ardra's drilling into his back.

Cidre rose from her seat. "I think Lien is needed here."

"How?" Samoht whirled around to face her.

"Nilrem," Cidre said. "Did you not tell me Lien saved Ardra's life? Did you not say he was bound to her until she returned the favor?"

"Aye, that I did," Nilrem said.

The child staggered back down the hall with a bread basket almost larger than she was. All but the sharp-nosed pilgrim fell upon the basket, stuffing the bread into their satchels.

Ardra maneuvered past Ollach and pulled the robe from Lien's arms. "I think Lien should stay right where he is. In truth, he saved my life three times, not just once."

Ralen, who had said nothing, pushed through the group and stood by Cidre's chair. "Why do you argue over him like dogs with a bone? He has a voice. Let him make the choice."

Everyone fell silent. Lien scanned their faces. Here was his opportunity to leave, to slip the noose of responsibility that Ardra was pulling tight around his neck.

If he stayed, he would have to help Ardra. If he left, he would probably never see her again.

Cidre answered for him. "Why not rest here for the day, pilgrims? I have a special feast planned and would be disappointed if any of you missed it. Lien can leave with you on the sunrising if that be his choice."

"Thank you," Lien said to Cidre. "I'll decide after the feast."

Ardra endured a few hours in the hall, listening to the didactic pilgrims. She noticed that Einalem had slipped away, but Lien sat with Cidre, listening carefully to the visitors.

He would leave.

She knew it. He would leave at the sunrising, garbed in rough wool, and she would never know . . . know what? How he felt about her? Where he had gone?

It would be obvious that he felt nothing if he left her. And his reluctance to look at her, even to turn his dark eyes in her direction, told her he would go.

It was as plain as the nose on her face, as the wiseman said.

How disappointed she was in Nilrem. Of course he was not a warrior, but she had expected greater valor in the matter of searching Cidre's herbarium.

She thought of a person who could visit the herbarium without suspicion. *Einalem.*

Ardra walked past some of Ralen's men. One of them made a remark about old men needing the mating dancers to service their young women.

She turned around. "You will keep a respectful tongue in your mouth. I imagine the goddess would take offense at that remark."

The man bowed and had the grace to look ashamed— and afraid. Although Ardra knew he had made the remark for her benefit, it suited the goddess's circumstances as well.

Ardra mounted the stairs to the gallery of bedchambers. The disrespect of the warriors would only grow worse the longer Samoht withheld her power. *Four days left.*

A serving woman pointed out Einalem's chamber. The door was slightly open. Ardra pushed it, took one look inside, then jumped back and eased it closed. She darted into her own chamber and sat on her bed couch with a thump. Her heart raced. Never in all her days would she eradicate from her mind what she had just seen. Never.

Ardra licked her lips.

Deleh opened the chamber door. "Ah, there you are. Ollach said you were most likely here." Deleh dropped her cloak over a bench and knelt by Ardra. "What is wrong, child?"

"I have seen something I cannot believe."

"Tell me."

"I cannot!" Ardra shot to her feet. She fanned her face with her hands. "Is it not hot in here?"

"You do not trust me, do you?" Tears welled in Deleh's eyes. "I am naught but a useless old woman."

Ardra sighed. She picked up Deleh's cloak and carefully hung it on a peg by the door. "You are not useless." She

Join the Love Spell Romance Book Club
and **GET 2 FREE* BOOKS NOW–**
An $11.98 value!
Mail the Free* Book Certificate
Today!

Yes! I want to subscribe to the
Love Spell Romance Book Club.

Please send me my **2 FREE* BOOKS**. I have enclosed $2.00 for shipping/handling. Every other month I'll receive the four newest Love Spell Romance selections to preview for 10 days. If I decide to keep them, I will pay the Special Members Only discounted price of just $4.49 each, a total of $17.96, plus $2.00 shipping/handling ($23.55 US in Canada). This is a **SAVINGS OF $6.00** off the bookstore price. There is no minimum number of books I must buy and I may cancel the program at any time. In any case, the **2 FREE* BOOKS** are mine to keep.

*In Canada, add $5.00 shipping and handling per order
for the first shipment. For all future shipments to Canada,
the cost of membership is $23.55 US, which
includes shipping and handling.
(All payments must be made in US dollars.)

∽∽∽∽

NAME: _____

ADDRESS: _____

CITY: _____ **STATE:** _____

COUNTRY: _____ **ZIP:** _____

TELEPHONE: _____

E-MAIL: _____

SIGNATURE: _____

If under 18, Parent or Guardian must sign. Terms, prices, and conditions subject to change. Subscription subject
to acceptance. Dorchester Publishing reserves the right to reject any order or cancel any subscription.

handed Deleh a linen towel and bade her wipe her eyes. "I will tell you what I have seen, but you must never speak of this, do you understand me? Never. This is *not* kitchen gossip."

"I swear by Tol's head."

"Oh, swear not by Tol. It is not that kind of matter. Nay, swear that if you speak of this, you will have to plait my hair each time I demand it—for a full conjunction."

Deleh grimaced, but swore.

Ardra snatched up a pair of tongs and poked the coals in the brazier so that she need not look at Deleh while she spoke.

"I opened Einalem's door just now, and Ralen was with her."

"Everyone knows Einalem services Ralen."

"I believe I understand that now, but, Deleh, what I saw was not mating."

"No?"

Ardra poked the coals with great vigor. "Einalem was on her knees before him and she was—"

"—feasting on his manhood?" Deleh asked.

"Deleh!"

"Ralen told Tol she was quite talented in the art."

"Art?" Ardra dropped the tongs on the floor with a clatter.

"Ardra, sit." Deleh pulled her to the bed couch and held her hand. "Pleasing a lover is an art. There are so many ways to enjoy the pleasures of the bed. I am disappointed that you do not understand this. Tol and I thought you had surely taken at least one lover."

"You may have lived among the Selaw for more than three conjunctions, Deleh, but you know so little of our people. A Selaw woman may not take a lover. The women of other chiefdoms might, but a Selaw woman will be cast on the ice if she dishonors her mate."

"You were far too beloved to be cast on the ice. You deprived yourself for nothing."

"And you must understand that there is a world beneath the one which a man or woman from Tolemac can see. It is the miners' world. The women can be merciless if someone they respect is dishonored, and though Tol was not one of them, they respected him as if he were."

"So, you had no lovers." Deleh patted Ardra's hand. "Tol would have been sad for you. He thought you and Ollach were close. The man is so attentive to your needs."

"Ollach!" Ardra screeched and clapped her hands over her face. "Say no more!"

"I will say but one more thing. Take a lover, but be sure it is not Lien."

Ardra raised her head. "Why not Lien?"

"He is wanted by another."

"Einalem?"

"Nay. 'Tis Cidre I mean. The goddess wants him."

Sickness rose in Ardra's throat. "How can you tell? Einalem watches him, so I thought—"

"Oh, aye, Einalem watches the pilgrim, but Cidre touched him. On the lips and chest. She wants him, mark my words."

Einalem opened her shutters to let in the fresh air. When she turned around, Ralen had climbed from the bed. She watched him stretch. "I want to be your lifemate, Ralen."

"Nonsense. You would despise my life." He dug in the bedding for his breeches.

"Perhaps in the beginning, but I could grow to like it." Why was he not succumbing to her wishes? She had given him half the powder in the vial and still he was aloof—nay, as cold as ever. What was wrong?

"I must see to my horses. They need exercise."

She walked across the room, slowly, to be sure he could admire her every move, her fine shape. She lifted her arms and piled her hair on her head, then let it cascade down, something he loved to watch. "Forget your horses."

His eyes darkened. But not much. He was sated.

"Let me pleasure you again," she said, stroking her hands up and down his hips.

He slid from her grasp and pulled on his breeches. "This is the last time I will seek your bed, Einalem, if you cannot accept one fact."

"What is that?"

"I have no wish to lifemate. When I do—if I do—it will be a chief's daughter, not a councilor's sister."

"You insult me."

"I am sorry." He lifted her chin and stared into her eyes. "You are lovely. You know how to please in bed, but I suspect my future will not hold the fate you would choose for me."

She could not stop her tears. "What fate is that?"

"A councilor's seat. It is what you wish, is it not? To be a councilor's lifemate? To be so honored?"

He had a musky scent after lovemaking that she had been unable to concoct in her herbarium. She had even bribed a bathhouse attendant to collect the oils and sweat of his body for her. Still, the power he exuded when aroused eluded her.

"You are the second warrior to disappoint me, Ralen."

"I am sorry. Now, if you wish to have me in your bed, you must forget this nonsense."

"Answer one question for me." She took up his tunic and held it behind her back.

"I am finished with your questions. Give me my tunic." He held out his hand.

She danced away. "Nay. Not until you answer my question."

But he would not play. He stood still and crossed his arms over his chest. "I have other tunics."

She hated him. "How will you feel when I give my favors to another?"

"I will miss you, but I will not share you. Cidre has indicated she is most willing to take your place."

185

Ann Lawrence

"Go to her, then. Lie with the goddess. May she curse your manhood. Nay, may she curse your sword arm."

In two steps he was upon her. He snatched her up and held her off the floor. "Never say such words aloud, do you hear me? Not even in jest. Call down the darkness on others if you wish, but curse me and I will visit it tenfold on you another day."

He dropped her and stormed from her chamber, slamming the door behind him.

"Go, Ralen. I am done with you," she called after him.

She paced, then flung his tunic to the floor. She tossed the pillows from the bed and tore off the stained linens. Finally, her ire spent, she went to her coffer. She tossed up the lid and pulled out the Vial of Seduction.

She did not understand why the potion had failed her. Then a thought flitted through her mind.

"Perhaps it failed because I do not truly want him. Perhaps it failed because when last we made love, it was someone else I thought of." The stone bottle was heavy, but she knew there was very little powder inside. It could not be wasted.

"That must be it. I did not truly want him. My thoughts of Lien interfered."

Ardra escaped from Deleh. This time, she made sure Ralen was elsewhere before she knocked on Einalem's chamber door.

"Enter," Einalem called.

Ardra did so and swallowed her surprise. Einalem sat on a stool plaiting her hair; she wore nothing but a smile. Her figure was as lush as the ones carved into Cidre's hearth.

"What can I do for you?" Einalem stood up and stretched, then walked to the bed. It was bare of linens, which lay by the bed in a heap.

Ardra stared in awe at what a storm of lovemaking must have taken place to cause the furs and coverlets to be on the floor.

"What do you want, Ardra? Surely you did not come here to inspect my chamber?" Einalem picked up an azure robe, which she belted on.

"I wanted your advice. I was in Cidre's herbarium and saw a few things I did not recognize."

Light filled Einalem's eyes. "Tell me."

"It occurred to me that I do not know what the Vial of Seduction looks like, nor the potion inside. Is it liquid or powder? What color is it? I may see the potion and not even recognize it."

"So, you have come to me because I would recognize something out of place in the herbarium."

"Aye, and you are the one person who could visit the herbarium without her suspicion."

Einalem lifted the lid of the gold chest on her table. "But not necessarily without Cidre."

"I was hoping you could think of a reason to exclude her."

"Let me consider."

Einalem cast off her robe and dressed in a serviceable blue wool gown and sturdy leather shoes. It was the garb of a healer who knew she might dirty her clothes or need to walk a great distance through harsh weather.

Ardra felt a pang of guilt that she so disliked the woman. Einalem was a healer who brought children into the world and eased pain.

Then Einalem wiped away the humble-healer impression by pinning turquoise beads in her braid.

While Einalem worked on her hair, Ardra inspected the small gold chest. It held rows of bottles with different stoppers, some wood, some gold. "What are these vials?" she asked.

"My herbs. Come closer and I will teach you a little trick."

Ardra stood on the opposite side of Einalem's table. She watched Einalem select a purple bottle. It was made of some smooth stone and painted with stars. The stopper

was silver. Einalem opened the bottle and tapped a turquoise powder onto a small white square of parchment. Next, she tipped the powder into a goblet.

"This is the night powder," Einalem said. "And this the night wine, brewed of grapes collected in the moonlight and washed in the fountains found beneath the capital, the same fountains that feed the bathhouses, though not the hot springs, the cold ones." She poured some wine into the goblet.

Ardra understood why Einalem had three packhorses if she had brought her own wine along. "I did not know there were cold springs in the bathhouses."

Einalem watched her over the cup rim. "Only initiated healers know where they are."

She drained her goblet. Next, she refilled her cup with the wine. She opened another bottle after sealing the first. This bottle was also purple, but it had no stars. It bore only a likeness of the sun at its most red. The stopper was gold. Again, Einalem tapped a powder, this one dusty red, onto the parchment, then tipped it into the wine. She drank.

"Now," Einalem said, "I will mix the potion for you. The night powder, I assume?"

"I do not understand."

"Then you must have no lovers." Einalem held up the two stone bottles. "The night powder is to prevent conception if you have made love at night. The day powder is for after-sunrise lovemaking."

Ardra turned away from the table to hide her face from Einalem. "I have no need of the potions."

The crumpled bed, the two potions, told Ardra that Einalem and Ralen had made love not only during the night, but also during the day. What was it like to make love in the brilliancy of the sun?

"Come," Einalem said. "I have thought of a reason to visit Cidre's herbarium."

"How?"

"You shall see."

Ardra accompanied Einalem to the hall.

Ralen and Samoht had their heads together over a board game. It contained a large gold oval consisting of smaller turquoise ovals interlocking with each other. They cast a die and then moved coins from oval to oval. It was a notorious game of chance. Much ill-afforded money changed hands among the ice miners, who enjoyed the game as much as these men of status.

Of course, the miners' boards were not this fine, their pieces small stones. But the money they bet on the outcome could mean a child's hunger and a woman's despair.

Einalem walked directly to the men and snatched a coin from the board. Samoht looked up and glared.

"Playing games again?" Ralen asked.

A vision of Ralen in Einalem's chamber flashed into Ardra's mind. She turned away, only to be confronted by the naked maidens on the mantelpiece.

"Nay," Einalem said. "I am done with games. How are your horses, by the way?"

"My horses are well. I am looking into adding a new mount to my stable, though," he said, leaning back in his chair.

She tossed the coin in the air. Samoht caught the coin, then rose and kissed his sister once on each cheek. "Now be off. We want to finish our game."

"We are looking for Cidre," Ardra said.

"Look behind you."

Einalem frowned. "Cidre is with Lien."

Lien and Cidre walked across the hall. The goddess touched his arm and pointed to the blue-hawk near the lofty ceiling. Her hand remained on his arm.

Ralen grinned. "Why should it matter whom he is with? He is celibate and she is not. There will be little going on there."

Samoht moved one of the coins on the game board. "I do not understand how a man can abstain from women. It is not natural."

Einalem crossed her arms and tossed her head. "He probably has an active hand."

Ralen and Samoht roared with laughter, drawing Lien and Cidre their way. Ardra did not understand the jest, but assumed it had something to do with pleasure. She took a deep breath and forced a smile. It would not do to appear ignorant.

"I bid you good day, Einalem," Cidre said. "I feared we might not see you at all before my feast."

"I love to lie in bed," Einalem said, and Ardra glanced at Ralen, but he seemed intent on his game.

Then Einalem put out her hand. "Lien. I wish to see your rash."

Lien rolled back his sleeve. The rash around his wrist had deepened to a wide red cuff. "It's a bit worse," he said.

"Oh, aye, this is much worse. The salve I gave you has done little to help. How I wish I had some . . ." Einalem broke off, then looked up at the goddess. "Oh, Cidre, you must have an herbarium. May I use your stores? I know of another treatment that may help our friend here."

Cidre bowed. "Of course. I shall accompany you."

Ardra followed Cidre and Einalem, conscious of Lien, who walked at her side.

Einalem stopped by Samoht and Ralen and touched a finger to her lips. "It seems to me, Cidre, that you do not trust me."

"Trust you?" Cidre's flawless brow wrinkled into small furrows.

"Aye." Einalem spread her hands out, palm up. "I have no need of assistance to make a salve, that I am sure you know, so I must assume you accompany me lest I disturb some work of yours."

Cidre smiled and swept out her hand. "By no means. I thought to watch you and perhaps learn something new, but if you think I lack trust, by all means, go alone. Use my herbarium as you see fit. Ardra has been there; she will direct you."

When they reached the lower levels of the fortress, Ardra took the lead and showed them into the herbarium. It was neither guarded nor locked up.

"So why don't you fill me in on what's going on here?" Lien asked Einalem.

"Sit down, Lien." Einalem pointed at a chair. "Ardra asked me to examine the herbarium for the Vial of Seduction. We are here to do so, quite alone, thanks to my quick thinking."

Lien straddled a chair, resting his arms on the seat back. "Really? Examining the goddess's herbarium? Looking for the vial? Now, why didn't I think of that?"

Ardra decided to ignore his tart tone.

Einalem washed her hands in a silver bowl, whispering a few words over the water as she poured it. Then, adding several ingredients, she cooked up a smooth, oily salve. Its scent reminded Ardra of the dew on a fresh apple.

While Einalem stirred and simmered, Ardra looked through every bin, box, bowl, and bundle. She saw much that puzzled her, but no small brown bottles, or powders that looked like dirt.

" 'Tis done." Einalem poured the warm salve into a bowl and then washed her hands again. "Take off your tunic."

Lien put out his hand. "I'll rub it on, thank you."

Einalem shrugged. "Do your wrists first. I will know immediately if it needs adjustment."

He rolled his sleeves and worked the salve into his skin. "It feels a bit better."

"It should have a cooling effect. May I look at your neck?"

Lien stood up, pulled his tunic over his head, then straddled the chair again.

"This has spread badly," Einalem said, and Ardra could not resist a peek. The rash which had encircled his throat now bloomed down his back in lines of dark red.

Knotwork.

The room shifted, darkened. Ardra put her hand to her temples and pressed hard. The air cleared.

It must be the warmth of the herbarium, together with the heavy scents of the spices and herbs, that made her feel faint.

She took a deep breath and moved closer. Nay, she was not faint. 'Twas as she believed. A tracery of knotwork overlay the honed muscles of his back. Yet Einalem seemed to see nothing in the inflamed skin.

"Einalem," she said. "I will put the salve on Lien's back while you search the herbarium."

"Yeah," Lien said. "Why is Ardra searching instead of you? She probably knows nothing about all this stuff. No one would know better than you what to look for."

"Well. That is true." Einalem smiled and slid her hand over Lien's bare shoulder.

Ardra tugged the bowl away from Einalem, but Lien put his hand under the bowl. "I can do it myself."

"Oh, you could never reach the center of your back." Ardra knelt behind him. She tipped the salve into her palms and took a deep breath.

The red lines were composed of tiny dots. His skin was hot where the rash was darkest. It seemed to run beneath his skin, not on top of it.

She placed her palms at his waist. He tensed. She held her hands there, not moving, until he relaxed. Then she ran her hands up the column of his spine, pressing her thumbs into the heat of his flesh. His hard muscles flexed beneath her fingers as she smoothed on the salve. She resisted the urge to trace the actual lines of his rash lest Einalem notice.

Ardra moved around in front of him, and he looked up at her. She could not read his expression in the dimly lighted herbarium, but when she set her hands on the inflamed circle of red about his throat, he closed his eyes.

His neck was reddest, the rash an angry collar like that worn by recalcitrant slaves in the warmer climes. If they

were alone, she would run her hands down his chest, touch his flat, dark nipples, and explore the line of hair that just showed at the edge of his breeches. But Einalem hummed in the background, so she worked the salve into the rash and remembered that he had no desire for little Liens. She knew deep within her that he would leave with the pilgrims after the feast.

Dispassion was what she needed. But she could not lose this last chance to memorize the feel of his skin.

As she worked, the rash faded, not completely, but it changed from dark red to a ghostly remnant against his sun-darkened skin.

Lien arched his back and rose quite suddenly. "That's fine, Ardra. Thanks."

"Did it help?" She cupped the bowl in the circle of her arms.

His chest was in front of her nose. So were the roses. So was the snake.

"Very much. My back feels a lot better than my wrists, though." He held out his arms.

Behind him, Einalem poked in a cupboard, lifting small linen pouches out and sniffing them. Ardra dipped her fingers in the salve. She examined the rash on his wrist as she had on his back.

There was no mistake. The rash formed of tiny dots did not run randomly across his skin, nor follow the path of his blood. It ran in a familiar pattern, thick as a manacle about his wrist. *The Shield*.

The salve faded the marks to a barely perceptible shadow on his skin.

He pulled on his tunic. She could not look away from his chest, nor forget the way his skin felt beneath her fingertips . . . or his thighs against hers when he'd sat behind her on the bed.

He belted the tunic and then touched her cheek. "Thank you," he whispered and turned away.

She pressed her hand to her cheek. To think that his rash formed the Shield pattern was madness.

"So, what's all this stuff?" Lien asked. He leaned an elbow beside Einalem. She slapped his hand when he poked a finger in a wooden box.

He sniffed a dark liquid that bubbled sluggishly over a wick burning in a dish of oil. "What's that?"

"Oh, a simple for a child who may be fevered."

Ardra's heart began to hammer. "We have been gone a long time."

Einalem ignored her. She moved methodically through the rows of bottles and dishes.

"Do you see anything unusual?" Lien asked.

Einalem tipped a bowl toward them. "A very large quantity of the herbs that prevent birth. She must have a very virile lover to need so much."

"They do not look like the ones you . . . have," Ardra said and glanced at Lien. He merely lifted his eyebrows.

Einalem smiled at her. "*These* herbs are taken before one makes love." Einalem lifted the bowl and weighed it in her hands. "In fact, I stand corrected. 'Tis the quantity needed to cause a birth to slip."

"What?" Ardra abandoned her spot at the door. She looked closer at the deep bowl filled with innocent green herbs. It could be a mix to season soup, save for the scent, which was that of the forest, not the garden. "What are you speaking of?"

"Looks like a salad to me," Lien said.

Einalem shook the bowl. "Do the Selaw women not rid themselves of unwanted babies?"

Ardra stared at Einalem and then looked away. *Did they?* She settled for a noncommittal shrug.

Einalem stirred the bowl with a wooden stick. "I would imagine 'tis the same where you come from, is it not, Lien?"

"Yeah. It's the same."

What else do I not know of a woman's world? Ardra wondered.

"This is a fresh mixture," Einalem said. "It looks ready to simmer. And this"—she moved to a wooden box whose lid lay by its side—"this is a very rare find."

"Is it the potion?" Ardra asked, resuming her place by the door, where she peered through the small crack, grateful to avoid more talk of babes, wanted or not.

"Nay." Einalem wet her finger, dipped it in the box, then licked her fingertip. " 'Tis a fine grind, this is."

"What is it?" Ardra hissed.

Einalem pursed her lips. "It is a spice to season food. Sometimes used to mask other tastes. If food is stale and so on."

Ardra abandoned the door again, but Lien clamped a hand over her wrist when she reached out to sample it. "Don't taste it," he warned.

"It is just ground nuts," Einalem said.

Lien eased his grip, and Ardra smelled the powder, then tasted it. "This was in the bread served to us before we retired."

"I believe you are right." Einalem replaced the lid and then moved about the chamber, setting it to rights.

"I have seldom slept so deeply. Do you think Cidre put it in our bread to hide a sleeping potion?"

Einalem laughed. "Sleeping potion? 'Twas just fatigue, my dear. Why should she put us to sleep?"

Lien answered for her. "So she could hide something without our interference? We did surprise her."

Einalem shook her head. "Nay. One cannot surprise a goddess. She has spies everywhere."

Chapter Fourteen

They left the herbarium without locating anything resembling the Vial of Seduction. How Ardra wished to arrange a repeat inspection with Nilrem, but he lacked courage.

Lien cleared his throat. "I'm going to have a chat with the pilgrims. Take a nap if you can; you look tired." He touched Ardra's shoulder, but for only a fleeting instant, then walked away.

She spent a moment watching how he leaned on his stick and remembering the fine, hard lines of his body beneath the tunic and leather breeches. A laugh dragged her back from useless dreams. Einalem's laugh.

Einalem had joined the men and Cidre at the hearth.

Ardra did not trust Einalem, but had to admit the woman had quickly identified each substance and its uses, finding nothing unusual save the large quantity of herbs to prevent birth.

Ardra skirted the hall. It was time to take the nap Lien had recommended.

She also wished to avoid the conversations that burbled around her like so much water over a dam. She could not

stay and watch Lien talk to Cidre, or the other pilgrims, for that matter. She did not wish to hear them laud the pilgrim life, nor did she wish to embarrass herself by disputing their claims.

In her chamber, she did as Lien had the night before: she jammed a chair beneath the latch.

She washed her face and hands. When she went to lie down, Lien's pack sat in the center of her bed. Curiosity bloomed like a troublesome weed. She dug in Lien's pack, but found only his tunic and a pot of oil she assumed was for his rash.

The tunic should be washed. She sat on the floor and pressed her face into the soft linen and breathed his scent. Something fell from its folds—one of the strips of cloth Nilrem had bound about Lien's wounds. The cloth was clean, and within its neat folds was the leaf from the Tree of Valor.

Lien had kept it. It felt as fresh as if it had just dropped from the tree. How was that possible? Did he know this heart-shaped leaf was once a token passed from one lover to another?

She pressed the leaf to her face and wept.

What a fool she had been to lie in bed with him. Had she not already made a fool of herself over another comely man?

Did Lien wear a false face? He made love, but wanted none of the consequences.

Why had she not heeded the warning painted on his arm? Now he would go. She should thank the gods that Cidre had put a sleeping potion in their bread. Else she might be wondering if she would bear another child who must live a hard life without a father to aid and teach him.

Someone pushed on the door. Deleh whispered her name.

"I cannot be found wailing like a simpleton over Lien's shirt," Ardra whispered. As Deleh wandered away, Ardra wrapped up the leaf and returned it to the pack. The tunic

197

went into a pile of her own garments that needed washing. To remove the signs of weeping, she splashed cold water on her face.

The pot of oil on the floor must be from Einalem, meant to ease Lien's rash. She opened it. Inside, the oil was thick, and she touched her fingertip to it and sniffed. She recognized the scent. She had a salve just like it to smooth on burns. Carefully she placed the pot in Lien's pack, retrieved his tunic, and folded it on top.

Was that how she had found it? Would he know she had gone through his things? She decided he was not so neat as to fold his tunic, so she pulled it out again and stuffed it carelessly in with guilty haste.

She curled on the bed and did as she had not done since her mother's death—she cried herself to sleep.

A hard rap on the door woke her with a start.

"Who is it?" she called.

"Samoht. Open this door. Now."

She dragged the chair away. He swept into the room and slammed the door behind him.

"What are you doing hiding in here? How can you find the vial if you are lying abed or primping?"

"I was washing my face. I was about to return to the hall when you arrived."

"What is this?" Samoht picked up Lien's pack. He rounded on her. "This is the pilgrim's, is it not?"

"Aye. He has no other place to keep it."

Samoht cast it aside. He was upon her in two strides. "You are lying with him, are you not?" He gripped her arms and shook her. "You press your knees together and protest when I touch you, but for him, a dark-haired freak, for him you will spread yourself."

He kissed her hard, stifling any protest she might make. He walked her back against the table and leaned over her. He was strong, aroused, angry.

She clamped her hands on his shoulders and tried to twist from his grasp. He gripped her wrists and jerked them apart.

198

"Scream, Ardra. Go ahead. Scream and summon help. It will surely be my men who come."

She choked back the shriek that was on her lips.

"Aye. Scream for help and I will see your Lien castrated, a common fate for a slave who dares to lie with his mistress."

He slid his hands over her breasts. "I will see your boy banished, and you"—he kissed her throat—"you I will chain to my bed until I am sated. Go ahead and scream. It will bring me great pleasure to punish your refusal."

Bile rose in her throat. He held her against the table, his body pressed between her thighs. He pulled up her skirt and ran his hand over her hip.

"Perhaps I should give your Lien to a few diseased outcasts. You know who I mean. The ones who prefer the favors of men to women. Then I will castrate him."

"Stop this, Samoht. You do not want me." She reached for her eating dagger. Her hand trembled. She would kill him before she would submit to him.

He gripped her chin. "I have wanted you since I witnessed your mating." He kissed her mouth. She whipped her face aside and he laughed. "Did Tol satisfy you? Or did you take lovers? How many? Ollach? I would like to castrate him, too."

"Ardra!" Lien burst into the room, tearing Samoht off her. He tossed the high councilor across the room and stepped in front of her. When Samoht came to his knees, Lien snatched up his stick and held it in both hands.

"You dare touch me! You dare threaten me!" Samoht scrambled to his feet and jerked his tunic straight.

Three men, Red Rose Warriors, crowded the doorway. Ardra snatched at Lien's arm to hold him back.

Samoht pointed at Lien. "Take this pilgrim and lock him up. He is charged with assaulting a councilor."

Ralen shoved his way into the room and stood in front of the guards. "What is the commotion here?" he asked.

Ardra hung on to Lien's arm.

199

"This man," Lien shouted, "was raping Ardra."

"Samoht?" Ralen slapped his hands flat on Samoht's chest to prevent him from lunging at Lien. "Is this true?"

"She was willing. Were you not?" Samoht stared at her, all his threats plain on his face.

"Aye," she whispered.

"Ardra!" Lien stared at her in disbelief.

"Lien, you misunderstood," Ralen said.

"You surely can't believe that. Look at her. She can't even look you in the eye!"

The warriors stepped back in wary silence. Ralen walked to Ardra and lifted her chin. "Look at me and tell me the truth."

Her mouth trembled. Samoht would castrate Lien. Harm her son. She had almost killed him with her eating dagger. Her life would be forfeit for such an offense. She gulped back her tears.

"Lien misunderstood." She stared at Ralen, but her words were for Samoht. "Please, Samoht, I beg of you, do not punish him. Nilrem made Lien vow to protect me."

Ralen gently moved the hair from her face. "I think there is more going on here than you wish to admit. But it would serve no one to continue this. Samoht, I think it hasty to have Lien locked up for defending Ardra."

Samoht stabbed the air in Lien's direction. "He came after me with that stick."

Ralen shook his head. "A stick? You wear a dagger, your men have swords. He can hardly do you much harm with a stick."

"I demand an apology for his mistake."

Lien opened his mouth, then closed it. He looked at Ardra. She wanted to beg him to acquiesce, but could not. Tears dripped down her face.

"Sure. I apologize," Lien said. He set the tip of his stick on the ground. "I was hasty. My mistake."

Ralen heaved an audible sigh. "Now, Samoht, send your men away. And Lien, fetch Deleh that she may tend to Ardra."

Samoht ordered his men away, and Lien walked out just behind them. Ardra wanted to hang on to him but could not.

The door shut. Ralen walked across the chamber to Samoht and kicked him in the thigh.

Samoht fell with a crash and lay there, writhing in pain. When he stopped gasping, Ralen pulled him before Ardra.

"Now the true apology will be made. Say the words, Samoht, or I will reveal a secret I am sure Einalem would rather remained hidden forever—something we both know need not come before the council."

Samoht jerked his arm from Ralen's and staggered back, rubbing his palm on his leg. The two men stared at each other. Ardra felt the heat and hatred streaming off Samoht as tangibly as if she could see it.

"Ardra," Samoht finally said. "Accept my apology." He turned and left the chamber, shutting the door with a bang.

"I would have killed him." She brought her hand forward from the folds of her skirt. In it was her dagger. With some difficulty, for her hand was shaking, she sheathed the knife.

Ralen took her hand. "I am heartily grateful to Lien that he interrupted. I need not tell you of the coil of trouble you would be in if you killed a councilor." He smiled. "Though I would have done the same in your place. I am sorry for Samoht's behavior, but I would not count on my threats keeping him in line. He is used to taking what he wishes." He lifted her hand to his lips.

The door opened. Lien stood in the threshold behind Deleh.

Ralen kissed her hand and then her forehead. "All will be well," he said and left the room.

Lien sat with his back to the wall outside Ardra's chamber. He clasped his hands around his knees, his stick across his lap.

He wanted a piece of old Sam. One part of him wanted a piece of Ralen, too.

201

Ann Lawrence

It pissed him off that Ralen had been the one to play the shining white knight. It pissed him off that he couldn't call the local sheriff and have Sam hauled off to jail for attempted rape.

Sam was the local sheriff, and Ralen his deputy.

The deputy was kissing the damsel in distress.

Damn.

Lien's rash pissed him off, too. It flared up when he was close to Cidre and simmered right down when Ardra touched him.

He shifted his shoulders against the rough stone wall. Ardra raised another itch he badly wanted scratched.

Deleh shuffled up the steps and into Ardra's room. The majestic concubine had deteriorated into an anxious old woman.

Ollach arrived. Lien nodded to him, and when Ollach knocked, Lien stood up. He walked in on Ollach's heels. He wanted company when he dealt with Ardra. A witness, so to speak.

Deleh began to comb out Ardra's hair. Lien found himself watching the motion of the comb. Her hair looked like a sheet of gold cloth. What was wrong with him? It was just hair.

"I have something to say, Ardra, and I'd like Ollach to hear it," he said.

She curtseyed.

He unloaded. "You are not to walk around this fortress alone, do you understand?"

"I can take care of myself." She brandished her eating dagger. Deleh gasped.

Lien merely lifted a dark brow, but he did not speak words of contempt for her boast. "A knife isn't the answer," he said. "Caution is. Do you understand?"

Ardra nodded. Lien was right. Had she been cautious, Samoht would not have caught her alone. And he never would again.

"A nod's not good enough. Say it."

With a sigh, Ardra complied, though she chose her words carefully so what she said was not a lie. "I will not walk around this fortress alone."

"You will not be in this room or any other without a bodyguard. And one of Samoht's Red Rose Warriors will not do."

"I understand what you are saying."

He jerked his thumb at Ollach. "Do you get it, too?"

Ollach bit his lip and shifted from one foot to the other, but nodded vigorously. Ardra imagined the poor man thought he must accompany her to the privy.

"Okay. Now, there's a feast downstairs. I'm sure you'd rather stay here, Ardra, but you're going. Stay where you can be seen—and as far from Samoht as possible."

He grabbed Ollach by the tunic. "You stick with her through the whole thing, understand? I don't care if old Sam pays your salary or not. You stick with her."

"As you wish," Ollach said, and Ardra wondered if he realized he was accepting a command from a pilgrim.

Ardra took a deep breath. "I am sure Ollach only understood half the words you said—"

"Mistress! I can understand his meaning. I am to protect you. Am I right?" Ollach looked at Lien, his eyebrows up, his hand on his sword hilt.

"You've got it. Now wait outside." Lien pointed at the door.

"You will both wait outside. I must change for the feast." Ardra tried to pretend she had no cares. She spoke as coldly as possible. She must distance herself from Lien. If she truly wished to prove herself able, she must take care of herself.

"You look fine in that, and we have to talk," Lien said.

She looked down at the rumpled gown. There were barely perceptible marks from her tears. Lien would not notice them, but a woman would. "I will not go to the feast in this gown."

Ollach tugged on Lien's arm. "Come. Women must have their way in some things. We will wait out here."

Ardra threw her shoe at the door after it closed. "Women must have their way in some things. I hope their swords go soft."

"Ardra! What ails you? Such words for a woman!" Then Deleh began to laugh. "I did not know you understood the necessity of having strong steel in a sword."

"Forgive me," Ardra said, but she smiled. "I am not completely ignorant, just weary."

Deleh arranged another overgown for her. It was ivory to match the underdress. Was it fortuitous that the gown had amber stitched along the hem of the sleeves and neck in the pattern of the Shield?

As she laced the gown, she realized it was one that opened in front, so a mother might nurture a child. It was a long time since she had needed it, a long time since she had seen her son. He was hidden now, with his nurse, who loved him quite as much as she.

Lien had no wish for babes.

She combed her hair again. She laced and unlaced her gown. She found a flaw in her woolen hose and took them off, then put them on again, tying the ribbons about her thighs. Last, she opened her pack and found a sheath and long dagger that had belonged to Tol. The blade was plain as was the hilt. She slipped it on the decorated belt that graced her waist and hips.

"Now, Ardra," Lien called from the hall.

She whipped the door open.

His hand was raised in a fist. He lowered it slowly. Would he challenge her right to wear the knife?

His gaze ran over her from her head to her waist, to the dagger, and back to her face. "You look . . . ready."

Chapter Fifteen

Cidre sat at the center of many long tables arranged in a T. The head table was raised up on a dais. Samoht and Ralen flanked her. Einalem sat next to her brother, Ardra between Ralen and Ollach.

Lien sat with the hoi polloi and Nilrem, too far away to be a part of the head table's conversation, but not far enough away from Pointy-nose to avoid the joys of pilgrimming.

Ardra hardly touched the jellied eels or something Nilrem raved about called the green goh. Goh looked like a plucked squirrel to Lien, but it was pretty tasty. Then he realized the pilgrims were not eating the meat and sighed. At least he could get in line with the spring water. It was clear, cold, and had apple slices floating in it.

He stood up and stretched. He needed a long run and a workout. What might a castle hold that he could use as free weights?

Pointy-nose (who had a name Lien couldn't begin to pronounce) tugged on his sleeve. "Lien, where are you going?"

The guests of honor were on the move. "Later," he said and pulled his arm away.

Cidre smiled at him when he sidled near the privileged few. "Lien, are you leaving my feast? We have had but one course."

Whoops. "Uh, no, I just wanted to thank you for including me."

One by one, the men and women took their leave, then returned in a few minutes. He hung around the table, making small talk. Ardra dutifully took Deleh with her when she excused herself. Lien was glad Ollach trailed her, for Samoht watched her every move.

Lien thought about inventing the flush toilet. A shower would be nice, too.

One of Cidre's guards, a man who had a damned fine set of overdeveloped biceps and a leather jerkin cut to show them off, brought Cidre a bowl of water in which she washed her fingers. She offered it to Lien, then directed everyone to shift down so that he might sit at her side.

It was an honor Lien knew he must accept, no matter how much his neck prickled.

Samoht never made eye contact, but Lien felt the animosity hopping right over Cidre in his direction.

The next course arrived by draped cart. A huge pig sat on it, apples and other fruit spilling out of its mouth.

"Ralen," Lien said while he watched how each guest carved his own portion of pork as the cart passed. "I want to make a request."

"You are not eating?" Ralen asked.

"I'm skipping the meat."

"What is it you want? Apple? Pear?" Ralen stabbed one of the pears as the cart moved away and held it out to him.

Lien took the pear, though it didn't look much like the ones from home. "My request concerns Ardra."

"Aye?"

"I've noticed that your men, or maybe they're Tol's men, are growing disrespectful to Ardra. I don't like it, and I'm hoping you're going to stop it."

Ralen speared a slice of pork and ate it right off his blade. He chewed a moment, then propped his elbows on the table.

"Let me understand you, Lien. You believe my men are not giving Ardra the proper respect, am I correct?"

"That's it. From what I've heard, she did a lot of good for the Selaw people. For that she is *owed* respect. She was also your brother's lifemate, and for that, *you* owe her."

Ralen nodded. "I agree. Look about. Can you point out any specific men I might speak with first?"

Lien scanned the lower table. "Yeah. The tall one at the very end. The man next to him, too."

"Done." Ralen lifted his goblet and signaled for more wine. "I will not do it because you ask it. I will do it because I should have from the start. If Ardra finds the vial, she will return to her fortress, and Tol's men will probably accompany her. I allowed my belief in the futility of her task to sway me and set the men to other tasks. It was wrong."

"You think she'll find the vial?"

Ralen shook his head. "I still believe the task impossible, but her determination is admirable. She has courage. Rare in a woman. Her son will be strong."

"What's her son's name?"

"Vad. He was named after a great man."

Vad. "Who was that?" But Lien knew who Vad was. Gwen's Vad was one man he could never live up to.

"Vad was a much-lauded Tolemac warrior who disappeared. 'Tis said he perished on the ice fields."

Lien watched Ardra. Her every move was elegant. Had she and Vad hooked up? Was Ardra's child Vad's son?

"How old is the boy?" he asked.

Ralen contemplated Ardra. The warrior was not as handsome as the notorious Vad, but Lien didn't know any women who'd kick him out of bed. He had tied his thick, blond hair at his nape much like Vad wore his.

"I am not sure," Ralen said. "Ask Ardra when her mating ceremony took place. The boy was conceived at that time."

So the child wasn't Vad's. Somehow Lien's relief was as troublesome as his jealousy.

Ralen interrupted Lien's musings. "She is beautiful, is she not?"

"Ardra?"

Ralen threw back his head and laughed. "Of course, Ardra."

"Are you interested in Ardra?"

Ralen tapped the tip of his dagger on the table. "I have greater ambitions, my friend."

"Than Ardra? The Fortress of Ravens?"

"My ambitions will not take me to the ice fields."

Cidre touched Lien's hand. "You are neglecting me. Please, tell me a bit about the land beyond the ice fields. I will wager they have naught so grand as this." She swept out her hands to encompass the feast.

Her fingertips were like nettles dragged across his skin. "You're right there," he said, glancing at the hearth behind her.

"What about your family? Have you any brothers as strong as you?" She ran her fingers up his biceps, and he stifled a groan.

She picked up her wine cup, and he took a shuddering breath of relief. Her eyes, almost sapphire blue in the torchlight, looked like cold, hard marbles.

"None. I have no family."

"I am so sorry." She licked her lips. When Ardra did it, his insides went haywire. Cidre caused not even a blip on the old radar screen.

Her hair, a strange mix of silvery white and gold, reached almost to her feet and right now was lying in a pool behind the bench like a bridal veil. If her figure was as good as it looked in the drapy green robe she was wearing, he would have latched onto her in an instant back

home. But here, each sweep of her fingers over his arm sent waves of irritation in its wake. Why?

"I appreciate your concern," he managed to say despite his discomfort.

Samoht said something at Cidre's ear, and she laughed and looked away. The loss of her attention was like cool water on Lien's skin. He took the opportunity to turn back to Ralen and slide a few inches down the bench away from the goddess.

"Look, Ralen, what's with you and Einalem?"

Ralen smiled. "Does there have to be something between us?"

Lien wondered how personal he could get. A few grueling miles on horseback didn't exactly make them friends. "No, I suppose not."

"Lien, you are far more interested in whether there is something between Ardra and me." He tore off a hunk of savory bread from a loaf and offered it, which Lien noticed he did each time he started in on something new to eat. Lien took the bread. It was coarse but excellent, warm and fragrant with herbs. No sleeping ones he hoped.

"Okay. Let's suppose I want to know what's between you and Ardra. Would you tell me?"

Ralen nodded. "I have nothing to hide. When Tol became ill, he often wrote to me on Ardra's behalf. It was his wish that I lifemate with her to protect her from Samoht."

"Will you?" Lien looked Ralen over. Both he and Samoht were Nordic minigods in their little world, but when you got to know the two, you understood that Sam was slime. Ralen was icy, but he had honor.

"It will not be permitted," Ralen said.

"That's it? Someone won't permit it, so you won't?"

Ralen smiled. "Oh, if I wanted her, I would fight the council, but in truth, she is not the woman for me. She is Selaw."

Prejudice ran deep here.

209

Ralen's smile became a frown. "Tol believed that if he set an example by mating with a Selaw woman, more would do so. The more ties between our people, the fewer hostilities. My brother was a dreamer. And two-faced."

"Really?"

"Aye. In truth, Ardra was never a lifemate in anything but the law's eyes. He mated with her for policy and peace. Their son will suffer for it if a strong warrior does not stand at Ardra's side."

"You could be that strong warrior." Saying the words was like speaking past a huge stone in his throat.

"Not I. I have other plans," Ralen continued.

"Which don't include a Selaw mate." Lien found the bread dry in his mouth. Just what would become of Ardra after the eight days were up?

"Tol thought Ardra needed a man her age, but it will not be me."

"Or Samoht. He is already mated, isn't he?"

"Aye. To a Selaw chief's daughter." Ralen eyed the young woman who brought a dish of greens swimming in some fatty broth.

"So Selaw has chiefs too?"

The girl leaned her breast on Ralen's arm as she spooned some of the greens into a bowl for him.

"Aye. Too many. Unlike Tolemac, which has been organized for many conjunctions into the council of eight, each chief in Selaw is a petty tyrant who will not agree to anything with anyone. Ardra's father was one such. He ruled the Fortress of Ravens and caused all manner of ills for his people."

Lien sipped at the broth and greens. It reminded him of a thin spinach soup. It was smoky and delicious.

A hulking guard stood up and sang while folks took another break. Lien figured the meal was going to last all night.

The singer was concert quality, although the song had a strange cadence. It reminded him of something by the later

Russian composers. He missed music. He had really enjoyed driving Gwen up a wall with classical music. She was a C & W kind of gal.

The song came to an end. The warriors banged their dagger hilts on the long tables in approval. The next song was a bit ribald and involved full breasts and soft thighs. Ardra, who was in deep conversation with Nilrem, didn't seem to notice.

A string of young women, all pretty enough to vie for Miss Ocean City, brought out trays of pastries. Ralen cut one open with his dagger and revealed apples and berries baked in what looked like a yellow pudding.

Lien decided it looked safe. While everyone forked up the dessert, wine was poured. Then Samoht clanged his dagger blade on his metal goblet, and everyone fell silent.

He lifted his cup. "I propose a tribute." The guests leaped to their feet, cups high. "To my lifemate," Samoht said. "It is my pleasure to announce she has proven herself by birthing a healthy daughter."

Claps, cheers, and whistles filled the hall. Lien thought Samoht might also be a bit drunk. His eyes looked mean and bleary as he proposed another toast to prosperity and peace on the border.

Of course, it was his army on the border threatening the peace, but no one remarked on that.

Ralen knocked the dull side of his blade on his goblet and leaned near Lien. "It has taken him five days to finally make the announcement. I suspect the news was behind his ill humor these last few days."

"Really?"

"The child is a female. And he failed to impregnate his mate at the mating ceremony. Always a matter of importance to a man."

"So only a son will do?"

"Aye. Tol loved to boast that he got Ardra with child at the ceremony and she birthed a son."

Ann Lawrence

The young woman with the large breasts and soup came by again, and this time Ralen hooked her into his lap. That ended all hope Lien had of knowing what went on at a mating ceremony.

He steeled himself to speak to Cidre, who was staring at Samoht with wide eyes as if the jerk were saying something important. Old Sam was rambling on about peace and ice.

"Cidre? Everything was great." Lien indicated the remnants of the meal.

"There is more." She patted his hand, and his wrist flashed hot.

"Really?" He lifted his goblet of water so she would remove her hand.

"Here it comes."

The cart was back. This time it held wheels of cheese. Some of it was bright blue.

"I overheard you and Ralen discussing Ardra's mating ceremony." Cidre offered Lien a slice of the blue cheese. He took a bite and it reminded him of plain old cheddar.

"We don't have mating ceremonies where I'm from, so I was curious about how it works."

She laughed. "It is not work, Lien. In fact, some find it quite . . . stimulating. I will be happy to tell you about it, if you wish."

"Please." She did the lip-licking thing again. It was way behind Ardra's hair thing.

" 'Tis simple. A great person's mating is of concern to many. The child, if a male, will gain much and will be raised to rule. Such a consummation cannot be left to chance."

"Oh no?" He glanced at Ardra. She was sitting between Ollach and Einalem now and looked none too happy about it.

"The consummation will not take place until the perfect moment, the moment most likely to conceive a son."

"How's that determined?"

She pointed to the windows overhead. One of the moons was just visible, on the rise. "It is a matter of the stars and moons and the turning wheel of nature."

Read old wives' tales, Lien thought.

"It is considered great good luck for both father and son if the babe is conceived at the first consummation. The stars are consulted, the old women. It is a very precise matter."

"I see. So you get told, tonight's the night."

Cidre giggled like a small child. "Precisely. Of course, we here in the Tangled Wood care little for sons. It is a daughter to whom we pass our wisdom."

"So you don't go through this process?"

"Oh, aye. We do, but we have our own ritual here in the Wood. Any consummation of importance is not a private thing. In Tolemac and Selaw, all who are concerned in the choosing of the moment attend, and representatives from each chiefdom if they hold an interest in the alliance. The chamber may be as crowded as this hall is at this moment."

Lien shook his head. "No."

"I would imagine Samoht's was just as well attended as this, Ardra's half as much. Her lifemate was not of Samoht's stature. Samoht would have representatives from all eight chiefdoms. Sometimes lots are drawn because the desire to attend is so great."

There was no way Lien could imagine maintaining an erection in front of a crowd like this. "You're telling tales."

"Not I." Cidre stroked the shape of her goblet's stem, up and down. It was a languid, sensuous gesture. It left him cold. "The deed is done, and the woman is separated from her mate, and all other males, until it is determined whether she has conceived. If she has, she is considered a well-chosen mate, and the child lucky, the father lauded for his virility."

"And if the woman doesn't? Do they go through this public bedding again?"

Cidre smiled. "Nay. The couple is left in peace to take their own time with the matter. We are not quite so cruel. But the fates have not smiled on the match if such be the case."

The young girl on Ralen's lap poured wine for him. Cidre watched them. "She is one of the mating dancers."

"What?" Lien could not help looking at the carved figures behind him.

"Mating dancers. During the ceremony, should the male find the matter"—she licked her lips—"shall we say intimidating, he is encouraged by the dancers."

Encouraged.

Cidre leaned forward. Her robe slid open a bit, and he could see clear down to her waist.

"Where's your consort?" he asked.

She shifted, and the robe slid a bit more to reveal a swollen, dusky nipple. "Venrali is unwell. I had hoped he would join us, but he did not feel up to the noise."

"Isn't a consort a mate?" Lien tried not to stare.

She moved, and the robe slid back into place.

"Nay," she said. "A consort is not a mate, although he goes through a mating ceremony of sorts. He is a specially chosen man who services the goddess in order that a daughter will be born and the wisdom of ages passed on. To be my consort is a great honor."

"I'm sure it is." And the poor old soul was about to get the boot for another man. An unwilling one, if that was why Cidre had stolen the Vial of Seduction.

Samoht shouted for quiet and left his seat. He held his cup high and wandered down the table. As he passed his men, the Red Rose Warriors stood up in a little mini-wave motion, and Lien realized they were sprinkled throughout the hall.

"I wish to propose a few tests of skill, Cidre," Samoht said as he reached the very foot of the long table and faced the goddess.

214

The men straightened up, and murmurs rippled down the tables.

"Men and their games," she said sotto voce.

"I challenge anyone who will take me up on the offer of a test of blades."

One of Samoht's warriors climbed away from the table and went to the open area between the long table and the double doors.

"I will accept the challenge," the man said. He pulled off his tunic and stood there, sweating, bare-chested, his hand on his hilt. He had three silver-hued rings on his right arm.

Ralen leaned near Lien and informed him, "If the man bests Samoht, he will become a lieutenant without having to earn the right in battle."

"I see." Samoht also pulled off his tunic. Though Samoht had a lean appearance dressed, he was well muscled. He had to be strong to wield the heavy sword he wore. Anger sizzled through Lien again when he thought of Samoht holding Ardra down.

The two men met in a clash of swords. It looked deadly. The hall hushed, everyone rising, gathering about the two. The crowd formed an oval a tad too close to the action for Lien's taste. He shoved spectators with his stick until he stood next to Ardra.

She glanced over her shoulder. Worry etched her brow. "He has taken too much wine," she whispered to him. "He only challenges when he is sotted."

"Then he won't do that well, will he?"

"He triumphs no matter what condition he is in."

The two men sparred back and forth for a bit, then Samoht slowly drove the challenger back until he fought right up against the crowd, which never budged.

Bets flew as coins were strewn on the floor—a problem for an unwary boot, but the two fighters seemed not to notice the bounty at their feet.

True to Ardra's word, Samoht lunged forward in a fluid motion and toppled the challenger into the spectators. He held the tip of his sword to the vanquished man's throat, then drew back, snatched up his goblet, brought to him by one of his warriors in anticipation of his success, and drank.

Everyone clapped and cheered. The warrior on the floor was helped up. He bowed and shook his head.

Lien looked at Samoht's arms. He wore three silver arm rings on his right arm and two gold on his left. Not an ounce of fat showed on his body, but Lien saw with satisfaction that his own six-pack was more defined than old Sam's.

Samoht drained his goblet and called for more wine. He held out his cup and scanned the crowd.

"Now it is his turn to choose an opponent," Ardra said. "It is the winner's right."

"How long will this go on?" Lien asked.

"Until Cidre calls an end to it or until everyone is asleep with drink."

"Lien." Samoht called his name, and the crowd before him parted. "I challenge you."

Ardra gasped.

Well, well. So the sheriff wants a showdown. "I'm a pilgrim," Lien called out. "We do not like to fight."

Cidre strolled with an almost dancelike motion to where he stood. "You cannot refuse."

"I have vowed I will not pick up a sword or dagger ever again."

"Oh, a sacred vow," Samoht shouted and raised his cup. "Let us drink to the sacred vow." Everyone followed suit.

"I do not like his manner," Ardra said.

Samoht walked toward where Lien stood with Ardra, sheathing his long sword as he came. "I will allow you to choose the weapon, pilgrim."

"You cannot challenge a pilgrim." Cidre took Lien's arm. His rash flared hot.

He disentangled himself as Samoht said, "As long as he is garbed as a warrior, he is a warrior."

The five pilgrims gathered around him and chattered protests at Samoht and Cidre.

Samoht shrugged, a crooked smile on his handsome face. It masked a sneer. "Am I right?" he asked. He spread his hands out to the crowd.

"Fine." Lien shoved the pilgrims aside. "I'll take your challenge."

Ardra opened her mouth, then closed it.

"What weapon, pilgrim?" Samoht asked. He planted his hands on his hips. He was pretty tanked.

"Sticks." Lien lifted his long stick a couple of inches and then let the tip drop with a rap on the floor.

"Sticks?" Samoht threw back his head and roared with laughter. His warriors joined in, but Cidre and those near Lien did not. They glanced about, sure there was some trick to come.

"Fine. If you don't think you're capable." Lien shrugged.

Samoht swallowed his laughter. "Not capable? Bring me a stick," he snapped and began to divest himself of his sword belt.

One of the Red Rose Warriors strode to Nilrem and tore the stick from the old man's hand. He sputtered a protest, but no one paid him any heed.

Cidre stepped into the oval of onlookers. "We must have some rules."

"The same ones for any challenge," Samoht said.

But the goddess shook her head. "Nay. These are sticks, not swords. Swords can cause death."

Samoht grinned and held the stick as Lien did, upright, one hand loosely around it near the top. "Then no rules. Anything goes."

"Agreed. Anything goes," Cidre said and smiled. "And no tunics, Lien."

"Women are always trying to get me out of my clothes," he said. Ollach and Ralen's men laughed. Cidre curtseyed to him. Ardra frowned.

217

Lien handed his stick to Cidre to keep her busy in case she decided to touch him. He didn't need the distraction of his rash.

Samoht wandered about the oval of spectators, riling the crowd. The five pilgrims cried out vociferously in Lien's behalf, but they were pretty much alone in championing him.

Lien dropped his belt and drew his tunic over his head. Ardra came forward and took it from him, folding it precisely and speaking near his ear. "I have seen him fight. Often. He likes a quick first strike and a low one."

"Thank you, Ardra. You can be my fight manager if I survive."

"May the gods smile on you," she said, then stepped back. Her knuckles were white as she squeezed his tunic in her hands. Briefly she touched the tunic to her lips, then lowered it.

He felt his heart begin to knock in his chest. Her serious manner reminded him this wasn't a game.

Samoht was standing hip-shot, one hand clasped about his stick, one hand around a goblet of wine.

The crowd was manic, a bit like the ringside crowd on the pro-wrestling network. Bets were flying, coins spilling on the floor by Samoht's feet. A couple of gamblers scattered some coins near Lien's feet, but damned few. Only those from the high table were standing in silence.

Lien figured he might as well give everyone their money's worth. Then he smiled, the pro-wrestling thought sparking an idea. He'd pretend he was in the ring.

He did as Samoht did. He wandered around his end of the oval, using the stick like a weight bar to give his shoulders a stretch, working out the kinks in his back and arms from sitting too long.

After that, he rested the stick behind his neck and held the ends loosely, so his arms were spread. A murmur ran through the crowd. He heard whispers about his tattoo and the roses. Somehow, he'd forgotten the roses around his

neck. But as Samoht stared at him, Lien saw his gaze drop to the chain over and over again.

"My stick's bigger than yours," he called out to Samoht. The crowd howled, and the councilor frowned.

"We shall see," he growled.

Lien brought his stick down and held it in one hand, the tip on the ground. As he hoped, Samoht did the same.

Lien smiled. "We shall see."

Cidre called that she, too, would like to see whose stick was bigger. Lien inclined his head to the goddess, lifting his stick.

He heard the word *snake* whispered. In its wake, a gold coin spun near his boots and rang on the wooden floor.

Samoht might top him by an inch or so, but Lien realized that he had a longer reach.

Samoht handed off his wine cup. Lien forced himself to remain loose. He wanted a piece of Samoht so bad he could feel the need flood his mouth.

Samoht stood with one foot forward. He stomped the ground with the end of his stick. Everyone's attention moved to the councilor. Lien shifted his stick so he held it loosely in both hands, horizontally in front of him.

Whatever wine haze fogged Samoht's mind cleared. Lien saw the change on his face. Samoht's gaze dropped again to the glass roses. Something flickered on the councilor's face. Confusion? It was time.

Lien clamped his fists on his stick and lunged forward. He thrust his stick between Samoht's legs and tossed him on his ass. Samoht's stick spun out of his hand and rattled across the floor.

Lien straddled Samoht and held the stick across his throat.

The crowd fell silent. Samoht kicked at him with his legs and twisted, growling, fists on the stick.

They were frozen, Samoht pressing up on the stick and Lien down. The stick shook. Lien held it in place, sweat pouring off him, ready to crush the councilor's throat, con-

Ann Lawrence

sequences be damned. Samoht gasped and choked. The long chain with the glass roses dangled inches from Samoht's face.

Cidre walked forward.

"The winner," she said, and placed her hand on Lien's shoulder.

Lien climbed off the councilor and away from Cidre's hand. Samoht rolled onto his side, gasping for air. The pilgrims burst into cheers. Ollach and some of Ralen's men joined in, but mostly the circle of spectators stood there in silence, staring at him—or rather, at his arm. The arm he held high in triumph.

Samoht came up fast. He snatched up his stick and whipped at Lien—low by the knees.

The blow stung, but Samoht didn't know his weapon. Lien did. He whipped his stick around and poke-checked the councilor once in the stomach and once on the shoulder as he went down, the wind knocked out of him.

Before Samoht could challenge him again, Lien bowed to Cidre and took a victory half-circle at the far end of the oval. He fisted his right hand around his stick and pumped it in the air. He made sure everyone saw his tattoo. If the snake could raise some fear, then by God he would use it.

A Red Rose Warrior helped Samoht to his feet. The councilor stood with his hands on his knees, gasping. Then he straightened and impaled Lien with a look as sharp as glass. He smiled. "Well done, pilgrim." He held out his hand.

Lien approached warily. He didn't trust the councilor. But Samoht was a true politician. He made the most of his defeat. He wrapped a sweaty arm around Lien's shoulder, and overwhelmed him with his wine-scented breath. "Come. Sit by me."

Samoht slapped his hand on Lien's chest and called for wine all around. It was an excuse, Lien figured, for him to examine the roses. The councilor hooked the chain and

rubbed a thumb over the earrings. He dropped them just as quickly as he'd snatched them up.

Lien's rash flared like an acid burn on his wrists and neck. Cidre stood by the hearth, her hand on one carved figure's hip.

She stared at him. An army of ants crawled down his back. He almost shook with the effort to control a mad need to claw at his skin.

"Lien." Ardra drew his attention from the goddess. "Your tunic." She held it out. Samoht let him go.

When Lien took his shirt, Ardra's fingers skimmed his, and his wrists cooled.

"You did well," she said. Then, as she moved to the side to make way for a serving woman with a pitcher of wine, she lifted her hand and placed it on his back. Firmly. Without a caress. The roiling heat subsided. The ants stopped crawling over his skin.

"Thank you," he said to Ardra.

"I but held your tunic," she said, but he read something in her eyes, soft amber now in the light of the torches, that told him she knew of his discomfort.

He raised his gaze to the hearth. Cidre was gone.

Was it Ardra's touch or Cidre's disappearance that brought such instant, blessed relief to his skin?

Chapter Sixteen

The songs grew ever more ribald, and Ardra took the opportunity to sneak away. What she had planned for her night hours would not meet with Lien's approval.

How magnificent he was with his dark hair and sun-browned skin.

Was she the only one who saw the pattern of lines that flared up from the waist of his breeches and spread across his back like wings? The warriors probably saw only the snake art, the women only his fine form, the strong spread of muscles as he raised the stick and stretched.

Ardra's chamber was not empty. Deleh lay on the bed. "I cannot sleep with all the singing, Ardra."

The old woman helped Ardra from her clothing and held out a silky lavender robe. It had a simple length of amber and lavender embroidered silk to tie it closed.

Ardra rubbed her temples. "Could you warm me a glass of honey and milk? Leave it by the door and then seek your bed. The moons are sure to be well up now. I know how you like the orb-glow."

"Aye, I will fetch your drink. But would you mind . . . that is . . . I have found another bed I would like to share."

"Another bed?"

Deleh, her eyes down, her toe tracing circles on the bare wooden floor, said, "There is a man here. He reminds me of Tol."

"You are free to do as you please, Deleh," Ardra said. "But you do know I will look after you always."

Deleh's eyes remained downcast. "Forgive me, but I do not think I will enjoy the fortress with Samoht as its master."

"You doubt I will prevail?" Ardra lifted her chin.

"Forgive me. Is there anything else I might do?"

Ardra sighed. "Just leave the milk on the floor outside my door." How could Deleh doubt her? And so quickly find a replacement for Tol? Were the concubine's feelings for Tol only as lasting as the protection he could offer her? Ardra chastised herself for such thoughts as Deleh fetched her comb. What were the insecurities of a slave compared to those of a free woman? Who was she to judge another?

Deleh combed Ardra's hair, then polished it with a soft cloth.

The hall had quieted. Ardra was filled with energy—a nervous energy, the kind that did not last, but still, energy it was. It was time to search beyond the herbarium for the potion.

"Listen well in the kitchens, please," she said.

"Of course. I will keep my ears open for you. You have only three days left. But why should I not bring your milk inside?"

"I may not be here, and I do not want you to lie if you are asked whether you saw me."

"What are you planning?"

"It is best you not know. Samoht and Einalem will do everything in their power to see that I fail. It would not serve me to have them find the vial or wheedle it from Cidre. It would not do to have Samoht think he can use you, either."

"What if someone sees you?"

223

"I shall say I cannot sleep, that I am looking for you!"

"Nay," Deleh said. She tucked Ardra's hair into her hood. "No one will believe such nonsense. Say you are looking for Lien—"

"Deleh!"

"You must. A woman would understand why you want to make love to the pilgrim. He will be gone at sunrise with the other pilgrims, after all."

Gone at sunrise.

"If you do not want to be suspected of searching the fortress, you must say you are looking for a man. That, anyone will believe. They may smile and talk behind their hands on the morrow, but the gossip will distract them."

"I will think about it." Ardra wished she were just a simple woman looking for a lover. Her nipples tightened against the cool silk as she thought of Lien. *Say you want to make love to the pilgrim.* She shivered and wrapped her arms about her waist, for her mind had conjured a vision of him lying in the mating position and her climbing astride him.

Another vision replaced it—Lien standing with his back to her, the ancient mark on his skin moving as his muscles moved. Molten desire flooded her body. The sensation had occurred in the hall as well, snatching her breath away. Unable to resist, she had gone to him, touched, felt the searing heat of his skin against her palm.

The sensation of the smooth silk robe sliding on her skin only inflamed the heat of her need.

Was Lien sitting outside her door right now? What would he do if she called him in? What if Ollach answered her call instead?

Ardra urged Deleh to her task. She must not waste the night hours.

When the fortress felt at rest, and no more men stumbled by her door, no more laughter rang out from the hall below, she left her chamber, wearing nothing beyond her

lavender bed robe. She hoped she looked like a simple woman seeking a man's bed.

Where was Lien? He was not outside her door. Neither was Ollach. And what had become of Lien's vow to watch over her?

The hall was dark and silent. A guard's footsteps could be heard outside the double doors as he paced, but otherwise Cidre had posted no men.

Snores and snuffles told her the pilgrims slept near the hearth. She wondered if their vows of celibacy were tested by the women carved into the hearth in voluptuous detail.

She worked her way through the kitchen storeroom, knowing what would be out of place there.

Thoughts of Lien's swift victory over Samoht intruded as she tiptoed across the hall. She feared Samoht's revenge if Lien did not leave on the morrow. The councilor would want Lien to pay in kind for the humiliation. She was not fooled by Samoht's laughing face after the stick fight. Lien would suffer for his triumph.

She heard a sliding sound. Behind her. Heart in her throat, she slowly turned. A shadow moved along the wall by the steps to the lower level, moving as furtively as she. A tall, thin male shadow. The pilgrim leader? Where was he off to in the middle of the night? There were no privies in that direction. Was he going to steal food from the kitchen? Thievery was a grave matter, one her father and Tol had punished severely.

Then she counted the pilgrims sleeping by the fire. Five. Who was this man who moved so quietly, and where was he going?

Curiosity overcame her. She followed. The man took the steps to the kitchen. He opened a door and walked quickly through the cook's gardens.

She did the same. He made straight for the little door that led to the orchard, but instead of cutting through the trees, he skulked along the outside fortress wall to the lake.

Ann Lawrence

The lake lay like a sheet of ice beneath the moons. Only two orbs had climbed the sky so far. They sat in the heavens like pale chunks of turquoise and painted the lake in green and white. A cool breeze ruffled the surface.

The man stood at the water's edge. He lifted his arms to the orbs in a silent exhalation. Then he bent and drew something from his robe. A cup. He dipped it in the water and drank.

The moons cast his shadow long and needle thin. Drawn to him, Ardra stepped closer. Her boot crunched on the pebbles.

He whipped around.

"Father!" A drumming and beat of wings filled her head. "But you are dead. . . ."

Chapter Seventeen

The man threw back his hood. Her father. Ruonail of the Fortress of Ravens. Dead more than three conjunctions.

He walked slowly toward her. "Forgive me, daughter. But I am not dead."

"Why? How?" She staggered back. Here stood a man she had mourned and hated equally from one day to the next.

Then she saw what lay on his chest. *The Black Eye*.

He put out his hands, but she could not touch him. He slowly withdrew his hands and tucked them into his sleeves.

"Come, daughter. Accept what your eyes tell you. I will not bore you with the trials I suffered to find my way here. Suffice it to say, I had prepared for the time when I might need to leave. There are those who will offer a haven for a price."

"A price? You are saying you had coin enough to find your way from the fortress to here?"

"Aye, child. Do not judge with such harshness. Would you have had me die? I think not. Rejoice with me that I

am well. Come. Give me the kiss of a daughter."

"Nay." The words caught in her throat. "I cannot. Your people suffered under your rule before you left, and it took over three conjunctions to set matters to right. If not for Tol—"

"You lost no time in taking a mate. And not a Selaw mate."

"You left me no choice. Had I not done so, our fortress would be ruled by Samoht!" She tucked her hands into her sleeves as he had. Every inch of her body ached with the cold. Never, not even on the ice, had she felt this chill, straight to her heart.

"What do you here?" Her father offered his hand again, but she could not reach for it.

"I could ask you the same question."

He drew himself up very straight and lifted his chin. "I am Cidre's consort."

Ardra shook her head in denial, but knew that what he said was true.

"I wear the Black Eye, a great honor, the mark of my status here. It is our hope that we will soon have a child. I believe Cidre is breeding."

"What are you doing out here? Why are you not with her?"

He turned to the lake. "I came to drink of the water. It is said to invigorate a man."

Ardra's mind seethed. Her father was alive. He was Cidre's consort. A sickening feeling lay like a stone in her belly.

"If she is breeding, what need have you of the lake water?" she asked before she could stop herself.

He shrugged. "It is a man's business and none of yours."

She saw him well, the orb-glow shining on his skin. He looked as if ten conjunctions had been stripped from him.

"Everything you do is my business. How dare you—"

But he spoke over her. "I dare because I intend to mate Cidre's child with your boy. With Cidre's abilities and my

blood, our daughter will be a formidable match for your son. And I will rule for them both until they are of age to do so on their own."

"Rule for them? You cannot even show your face." The words were arrows to her heart. He had discounted her as if she were nothing.

"I have a plan."

Ardra wanted to scream. She knew well her father's schemes.

"And should Cidre birth a son?" she asked as calmly as she could.

"Goddesses have rarely birthed sons. Now, quickly, is there anyone of your party who would recognize me?"

She studied him. When she had last seen her father, he had looked old, his amber eyes dull, his skin dry, his white hair lank and lifeless. Now, although his hair was still white, it looked thick and luxurious, swept back from his brow. He radiated energy.

Ardra shook her head. "Nay. I have only Deleh with me, and she came to the fortress with Tol. Will Nilrem know you?"

"The wiseman is here? Nay. I think not. We have never met, though he would know me by reputation."

"Samoht will only need to hear your name and—"

"I have a new name along with my new life. I am no longer Ruonail of the Fortress of Ravens. I am Venrali, consort to the Goddess of the Tangled Wood. Is she not beautiful? Is she not magnificent?" Pride shone in his face.

"Why can you not be content in this position, *Venrali*, and leave my son and me alone?"

"I am not such a great age as to be content in the shadow of a woman. As for your son, he needs someone to guide him to manhood. Who better than I?"

Ardra saw the light of ambition aglow on his face.

"Now, what do you here?" Venrali asked. "Such a feeble tale, hunting a love potion. Nonsense. Cidre was concerned

229

that you might have discovered I was here and come to unmask me."

"We seek the potion, nothing more."

Her father walked along the shore a bit, and she followed in his path as she had so long ago, as a child, when he had been a revered man, a loved one. Now he was a consort to evil.

"I am sorry, Ardra," Venrali said. "Cidre cannot help you. She knows naught of the potion. And has no need of it."

"Are you sure?"

His look was cold. "You doubt your father's word?"

Their steps led them back toward the garden gates and the fortress. Ardra searched for an answer to his question, but none came, so she remained silent. She had doubted her father's word long before his disappearance.

"I must go. I have somewhere I must be," he said. "Now that I know who is among your party, I will join you for meals. It is an omen, our meeting. It bodes well for the fortress and my return. It is good. When Cidre is delivered of her babe, I shall make my way back to the fortress and rule through your boy."

"Father, I have learned to rule—"

He patted her shoulder. "Nonsense. A woman may not rule."

"Cidre rules her fortress. Why should I not rule ours?"

A smirk appeared on her father's thin lips. "There are some aspects of responsibility a woman is suited for, but the ability to rule is a man's. Cidre appears to rule, but it is in appearance only. I rule. I will send for you soon. We shall talk about my return."

Ardra watched him slip through the garden door. Her mind seethed with emotions she could not control.

His return?

She looked up at the glowing orbs overhead. If she did not find the vial, she would find Samoht in control of her fortress. Her father would never challenge Samoht's army.

Yet even if she found the vial and was awarded rule of the fortress, her father would descend. It seemed she was doomed to be a pawn either way.

Ardra wandered, unsure where she was, unsure of what to do or what to think. How could she serve both her father and her people?

She looked around. The rich scent of apples filled the air and drew her into the orchard. There were no orchards near the ice fields, yet the ice ensured that her people knew the fruit. She huddled on the bench where she, Lien, and Nilrem had talked that morning.

The orchard reminded her of the bounty that life had to offer. She saw branches weighed down nearly to the ground, smelled the sweet scents of wood and fruit. Yet she could only shiver. If her father returned to the fortress, there would be no bounty, no sweet gift of life. Only one man's ambition would find fruition.

Her father said Cidre did not have the vial. Was he in Cidre's confidence? If the goddess did not have the potion, then Ardra knew it mattered not how many days she was given; she would fail, and Samoht would control the fortress.

And what would her father do if Samoht took the fortress?

Would her father try to rally the Selaw behind him? Would it mean war? What would become of her son?

She touched her forehead. Was she fevered? Had she imagined her father? Would she wake on the morrow to find that the goddess had slipped another potion into her wine?

If her father was real, he could return and remain hidden, plotting in the labyrinth below the fortress.

Tears ran down her face. She would be his hostage, acting on his orders, and her people, her son, would suffer for it.

A hand touched her arm.

"Lien!"

He pulled her from the bench and into his arms. His voice was soft and low at her ear. "What the hell are you doing out here?"

"I—I could not sleep," she said.

"You're freezing." He ran his hands down her back, then set her away from him.

He pulled off his cloak and wrapped her up before leading her to the small door into the fortress and across the hall. His grip was unyielding.

They reached her chamber. The door thudded against the wall when he flung it open.

"Didn't I tell you not to go anywhere without a guard?"

"You said around the fortress. I went to the orchard." Even she heard the quiver in her voice.

"Come here," he said, gently this time.

"I took a walk to think. I have only three days left, you know. And why were you and Ollach not here to guard me as you claimed you would be?" Better to attack than defend.

"We were delayed by old Sam. He ordered us to the stables to work with the horses."

"The stables! You are not grooms."

"Ralen had disappeared with Einalem or I'd have refused the order. As it was, I figured that if I refused, I'd be facing another challenge. I assumed you would remain *safely* with one of your men, but when Ollach and I came back, we found everyone in bed and your room empty. Why didn't you wait for one of us?"

"I am sorry," she said.

His pack sat on her table. Across it was draped a robe. A pilgrim's robe.

"Lien." She picked it up. The wool was coarse, scratchy. She clutched it to her breast and whipped around. "Do not do this."

He shook his head.

Tears welled in her eyes. "Not yet. Not now," she whispered.

"I have to make a decision, Ardra."

"Not this one." She held out the robe. "Choose to remain as you are."

He took the robe and draped it over his pack.

They met in the center of the chamber.

"If you leave me, I will have no one." She took off his fur-lined cloak and dropped it on the floor.

He said nothing. She covered her mouth with her fingers.

"Ardra." His hands fell on her shoulders. She pressed her face to the beat of his heart.

He tipped up her face, skimmed her mouth and wet cheeks with his thumbs. "I want to touch you so badly."

"Lien." She wrapped her arms around his neck.

They rubbed foreheads, cheeks, then lips. She held him close, drawing in his breath, his taste, reveling in the scratch of his dark beard. He lifted her and kissed her between her breasts. She held him, her arms tight around his head.

"Do not go, Lien. Please, do not go."

"I'm not going anywhere." He placed her on the bed.

Her robe fell back, baring her breast and leg, but she did not close it. Instead, empowered by the look on his face, she reached up and tugged his belt open. The smooth leather slithered through her hands, heavy and warm. He shed his tunic.

She could wait no longer. She cast his belt aside, climbed to her knees, and wrapped her arms around him. His skin was hot wherever the tracery of knotwork appeared.

With a boldness that suddenly came easy, she ran her hands over his shoulders, his throat, followed each caress with her mouth. From one moment to the next, her cold dread faded along with the red lines on his body.

The heat of his hands drew her mouth to his wrists, to lick across his veins, to press a kiss on the disappearing symbol of ancient goodness.

233

She sat back on her heels and looked up at him. His eyes were dark pools of uncertainty. "I want more than kisses, Lien," she whispered, and tugged on the laces at his waist.

He watched her hands, breathed the flower scent of her, no longer fought the flicker of flames stoked by her touch.

She made a small throaty sound when she stripped his pants down over his hips. When she gathered him into her palms, her mouth was greedy. He threw back his head, gasping, wanting to be inside her, wanting what was not going to be—ever.

"Ardra. Ardra. Stop."

She fell back onto her heels, her amber eyes wide.

He cupped her face and licked her lips, ran a thumb over her nipple. A guttural, animal sound came from his throat.

She lay back as he came down over her.

She saw all of him, saw the long line of his body from smooth dark chest to paler waist, to the line of dark hair on his belly that led to the thatch around his manhood. She palmed his stomach, moved her hand over him, touched forbidden places, wanting the exploration to last all night.

"Why did you stop me? I want to feast on you," she said.

"Oh, my God." He shook his head. "No. No. It'll all be over in an instant if you do."

"Nay, Lien. I want to learn this art of lovemaking." Her fingers ran over him. "All of it. Now."

He groaned and guided her head with his hands. He lost sight of his protests. Forgot why she shouldn't. Buried his hands in her hair. Fell back, conquered.

She caused almost as much pain as pleasure, learning what made him moan and what didn't. Every touch of her fingers, lips, teeth, every lick of her tongue, made him want to scream. It was unbearable and perfect at the same time.

Then it was over. Exquisite ecstasy twisted through him like a strike of the snake on his arm. It burst through his

system, a sweet venom pouring out of him. It paralyzed his breath, his mind, his every sense.

"Lien." She moved up him and straddled his body. Her hair fell in a tangle, pooled on his chest.

He stared up at her. A pulse beat visibly in her throat. Flames from a candle flickered in her gold eyes and glossed her wet lips. Wet from him.

"Did I please you?" Her voice was a hoarse whisper.

"Beyond the power of words," he managed to say.

He wrapped her up and rolled her beneath him, her silky robe caught between them. He shifted the gossamer fabric off her hip to touch her. Her flesh was hot and slick, swollen. He imagined her taste, her scent.

"Oh, Lien," she said, and buried her face against his chest. "Teach me what else I may do to please you."

"Your turn," he whispered at her ear, but she pulled out of his embrace and sat up.

"Nay, Lien. I want to give you more happiness."

Cold thoughts doused his ardor. "Ardra. Do you think that if you please me here in bed, I'll stay with you?"

Her eyes shifted away.

"Damn it. So this was—"

"From my heart, Lien. Nothing more."

"Sure." He moved her hand off his thigh and stood up. He paced the chamber. Her silence screamed the answer he dreaded.

When he reached the bed, he lifted her chin and ran the ball of his thumb across her wet lips. "You've never done that before, have you?"

Her negative was no more than a shimmer in the gold fall of her hair.

"Great." He sat down and dropped his head into his hands.

She knelt beside him and touched his knee. He could smell her. Flowers. Woman. Heat.

"What is wrong?"

235

"Look, Ardra. A man wants to think that when a woman does something as intimate as what you just did, it wasn't a payment for services rendered."

"Is that what you think? I am paying you as I might when I hand a purse to Ollach or . . . or—"

"Exactly. Here's how I see this. You think, 'Gee, maybe if I lie down for him, he'll stay.' "

Ardra pulled the robe about her. "Your words are hard."

"You're that desperate?"

"Desperate?" She climbed off the bed and walked away from him. She was desperate, but not as he implied.

It was on the tip of her tongue to tell him of her father. But the words would not come. If it got about that her father was alive, Samoht would have him captured and killed. She might not want her father to rule, but neither could she be the instrument of his death.

"I must tell you how desperate I am, Lien. I have but two more days. Each movement of the shadow on the sundial marks the time until Samoht takes all I have. If you want to understand payment, understand how I paid for my people at my mating ceremony. What I did with you, I did with joy in my heart."

Lien stood and tried to take her into his arms. She avoided him, hugging her waist, stepping away out of his reach.

"Cidre told me about your mating ceremony. It was barbaric."

"Killing men and women to enlarge the boundaries of one's chiefdom is barbaric."

"Can we start this conversation over again?" he asked.

"Which one? The one where you tell me that what I did insulted you, or the one where you tell me how pathetic and desperate I am?"

"The one where I humbly apologize for misunderstanding."

A smile traced her lips. "We have not yet had that conversation, Lien."

"Then I'll start. I insulted you. I humbly apologize."

"I do want you to stay. I will not pretend otherwise."

He took a cautious step toward her and was thrilled when she stayed in place. "And I want to go back to the spot where we were a few moments ago before I put my foot in my mouth."

She smiled. A real one this time. "Impossible. Your feet are so huge."

"Come here."

Ardra stepped into his embrace. Her shoulders were stiff, her back rigid under the sweep of his hands.

"Ardra, what you did to me was . . . words can't describe how it felt."

He boosted her onto the table. Some of their frenzy had died. He wanted it back.

Before she could object, he lifted her hair away and kissed her throat, edged her robe off one shoulder, kissing the flesh he bared.

"Lien." She stroked her fingers through his hair. "What you will do to me—is it payment for your mistake just now?"

"What?" He straightened up and frowned.

"You were about to give me happiness, were you not? Were you doing so because you are sorry you insulted me, or because you truly desire me?"

"Ardra. You think too much. Try to be more like a man. We hardly ever think." He put his hands on her knees and moved them apart. "I think it's pretty obvious I desire you."

Her gaze dropped. She shook her head, and her hair flowed over her shoulder. Her eyes widened.

"I really like your hair," he managed to choke out.

"Some men would say it is not the lovely color of a Tolemac woman's."

He scooped her up, and she wrapped her legs around his waist. He deposited her on her back on the side of the bed. "Some men must be mad," he managed when he sat

237

back on his heels and contemplated her body, displayed for him, the lavender silk robe half on, half off, one breast exposed, one covered. He felt humbled.

He leaned forward and kissed her inner thigh. "If I give you happiness, it's because you've renewed my belief that a woman can be as good inside as she is beautiful outside."

Her thighs quivered. Gently, so he didn't scare her, he lifted her legs and placed over his shoulders. When he touched her, she gasped and locked her hands in her robe.

"You must be magical," he said before sliding his fingers over her swollen flesh. "You've conjured some sense of responsibility out of my hard, cold soul. And cured my rash."

He blew against her skin, held her hips for a carnal kiss that arched her off the bedding, hard against his mouth.

"Lien," she wailed. "What are you doing to me?"

But he couldn't answer. Her essence seduced him, the scent of her, her taste, the gasps from her lips as he touched and kissed her.

He fought the need to stand up and push himself inside her, won the battle only because after she came, she sat up abruptly and wrapped her incredibly hot hands around him and pulled him between her breasts.

A pearl necklace it was called.

And he would remember it forever—her amber eyes wide, the lavender silk robe half off her shoulders, her nipples small, hard marbles, and the drops of his essence across her skin.

Chapter Eighteen

Ardra watched Lien sleep. He reminded her of an exhausted child lying on his belly, his arms and legs stretched out so she had but a small corner of the bed to claim.

He had long limbs and strong muscles. All signs of his injuries had disappeared, though his skin was far from flawless. There were brown dots clustered on his shoulders and sprinkled through the dark hair on his legs. She resisted an urge to run her fingers in one continuous journey from his shoulder to the callused sole of his foot.

She could not sleep any longer. It must be near sunrise. Two days left.

She edged her way from beneath his arm.

"Where are you going?" He hooked her wrist.

"To bathe."

He released her to the task, but rolled over, drawing a fur over his body. She felt his scrutiny as she bathed in the cold water of her basin. Each sweep of the linen cloth reminded her of the touch of his hand and mouth. Aches tingled in the oddest places as she patted her skin dry. When she placed the block of soap in her coffer, she saw her silver pendant.

"What's wrong?" he asked.

When she returned to the bed, she showed it to him. "This is not just a pretty bauble. It is the key to negotiating the labyrinth beneath my fortress. My son hides there now."

"You have a labyrinth?"

"It is not truly mine, Lien. It existed long before the fortress was built. Many suspect it was made by the ancient ones to escape the cold. There are hot springs beneath the ice. A man could hide there for years and never be found."

He closed his fist over hers. The pendant's edges were sharp in her palm, as sharp as the pain in her heart that her father would return and undo all she and Tol had accomplished for her people.

Lien said, "It will all work out. We will find the vial and cut Samoht off at the pass."

She dropped the pendant over her head. It lay on her chest as his glass roses lay on his.

"Where do we look next? We have searched the herbarium. I have Deleh listening to gossip. What hope is there? Cidre must be persuaded to give up the vial—or tricked into it, for I have nothing with which to bargain."

"If Nilrem is correct and Cidre is looking for a new consort, she must have someone in mind. It's not as if caravans of prospects were coming by for her approval."

It was on the tip of Ardra's tongue to tell Lien that her father was Venrali. How she wished to lay her troubles before Lien, to ask him what he thought would become of her father when Cidre cast him aside. And tell him, too, her fears of her father's fury if he was passed over for another man.

But she couldn't tell Lien any of it. It would mean revealing all the shame of her father's reign at the fortress, all the shame of his final days. Then Lien might think what Nilrem sometimes said. "Like father, like daughter." Would she be painted with the brush of her father's crimes?

Instead she said, "There may be no caravans of prospects, but there are so many here *now* who might please her. You, Ralen, Ollach, other warriors."

"But to use the potion against us would be dishonorable. I can't speak for Ralen and the others, but I'm not going to be Cidre's boy toy."

Ardra touched his cheek. He cupped her palm and kissed it.

"Boy toy? Such unusual phrases you have in Ocean City! You are a riddle," she said. "You profess no wish to be involved, but when you speak, you are so decisive." She sat on the edge of the bed. "Men can be that way. They can say, 'This is what I think, or this is what I will do,' and everyone accepts the decision because the words are spoken by a man."

"You said Tol allowed you to rule. Didn't you speak your mind?"

Ardra jerked her hand away. "Allowed? He did not *allow* me anything."

"I'm sorry if I offended you. Again." He sat on the edge of the bed, the fur over his lap.

She bowed her head. "You need not apologize. It is what most men would think."

"Ouch. I don't like to think of myself as most men."

"Aye, Lien. You are not as other men. You say things no Tolemac warrior would ever say. You . . . are so alien to me and what I know.

"As much as I might wish to take credit for all the good that has come to pass in the last three conjunctions, I cannot. Tol used the force of his position to bring order and peace to the border. Then he taught me to rule."

"And you want that responsibility?"

"Who else can take it?" She stood before him clad only in her hair, and yet felt more naked inside than she ever could on the outside.

"Hand it off to someone else," he said.

She shook her head. "I cannot."

241

Ann Lawrence

He put out his hand.

It was symbolic of what he had told her to do. *Hand it off*. She could not. And he wanted no part of her dilemma.

To take his hand meant only a physical giving. She knew he wanted her. But she had not the will to place her hand in his, to drain all her strength in such a way again.

When she did not move, he slowly dropped his hand to his lap.

"Lien, I may not have shared Tol's bed, but I shared the table when he judged the matters of the fortress. Over time, he deferred small matters to me, so my people would begin to accept my decisions. They distrusted me not only for my womanhood, but for being my father's daughter."

She put on her robe, now a wrinkled mess. "At first the matters involved the women or servants; then they became more complex matters of mines and treaties."

Lien shrugged. "Better you than me."

"You said you were once a warrior and now a merchant. How did you choose that path?"

"Oh, I went to a huge city, like the Tolemac capital, and sold something called stock—shares in businesses that make or sell other stuff. But I hated the job. Then my mother got sick, and it seemed a good excuse to leave that job and return to Ocean City. It gave me a chance to go back to school and learn to do something more appealing—like teaching. Graduate school, it was called."

"You went to school with children?" She tried to suppress a smile, picturing Lien on a bench before a wiseman.

"Where I'm from, there are schools for all ages. You can keep learning even into old age. However, I had to quit school—my mother took so much of my time—so I looked after her and worked in a shop I own with a woman."

"You owned a shop with a woman?"

He touched her chin. "Close your mouth. Yes. Where I come from, a woman may own a shop. You know the owner. Gwen."

Ardra gasped. "Gwen? Vad's Gwen."

"The same."

Ardra clasped her hands and touched them to her lips. "I prayed they had survived. So, it is possible?"

"What?"

"To cross the ice fields?"

"That statement says you don't believe me. Maybe I am what Samoht said—just a runaway slave."

His eyes were cold. She took his hand. His fingers did not close around hers. "Nay, please, Lien. I believe you, but you must realize that what you say is the same as if . . . as if you said you had come down from one of the moons. 'Tis so hard to accept."

"Accept it, Ardra."

And she knew, in that moment, that he could be as unyielding as any other man.

"Lien." She stared into his dark eyes. "Do not be angry that I am doubting. I doubt everything. Everyone."

His shoulders shifted. He pulled his fingers from hers, and she felt the rejection almost as a physical pain in her breast.

Then he reached up and tugged on her hair. "Come closer."

The temptation, his physical arousal, a need for his strength, drew her down on her knees by his side.

He stroked his fingers through her hair. "You are far too vulnerable. You need to grow a shell."

"I may have no shell, Lien, but I have one thing. I am right and Samoht is wrong. Should not right triumph?"

"Sadly, if often doesn't."

She needed to change the subject or she would weep for the loss of her freedom and that of her son. "Tell me about your crossing, Lien."

"I can't tell you. I don't remember what happened. I just woke up here."

"But Gwen and Vad crossed. What tales did they tell?"

"Yes, they crossed, but it is an experience that leaves you without any sense of how it happened. I guess the cold affects your brain or something."

243

"If Samoht believes you are from beyond the ice fields, it is no wonder he is so anxious to take my fortress. It puts him in control of the way across. Is it not true you have fantastic weapons there?"

"We have some pretty devastating weapons, yes."

"And those weapons could subjugate us to Samoht's will."

"He's not going to succeed. The ice is too treacherous." Lien tucked some of her hair behind her ear.

"You are living proof he can do it," she said. "You need never fear he will kill you, Lien. To do so would be to lose the one being who could lead him across the ice." She bit her lip. "Could Samoht convince you to take him across the ice fields? To gather those weapons and return to conquer us?"

A tear ran down her cheek. He skimmed it off with his thumb and touched it to his lips. She must not let him see her weakness.

"No."

"What a simple answer. But life is never simple. What if he put you to some terrible test? Threatened to cut off your—"

"Shhhh. Just stop. Let's deal with each problem as it develops. Concentrate on the Vial of Seduction."

A terrible thought swept through her.

"Did you sell those weapons, Lien?" she whispered.

He cupped her face and brushed his lips across hers. "I didn't sell weapons. I sold games."

"Games?" She pulled back and stared at him. "You jest."

"That's what I sold. Games."

"Such as the one Samoht and Ralen played in the hall?"

"More or less. Where I'm from, there are more games than you could possibly count."

"I have no time for games."

"Neither do I."

He pulled the fur from his lap and let it slide to the floor. She felt heat rush through her. He was aroused. When he took her in his arms and drew her down on her side, she forgot her resolve to keep her distance.

"Ardra."

It was all he said. His mouth said the rest. He cupped her buttocks and pulled her against his rigid manhood. This time, she mimicked his actions, spreading her palms on him. Would she ever again feel the wondrous sensation he evoked with each caress of his hands and lips?

They rolled over one another, mouths hungry, trying to remove her robe, but only knotting it more securely. She ended up flat on her back with him on top of her. Laughter died in her throat when he finally released the tie and spread the silk open. His gaze was as tangible as a touch on her breasts, hips, and thighs.

She needed to bite the coverlet to stifle a cry as he ran his hands over her.

Then he put his hands on her knees and separated her thighs. He explored her with his fingers, each touch spreading warmth and anticipation. He kissed her breast. Heat flowed from his mouth like a fire that had jumped its hearth.

She smoothed the soft short hair around his ear and squeezed her eyes shut. A moan escaped her lips as he found the slick wetness within her. The languid caress of his fingers became more urgent, moving in and out of her in deep strokes. A small harbinger of that greater sensation rippled through her, and she arched against the thrust of his fingers.

"I want to be inside you," he said. He stared into her eyes, his so black in the dim light they were like an abyss, a place to be lost in forever.

She saw the dark hair of his beard, the strange hole in his earlobe. Fear and desire entwined through her being, as knotted together as the design on his arm.

"It is not possible," she whispered. "If I bore a child—"

245

"You would be in deep trouble," he finished for her. His hand fell still.

All she could do was close her eyes against his intense scrutiny. "If I quickened, Samoht would use it against me. I would be called wanton—may yet be if he learns you are here with me now."

She held her breath waiting for Lien to withdraw, but instead he drew her on top of him, settled her thighs about his hips so she straddled him, and nestled his manhood against the wet folds of her femininity. She shrugged off the robe, letting it drop to the floor.

He lifted his hips. His eyes closed, his lashes thick and black on his cheeks. She saw the serpent on his arm shift and ripple as he gripped her hips and held her down. This time she felt no fear.

She leaned over to kiss the warm column of his throat. He entwined his hand in her hair as she licked along his shoulder, his arm, to the snake.

A swirl of heat and energy surged through her body. He gasped, and his hand tightened on her scalp. He tried to move away.

"Nay, Lien. There is something between us. Some magic."

"I don't believe in magic." His shoulder and arm muscles were clenched tight, his fingers in a fist.

"Nor do I." She explored not the design this time, but the contours of his fine musculature. His muscles tensed and flexed as she laved his skin. She lingered in the warm hollow of his elbow, licked the skin there, breathed in his scent.

When she returned to the snake, she was ready for the surge of heat, absorbed it into her being, and knew they were as connected as the lines that twisted along the snake's coils.

Sweat broke out where his skin touched hers. He held her hips. Her skin was so white in contrast to his hands

and chest; the hair at the apex of her thighs was gold against his black.

She rocked on his manhood, soothing an ache between her thighs that made her feel wanton, wild, and wonderfully wet.

When she gripped his arms, her hands spread over the design, anchoring her against the storm building within.

The strange pulse ran from her hand straight to her heart. It rippled down to where their bodies touched so intimately.

"What is it like to be inside a woman?" she whispered.

"Like being in a very warm, snug glove," he said. Then he arched, pushing up as she pressed down. He cupped her breasts and captured her swollen nipples between his fingers.

Ardra hung on as heat whipped through her. "I feel it. There is something happening between us."

"It's all in our heads, Ardra." Then he arched again and gasped.

He spent himself, but she did not see it happen, nor know it.

Her heart had stopped beating. Her world had gone white hot.

When she could speak again, Lien had left the bed. He was using her basin of water, hastily, not looking at her. She stretched and pulled a coverlet near. It was wet, and a moment later he took it from the bed and dropped it beside her wrinkled robe and the other garments Deleh would have the washerwomen tend.

"Does every glove fit every man?" she asked.

He covered her with a fur, but he seemed distant now. His eyes did not meet hers. "Sure. Men are pretty indiscriminate."

So, only she found what they had done unique. "Have you worn many gloves?" She wanted to snatch the jealous words back into her mouth.

247

"Not too many . . . all things considered." He pulled on his breeches and laced them.

"Lien. It is best we not do this again. We might . . . complete the act next time. I cannot bear a child without a lifemate."

"What happened to all your talk of herbs?"

"Do you wish me to ask Deleh to get them for me?"

Lien smiled, but he looked at the pendant around her neck, not her eyes. "No. Not necessary. You won't need them."

Lien sat on a chair by the door and waited for Ardra to wake. He probably shouldn't have let her fall asleep again, but she'd looked exhausted.

And he had needed to think.

Finally, she stretched, yawned, and sat up. "What are you doing?"

She shook her hair from her face. It cascaded all around her, and it was her hair, so wild, her small breasts pushing through the mass to tempt him, that told him he was doing the right thing.

It was as inevitable as the rising of the Tolemac sun outside that he'd come inside her next time. Then he'd be so tied in knots he'd never get untangled.

"I'm going to put on this robe." He nodded to where the robe lay over his lap, his stick on top of it.

"Nay," she whispered, and knelt on the end of the bed.

He had watched her sleep, how she had tossed restlessly, so filled with energy, needs, and frightening possibilities.

"Why?" She bent her head and clasped her hands on the edge of the bed, not trying to cover herself in any way. She had grown too comfortable with him, shared too many intimate acts.

"To make you understand, I'm going to tell you a story. A true story. I once had a lover named Eve. We both thought we'd get married—that's lifemated to you." He

ran his hand over his head. "Let's see. How do I make you understand?"

"Aye, Lien, you must make me understand."

"Then my mother got sick, not old-age sick, but something lingering, something not solved in a day. There's no one to look after her but me. She's . . . self-destructive."

He slid his hands along the smooth stick. "And let's say my intended lifemate can't understand how responsible I feel. That I just can't let my mother wander off into oblivion without trying to help her. Let's say that woman finally says, 'Choose,' and I pick my mother instead of Eve. What do you think about that?"

"I think you have an obligation to your mother. Your lifemate should understand that or she is not worthy of you."

He raised his eyes to the ceiling. "Yeah. Maybe here. But where I'm from, it didn't really work out that way. Eve left me. She said my mother had made her own problems, and I needed to let her find her own solutions."

"I do not admire your intended, Lien."

"Yeah, well. I told Eve I wanted to feel that I'd done everything I could. So Eve left."

"I am sorry, Lien."

"I feel like I'm at that same decision point again."

"I have not asked you to choose."

He sighed. "I've come to realize over the past few days as I've watched Ralen that he wouldn't run away from the challenge of helping you. He might stick with you for reasons that are self-serving, but he would stand by you. So I feel I have to do this, see this quest thing through." He touched the robe.

"But why as a pilgrim?"

"That's the other half of my story. See, where I come from, things are not black and white the way they are in Tolemac. Here, something's honorable or it's not. Something's right or it's not. I've been sitting on the fence as if I were at home. I've been saying, 'Okay, I don't want any

hassles over my lack of arm rings, so I'll hide behind the idea I'm a pilgrim.' That's what I've been doing, Ardra. Hiding who I am."

"And who are you, Lien?"

"I'm either a pilgrim or I'm not. I'm not going to be *unknown* any longer."

"Lien. You can't do this. Put aside the robe—"

"Stop. One day you'll meet the perfect man and he'll—"

"The perfect man. Not you," she whispered.

He walked over to the bed and pulled her up into his embrace. "Earlier this evening you asked me not to leave you, and I said I wasn't going anywhere. I meant it. I'm not leaving you."

"But why a pilgrim?"

"Because I'm not going to sit on the fence anymore. I'm going to put on this robe and *be* a pilgrim, with all the problems and deprivations that come with that status. It's the only way I can help you. If I remain as I am, I will make love to you again."

"Love. Was it making love?" she asked. A tremor ran through her that he might love her.

"Call it whatever you want, either way you will suffer because of what we do here. Samoht will use your behavior—sleeping with a man who's not your lifemate—to prove you're not the fine woman I know you to be."

So it was merely copulating, not lovemaking, to which he referred. The room was suddenly cold. "Lien—"

"If I don't choose this path, Samoht is going to challenge my status again, and I'll no longer be able to help you."

"You bested him at the feast."

"I didn't best him. I took advantage of your advice and the fact he'd had too much wine. Next time, he'll insist on swords. And he'll be sober."

She shook her head. "To kill a pilgrim is—"

"Bad luck. True, and you said he won't kill me because he might be killing his only way across the ice fields, but I

saw his face when I knocked him down. He wants blood. He won't let anything stop him."

"So you will play the pilgrim."

"I will not be playing. As long as you have nothing to bargain with, you have only the vial to save your fortress. And while you search for it, I'll try to protect you."

The pilgrim robe would separate him from her forever. Tears welled in her eyes, so she turned her head away that he would not see her grief.

Nothing to bargain with . . .

Lien was wrong. She did have something to bargain with now.

Cidre hummed a song as she dropped some morning dew into her persuasion spell. Ardra must be put out of the way. It was obvious that Lien would never accept his place as consort if Ardra remained available.

A shiver of desire ran through Cidre's veins, a desire she had not felt with any man—ever. It was so strong, she had to pause and lean on the table to wait for her body to return to a serene state.

It was Lien's dark hair, his nearly black eyes, that drew her. What powers the Daughter of Darkness would have if she was conceived of such a man's seed.

After the persuasion spell simmered precisely one rise and fall of the night orbs, she could put her plan into action.

Cidre lifted a goblet and sipped another, more bitter, brew. She must be sure that no child already took root within her. No child of Venrali's could equal one of Lien's.

Lien would not easily come to her bed. If she had been able to get to him before he'd spilled his seed over Ardra, then perhaps the usual persuasion spell would have lured him to her.

But it was too late to rue such misfortune. Deleh had told her of Ardra's time with Lien. Deleh was so easily persuaded. Cidre had needed little of the spell to get Deleh to turn over her mistress's secrets.

Now Cidre knew that even if Lien and Ardra were under the persuasion spell, they might not do as she directed. Ardra might not refuse Lien's advances, and even if she did, Lien might not turn to another. The spilling of seed between lovers created a powerful lure of its own, hard to counteract.

A knock came at the door. Cidre glanced about. There was nothing to indicate she was preparing a persuasion potion.

"Come," she called out.

Einalem, garbed in a turquoise and ivory gown with chains of gold at her waist, glided into the herbarium. "I bid you good day." As was proper, Einalem curtseyed and waited for the touch of greeting on her shoulder.

"Sit. Rest a moment while I finish my work," Cidre said.

Einalem curled her feet beneath her as she sat in Cidre's favorite chair, a broad one with wide arms. "What are you brewing?"

"Oh, just something for one of the kitchen boys who burned his thumb." Cidre lighted the wick beneath the persuasion spell, then stood back with a smile of satisfaction. For a moment she lost herself in contemplation of Lien's passion. She could almost taste it on her tongue.

To cover her delight, she drew up a stool. She sat lower than Einalem to give her a false impression of importance.

"Now"—she patted Einalem's hand—"how may I help you?"

"I have done a very bad thing. Or a good thing, as some may view it."

"Ah. Am I one who will be pleased with what you have done?"

"Aye. You see . . . that is, I have the Vial of Seduction."

"By Nilrem's knees!" Cidre forced herself to show the proper dismay. Why had she not guessed? And how could Samoht be so blind as not to see the thief in his own nest?

A little tear ran down Einalem's cheek. "I regretted it the instant I took it. You see, I had shamefully peeked in

on the council session the day they were discussing the fate of the treasures." She chewed her thumbnail. "It tortured me, that potion. But I *did* resist for a very long time."

Cidre held Einalem's hand still. "What made you succumb?"

Einalem leaped to her feet. "I could no longer stand it. All around me, men and women are making love—feeling some tender emotion that eludes me."

"Surely you have many fine lovers? Ralen? Is he not one of them? He is very fine."

"Ralen!" Einalem said. "It was Ralen who pushed me to steal the potion." She sank into the chair and leaned forward. "It is Ralen who is to blame. If he had but understood the great honor accorded him if he lifemated with me . . . but nay, he must reach higher. It is his fault, is it not?"

"Oh, aye. 'Tis Ralen's fault. How could he not want you?" Cidre smoothed a finger over Einalem's furrowed brow.

"I do not understand what went wrong. I please him in bed. But he makes love as he makes war—"

"He is cold."

"As cold as Ardra's ice."

"Then it is not your fault," Cidre said. "It is a fault of Ralen's that he cannot give you his heart. And so, you stole the Vial of Seduction to turn Ralen's heart warm."

"Aye. I knew just the size and shape of the bottle. I asked my brother to show me the treasures, and when he was not looking, I substituted another, similar bottle. It was almost a conjunction before anyone noticed the switch."

"But the potion has failed."

"I have used it on Ralen twice. There is so little of the powder left that I feared if I did not seek advice, I would waste it. When I heard that Ardra was coming to you for the vial, I was amused. Then I thought 'twas an answer to my prayers. You alone might be able to help me. When Ralen insisted he should escort Ardra, I begged to come

along. I thought you might help me find a way to make the potion work."

"What of your brother? Has he any inkling you have the potion?"

Einalem's eyes welled with tears. "Samoht has no idea I have the vial. He is sure you have it."

Cidre looked at the potion bubbling on her table. It was like water to the power of the powder in the Vial of Seduction.

Once administered to Lien, Ardra could crawl on her knees naked to him and he would kick her aside. The image snatched Cidre's breath.

"I will help you use the potion, Einalem, but for a price."

"Some of the potion."

"Ah. You understand the value of what you have."

"I will share, but can you make the potion work?"

Cidre took Einalem's hand. "You poor woman. Did no one tell you that only an honorable person can use the potion? Just by stealing the vial you ensured you could never use it."

Einalem's shock amused Cidre. What a stupid woman. To steal something without understanding its true nature.

When Einalem had recovered, there was a tremor in her voice. "How will we make it work, then? How? It seems impossible."

Cidre found it amusing that Einalem assumed she, too, could not use the potion. She said, "Oh, I shall find an innocent to administer the potion for us."

"How can any woman, innocent or not, give the potion to a man, exchange a kiss with him, and then stand aside to allow his seduction by another?"

Cidre stood up. She adjusted the wick beneath her persuasion potion. "I will think of something. Come here after the midday meal on the morrow and I will have an answer for you. Ralen will soon be yours."

Einalem went to the door. On the threshold, she turned back. "Oh, Cidre, it is not Ralen I want anymore. Nay. I have found another."

Cidre shook her head. Inconstant woman.

"I feel as if I will die of the want if I do not have him. He invades my thoughts even when Ralen is in my arms."

"Who is this man more alluring than Ralen?" Cidre asked, though she cared little.

"Lien. No other will do."

The air hissed into Cidre's chest. She gripped the stirring stick so she did not thrust it into Einalem's eye.

Cidre waited until the door closed to give way to her anger. She threw a dish of flax seeds against the wall and stabbed a goh carcass again and again. Finally, she calmed. "Oh, Einalem, you will die of want. For you shall not have him."

Chapter Nineteen

Lien took a deep breath and walked to the grotesque hearth, Ollach in his wake. The day was very new, the light just filtering into the hall. A few torches still smoked in the wall brackets. Cidre, on her carved throne close by the warm hearth, sat amidst her new best friends, the fawning pilgrims.

She was garbed in a pale green gown much different from her other loose dresses. This one was fitted from stem to stern. A lacy gold chain encircled her waist, the ends falling to the hem of her dress. The lush body promised in the loose dresses was realized in this one. Her hair had pale green threads wrapped around some of the strands.

Ralen and his men had ranged themselves about the hall, their black and white in harmony with Samoht's strictly black-clad men. Einalem must still be in bed, and Nilrem snored on a bench in almost the precise place he'd been found yesterday.

When Cidre greeted Lien, the hall fell silent.

"Have you made a decision, Lien?" Cidre asked him.

"I have." He bowed to the goddess.

Samoht, who sat at the table near Cidre, picked his nails and affected a look of boredom. The effect was ruined by the two-foot-long dagger embedded point down in the table by his elbow.

The sight of the dagger cemented Lien's resolve.

Tomorrow Samoht might go after Ardra with something sharper than his raised voice and overwhelming personality.

Lien made a show of laying out the pilgrim robe before Cidre.

"So you eschew the pilgrim life," Samoht said. He brushed his nail parings off the table, scattering them at Lien's boots.

Lien didn't answer. Instead he undid his belt, placed it beside the robe, then took off his tunic.

Samoht frowned. A few serving women gasped when Lien pulled the pilgrim robe over his head and settled the hood down his back.

"Stick," he said, and Ollach slapped it into his hand as an operating nurse might.

"So you go, Pilgrim?" Cidre said. "I am sorry. I found your company amusing. As did others, I am sure."

The goddess looked up, and he followed her gaze. Ardra stood at the top of the stairs, garbed in the long gold column she'd worn the first time he'd stepped over the invisible boundary—the invisible boundary that Ardra was starting to recognize. The invisible boundary he had been too jaded to have thought important until he'd stepped across it. Her face was a portrait of want and need.

He turned away.

Samoht pulled the long knife from the table and sheathed it. "Aye. We will be sorry to see you go."

Lien smiled. "Oh, I'm not going anywhere. I'm just changing my clothes."

"What are you saying?" Samoht rounded the table and stood toe to toe with him. Threads of red in the whites of

Samoht's eyes testified to the world-class hangover the man must have.

"I'm saying I'll be here for a while yet. Nilrem said I was to stick by Ardra's side, and that's what I intend to do. And in case anyone forgets my status, I thought I'd follow your advice, Samoht, and take advantage of the kind offer of this robe."

Cidre threw back her head and laughed. "You are a puzzle, Lien." Then she turned to Pointy-nose. "It seems our friend will not be completing his pilgrimage at your side. I bid you good journey." She pressed her hands together palm to palm and curtseyed to each pilgrim in turn.

Her dress really hugged her every move. Pointy-nose looked as if he had a little fire going on under his robe, but he dutifully moved off with his comrades.

The pilgrims strode away as a unit, and Lien could not say he was sorry to see them go.

He looked up at Ardra. Did she regret what he had done?

Her face was expressionless, her back ramrod straight. Ardra, the woman who could rule a fortress, now stood there looking determined. Turning her back to him, she disappeared from the hall.

"Everyone sit. Sit." Cidre clapped her hands "Eat."

Lien shook his head when Cidre swept out a hand, inviting him to sit by her side. His skin, clear of the rash since Ardra's embrace, now prickled with the harbinger of its return.

Instead he walked to the lowest position at the far end of the table—a seat that placed his back to the door—a pilgrim's kind of seat. Ollach settled at his side, saying that Ardra had ordered him to suffer the same indignity as Lien by sitting in a position reserved for the least of diners.

Lien smiled. He wanted to appear to Samoht as the least of men. One who might have bested a councilor when that councilor was drunk, but not one to worry about when sober.

Underestimation was one of Lien's few weapons.

A trail of serving men and women brought out platters of bread, cheese, and fruit and ewers of wine and water. As Lien raised his cup of water to his lips, a ripple of sensation passed down the hall. His heart began a little dance when he lifted his eyes to the top of the stairs.

Not Ardra.

Descending the stairs was a tall, thin man with a magnificent head of white hair. He wore a dark green robe open over a loose tan tunic and buff breeches. Around his neck he wore the heavy gold chain and black gem Cidre had worn the night of their arrival.

The Black Eye. A symbol of evil, according to Ardra.

Everyone jumped to his feet. Cidre walked to the foot of the steps and dropped into a very deep curtsey. The man placed a hand on her head. When she rose, they walked side by side to the high table. Before they sat, Cidre kissed the man on each cheek. The motion drew Lien's eyes to her consort's.

They were Selaw amber.

Lien realized he'd stopped thinking of Ardra's eyes as anything but beautiful. Now he noticed them again as something that separated chiefdoms.

"I am so pleased," Cidre said, "to present my consort, Venrali."

Venrali bowed, kissed Cidre's hand, and bade everyone to sit. Lien observed the man with intense curiosity. Finally, he had met the goddess's mysterious sperm bank.

"What a bore for a beautiful young woman to ride such an old mount," Ollach whispered.

"That is disrespectful to your mistress."

"Ardra? She was given no choice. This woman chose deliberately."

"Then maybe she loves him."

Ollach coughed into his wine goblet. "A man loves his concubines, not his mate."

Lien saw Nilrem yawn, stretch, then head in their direction.

Nilrem pushed his way onto the narrow bench on which Lien sat. The wiseman prodded every piece of fruit and sniffed each cheese before nibbling on his selections.

"What do you think of Venrali?" Lien asked.

"What do you think of a woman who chooses such a man?" Nilrem countered.

Lien shrugged. "Maybe they're in love."

"If she is truly the Goddess of *Darkness*, she is evil and he may be as well. It would be prudent to be wary of them both, though she may be the more deadly."

"I think Venrali looks pretty fit for a man his age."

Nilrem patted his chin with the end of his beard. "I would like to be so fit. Then I could have such a beautiful woman to tend to my needs."

"So you wouldn't kick Cidre out of bed?"

"Me?" Nilrem cackled a long laugh, then began to cough and choke, spraying bread crumbs across the closest diners, a few of Ralen's warriors. They shot ominous looks at him.

Lien said, "Whatever illness kept Venrali hidden away until this moment doesn't show."

"I need not tell you that some illnesses are not very apparent to the naked eye. Still, he looks remarkably healthy. Do you think he might have been hiding for some reason?"

Lien chewed the nutty bread. "Why should he hide? Unless old Cidre is poisoning him at a slow rate. You know, found a way to knock him off so she can consort with a new consort—"

Nilrem clutched his sleeve. "That is it."

"Shhh," Lien cautioned, but no one was paying attention to them. He quickly ate a few more slices of bread and cheese as well as three apples. "Where's Ardra?" What kept her hidden? Her anger with him for choosing to be a pilgrim?

"Searching for the potion. Everyone is here save Einalem. What a wonderful opportunity to go through coffers—"

"Searching!"

Nilrem clamped a hand on Lien's arm. "Do not jump up like a suitor whose robe is afire. You cannot rush off after her."

"Why not?" He jerked his sleeve from Nilrem's grasp.

"Do you think she will appreciate your faith in her to manage her fate, let alone that of her people, if you cannot leave her alone for an hour?"

Lien picked up a fourth apple. He took a bite, but it was ashes in his mouth.

Ardra must make her own way.

"What about this idea you have that I should stay with her until she saves my life? How can she save me if I'm sitting here with you? I might choke on this apple."

"Oh, I do not interpret such things. Hush now. The goddess has something to say."

Lien opened his mouth, but closed it. Ardra stood again at the top of the stairs, frozen, her eyes on Venrali and Cidre.

Cidre tapped her dagger on her gem-encrusted goblet. Ardra remained poised, one foot on the step, her hand on the newel post. Lien willed her to look down at him, but her gaze was fixed on the high table.

Cidre said, "I wish to celebrate Venrali's return to good health and the arrival of our most illustrious guests from both Tolemac and Selaw with a magnificent hunt."

A burst of cheers and clapping resounded about the hall.

Cidre smiled, and when the noise subsided, spoke again. "We will hunt the boar. Eat. Eat that we may make our way into the forest without further delay."

Oh, great, Lien thought. *A boar hunt.*

Ollach leaped up and hurried to Ardra to act as bodyguard. Lien felt more than a tad jealous, but Ollach wore a sword whereas he only had a stick.

261

Ann Lawrence

"I'm staying here," Lien said to Ralen, who had drawn near. "We pilgrims don't like killing little forest creatures."

"Little?" Ralen laughed. "A boar is not a little creature. And if we take the goddess's totem, the sow, 'twill be the best of omens for us all."

"And what of Ardra's need to find the Vial of Seduction?"

Ralen planted his hands before Lien on the table. "There is no vial to find. It is gone. Or if it is here, it is hidden away where no one can find it."

Lien shrugged.

"Ardra will not be hunting a vial, she will be hunting boar. I intend to take her with me and watch over her," Ralen said.

Damn.

Chapter Twenty

A knock turned Samoht away from his maps, but when he saw Einalem in the doorway, he went back to the parchments.

"Brother, we must speak."

Samoht looked up. There was a touch of agitation in her voice that made him pause. "Come, sit." He set aside his map and took a chair while she perched on the end of the bed.

"I have something to tell you. Something that will anger you, but I pray you will listen and try to understand."

He leaned forward and took her hand. "You have been angering me since we were children. Why should this day be any different? I shall still love you."

"Oh, Samoht. I have changed my mind about Ralen."

Samoht grinned. "*That* I could have predicted from the moment you first took him to your bed."

"Did you know he wants a chief's daughter?"

"Of course. I tried to tell you that when you first saw him, but you would not listen."

Einalem slipped her hand from Samoht's and went to his maps. "You are still trying to figure out where we are?"

"Aye." He joined her and pointed out the area he had marked with an ink tinted red. "This is where we are supposed to be, according to Ralen. But there is no rise in the land, nor a lake. He says we must correct our maps. I say we are farther east." He tapped the map.

"There are no lakes there either." Einalem shrugged.

"The mapmakers will charge me a fortune to survey and correct the mistake, no matter which of us is right."

"Make a wager on the matter with Ralen. If he truly believes he is right, he will take the wager. If he is not sure, he will not. Then you need not go to the expense of sending the mapmakers, just change the map to suit what you think."

"You did not come here to discuss maps, nor to tell me you are tired of Ralen. What have you done to make me angry? Get it out on the table." He slapped his hand to the table top to emphasize his impatience.

"I have known for more than a day who has the Vial of Seduction but never told you."

His heart began to beat fast. If this was true, he could have Ardra as his concubine, a willing lover, even washing his feet in the hall should he wish it.

"You have disappointed me, Einalem." He kept his voice calm and controlled. "Tell me everything."

"The goddess has the vial, as the slave gossip said, and I have made a bargain with her to show me how to make use of its precious potion."

"Indeed," he said. He would have Ardra's fortress without a drop of bloodshed.

"Why do you smile?" she asked, sitting on his bed.

He swallowed the grin. "Why, I have just realized that if you can get Cidre to use the Vial of Seduction, she has solved the honor problem. How has she done it? Tell me."

"Cidre will not tell me. She merely said she knows the answer to the riddle."

"So, you were able to get her to admit she has the vial?"

"Aye. Are you not proud of me?"

"Greatly so. Why did you fear I would be angry? Why, I shall put it to the councilors that you be rewarded. You have made real what was naught but slave gossip until this day. Would you like a legacy of land in the chiefdom of your choice?"

"Oh, I will think of something."

She did not meet his eyes. He wondered what she was not telling him.

"Just as there will be rewards for the vial's return, so there must be punishments," he said. "How did Cidre get the vial in the first place? Which councilor stole it?"

Einalem shrugged. "She would not say, but I suspect 'twas Tol, and he is certainly beyond punishment. He probably tried to trade it for some elixir to cure his illness. Sick people can be desperate."

"There is more to this, is there not?" He grasped her chin and forced her to look at him. "You have done as Ralen could not, Sister. You do realize that? You have gotten Cidre to admit she has the potion."

"I have." She looked at the center of his chest.

"We must persuade her"—he chuckled over his choice of words—"not to admit the truth to anyone but us. That way, we can let the eight days flow by and Ardra's fortress will be in my power without a drop of bloodshed."

"I have already convinced Cidre it serves no one to admit she has the vial. I told her even you must not know."

He lifted a brow. "Why may I not know?"

"Three can keep a secret if one of them is dead. Has not Nilrem said that often?"

"Ah. That is true. So you told Cidre it will be—"

"Something between women only," she said.

"And how did you discover Cidre had the vial?" Samoht watched his sister's face. She bit her lip and looked at her hands.

"While making a salve for Lien's rash, I had an opportunity to look about Cidre's herbarium. I recognized the

bottle." She looked up and met his gaze. "You showed it to me once, remember?"

"Aye, and a good thing, too. Were you alone when you found it?"

"Nay, Brother, Lien and Ardra were there, but they were too intent on his rash to suspect what I had learned. Ralen would have found it had he been trained to recognize what was out of place in a healer's realm."

Samoht frowned. "So I should have sent you with Ralen the first time. You did suggest it, but I ignored you."

"Aye," she looked up, and her face registered her anger. "Aye, Tol allowed Ardra to make decisions beyond a woman's place. Why do you never see that my thoughts have value?"

He cupped her face and kissed her nose. "Because you so often come up with something ridiculous like wanting to bed some highly inappropriate man. That shows me you are ruled by womanly desire, not reason."

She jerked away. "And you are not ruled by your manhood?"

"Nay, Sister. And I pray you have not come to tell me you want some inappropriate man in your bed."

Einalem hugged her waist. "I have asked Cidre to persuade Lien to my bed."

Samoht caught his breath. "Lien?" He forced himself to remain still and calm.

"Aye." Einalem gripped his arms. "I cannot eat or sleep for the want of him. Cidre has persuasion spells she can use to make him amenable to my advances, but they are not powerful enough for lasting seduction. I need the vial for that."

"Then you have not yet used the Vial of Seduction on him?"

"Nay. She has yet to give it to me."

Samoht shook her off. "Why would she? Why would she not keep the potion for herself?"

"When I told her I had seen the vial, she was quick to bargain with me for my silence. She will require some gold, perhaps larger shipments of ice."

It annoyed Samoht to see Einalem evading his gaze. There was something hidden here. "Let me see if I understand. Cidre has promised to use the Vial of Seduction to bring Lien to your bed. Am I right?"

"Aye."

He walked away from her to the long window that looked out over the lake. He pushed open the shutters to take in a breath of air and calm himself. "It is a waste of a treasure, Einalem. A waste!" he shouted, his anger slipping free.

"It will not be wasted. Please—" She backed toward the bed. "I will not allow it to be a waste."

Samoht strode to where she stood. He gripped her arms. "To give some of the seduction potion to a vile slave is a waste." He lowered his voice. "You are as base as the fornitrix who ply their trade on the bathhouse steps."

She burst into tears. The sight of her tears, so rare, so copious, shot a dart of shame to his heart.

He pulled her into his embrace. "Einalem, I have never forbidden you any man's favors. But never have you chosen so unwisely. The man is surely a slave, no matter that he wears the pilgrim robe."

"He also wears your roses."

With a slight push, Samoht set her away. "That is the only reason I did not kill him at the feast. I will stay my hand only until I discover how and why he wears them." He shot a hand out to the window. "They are made of glass, according to Nilrem. Glass! We have few who can make the substance into large pieces for windows, let alone such a tiny gemlike creation. It is another reason you should distance yourself."

"I cannot. It is my belief the roses are a sign I should pursue him. It is your symbol, Brother."

267

He shook his head. "You will make a fool of yourself. He is a man unlike any you have seen, that is all. It is his odd hair color. I once saw a woman much like him. She caused chaos, and we lost a valuable warrior because of her. This man reminds me too much of that one. Evil she was, and evil Lien may be."

"Lien is not evil." Einalem clasped her hands together in supplication. "I never ask you for anything. I ask you now for your indulgence. Let me have him."

"Let you have him? Is Cidre not going to use the Vial of Seduction to help you? What need have you of my permission? It sounds as if you have already done what you wish."

"I will not use the potion without your permission. Have I not always sought it when the man is—"

"Unsuitable? Let me see, how many have there been? A simple warrior with no lineage. A warrior who wishes a chief's daughter? My stable master? How many must I name?"

"You have indulged me in all these matters; why not now?"

"Do not whine." He walked to the maps and unrolled the largest one, which showed the eight chiefdoms. "The chiefs have no sons to whom I might mate you. There are no brothers free. That unfortunate reality is the cause of your unrest. You have tired of Ralen, having sought his bed too early in the game." His insides felt as if he had swallowed a cinder from the fire. "I am going to give you an order, and I will have you stripped and flogged in my hall when we return should you defy it."

Einalem gasped. He turned and pointed his finger at her. "You will use the Vial of Seduction to bring Ralen to the question. And only Ralen. I will see that he takes Tol's seat whether he wants it or not. You will then be mated to a councilor. Your children, if you can still birth them after all the herbs you have taken, will be raised to rule. If I find that anyone but Ralen has warmed your bed . . ."

268

He paused and watched her eyes narrow. "Nay. You will try to get me on my words. If I find that any man but Ralen has spilled his seed within you, I will have you publicly flogged and the man castrated."

She dropped to her knees. "I no longer want Ralen. I beg of you. Do not do this."

Her pitiful entreaty left him unmoved. "Enough of the playacting. You were never one to beg. You came to me and told me of your desires and now must live with the consequences of my decision. When Cidre gives you the seduction potion for Lien, you will give it to Ralen instead. Drink of it yourself, by the gods, and have done with it."

Einalem rose and flew at him. She struck out at his face with her nails. He caught her wrists and held her off. "Shall I send for Ralen now? You can spend this anger on him. Claw his back, bite his neck, but forget Lien."

She struggled in his grip for a moment, then went limp. "I will not be able to forget Lien."

"Then I will have you flogged. I most enjoy a woman's flogging. In fact, I am thinking of ordering Ardra punished when her eight days are over. I will call her to the center of Cidre's hall and tell her how disappointed I am in her failure. Then I will have her stripped and whipped."

He felt a hot surge of arousal at the thought. The idea of Ardra held by two of his warriors, arms outstretched, as a third punished her hardened him. Perhaps he would wield the whip himself.

He set Einalem away. "Do you understand me? You may not give the seduction potion to Lien."

"You are just jealous." She rubbed her wrists where he had gripped her arms.

"Am I? Not about Lien."

"Aye, you are. Ardra wants him, and you cannot bear that. You challenged him because he stood in your way. I heard what you were about in her chamber." She tossed her head and ran for the door. She fumbled at the latch.

269

Ann Lawrence

Samoht realized he had not gleaned the most important information from her yet. And now, after his harsh words, he might never have it. He ran after her and planted a hand on the door to hold it closed. "Forgive me. I do not know what possessed me to be so hard on you."

She stood, her hand on the latch, unmoving, stiff with anger.

"Come, let us strike a bargain," he said.

He drew her away from the door. Her head was high, her pride challenged.

"If you will secure the seduction potion for me so I will have Ardra as a willing concubine, and if you will use it on Ralen yourself, I will see that the council gives you a most attractive reward."

"What reward?"

"Lien. I will have the council declare him a slave, no matter his pilgrim status."

"How does that help me?"

"If the council declares that Lien is a slave, he can be given to you. He will be yours to do with as you wish. If he tries to flee, we shall have him shackled. I believe he has worn chains before. Did you see the redness on his neck and wrists when he fought at the feast?"

Einalem put out her hand. He took it between both of his.

"Promise me, Samoht, that you will keep this promise. Else I will spend my life with a man I no longer want."

"I promise. You will be a councilor's lifemate and have the man you most desire in your bed whenever it suits you."

She kissed his cheeks and smiled.

Now for a bit of chatter and then he could ask the most important question. "Are you ready for a hunt? I have not taken a boar in many a conjunction."

"One of the ills of ruling, Brother. One must spend so much time in the capital."

Samoht threw up the lid of his coffer. He drew out a black cloak stitched with a border of red roses. "I believe I shall wear my personal emblem today."

"Shall I wear it too?" Einalem asked.

"That would please me. What do you think Cidre will wear to the hunt?"

"Something green."

They shared a laugh, and Samoht knew she was ripe for his question. "So, whom do you think Cidre will give the seduction potion to?"

"Not the old man. Deleh told me she heard Ardra say the goddess needs a daughter to carry on her work. Perhaps the illness that kept Venrali from our table the first night has prevented him from getting her with child. It is said he has worked at it for several conjunctions to no avail."

"Hmmm. Then Cidre stole the potion to seduce a new consort?"

"Deleh thinks so. She says Venrali has angered the goddess, or so the kitchen slaves say. He has fathered at least two sons on slaves. Deleh thinks the goddess must choose a new consort before she is too old to raise and train a daughter. It takes a lifetime, you know—"

"Aye," he interrupted her, not caring about goddesses and daughters. "I am sure 'tis a long process. But whom do you think she wants the Vial of Seduction for?"

"Whatever man she can find who has proven he is virile and can produce a female child."

"That could be any man."

"True. I suppose any virile slave would do. But Deleh says the kitchen slaves believe the man must be special. He must be a powerful match, her equal."

"There are few to equal her status."

Einalem went to the door. She pulled it open and smiled back at him. "I cannot think of many who would fit her requirements. A councilor would do. A warrior of Ralen's status, perhaps. Why, you are not only a councilor, but you

271

have proven your mettle on Boda. You have a daughter."

"Nonsense. Cidre cannot mean to use the potion on me."

"Why not? I would watch what you eat and drink, Brother."

"What a ridiculous notion. If she used it on me, I would slice her throat." Despite his words, he felt a shiver of distaste. He glanced at the map table and the goblet of wine he had been drinking.

"But if you are seduced, Samoht, you will not want to kill her; you will want only to bed her."

Samoht stared at Einalem a moment. "What you say holds merit. I shall have one of my personal guards taste my food and drink."

Einalem left, and Samoht returned to his table and the allure of his maps, dismissing Einalem's concerns from his mind. He smoothed his hands over the map of the eight chiefdoms. There on the edge he saw the border between Tolemac and Selaw.

"Aye, Einalem, I shall give Lien to you as a personal slave. He will be compliant to your wishes as you will be compliant to mine. When all of this is over, when Ralen is lifemated to you, I shall take your very compliant slave and direct an excursion across the ice fields. Lien can show me the wonders of his chiefdom. And then we shall see how long the Selaw hold out against me."

Chapter Twenty-one

The hunting party made too much noise, in Lien's opinion, to catch a damned thing. They were a formidable quantity of people that included at least a dozen slaves and one packhorse. Any self-respecting boar within twenty miles had long since found a nice cozy hiding place.

Cidre, her hair braided into loops and covered by a gauzy green veil, kept up a running commentary on the trees. Some were pines, or tall oaks, a welcome straight line among all the matted twisting of the other trees.

Nilrem jostled along in his saddle, looking as miserable as a rider could be. Venrali listened to the goddess as if he'd just arrived yesterday and repeatedly asked for some woodland fact. Samoht and Einalem, dressed like twins in black with lots of roses splashed on their hems and sleeves, oohed and aahed, asked questions, pointed, and generally sucked up to the goddess.

Ralen had fallen into a hard silence. Ardra rode beside the warrior, likewise silent unless someone spoke to her directly. Her back was straight, her hair a sheet of gold down her back. Lien imagined she must be screaming in-

side, to spend the last of her eight days on a boar hunt.

As far as Lien was concerned, it was not a hunting party but a social ride through the trees. He wondered what the true purpose of the journey was.

Lien decided it was time to find out what was going on, but Venrali lifted his hand and the party halted in a broad glade filled with coppery sunlight. Bright white streamers of cloud floated in the purple sky overhead.

At Venrali's order, everyone dismounted. Ralen muttered under his breath as the slaves dashed about setting out cloths and opening saddlebags containing roasted birds and fruit.

Lien could not eat. Ardra walked right by him to Samoht. Lien watched her touch the councilor's sleeve and sweep out a hand in the direction of the horses. The two strolled over to the string like best friends. What the hell was going on now?

Ardra looked up into Samoht's lean face. He was comely if one looked beyond the lines that years of frowning had etched on his face. "I have a bargain for you, most Esteemed High Councilor."

"When a woman uses my title, I grow cautious," he said. He rubbed the nose of his horse, a horse the color of thick cream, a horse whose saddle had red roses carved into the leather.

"I use your title so you will know it is a council bargain I want to make."

"Go on. My curiosity is piqued."

"I want to trade myself for an assurance."

His eyes grew wide. "Indeed?"

"I could wait until the morrow to admit I will not find the Vial of Seduction." She wondered if she had his full attention as his gaze flicked to where Einalem sat alone in a pool of black skirts with red roses on the hem. Ardra hurried on, "But we both know how likely it is that I will fail. So I thought I would make my bargain now."

Samoht dragged his eyes back to her face and said, "If I wait until the morrow, I will have your fortress without making any assurances."

"But you will not have me. Not willingly. Not wanting to please you. Whenever. Wherever." She lifted her chin and dared him to make a biting insult as was his habit.

He said only, "What assurance do you want?"

"I want you to write out an assurance that upon its signing, you will withdraw your army and go home. Leave my fortress under my rule to be governed by the treaties already negotiated by the council."

"And for this *written* assurance, I get you."

"Aye." She kept her eyes on his face and forced herself to forget Lien and every moment in his arms.

"Unconditionally." Samoht raised one eyebrow.

"Unconditionally."

"As my concubine? Available to my every whim? When I withdraw my army, you go with me? Openly?" He reached out and ran his fingertips along her cheek.

She forced herself not to flinch. "Aye, I will leave a regent to rule for as long as you desire me."

"I will think about it. You ask much. I am not sure you are worth it." He walked away.

Lien watched Ardra and Samoht. The councilor looked like a fox who'd made it into the henhouse. Ardra looked as cold as her ice.

What the hell had gone on between the two?

Samoht strode back to his sister. A slave offered them fruit, and Einalem laughed over something Samoht said as he plucked an apple from the bowl.

Lien thought about the alternative to being a pilgrim in this world. *Slavery*. Handing bowls of fruit around, or worse, sold anywhere to anyone for whatever purpose. If slavery appeared to be his lot after Ardra's eight days were over, he was going to leave. Permanently.

There wasn't much in Ocean City to draw him home, but he would be of little use to Ardra in chains.

Did he want to be of use to Ardra after this? And how could he sleep at night in Ocean City worrying about her here in this world?

Even if he avoided slavery, he had little chance of passing himself off as anything other than what he now was—a man on a pilgrimage. He had no skills with weapons other than a stick.

As for allies . . . Ralen would follow Samoht's orders. It was what soldiers did. Nilrem would only commiserate and advise. Ardra would do what she must to save her fortress from Samoht.

She would do whatever she must. Bargain with the devil if need be. *Damn.* Lien cut across the clearing toward Ardra.

Cidre intercepted him. "You do not eat, Lien. Are you not hungry?" She smiled at him. She rubbed a finger across her lower lip. The rash on his neck and wrists flashed hot; darts of pain ran down his back.

"Thank you, but no, I'm not hungry." He sidestepped her and joined Ralen, who headed for his horse, which was tethered to the one Samoht had ridden, just one of many in a long string.

Ralen refused a cup of wine a slave offered him and said, "I wonder if this boar hunt is an excuse to close the forest, trapping us all here."

"How can someone close a forest?" Lien looked overhead and imagined the branches leaning in on one another, locking together in one solid mass.

Ralen lowered his voice. " 'Tis said the goddess can cause the paths to vanish, the vines to choke each passage. 'Tis said a victim will wander until he starves to death. Some say they have seen hapless victims roped to the trees in vines."

"Why are we standing here, then?"

Ralen shrugged. "We have little choice. Samoht certainly gave *me* no choice about joining this hunt. It is a waste of time. Cidre has led us around in circles."

"Can I ask you a question?"

"You are full of questions."

"If a pilgrim wears only this robe, what does he do when it gets really hot outside?" He resisted an urge to claw at his neck where the robe chafed his rash.

"He sweats," Ralen said and grinned.

"Great."

"Look—"

"Where?" Ralen asked.

"No. I didn't mean actually *look*. I meant . . . never mind. Ardra and Samoht were just talking. I think some agreement was made between them. He looked way too smug when she walked away."

Ralen's whole body went stiff. "Agreement? What agreement could they possibly—"

"Exactly. What bargain would they—"

"She has nothing to offer except—"

"Herself," Lien finished as the idea popped into his head. His stomach lurched almost as if he were on a roller coaster. "I'm going to talk to Ardra." He shoved past Ralen.

Men burst from the trees. They rushed in from the far side of the clearing, swords and axes raised.

"Rebels!" Ralen shouted.

Lien whipped around. Ardra was across the clearing—too far away. *Too far.* He set out anyway.

Einalem screamed and threw herself at Samoht. Cidre stood frozen beside Venrali. Ollach swept Ardra behind him.

Every warrior drew his sword and met a rebel head on.

Noise burst over Lien, his way clogged with fighting men. Shrieks and screams echoed through the clearing.

He ducked beneath the rope holding the horses. He dropped to the ground, crawled to his horse, and jerked his

staff from the saddle. When he shoved his horse's rump aside, he stared in disbelief at the carnage around him.

The attackers slashed and chopped at Ralen's warriors. The clearing swirled in a chaos of men and swinging weapons. Lien was pinned near the stomping hooves of the heaving string of horses.

Einalem and Cidre huddled together behind Samoht. The councilor held off two rebels with ferocious slashes of his sword.

The horse behind Lien reared. He pivoted just in time to see a hairy man raise an ax. He thrust his stick up under the man's arm into his chest and snatched the ax as it fell. He heaved the ax into the dense woods.

He felt a blow reverberate along his stick into his hand and shoulder.

He staggered around. Another man raised an ax; Lien jammed his stick into the man's throat. Blood gushed from the wound. With a look of surprise, the man collapsed on his back.

Another marauder ran at the horses, who reared and slashed with their huge hooves. Yet another man crawled on the ground toward the mounts, a knife ready to cut them free.

Lien cracked his stick down on the man's wrist. He howled and scrambled back amid the horses' hooves. In moments, the man was a bloody wreck.

Ralen's men formed a protective shield around the women and Nilrem. The warriors fought, outnumbered two to one. Then Ardra pulled out her eating dagger. She plunged it into the arm of a man who had breached the warriors' defenses. The man howled.

Cold cascaded through Lien. He used his stick to move forward—to fend off another rebel's advance on the horses.

There was no way to get to Ardra. Slaves huddled between her and him. Undefended slaves. Slaves cut off from the rest of the party.

A rebel turned on the slaves, his ax upraised. Lien stepped behind the attacker and jabbed his stick into the man's kidneys. The man dropped to his knees. An intrepid slave with a gap-toothed grin bashed the gasping man on the head with a stone.

A moment later, the end of Lien's stick was lopped off by the swinging blade of another rebel. It happened in slow-motion, the blade sweeping down, leaving the stick half its former length.

Lien raised it to parry another blow, then at the last moment rolled aside. The rebel turned on the cowering slaves.

Two warriors ran past the slaves and joined the defense of Samoht and Einalem.

The charging rebel grinned through his ragged beard. He gave a low laugh and slashed at the slaves with his sword, taunting the men who were unable to defend themselves.

Without thought, Lien swung his stick across the back of the man's knees. The rebel fell. When he rolled onto his back, Lien planted his boot in the man's groin.

Another rebel rushed the defenseless slaves. Lien faced him.

He held the howling rebel off, parried the man's sword blows, jamming his stick up under the man's swinging sword.

Suddenly the rebel reeled back, and Lien hit him in the chin. The man sagged, blood gushing from his mouth, and lay still.

The gap-toothed slave jerked the sword from the rebel's grasp. He joined Lien in holding off the rebels attacking either the horses or the slaves.

The rebels fought with ferocious intensity, driving the women and warriors along the path. The ragged company howled and pushed, slashing their axes indiscriminately into the flesh of horses and men.

Einalem broke from the circle of protection. She ran across Lien's path. He grabbed her cloak and tossed her

behind him into the kneeling slaves just as an ax embedded itself in a tree by her head.

A giant man with a huge sword ran like a madman after her.

Lien met him, just as he would an opponent running full-tilt toward the goal. They hit in a clash of bodies. Lien parried every sword thrust with his stick, using only instinct to hold the man back. If the rebel got by, the slaves were dead.

Lien's stick shattered, carrying him backward to land with a thud on his back.

The giant raised his sword and grinned. Then his eyes went wide. He slapped his hand to his neck where a small blade protruded. Lien took the opportunity to lift the shattered end of his stick and crush the man's hand. His sword fell from his grip. With a gurgle of anger, he bent down, groping for his blade.

Ralen ran up and with a mighty swing of his sword, ended the rebel's life.

The warrior thrust his dagger into Lien's hand. But it wasn't needed. The rebels had lost their will with the giant's death. They backed away, disappeared among the trees, and sprinted off on nearly invisible paths.

Cidre ran to Lien. Her eyes were bright blue and wide, her hands questing over his bloody robe. "Did he hurt you?" She glanced at the giant by Lien's feet.

"No. I'm fine. But others aren't." Lien carefully disentangled himself and set her aside, removing the acid burn of her hand.

He turned in a haze and looked for Ardra. She knelt by a warrior, bandaging an arm. Something ferocious inside him settled.

Then he saw it—the small dagger protruding from the giant's neck. Lien's legs were suddenly shaky. He bent over the giant and jerked the blade from the man's neck.

It was Ardra's eating dagger. Adrenaline pumped its way through his body again. *Ardra* had thrown the knife. And saved his life.

He wiped the blade on his sleeve, walked straight to Ardra, and touched the crown of her head.

She looked up. Her amber eyes were liquid gold, wide, not dazed like those of the injured man she helped, but determined.

"Thank you." It was all he could say as he gave her back her knife.

Ralen walked by them toward a horse that had managed to get loose. He stumbled. A hole yawned at his feet. Lien grabbed for Ralen's tunic. They slithered in wet leaves straight toward a void. The horse whinnied and scrabbled backward.

The ground gave way—straight into a pit.

It was over in moments.

Lien stared up at the purple sky. Shocked faces stared down at him from the rim of the hole. He tentatively moved his limbs. A groan nearby shook him out of his lethargy.

When he took a deep breath and sat up, he saw Ralen on his side, blood in his hair.

"Ralen, are you all right?" Lien crawled to the warrior. His eyes were wide open, and for a moment Lien thought he was dead. But Ralen groaned, and his eyes closed in a brief spasm of pain. "Where are you hurt?" Lien asked. His own body felt bruised and battered.

He realized there were rocks beneath a thick mat of muddy leaves. Ralen shifted to his back, and his left hand shot out to grasp Lien's arm. He closed his eyes. For Ralen not to speak, he must be very hurt, impaled on his sword perhaps.

"Is he alive?" Samoht called from above.

Quickly Lien ran his hands over Ralen's tunic, searching for blood, seeing only what stained his hair. But his arm was bent at an awkward angle.

"He's alive, but his arm's broken."

Samoht swore.

"Can you sit up?" Lien asked. Ralen nodded but didn't move.

"Damn." Lien looked up. The pit had sheer sides cut with a digging tool, not caused by a collapse of nature. "Is this some kind of boar trap?"

"A man trap," Ralen said, then hissed in his breath.

Lien stood up and called, "Make some rope out of those vines and get it down to us. Be quick about it." The fear that the rebels were rallying their forces made him order the onlookers as if he were in charge and not Samoht.

"Do you want me to do something about this?" He touched Ralen's arm.

"Nay. Leave it to the women." Ralen opened his eyes, then licked his lips.

Although Ralen's face had not paled, there was a look about his mouth that told Lien that speaking was an effort. Sweat slicked his brow, but his skin was cold. He was going into shock.

Lien elevated the injured arm. Ralen's body jerked and his eyes opened wide, but he made no sound, his lips clamped shut.

"Sorry. I had to raise your arm; your fingers are really swelling."

"Thank you." Ralen grimaced. "I will have someone's head for this."

"We have that same expression where I come from," Lien said.

"It is not an expression. I will have someone's head for this." Then Ralen grinned. It was not much of a grin, but it was a sign he was not slipping into unconsciousness.

"So this is where the rebels were herding us," Lien said.

"I believe so. They would have culled the ones they wanted and left the rest of us to rot."

Samoht looked over the edge of the pit. "We are dropping rope and vines. The women have conferred over Ralen's injury, and Nilrem will instruct you."

Nilrem gave quick directions. Lien pulled Ralen's belt from his waist.

Ralen groaned, his eyes closed.

"Look. Nilrem says I'm to tie up this arm or there's no way you're getting out of this pit."

Nilrem looked down from the rim, nothing but a nose and a thatch of wild gray hair. "We need to get you out as quickly as possible lest the rebels return." There was a quiver in the wiseman's voice.

The bloody garments a warrior tossed down must have come from a corpse. But beggars can't be choosers, so Lien used Ralen's dagger to slash one of the tunics into strips. He padded Ralen's arm with the other. While Lien worked, the warrior said not one word, but sweat dripped down his face and his skin was clammy cold.

Next, Lien lashed Ralen's arm to his chest. The warrior groaned as Lien moved the limb, but did nothing to hinder the effort. Lien wondered if Ralen would be able to get to his feet.

A thick braid of rope and vines dropped at Lien's side. He tested the line and hoped it was tough enough. Ralen was no light weight and neither was he.

He heard a rustle behind him. Ralen was struggling to his feet. He swayed a moment, then with visible effort straightened up. Lien said, "Don't pass out on me now."

Ralen gripped his arm. "This was a planned attack." He leaned heavily on Lien and groaned, then said, "Did you notice it was women and slaves who were the targets?"

Lien shook his head. "I barely saw beyond my stick."

"You have to get out of this pit. Now. Protect Einalem; I am useless like this." Ralen's hand grasped Lien's sleeve again. "Let some of my men get me out. You must get up there and tell Samoht my suspicions. Cidre has to be behind this."

"I can't believe it." Lien made a sling out of the braided vines and rope for Ralen, then made a similar one for himself.

Ann Lawrence

Ralen's men hauled Lien up the steep sides. Mini-avalanches of mud showered down as he scrambled his way over the top.

Once there, he instructed one of Ralen's men to go down into the pit and aid Ralen. He outlined the safest way to haul an injured man out of a pit, pretending he knew what he was talking about when, in truth, he had no idea if the warrior was even strong enough to hang on to the rope.

While a trio of men worked at getting Ralen out of the hole, Lien looked for Einalem.

She knelt by a wounded slave. As Lien watched Einalem work, he saw a shiver in the tangled roots beside her. He snatched up a rock and pitched it hard into the foliage.

A strange thrashing sound burst from the foliage along with a jet of slimy fluid. It cascaded over Einalem and the wounded man.

Einalem fell across the slave in a dead faint.

A creature burst from the tangled roots.

A dragon. A six-foot-tall, scaly, green dragon with a barbed tail.

Lien stared in disbelief. All about him, slaves and warriors alike stood in silence. Some warily began to back away. No one spoke.

A second creature, half again as tall as the first, emerged from the greenery. It swung its head in Einalem's direction. A viperlike tongue flicked out to test the air.

"What next?" Lien muttered. He glanced about for a weapon. The damned creature had talons. It shifted closer to the prostrate Einalem. The slave beneath her rolled his eyes.

In another moment someone was going to move and the things would attack.

Something did move—in the trees and vines behind the dragons. A snake. Then another. And another. They were three long ropes of slick, shiny black, with red, hooded eyes. They twisted their diamond-shaped heads in Lien's direction.

284

The dragons did, too.

Lien concentrated on the serpents. His tattoo pulsed as if the veins in his arm were suddenly too narrow for his blood.

One dragon thrashed its tail, smacking the roots behind it, causing the slave beneath Einalem to shriek.

The dragons thundered forward. Slaves and warriors trampled each other, shouting, running, stumbling over one another to escape. The dragons charged the clearing, past Einalem, past Lien, after the running men.

Lien pointed to the dragons and shouted, "Stop them."

Like magic, the black snakes dropped from the trees and skidded along the ground. They darted between the dragons' feet. One moment the dragons were charging slaves, the next, they were biting and hissing and spewing slimy fluid on the black vipers at their feet.

The first snake swelled. It reared its head and darted forward, biting the dragon on the neck. The other two snakes attacked it too.

The dragon shrieked. Its companion crashed into the trees, disappearing.

Lien watched in awe as the dragon turned and twisted, slashing with its jaws at the snakes that had clamped onto its feet. Men jumped away from the creature's swinging tail.

The poison worked its way through the dragon's system. The creature slowed its dance. Slime dripped from its open mouth—a mouth filled with jagged teeth. It shuddered, made one last snap at the snake, then stood still. It trembled, rolled its eyes, then fell to its side with a crash.

The snakes let go. Slaves cowered as the vipers slipped through the trampled grass toward Lien. They lifted their heads like cobras before a snake charmer. He found his hand steady when he pointed after the surviving dragon. The snakes zigzagged off into the brush.

Everyone in the clearing stood still, staring at the felled dragon. No one even looked in Lien's direction. He took a

deep breath, then went to where Einalem lay across the slave. Ardra reached her at the same time. Lien's eyes met Ardra's as he helped her pull Einalem off the slave. They placed her gently on her back. Her eyes fluttered.

The slave shook. Lien went down on one knee and checked the man's bloody arm. The slimy stuff was all over him—sticky, smelling like a sewer. Lien called over his shoulder, "Hey, bring some water to wash off this slime."

Slaves ran to do his bidding. He found himself unnecessary as Cidre and other servants bathed those who had been slimed.

Ardra placed her hand on his shoulder. "The venom can rot the skin. It is imperative we wash it off."

While the women sluiced the dragon venom off Einalem and the slave, Lien nervously checked himself for splashes but found none. Then he helped Ralen onto one of the horses. The warrior's eyes spoke eloquently of the pain he was in.

When Lien handed Ralen the reins, Ralen said. "I saw your command of the snakes. Is it something you want others to know?"

Lien looked over to where Ardra stood with Einalem, who was dressing a small wound on her brother's leg. "I don't know what you're talking about."

"As you wish." Ralen grimaced and wrapped the reins about his good hand.

"Lien," Ardra said, hurrying toward him. "You must wash. You touched the slave."

She held a pitcher. He was surprised to see it was wine she poured over his hands. It ran as red and warm as blood through his fingers, pooled in his palms. He rubbed it into his skin; then she poured the wine over his hands a second time. It splashed down her ivory gown.

"I'm sorry," he said.

Ardra met his gaze. Her eyes were full of concern. "Better some wine than the venom."

"Ardra, what were you and Samoht talking about before—" He spoke to the air as she walked away, offering the wine to some of the men who had been near the dragon.

He watched her move around the clearing, organizing the slaves and even the warriors. She designated a man to ride behind Ralen and curtly shut Ralen up when he tried to protest he was able enough to ride alone.

"We need to leave immediately," she said. "What if the rebels regroup? Or the commotion disturbed a nest of dragons, not just these two?"

A nest of dragons? Lien glanced around. Which was worse, rebels or prehistoric dinosaurs spitting venom?

Ardra mounted up behind a small slave woman who had done nothing but weep since the first rebels attacked.

Nilrem came to Lien's side. "We have treated all those who are injured; we must go."

"Looks like we're moving out now." He helped Nilrem onto the horse and climbed up behind him. The old man was exhausted, and Lien thought that if he let Nilrem go, he'd fall right off.

Nilrem craned his neck in all directions, his beard blowing in Lien's face each time he turned.

"What happens when Ardra's eight days are over?" Lien asked to distract the old man.

"Samoht takes her fortress. He will see no need to honor the treaties between Selaw and Tolemac. And why should he? He will have what Tolemac needs, a direct path to the ice fields and whatever lies beyond. And, of course, the ice. Let us not forget the joys of the ice itself." The old man whispered, " 'Tis said Einalem much likes a shard of ice rubbed on her nipples."

"More information than I need to know," Lien said.

Cidre led her horse to their side and inquired after Nilrem's health. Lien's rash heated and the ant dance began again. He could no longer deny that it was a signal of some sort.

The return was torturous, and not because of his rash. Lien suspected it took so long because to go straight back to the fortress would demonstrate that they had ridden in circles.

Lien helped carry the wounded into the hall, which quickly became a hospital.

Venrali stood on the high steps and declared to all that their attackers wanted the horses. Samoht countered with the opinion the rebels were trying to kill him. The two men argued the issue while everyone worked around them.

Ralen's words that the attack was planned ran in Lien's brain like a hamster on a wheel. What did Cidre gain if Einalem and Ardra were dead?

The sun began to set, a reminder of the carnage, dripping its scarlet gleam over trees and vines. The courtyard was deserted except for Ardra, who remained until the last man was taken inside and the last horse was assigned a groom to see to its care. It was she who ordered a group of men to return to the clearing for the dead.

Lien watched her. She knew how to lead. There was something in her voice and manner that made everyone jump to follow her directions. Even the men from Tol's guard who had been insolent obeyed her orders. That might be Ralen's doing, but still, Lien couldn't find fault with any of her decisions. This was another side of her, different from the softer woman who'd spent the night in his arms.

This woman didn't need anyone. And had probably struck a bargain with the devil to get what she wanted for her son and her people.

Not once did she look in Lien's direction for help—or to any other man either. He worked in the stable, which had an open front, so he could keep tabs on her.

She assumed a central location from which to marshal the slaves and warriors, one arm extended, pointing out tasks to be done. Her skirt was splotched with blood. Her hair was a tumble of snarls. There was a smudge of dirt on her chin.

A hard realization hit Lien like a fist in the chest. He loved the very things about Ardra that he'd sworn to Gwen did not attract him—Ardra's slim figure, her serenity, and what had appeared in the game as coldness but was in fact an incredible self-possession evident even during the attacks in the forest.

She had not run or screamed. She had drawn her eating dagger and stood her ground. It was a damned good thing he was a pilgrim, or he'd be working off the adrenaline rush of the fight between the sheets, probably making little Ardras and Liens in the process.

Then he'd be stuck here forever.

The gap-toothed slave who'd fought for a moment at Lien's side touched his arm. Lien tore his gaze from Ardra and looked down.

The slave held out the confiscated rebel sword. "Would you have it?" he asked.

Lien shook his head. "You should give that to one of Ralen's men. I don't need it."

"I think you chose the wrong path," the man said.

"What's your name?" Lien asked.

"Inund. I come from the sea." He gestured off in what Lien would call a southerly direction. "We have dragons that swim where I come from."

Great. Loch Ness monsters. He glanced nervously toward the lake. "How'd you get here?"

"My father is a free man, but enjoys the grape too much, if you take my meaning."

"Sure do."

"When he lost his living—repairing fishing nets—he sold me to our Esteemed Goddess's mother."

"I see. Did he get much for you?"

The man smiled. "A side of boar delivered once a conjunction. I have fed my family well for half my life."

"What would have happened to them if you'd been killed back there?"

289

The man lost his smile. "I suppose my father would sell my sister." He bowed and departed. When Lien looked up, Ardra was gone.

"Damn." He headed for the hall.

It was a mini-hospital. Shaken slaves poured water and wine while others huddled in corners and whispered. Einalem moved about like Florence Nightingale, while Cidre wandered, not paying much attention to anyone. When Cidre saw him, she perked right up and hurried over.

"Lien. Come. You must remove your robe and let me see if the dragon venom touched you anywhere."

"It didn't."

"It did." She pointed to his boots, and he saw what she meant. There were holes here and there as if acid had burned them. "Strip off everything," she said. "Leather is no protection."

"Later." Where the heck was Ardra? He didn't see her anywhere. And there was no way he was getting naked with the goddess.

"Later may mean death," Cidre said.

Lien heaved a deep sigh. "Thanks for your concern. Later." He walked away, through the hall, up into the corridor of chambers. No Ardra. He opened doors on empty chambers; everyone was occupied in the hall.

One door revealed an opulent chamber fit for a sultan, and he recognized Cidre's scent and Venrali's robes. With a glance at the door, Lien did a little vial-hunting, running his hands through the clothing in coffers, feeling under mattresses, looking in pots, sniffing bottles. The seduction potion could be in any one of them and he'd never know it, although he saw nothing that looked like the dirt Nilrem had described.

He flipped back the lid of a wooden box about twelve inches square. It was quite plain in comparison with the richness of the room. Inside, nestled on a green silky cloth, was a pile of rusty chains attached to wide metal bands. He picked them up and stared. It was a set of shackles.

Chapter Twenty-two

Ardra met Deleh at the door to the kitchen. Deleh held out a cup. "Come, Ardra, you have eaten nothing all day. Drink this milk or you will faint and be of use to no one."

Ardra took the cup and drank. She wiped her mouth with the back of her hand and stared into the cup. The milk tasted strange. "Deleh, did you make this yourself?" she asked.

"In the kitchen with my own hands." Deleh took the cup back.

"It has a funny taste."

"Oh, 'tis probably what Cidre added to it."

Ardra grabbed Deleh's arm. "What did Cidre add?"

"Just something to give you strength."

The door closed behind Deleh. Ardra ran through the kitchen and into the garden. She stuck her finger down her throat, gagged, and coughed up some of the milky drink. Although she tried several times, she could not disgorge it all.

She stood among the vegetables and tried to assess how she felt. Was her skin warmer? Were her hands tingling?

What of her fatigue? Was she more tired or less?

Why would Cidre poison her?

With relief, Ardra realized she felt as she always did. Lifting her hem, she went back through the kitchen and to the lower levels of the fortress.

She saw Cidre coming, a leather pouch in one arm and a basket in the other. Ardra stepped backward into the shadows and waited for the goddess to pass her. A chill air swirled after her.

Unable to resist looking inside the herbarium once more, Ardra tiptoed down the corridor and past a smoking torch.

She opened the door and froze. "Oh, I thought this chamber was empty."

A young girl stood still, a spoon in her hand, a vacant look on her face. It was the girl from the orchard. The one Lien claimed Cidre put them asleep to protect. She was beautiful.

"My name is Ywri," the girl said, smiling shyly. "Your face is very dirty. It is not pretty like mine."

Ardra touched her cheek. "I'll have to wash it." How was she going to get this young woman to leave the herbarium? "I think Cidre could use your help in the hall . . . or the kitchen," she said, fumbling for a reason to send the girl away.

Ywri curtsied and smiled. "I will go to the kitchen."

A moment later, Ardra was alone in the herbarium. She pressed a hand to her heart to still its rapid beat.

The herbarium was brightly lighted with ranks of oil lamps giving off a myriad scents that somehow blended into a soothing, sweet whole.

A mixture bubbled over a candle. It smelled and looked like stewed berries.

Ardra scanned the chamber. It was useless. Everything looked as it should. She was turning to go when a breeze kissed her cheek.

Along with it came a spicy, exotic scent. It appeared to come from a tall cupboard that held bunches of dried herbs.

With a sniff she determined it was not the stuff in the cupboard that gave off the seductive scent.

Cool air washed over her, bringing the strange scent again.

She waved the candle back and forth before the cupboard's shelves and watched the flame flicker. The breeze came from the back of the cupboard.

A line of uneven wood ran along the corner. She followed it with her eye and realized the back of the cupboard was actually a small door with what looked like a bent nail as its latch. A tug on the nail caused the shelves to swing forward away from the back wall. Before her yawned a dark, narrow space.

With a backward glance to assure herself that Cidre's herbarium door was closed, she stepped through the cupboard. To her right was a winding staircase. The air was filled with the unusual spicy scent. She mounted the steps.

The scent of the forest mingled with the spice the higher she climbed. The air grew cooler, the way more narrow. Her shoulders brushed the walls. She knew that a staircase such as this was often the one used by masons to carry materials to the higher levels as a fortress was built. But this passage was not closed off as the ones in her fortress were, nor dusty with disuse.

Nay, the scent of fecund earth and plants grew stronger the higher she went, twisting into the upper reaches of the hall. The exotic scent filled her head.

Another door, this one with an ordinary iron latch, opened quietly on well-oiled hinges and gave entry to the upper reaches of the fortress.

When she lifted the meager light of the candle up high, she gasped. Here, in this hidden space, was the rest of Cidre's tree. Far overhead, almost disappearing in the black shadows, was the flat roof of the fortress, the roof whose lines could be seen from the hill on approach. And here, confined and twisted, bent down in ponderous majesty, did the mighty branches end.

Ann Lawrence

Here were the leaves, big as her hand, some even as large as meat platters. Flowered vines wrapped around the majestic arms. The scent of moist earth drew her forward in wonder. With the candle held high, she walked across the attic floor, which was deep with loam formed from generations of leaves falling and decaying. How did the monolithic tree survive without sunlight?

She touched a bright white flower that gleamed in the light. Nestled in the petals were two red centers as shiny as gems. She held the flower close and breathed deeply of its scent. Herein was the source of the exotic smell.

She wove her way between the branches that erupted from the earth and the lovely entwining vines that looped over limbs and draped the air in every open space.

Closer to the heart of the tree, her candle lighted only a small circle of the darkness, a circle she carried with her, a warm circle in the cool and lovely space. She thought of the labyrinth beneath her fortress and thought that Cidre had her own here above her hall.

Ardra stood still. She was at the heart of the tree. Was it her imagination that she could hear its throbbing beat? A rustling sound drew her around the thick central trunk.

Lien reclined there on a twist of matted branches. He had put off his pilgrim robe and wore only breeches and boots. His breeches hugged his lean limbs. She could not tear her gaze from his spread thighs.

"Lien," she said, her mouth dry, as dry as it had been the first time he had touched her with passion.

Smaller branches, still thick and smooth, supported his arms like a throne might. She stood by his feet, her heartbeat echoing in her ears.

He smiled. How tempting his lips looked. She remembered how they felt on every part of her body.

"Come here, Ardra," he said. His voice held the husky quality of passion.

"I cannot, Lien. You have made a pilgrim vow. You do not want me. And I have offered myself to Samoht."

"Come here," he whispered.

Her candle hissed and flickered in a stir of air that rustled the leaves and lifted her hair.

Though the air was almost cold in the attic forest, sweat dripped down Lien's brow. She watched a single drop trace the hard line of his jaw, follow the long, smooth skin of his neck, and course between the honed muscles of his chest. It moved slowly, so very, very slowly, before it disappeared into the line of dark hair at his waist. She took a shuddering breath along with a step back.

She tipped some wax on a broad branch and set her candle down.

"Come here, Ardra," he repeated.

She stepped between his feet. "What are you doing here?" she asked. "How could you choose the pilgrim way? I can never touch you again."

"Come here." He lifted his hand to her.

"I can never touch you again," she repeated.

A vine slipped from a branch. It dropped across his upper arm and wrapped around it to conceal the snake design there.

Suddenly he was naked, though he had not moved.

Her throat was as dry as the Scorched Plain. Her head pounded. The cloying greenery and flower scents were as tangible as a taste. She closed her eyes. Opened them. He was still naked—and aroused.

Another vine shifted and dropped onto his hip, and she gasped as it teased his groin, ran down his thigh, and wrapped around him just above his knee.

"Lien. Move, Lien." When he merely stared at her, she wondered if she had said the words aloud.

"Lien. Move. Now." She stepped within the embrace of his thighs and pulled at his arm, but she was too weak. And he too strong. The vines shifted and slithered around him. "Now, Lien. Now. Please move." She grabbed his hand. A vine dropped on her wrist and whipped around her arm and his.

295

"Lien!" she cried, but he only stared at her.

Vines looped around her arm, hips, and waist.

His eyes were glazed, staring, the centers so huge they resembled Cidre's Black Eye.

"Lien, help me!" She slapped his face with her free hand.

Bark scraped her palm.

He was gone. Vanished in one heartbeat.

"Nay," she cried, too late to break away from the tree. The vines tightened about her waist. More vines dropped upon her, entwining her as they had appeared to entwine him. The slick vines pulled her closer and closer to the trunk. Its bark grazed her cheek.

Finally, the rustle of foliage fell silent. Her candle hissed and died.

Ardra wept. She would die here. Lost in the darkness, her fate unknown to anyone. And surely 'twas her enchantment with Lien that had drawn her into this cold embrace.

Lien knew the shackles weren't for mattress games. Venrali might agree to a little bondage, but the chains Lien coiled back into Cidre's box were a serious set of tools for holding someone hostage.

They were not a game.

He opened a door he found behind a tapestry depicting the Tangled Wood. It was a private privy. Like the more public one he used, it was a simple wooden seat on a stone box with a chute to the deep, silent recesses of the earth. Some clever ventilation system kept the room smelling pretty innocuous.

Scented dishes of oil burned in wall niches. A table held cloths, soaps, a basin, and a pitcher of water for cleanliness. He poked around some bottles filled with flowery scents but doubted Cidre would keep the vial where Venrali might use it.

He returned to the hall, but there was still no Ardra.

Venrali and Samoht continued their argument, Einalem and Cidre their nursing duties. Ralen moved among his men.

Ollach offered Ralen a goblet of wine, and Lien noticed that Ralen's good hand shook as he drank while his broken arm was now splinted and tightly wrapped in clean bandages.

A serving woman passed with a tray of folded material.

"May I have one?" Lien asked, snagging a length of cloth.

She shrugged and continued on. Lien folded the linen, which he assumed someone was going to cut into bandages, and walked over to Ralen.

"This might make your arm more comfortable." He didn't wait for permission but slid the sling under Ralen's injured arm.

"Where's Ardra?" Lien spoke softly so only the warrior could hear. "I can't find her."

Ralen scanned the hall while Lien tied the sling over his shoulder. "I have not seen her, but Samoht has not moved."

"Yeah. But he has a bevy of guards at his command."

"Granted."

Lien left Ralen and decided to search the kitchen next. Ardra wasn't stirring soup and hadn't been through there, according to one cook. He went down to the storerooms, snagging an apple, then headed deeper into the depths of the fortress, peeking in various rooms. Most were simply for storage.

In one room he found a young girl sitting alone. Although this area of the fortress seemed reserved for sacks of grain and hanging slabs of smoked meat, hers was fitted up as a bedroom. He knew her in an instant. It was the beautiful young woman Cidre had spirited away on their first night at the fortress—Ywri. Lien thought of her hidden here for the length of their visit.

She was stitching on a length of cloth, a candle by her side, even though if she'd gone upstairs, she could have worked in bright sunlight.

When he pushed her door back, she stood up and stared at him, her mouth slightly open. She was beautiful. Her breasts were very large, her waist tiny, her hair coiled and twisted with multicolored ribbons. She was all dressed up with no place to go.

Her eyes were as vacant as a deer's caught in headlights.

"Hi." He smiled to reassure her he was harmless. "I'm looking for Ardra. Have you seen her?"

"Ardra? The one with the golden eyes? Her face is dirty." Her voice was low and soft.

"That's her."

The young woman smiled. "I have seen her. She went into the herbarium. I have a new gown." She held her green skirt out with both hands and turned for his inspection.

"It's very pretty," he said.

"My name is Ywri. It means pretty."

"I have to go now," Lien said.

She sat down, picked up her sewing, and began to hum. Slowly Lien backed out of the room.

The lower levels of the fortress were deserted. Lien went straight to the herbarium.

"Ardra?" he said and pulled open the door to Cidre's special place. Immediately he smelled rotting foliage. It was a thick, cloying scent in the small room and originated from behind a cupboard door. When he pulled it open, he gagged. Before him was a dark, narrow staircase, filled with the fetid smell. Cold air swirled down the steps.

A heat pulsed through his arm. It coiled on his tattoo. He went back into the herbarium and grabbed a candle.

When he stepped into the cupboard, a gust of noxious air blew the small flame out. He retreated a moment, then went back into the passageway and took down a torch.

It smoked and hissed at his ear while he climbed the narrow steps. The rotting odor grew more powerful. His heart began to pound. He drew up the loose neck of his robe and covered his mouth and nose.

At the top of the steps, a small door stood open. A white animal, almost a rat but not quite, ran past him and down the steps.

Blood pounded in his temples.

He coughed and pushed past the door. The light of his torch lit only a tiny corner of what he suspected was an attic the size of Cidre's hall. It was filled with the rest of Cidre's tree. It burst from a floor covered in muddy soil, and then crowded the attic with tortuously twisted branches. Vines draped over every available space. He had to duck to prevent them from touching his skin.

The rotting scent was nearly unbearable as he moved cautiously through the maze of limbs and vines.

The white flowers hanging on the vines were spotted brown and black, dripping slime on the muddy ground. Small rodents scurried away from his boots.

"Ardra," he called. His tattoo pulsed like Ardra's heartbeat. He forced himself deeper into the attic.

He found the heart of the tree where the limbs sprouted in twisting profusion. A moan came to him over the rustle of leaves.

"Ardra." He stared a moment. She looked as if she had been spun into a dark green web. Her head sagged to the side. He touched her throat. Her pulse throbbed. "Thank God," he whispered.

He tore at the vines with his fingers. They resisted every effort. When she groaned, he realized that every time he pulled on a vine, it tightened up as if punishing her for his actions. He set the tip of the torch's flame to one thick vine.

It recoiled and shifted. He ruthlessly held the torch to the thicker vines. They slithered back like snakes, releasing her. Ardra sagged against the tree. He wrapped one

arm around her waist and took her weight against his shoulder.

Finally only one vine, a thick one about her ankle, shackled her to the tree. He was afraid to lay her down in the slimy mud or bring the torch too close to her foot. He jerked off her slipper and made a hard pull. Her small foot slipped from the vine's possession.

He stumbled back. He scooped her and the torch into his arms and hurried toward the staircase.

The leaves rustled and splattered them with the rotting-flower slime. His rash throbbed and pulsed with every step.

Ardra looped her arms about his neck. He feared the tree would stop them from reaching the steps as vines slipped from branches and the rotting flowers rained slime down on them.

He waved the torch back and forth, singeing vines, then burst through the door and half slid down the steps. In the herbarium, he paused to close the door.

Ardra murmured his name the instant they left the herbarium. He carried her through the kitchen, now filled with workers tending pots. Though they stared, no one tried to stop him as he burst from their domain and out into the gardens.

When the cold air hit them, she opened her eyes. "Lien. I cannot have you."

"I know," he said softly.

"I have offered myself to Samoht." Her eyes fluttered shut.

Sweet God. Samoht.

Without stopping, he carried Ardra to the lake and into it. He walked straight ahead until only her head was above the water. He dunked her beneath the cold, clear water and said a fervent prayer of thanks when she came up spluttering and gasping for air.

He took her face in his hands and kissed her hard. Then he remembered what he wore and what she had done. He set her away.

"Lien?" She stumbled on her skirt and went under. He hauled her upright and helped her slosh back to the pebble beach. They stood there in water to their knees, chests heaving, staring at one another.

"What took you to the attic?" he asked.

She smoothed her wet hair from her face. "You were there. Sitting among the branches. When I . . . went close . . . you were gone."

"What possessed you to enter such a rotting, vile place?" He shook her by the shoulders.

She tipped her head. "Rotting? It was beautiful. Filled with the white flowers"—she pointed to the vines draping the outer walls of Cidre's fortress—"and the sweet scent of perfume."

"Ardra. When I found you, you were lashed to a rotting tree. The flowers were rotting, the vines, the place reeked of slime. You were—"

"Cidre." She turned away and splashed water on her face. "Deleh gave me a drink of milk and honey. She said Cidre put something in it to give me strength."

"So it wasn't magic. You were drugged to see what Cidre wanted you to see. I'm sure that if she wanted me in her attic, she'd make sure I had something to help me enjoy the experience, too."

Ardra walked toward him. Her dress was heavier than Einalem's had been back at the stream, but wet, this woman beat Einalem hands down. She was as slim as a wand, her breasts firm mounds which he knew fit in his palms as if created for him. He ruthlessly pushed the intrusive thoughts aside.

"You said some stuff when I carried you out of there." His tongue felt too large for his mouth. "Is it true?"

"What?" She gathered her hair and wrung out the water.

"That you've offered yourself to Samoht."

She splashed water on her face but did not look at him, and he knew her words had not been the ramblings of an unconscious woman.

301

"I had to do it," she said.

"No, you did not."

"There are no more choices, Lien. And he has not agreed. He is weighing my worth."

Lien gripped her arms. "Weighing your worth? Fuck him. You're worth a hundred of him. Ardra, don't do this."

She jerked out of his embrace. "You lost the right to tell me what to do when you put on that robe. You can protect me if you feel the need, but that's all."

He got a grip on his anger. They stood together in the cold water, hot emotions sizzling between them, and he was powerless to do anything about it. "I know this sounds crazy, but I don't want Cidre to know that she succeeded in getting you trapped in the attic, or that I took you out. I don't know why, but I want to keep her guessing. There's a young woman who saw me—"

"Ywri. Lovely, but simple?" She held out her wet skirts with a scowl. Water lapped their knees. "She saw me too."

"I asked after you, and she's the one who directed me to—"

Their eyes met. "Ardra, I know you're thinking what I'm thinking."

"Aye," she whispered. She dropped her hem and put out her hand as if harsh words hadn't come between them.

He entwined his fingers with hers. "She's innocent, Ardra. Beautiful. A man wouldn't expect her to do anything deceitful."

"She might offer a drink . . . food, and a man might take it."

"Yes. He might."

"And if she offered a kiss after?"

"We have to talk to Nilrem."

Lien tugged Ardra through the water toward the pebbly beach.

"Lien! What are you doing?" Ollach stood near the shore like a disapproving nanny.

Lien dropped Ardra's hand, bent down, and splashed water on his face. "Say we had dragon venom on us. Say it was burning your skin."

"And if no one believes us?" Ardra did as he had, washing her face and neck.

"We'll cross that bridge when we come to it."

"We have that same expression here. We say we will jump that fence when we get to it." She stumbled on her long skirt.

He took her elbow. "Ardra, where do you get those little expressions?"

"Mostly from Nilrem. Of course, *he* got them from the wisemen who came before."

"Of course."

Lien drew Ardra up the beach, where Ollach joined them. The warrior commiserated with them about dragon venom, showing a spot on his sleeve where it had eaten a hole clear to his skin; then he headed off to the stables, while they continued toward the kitchen door.

There they met the gap-toothed slave who had wielded the sword.

"Lien, I must thank you for saving my life," Inund said.

"Look, you can show your thanks by making sure no one in the kitchen remembers seeing Ardra and me."

The man waggled his eyebrows, but bowed and opened an iron-strapped door. When Lien peered out, he saw another small set of steps. He sniffed the air but smelled only wood.

Before he entered the dark space, he drew back and said to the servant, "Do you think you can find me a dry robe?"

"Without doubt. Where will I find you?"

"Uh—" he said, but Ardra interrupted him.

"You must bring the robe to my chamber. No one would think to disturb us there."

Lien felt his cheeks flame as Inund grinned and hurried away. Cautiously Lien led Ardra up the winding steps to

303

discover that the way was nothing but an innocent servants' staircase to the bedchambers.

Once in her room, Ardra immediately began to strip off her wet clothes. Lien turned his back. He eradicated the vision of her slim form from his mind, concentrating instead on the fact that he had nothing to wear again. A tap at the door made him whip around and hold a finger to his lips.

Ardra wore only a thin linen shift that reached to her ankles. It had skinny straps and was tight across her small breasts. Damp, it molded her body, heightened the shadows, outlined her delicate bones. He swallowed. Mesmerized, he could not tear his eyes from the dark shadow of her navel. He wanted to bury his face against her and breathe in her scent.

The tap came again. Ardra walked to the door and cracked it open. A pile of clothing was thrust through the opening.

She stood a moment, head bowed, the clothes in her hands. Without turning around, she dropped the garments on a chair near the door.

"I will wait for you to dress," she said.

The shift clung to her buttocks and legs. Lien no longer tried to look away. As he stripped and dried off, he watched her. He had a raging erection, but knew he was going to do absolutely nothing about it.

Samoht would see her like this. The thought riled something very cavemanlike in his nature.

Inund had donated a pair of long trousers and soft boots which he cross-gartered above and below his knees as he'd seen some slaves and warriors do. The trousers were a bit tight, but he laced them as best he could.

The robe, while similar to a pilgrim's, was made of a softer, smoother cloth. It had a rough rope belt and a hood.

"Okay. I'm done," he said. "You can turn around."

She did. And gasped. "Your hand."

He looked down. The rash on his wrist had darkened in places and faded in others. "God."

The rash hurt no more than it had before, but what he saw was beyond his understanding. It was the same knot-work as on his tattoo.

"The pattern is called the Shield," she said. "It is a sign. You are good."

He took her hands and pressed them together. "Stop it. I'm no better than anyone else. It's not a sign of anything."

Ardra shook her head. "It is a sign that you can feel evil. It darkens when Cidre is near. It spread across your back when you fought against Samoht." She shivered.

"You're cold. Get changed." He had to pretend that what she said was unimportant. He couldn't tell her how his tattoo had pulsed in the attic like her heartbeat.

He pulled his hands away from her and went to his pack. He needed something to do, so he tucked the bandage with the leaf Ardra had given him up under his robe, inside the front of his trousers. The cloth buffered his skin from the rough laces.

"Lien." Ardra came to him. "Please wait for me."

He nodded, one hand on the latch. He kept it there so he would not be tempted to take her in his arms. When she was finally ready, she looked none the worse for wear. Her clean gown was ivory with a serviceable brown apron thing over it. One tie was hanging loose. "Allow me," he said.

She turned around. He lifted her damp hair and gently placed it over her shoulder. As he touched her, his wrists cooled. He spread his hands on her shoulders and tried not to gasp as the fiery pain receded.

"I can braid my hair on the morrow," she said.

As he crossed the ties behind her waist, he realized it was her way of saying her eight days of mourning would be over. When he brought the ties to the front of her gown, she covered his hands and held them hard against her.

"What will you do when I braid my hair?" she asked.

The simple statement shook him out of his trance.

"Ardra, no matter what happens about the vial, don't give yourself to Samoht. I can't leave thinking you will be in his power."

"But you will leave."

Her hands were cold. He disentangled his and tied the apron securely for her. "I'll finish my pilgrimage."

"We must tell Nilrem what we think about Ywri." She left the chamber, regal as a queen, her thoughts and emotions much better controlled than his.

Lien took the back steps, cutting through the kitchen and arriving in the hall before Ardra. He made a beeline to Nilrem.

"Ardra and I think we know how Cidre will administer the seduction potion."

Nilrem raised a shaggy brow. "Tell me." He leaned close so they could speak without being overheard.

"There's a young woman named Ywri whom Ardra says is simple. She's also beautiful."

"Say no more." Nilrem patted Lien's arm. "We have but to watch for her and to whom she offers food or drink."

"It's too easy," Lien said. "There's a catch somewhere."

Chapter Twenty-three

Ardra felt the difference in the hall as soon as she started down the stairs. No one spoke above a whisper. Among the slaves who brought out the platters, many wore bandages and several limped.

Ralen sat by Cidre, his arm wrapped and strapped to a splint. "This is clever." Ardra said and touched the halter of cloth that supported his injury.

"Lien fashioned it for me."

"Oh." She touched the tips of Ralen's fingers to assess the color of his nails to decide if he was bandaged too tightly. "Does this hurt?" she asked. A few conjunctions ago, she would not have known how to care for an injured man.

"I have had enough wine so nothing hurts." He grinned.

"I want to tell you how sorry I am for your injury."

"There was nothing you could have done to prevent it."

"Nevertheless. You were helping others."

Ralen adjusted his arm a bit, and Ardra suspected the wine had not completely relieved his discomfort.

"I will soon be wielding a sword again, so stop worrying," he said.

She kissed her fingertips and touched his injured arm very lightly.

Lien stood with Nilrem. He gave a barely perceptible nod, and she knew the wiseman had been apprised of their suspicions regarding Ywri. As soon as Ralen separated himself from Cidre, she would warn him too.

She walked toward Samoht. She could feel Lien's emotions across the hall—they rolled off him in waves. Or was it just some hope within her that he felt more than he did?

Would Lien remain with the wiseman when the eight days were over? She tried to imagine Lien as a pilgrim on Hart Fell, living in deprivation, eating whatever was donated, spending his days in contemplation.

Would Lien leave her to Samoht's bed? Sorrow filled her that she would never lie in Lien's arms again. His celibacy negated all hope. Part of her was angry with herself for feeling more than he did. If he had felt the depth of emotion she had experienced, he would not have chosen the pilgrim path. He would have thought of another way.

What way?

Samoht watched Lien as a blue-hawk might watch a goh. It reminded her of Lien's words that Samoht wanted blood. She must find a way to extend her bargain to include safe passage for Lien.

Ardra remembered how she had once thought she loved a man. She had thought of the man in her idle moments and had felt an inner thrill when he had once tried to kiss her, but now that she had experienced physical pleasure with Lien, she knew that small thrill meant little when compared to what she had discovered in Lien's arms. How would she bear Samoht's embrace?

She crossed her arms, and when she wrapped her hand about her upper arm, she felt the hard metal of her arm rings. It was all that separated her from Lien.

Two rings of metal. Generations of tradition and close-mindedness.

Then she realized that it was not their shared passion that made her regret parting with Lien; it was the fact that he offered her something no other man had ever offered her, Tol included.

Lien thought her capable of all she hoped and needed to do. He did not doubt her. He encouraged and supported her. He had no wish to rule her life and thoughts.

Her steps led her to Samoht.

"Sit with me, Ardra." Samoht's smile was warm. Nothing was evident of the callous man who had attacked her. "If we are to share a bed at some time, we could at least share some food. Now, what pleases you?"

Ardra blindly took slices of meat and roasted onions from the platter Samoht passed her. She could not eat, but she recognized the gesture of a councilor serving a woman as an extraordinary one she should not scorn. "I wish to petition you to grant Lien unconditional safe conduct."

"Free men have safe conduct."

She waited, fear for Lien making her throat feel tight.

After a few moments Samoht shrugged. "If I agree to your bargain, it will be done."

She put her hand on his sleeve. "When will you make your decision?"

He covered her hand and squeezed her fingers. "Soon. I have thought of nothing but your bargain. Of you beneath me. Ready. Willing. Begging me to—"

"Ardra," Lien interrupted them. "Ralen needs you."

"Go away, pilgrim." Samoht jumped to his feet.

A flush ran over Lien's face.

"Lien," Ardra said. "Tell Ralen I will join him in a moment."

Lien walked away. He had broken the moment. She could no longer sit with Samoht. "I will be back after I have looked at Ralen's arm. He is not one to complain, I imagine."

She swept away from the table. Ralen looked surprised when she sat beside him for the second time. So Lien had lied.

"I would like to check your hand again." She picked up his fingers and examined his nails.

"Ardra," Ralen said. "Might I make a suggestion?" When he lifted his wine to his lips, his hand shook. He quickly set the cup down.

"I appreciate your thoughts on any matter, Ralen." She pretended she had not seen his weakness.

"Of course. You have been raised to understand your place."

If he were not injured, she would kick his shin for such a remark.

Ralen nodded in Lien's direction. "Why do you not petition the council to grant you Lien?"

"Grant me Lien?" she asked. "What do you mean?"

"He will eventually be declared a slave, no matter the snake that coils three times about his arm. At that time, and I suspect Samoht will push the matter, if your petition is registered first, the council will have to consider your request before any others." He leaned close to her and glanced at Samoht. "You can ask for Lien as your protector, citing how he saved your life—"

"Four times."

"Three times. You saved *his* life today."

"Three times," she echoed. But it was four times. Ralen would never know of Lien's rescue in the attic.

Her own act during the rebel raid had been pure instinct. She would have fought the rebel with her bare hands to save Lien.

She knew the taste of Lien's essence, knew the touch of his hand in intimate detail. Lien was as much a part of her as if he had spilled his seed within her and quickened her with child.

There would be no other man for her—ever. She might be bargaining her body to Samoht, but her heart was Lien's—forever.

"The council will be strongly inclined in your favor, no matter what other petitions might be made after yours," Ralen said.

"Who else would make such a petition?" She cut small slices from the roasted mutton and placed them piece by piece on his plate that he might eat with only one hand.

"Einalem."

Ardra continued to cut the meat into ever smaller pieces. "Einalem?"

"Oh, I know her well, which I am sure *you* know. I have seen the signs. She wants Lien, and with her brother as high councilor, she will likely have her way. Once Lien is declared a slave, she will go for ownership."

Einalem wanted Lien? "What hope have I against a councilor's sister?" She had difficulty remaining in her seat. "And Lien would never accept slave status."

"He may have to go on the run, then."

She would never see him again. "Ralen, we cannot let this happen."

He gently stopped her from cutting his meat into tiny specks. "Then warn him to adhere strictly to every pilgrim convention."

Every pilgrim convention. *Celibacy*. Her heart ached.

Ralen got to his feet. He bowed at Lien, who was approaching the table. It was a mark of great respect, but was ruined when he swayed. "I must thank you for fighting at my side, Lien. Many owe you their lives."

"I just did what was necessary," Lien said. "How's your arm? And your head?"

"Passable. You have fought before, have you not?" Ralen said. "You told the truth when you said you had once been a warrior."

"Uh. Sure."

"How do you know Lien was a warrior?" Ardra asked Ralen.

"Lien knows where to place himself when confronting an enemy. He knows how to adjust his position when another man joins him in the fight."

"Thank you," Lien said, and Ardra suspected he wanted an end to the discussion.

"Perhaps it was luck," she said.

Ralen shook his head. "It is often a matter of footwork. You displayed excellent footwork, Lien."

"Thanks again. Where I'm from, we divide up into attack and defense players—uh, warriors. I was in the defense group for years, and then my coach—my leader—changed me to attack. But once a defenseman, always a defenseman, I guess."

"So you prefer to defend rather than attack," Ralen said. "I have men who excel at one over the other. It is important to know their strengths when deploying the men in battle."

"I was good at attack, an All-American to be exact, but I have to say I much preferred defense."

"I do not know this term 'All-American,' but I assume 'tis an honor." Ralen smiled down at Ardra. "You see, it is no surprise Lien saved your life so many times. There is something within a man that leads him down one path or the other. I suspect Lien will not start a fight, but will delight in drawing it to a close."

"It matters not. Lien has chosen to set aside his warrior ways."

Lien acknowledged her words with a bow but was saved from speaking when a slave rang a bell. Its deep, sonorous tone caused everyone to fall silent.

A commotion at the entry to the hall drew their attention. A line of slaves, many leaning on one another, filed into the hall. Lien went to the far end of the table near Nilrem as the band of slaves approached Cidre and Venrali.

The man at the fore was the gap-toothed slave, Inund. He bowed deeply to Cidre and waited for her to acknowledge him.

"What honor is this that all my servants have come to the hall?" Cidre stood up, and so did Venrali.

Ardra could not get used to seeing her father here in this hall. Nor could she get used to the idea that he never

looked in her direction. Not once had he looked at her in the forest. She had kept her eye on him. He had defended only Cidre. The knowledge hurt. If only she could confide in Lien.

Inund said, "Most Esteemed Goddess, we, your slaves, wish to offer a gift to Lien, the pilgrim, for his valiant defense of us."

"Lien." Cidre said the name softly. "Come, pilgrim, join me here. My people wish to honor you."

Lien approached her, and Ardra knew the pain it must be causing him, for the skin around the open neck of his robe was as red as the Tolemac sun. The stain was the color that painted his face during embarrassment or passion. Though 'twas his proximity to evil that flushed him so at this moment.

Her father frowned. His displeasure jerked Ardra from her thoughts. Did he think as Nilrem and Lien did, that Cidre wanted a new consort? Ardra looked from Venrali to Cidre to Lien, who now stood at the goddess's side. The goddess smiled up into Lien's face.

A terrible truth dawned on Ardra.

Deleh was right. *Cidre wanted Lien, too.*

The slaves huddled behind their leader like whipped dogs cowering before their master. Ardra hated their subservience. No one cowered in her fortress. Or not since her father left.

"Here is Lien," Cidre said to Inund. "What gift have you for him?"

The slaves handed Inund a long, wooden stick, adorned like no other stick she had ever seen. From tip to end it was wrapped in metal—shaped like a snake's body coiled about a branch. A serpent ready to attack.

"I have seen nothing like this in my life," Ralen said to Ardra. "It is magnificent and echoes that paint upon his arm. It reminds me of those snakes in the woods today."

"What of the snakes in the woods?"

"The snakes that did as Lien bade," Ralen said.

"You have had too much wine."

He shrugged. "I forgot . . .'tis a secret." He sat down abruptly.

Deciding that Ralen was too sotted to make sense, she turned to hear Cidre address Lien.

"My people honor you." She curtseyed to Lien as he took the stick. "It is oak, the straightest of trees, rare in the Tangled Wood, and clad in metal strong from the forge."

"I am honored. It is a fine gift." He bowed deeply to the slaves, then to Cidre.

Ralen leaned near Ardra again. "He is the only person who fought for the slaves. No one will say so, for it would insult the rest of the warriors, but sadly, I realized a bit too late that Lien alone fought for them."

"Slaves are often forgotten in battle." It was all she could manage as the significance of the gift struck her.

"Lien, you must say a few words," Cidre said.

Lien's cheeks flushed red. "I only did what was necessary, as did many others. I'm sorry we could not save everyone."

Nilrem pushed his way forward. "Wait, Lien. Before you accept the stick, I have something to say."

Venrali and Cidre nodded to the wiseman, and Lien stood aside.

Nilrem took the tall, snake-wrapped stick from Inund and ran his hands over its surface. "Many wonder why wisemen always carry a stick. It is not a weapon to us. We carry it because it is the ancient symbol of a shepherd." The slaves all nodded. Nilrem continued, "The shepherd leads and defends his flock. To carry a staff of sacred oak, even one so decorated, is a symbol that one is respected for his honor and his defense of those less able." Nilrem held the stick before Lien, balanced like a sword on his open palms. "It is a fine gift, but one that carries much responsibility."

Would Lien take the staff? Ardra held her breath. He wanted no responsibility. He had said he would run in the opposite direction. He had said he did not want even the smallest tie to bind him.

Ardra knew that the frown she saw on Samoht's face was etched on her own as well. She imagined that the councilor did not like the symbolism of Lien as shepherd to the slaves.

A hush fell over the hall. Without a look at anyone, Lien reached out, gripped the stick with both hands, and took it from Nilrem.

Lien bowed to the company of slaves. A murmur ran among the warriors, for no one bowed to a slave. Inund bowed in return and backed away, his hands pressed together palm to palm.

Lien set one end of the stick on the ground with a decisive thump of metal on wood.

Ardra watched Lien accept a pallet by the hearth with a few of Ralen's warriors. When everyone was asleep, she would approach Samoht to learn of his decision. She imagined that the councilor would demand some proof of her commitment to the bargain. Perhaps he would want to bed her this night, but she would not give in to him until the bargain was written out and signed by witnesses. Then . . . then she would do whatever was necessary.

Would she ever see her son again? Or would she travel about with Samoht as he performed his duties for the council?

She touched her face with her fingertips, rubbed her temples.

"What is wrong, Ardra?" Ralen asked. He was slumped in a nearby chair.

"Ralen, what causes one face to be more appealing than another? One man or woman more desirable? Or one less so?"

Ralen shrugged. "It is all nonsense. As far as I am concerned, one woman is as good as another." He grinned. "Or she is when the candles are out."

"Have you taken anything for your discomfort beyond the wine?"

His grin remained in place, but there was a stiffness to his mouth. "Nilrem gave me something which he said will dull my pain but not my wits. If I could find a woman to warm my bed," he said, reaching out with his good hand for a passing servant, who giggled and skipped away from his grasp, "I would feel quite fine."

"I bid you good rest," Ardra said and curtseyed to him. "There is little point in holding a conversation with a drunken man," she muttered. "And sometimes little point even with a sober one."

Next she stopped by the kitchen, for she was suddenly hungry. She realized she had not eaten anything but the milk and honey given her by Deleh, but when she entered the kitchen, the heavy, smoky air chased her appetite away.

Nilrem sat beside Inund as he worked scrubbing a large pot. His bandage had slipped over one ear.

She retied it for him as an excuse to speak with him. "You bestowed a great honor on Lien."

"He deserved it. We would all be dead if he had not aided us."

Nilrem held his hands out to the flames in the hearth. "Lien is a good man. Strong and valiant as any Tolemac warrior."

"Or Selaw," the slave quipped.

"He is a pilgrim now," Ardra said.

"Oh, aye, but a man can change." Nilrem patted her arm.

Ardra doubted it. "Has Cidre ordered any particular food or drink for Lien?" Ardra asked.

"Why?" Inund stopped scrubbing and eyed her up and down. It was not an insolent look, but curious.

Nilrem answered the man. "There is a potion missing, and we fear it is in the goddess's possession."

"You mean the portion Ralen came in search of? He must be very lonely to come here twice for love." Inund rolled his eyes. "The goddess was very angry at Ralen's intrusion the first time. She punished every mistake with twice the fervor."

Ardra placed her hand on the slave's thickly muscled arm. "We are sorry for it, but we still believe she has the Vial of Seduction hidden here at the fortress."

"The w-w-what?" Inund's hand slipped off the pot, his features blank with horror.

"The Vial of Seduction. 'Tis what we seek now and what Ralen sought on his first visit."

"We heard only that Ralen wanted a love potion." He bit his lip and then began to tremble visibly.

"What is it?" Nilrem asked. He poked the man's arm, and Inund hastily resumed his work lest the other slaves in the kitchen turn their attention on them.

"How can you be so calm? 'Tis a terrible thing, a catastrophe," Inund said.

"Aye, 'twill be a catastrophe if Cidre seduces the wrong man," Ardra said. "She has one consort already to do her bidding; why does she need another?"

"A daughter, Ardra," Nilrem said. "I need not remind you. She must seduce a new consort, and I believe she has chosen Lien."

The gap-toothed slave shook his head. "Nay. Nay. The potion is not used to seduce the consort. It is used to *make* the consort."

"Make a consort? What do you mean?" Ardra asked.

A tear ran down Inund's cheek. "If our goddess has chosen Lien . . . nothing will save him."

"From her seduction?" Nilrem asked.

"Do you not know the true nature of the Vial of Seduction? Can it be only slaves who know its nature?"

Ardra exchanged a glance with Nilrem. What was this man babbling about? Nilrem knew its nature. Did he not?

The slave scurried to the doorway and waved for them to follow him, out into the indigo night, deep into the goddess's orchards.

"I know 'tis only slave lore . . . but often it is the tales of the slaves that hold the truth, not the white-washed versions told to those who wear arm rings."

Nilrem nodded. "That is so. What is it we do not know about the potion?"

"Can I speak with freedom from punishment?" Inund directed his question at Ardra.

"You may. Quickly," she said. The man was agitated, glancing about, sweating though the air was cold here in the dark shadows of the orchard.

The slave jutted out his chin and took a deep breath, then spoke. "The Vial of Seduction has nothing to do with love."

Chapter Twenty-four

The wind lifted. A mist rose to block Ardra's view of the lake. A chill came with it, a portent of some evil.

Inund paced, his hands in fists. "The potion has naught to do with love, though 'tis seductive in the truest sense," he said.

"What is it, if not a potion to cause a man to fall in love?" Ardra asked.

" 'Tis said in slave lore that if the powder in the Vial of Seduction is mixed in liquid and then imbibed, it will cause the drinker to see all."

"All?" Nilrem and Ardra said together.

"All. All that is past. All that is present. All that is yet to come."

Ardra shivered. Nilrem took her hand and said what now coursed through her mind. "And to know everything is—"

"To be all-powerful," Ardra finished for him.

"To be all-powerful is the ultimate seduction," Nilrem said. "No man can know everything, be all-powerful, and not be drawn to the dark side." Nilrem's fingers were cold in hers. "There is a saying handed down from one wiseman

to another, that all power corrupts, and absolute power corrupts absolutely."

"Nilrem," Ardra said softly. "That means that whomever is given the potion will be a truly dark and evil consort for Cidre."

Inund nodded. "The potion will give the goddess what she most wants—a fiend for a mate."

"What is to be done?" Ardra murmured. She wrapped her arms about her waist and whispered a silent prayer.

"It is said in legend that only the sap from a leaf of the Tree of Valor will save a man once he drinks the seduction potion," Inund said.

"The Tree of Valor?" Ardra stared from Inund to Nilrem.

"Aye," Inund said. "But the tree does not grow in the Tangled Wood."

"It would not dare," Ardra said, but with a smile. "This is magnificent. I know just where to find such a leaf."

Nilrem smiled too and clasped Ardra's hands. "Then all is not lost."

"Thank you," Ardra said to Inund. "You must return to your tasks before you are missed."

When the slave turned to go, she called him back one last time. "Wait. May I make a request?"

"Ask anything of me if 'twill protect Lien."

She smiled. "You are a good man. We think Ywri will be asked to give the potion to someone. Perhaps Lien. Perhaps Ralen—"

"What of Samoht?" Nilrem interjected. "He has begotten a daughter. He has proved his virility."

Ardra nodded. "Perhaps Samoht, but I saw a look on Cidre's face that makes me believe she wants Lien. Inund, will you keep an eye open for Ywri? Let us know if she is given something by Cidre to offer any of our men?"

"It makes great sense that Ywri would be the vessel for our goddess's intent. Ywri is the goddess's daughter, you know."

Ardra and Nilrem exchanged a glance.

"The goddess ofttimes hides the girl away when men are about for fear that one may take advantage of her. We believe it was once our goddess's greatest hope that, over time, Ywri would change, but it was not to be. Though Ywri is now a woman, she is yet a child. I will watch her, but if the potion is prepared in the herbarium, I will have little knowledge of it."

Ardra looked up at the indigo sky, but saw it was choked now with green-black clouds that reminded her of Cidre's gowns.

She must warn Samoht as well. She could not keep her self-respect if she did not warn Samoht of the dangers of the potion. Her first thought was that he might wish to be all-knowing, but then, on further contemplation, she suspected that even Samoht would understand the evils of such power.

In the meanwhile, she realized, Lien slept in the hall, oblivious to the nature of his danger. "I must go," she said to Nilrem.

She ran past astonished guards, through the sleeping folk in the hall, to the hearth.

Lien's pallet was empty. She fell to her knees and placed her palm flat on the woolen blankets. They were cold. She shook one of the warriors nearby. "Where is Lien?"

The man smirked, but answered. "He went off to the privy. He will not thank you for following him there."

Ardra lifted her hem and ran back through the kitchen. She darted among the trees a bow-shot's distance from the gardens, where stood a long, low building—the common privy. She flung open the door. Wicks in dishes of scented oil flickered in the breeze.

No one was inside.

Ardra bit her lips in frustration. She must tell Ralen, but first—she hurried up the stairs to her chamber. When she opened the door, she saw Lien's pack on the bed. Without

321

hesitation, she opened the pack. First she must get the leaf from the Tree of Valor.

The pack was empty.

Cidre did as she was sure Einalem had. She spooned the powder from the Vial of Seduction into a cup. This time it was not wine she poured over it, but a clear spring water in which she then dropped a few thin slices of apple.

Would Lien drink from the cup if Ywri offered it? Perhaps. If he was thirsty enough.

She mused on the matter and added a touch of her persuasion potion to another goblet—her own. If he wished to switch goblets, she would comply. The persuasion potion would then make him more compliant.

"Ywri," Cidre called.

When Ywri entered the herbarium, Cidre settled her on a bench and offered her a small sweet cake. When Ywri had finished eating the cake, Cidre leaned forward and kissed her on the lips. Cidre stood back and smiled. "You look lovely. Your hair is very pretty." Ywri smiled vacantly.

A shiver of anticipation swept through Cidre. It must be now. This day. All that had been denied her must be hers before Ardra's eight days were over. For when the sun rose on the morrow, Samoht would take his party away—and Lien with it. All her hopes for a new goddess would be dashed.

Venrali expected to share her bed this night. Unfortunately, the battle had raised his ardor, and if he got her with child, it would ruin everything. She wanted to tell him without equivocation that he had been supplanted by another.

She would prepare Venrali's favorite hot wine drink, and after he drank it, she would tell him. She would insist he leave with Samoht's party, and if Venrali refused, she would tell him he should expect poison in his meals at any

time, any day. That should get him packing his belongings quickly enough.

"I have something special for you to do," Cidre said to Ywri.

"Special?"

"Aye. I want you to offer a pilgrim a drink. It is a very, very special thing you will do. And special things require a kiss, do they not?"

Ywri smiled. "You always kiss me when you give me a special cake."

Cidre fixed a curl on Ywri's forehead. "Just so. After you offer the pilgrim the drink, you will give him a kiss."

Chapter Twenty-five

Lien woke, the scent of earth and leaves filling his head. He lay with his back against the rough bark of a tree. Was he in Cidre's attic again? No. The smell was fresh and clean.

He tried to sit up, and chains rattled. "Shit." He was not only shackled to a tree, he was also naked as a jaybird. He struggled to his knees but couldn't get to his feet. Bands of metal encircled his throat and wrists. The shackles were connected by looped chains to a tree. He was chained like a dog on a very short leash. "Now, why should this surprise me?" he asked aloud.

"Aye. Why?" Cidre stepped from between the matted roots as if they were cobwebs, her greenish-black robes swirling about her body. "A man who can be surprised is a man who is not thinking."

"So how'd I get here?" he asked.

"One of my guards hit you over the head outside the privy."

"I hope it was on the way out and not on the way in." He grinned and resisted the urge to lunge for her. But she stood just outside his reach.

"I am pleased you did not suffer much from the blow."

Actually, his head hurt like a son-of-a-bitch, but it was a small matter compared to the acid burn rising on his rash.

A thrashing of undergrowth revealed two of Cidre's guards. They took up places on either side of him. Frick and Frack.

Only then did Cidre wander close enough to skim her fingertips along his hip. It was like being stroked with a hot needle.

"What is this mark?" she asked about a bruise on his hip now purpling from his fall in the pit.

"I'm rotting."

Her laughter filled the air. "Such an outrageous notion will not free you."

"Too bad."

Her hand was warm when she cupped his genitals. "You are not rotting here," she said and released him.

"So why'd you tie me up?" he asked, hoping she wouldn't touch him again. He might not have the rash on every inch of his body, but pain filled him wherever she touched.

"I need you."

"So you had me hit over the head?"

"I did not think I could get your attention in my hall."

He jerked against his bindings. "You have my attention now. I'm all ears."

"All ears. How delightful." She laughed again. One guard, Frick, placed a heavy hand on his shoulder—as if it were necessary to restrain him further.

"Each goddess has passed her knowledge down from generation to generation," Cidre said. "It is my turn to do so."

"What do you need me for? Want me to find you a guy?"

"A guy? What is a guy?"

"A man."

"Exactly. A man, though you need not find one for me. I have found one on my own."

Ann Lawrence

"Venrali?"

"Nay. I thought he was the answer to my needs, but I have found him inadequate."

"Can't get it up, huh?" He felt no give in his chains, and the two guards were too close for any tricks.

Cidre shook her head and made a tutting sound. "You insult a fine man. Venrali is virile enough. That is not the issue. He has failed with *me*."

"Ah . . . but not with some other little slave girl somewhere."

Her brow furrowed with what appeared to be only minor irritation, but somehow Lien thought it was a deeper humiliation.

"Well, my advice—not that anyone ever takes advice— is try, try, try again." He flexed against the chains, then fell still when Cidre dropped her gaze to his thighs.

"You do not understand, Lien. A man who fathers sons is useless to me. I need a daughter."

"Old Samoht might help you out," he suggested.

"He might, but the moment I saw you, saw your dark hair, your beautiful eyes, I knew who would father my child."

"Even if you have a daughter, won't it take a long time to raise her and train her? Twenty, thirty conjunctions?"

"That is why I cannot delay any longer."

Lien had seen enough movies to know that the best way out of this kind of situation was to keep her talking and hope for the cavalry to arrive. "So how do you train a baby goddess?"

"I believe you are uncomfortable." She set her hand on his wrist. Pain radiated from her palm. "I shall see what I may find for your relief. A goddess is a healer, you know."

"No, I didn't. I just thought you hung out and looked good. Where I'm from, a goddess is just a beautiful woman. Nothing more."

"Here a goddess is worshiped. Honored. She need not be beautiful. Such empty reverence insults me."

"So what does a goddess *do* specifically?" He worked his wrists in the shackles, but found no way to slip out of the metal bands. His efforts drew the attention of Frack, who placed a boot on a loop of the chain, dragging Lien's arm straight down at his side.

Cidre made languid circles on the inside of Lien's thigh with her fingertip. "What would you like? Power? Wealth? All may be yours through me."

"Pilgrims aren't too interested in power and wealth."

She shrugged. "You soon will be. Now I must go. My guests must wonder what has become of me. But know that I will have you. I knew the moment I touched your hand that you would be mine. You reek of power, leashed power. And I intend to release it. I shall be back, and these kind men will take you to a comfortable place where we may indulge our desires."

After the goddess walked off into the foliage, Frick and Frack unlocked his chains and half dragged, half carried him along a path deep into the Tangled Wood.

Ralen opened his chamber door to find Einalem in his bed. He tossed the blanket covering her onto the floor. "Come, wake up."

She rolled over and smiled. "I would prefer to return to my dream. In it, you were making love to me . . . along with several of your men. All as well endowed as you."

He tried to concentrate on what he needed to say. His throat was parched from the wine, but he saw no water in the chamber. "I would love to join you, but Ardra has discovered that Lien is missing."

"Lien? Missing?" Alarm filled her face.

"So, I am right. You would like Lien for yourself. Well, help in the search, or it will be Cidre who gets him."

"How can I help?" She slipped out of bed, but for once, her nakedness did little to arouse him. It was always so; once he knew a woman's ways, he lost interest in her.

"I found a slave who saw one of Cidre's guards hit Lien over the head with a club of some sort," he said as Einalem threw on a turquoise and ivory gown. When she turned her back that he might lace it, he tersely reminded her he had but one functioning hand.

She made a dismissive gesture and did the best she could alone; her words tumbled from her lips in agitation. "Cidre and Lien? I cannot believe it."

"Could you question a few of Cidre's men? I think they might offer more information to someone like you"—he cupped her breast—"than someone like me."

Lien sat on a soft bed in a small, one-room, thatched cottage. The cottage was bare except for the bed and an open fire pit in the center of the room. A cauldron bubbled over it.

The bed was neatly draped with linens stitched in a pattern of tangled leaves and vines. A thick white fur was folded at the foot. There was no pillow.

Frick and Frack had dragged him to the bed and locked his chains to an iron ring on the wall so he was forced to sit on the edge. They had left him alone for the rest of the night, then returned to check his chains before stepping aside for Cidre.

She gave him a smile and opened the shutters to let in air and the coppery glow of sunlight.

Lien's tongue felt thick in his throat. He didn't fear the potion; she couldn't make him eat or drink, but he feared the writhing, cramping pains that ran up his arms and across his back.

The goddess went to the cauldron. Smoke twisted up in a column through a smoke hole in the peaked roof.

"Making a witch's brew?" he asked.

"A simple soup, Lien," Cidre said. She stirred the contents with a long, smooth stick. The cauldron was etched with figures that danced in a naked chain, covered only by flowering vines.

"Look, you're just making trouble for yourself. Venrali will be pissed, and Samoht and Ralen will bring their warriors here and tear this cottage down around you."

Lien's hands were stiff, but not from being shackled. They were locked in a rictus of pain caused by the rash that tormented his body. The agony had ebbed when Cidre left but had now redoubled. He could no more fight her guards or run away than if she'd broken his arms and legs. Each movement of his body was agony, the pain and cramps escalating each time Cidre wandered near to stroke his body. And she wandered near often.

"The men will not miss you. The women—well, they might," she said, tasting whatever she was cooking up.

"What women?" He didn't like the way she said "the women." Was Ardra in danger? And who else was Cidre referring to? Einalem?

She trilled a laugh that sent waves of pain up his neck into his head. "Ardra. Einalem. But they will not have you."

"Fine with me." He groaned and leaned forward. Nausea crowded his throat. "The one's a cold stick, the other a scheming bitch."

"You do not desire Einalem? Or Ardra?"

There was an emphasis on Ardra's name that tormented him worse than any bodily pain. Then Cidre was next to him. She ran her hands over his bowed head and lifted his face to her. "You will drink my potion and be filled with—"

"Desire for you," he managed in a low tone. "I already desire you." Would she believe him and leave Ardra alone?

"Nay. Knowledge. *All knowledge*. All knowledge from the past, the present, and the future. Only the ill-informed think the Vial of Seduction holds a love potion. What simpletons you all are. I have persuasion charms to bring about love. Nay, I want you worthy of being called Consort to the Goddess of Darkness."

"You can't make me eat or drink anything," he said through clenched teeth. He suddenly understood why the

vial had been locked up in the Tolemac vaults.

"Nay, and I shall not try. You will receive the blessings of the potion through another. When the cup is offered, you *will* drink. You will be so thirsty, you will not resist."

Lien was grateful he knew about Ywri. If not, he might have taken something from her. Involuntarily, he shuddered.

Cidre ran her hands over his hips, her nails scratching at his skin. "Our child will be filled with the black depths I see in your eyes." Her breasts grazed his chest when she touched her lips to his eyelids, first one, then the other, slowly drawing her tongue across his eyelashes.

He buried a scream that threatened to erupt from his lips as each sweep of her tongue burned like a live electric wire on his skin.

"You are mine, Lien. Mine." She licked her finger and put it on his wrist, then drew it up the inside of his arm to his tattoo. She gasped and jumped away from him, her hand to her mouth. "Fiend," she whispered, eyes wide.

He forced a smile. "Seems my snake doesn't like you."

"It is a warrior's mark. It centers your male vigor."

"Just don't touch it."

She sucked her fingertip like a small child. "A man's strength is not just in his manhood." She kissed his lips.

"More," he whispered. He must convince her that she had nothing to fear from Ardra.

She smiled. "So you are just like any other man, are you not? And you will be ready here"—she gripped his sex—"when I am." He wanted to vomit.

"Let's do it now," he managed to say through clenched teeth.

Cidre laughed. "Not yet. But we can sample the pleasures if you wish." She slipped her robe off and dropped it beside his feet. She planted her hands on his thighs. Her breath was warm when she pressed her lips on his.

His muscles locked in cramps, but he forced himself to put his arm around her neck. He held her hard against him

in feigned desire. Pain radiated in excruciating waves from every point their bodies touched. The idea of Ardra being in danger from this woman gave him focus. He tightened his arm around her throat and bit her lip; the metallic taste of blood filled his mouth.

She screamed and tried to break away. He locked his hand over her wrist and pictured Ardra.

Frick and Frack barged into the cottage and tossed Cidre aside to get to him.

"Nay!" she screamed. "Do not harm him."

Her men stepped instantly back. "He would have killed you," Frack said.

But Cidre waved them back after shrugging into her robe. " 'Twas my foolishness to approach so closely. My stupidity. He did what all warriors are trained to do."

"He tried to strangle you," Frack persisted, and set himself between her and the bed.

Lien dragged air into his lungs. He tried to stretch out the knots in his arms and legs. When his chains rattled, Cidre stepped past her guard. "Warriors kill. Now go."

The men left the cottage, but Lien imagined they weren't far from the door. Cidre rubbed her throat. "You might have killed me, but you would have bled to death on these sheets soon after."

He said nothing because he couldn't speak. The pain had stepped up with her anger; his body was crippled with it.

She smiled and smoothed a hand over his hair. "We will have a mating ceremony, Lien. You cannot prevent it. You will be filled with all knowledge, and I with your seed. I will have my daughter. Why fight it?" She released him. "Oh, and there will be no women of status in attendance . . . they will be . . . gone by then."

Einalem closed her eyes and conjured up Lien's face as one of Cidre's guards grunted over her. He took an inordinate length of time to finish, so she hurried him a bit with feigned moans.

Finally he found his pleasure and climbed off her. She sat up and smoothed her skirt down. "Is our bargain met?" she asked.

"With wondrous joy, mistress." The guard laced his breeches and held out his hand.

Einalem took it and smiled. "You have had what you wanted, now I shall have what I want."

He helped her off the bed and with a touch of shyness held out her cloak to her. "With pleasure, mistress. I will sketch you a map. 'Tis not far."

Ardra prayed that Tol would forgive her for the disrespect to his memory as she braided her hair into one thick plait down her back.

She shook out the groom's garb that Inund had brought. "Turn around." While the slave did as bade, she switched her gown and soft undergarments for those of a stable groom. The boy was slender, and the clothing, a linen shirt and well-worn breeches, fit her well. She cinched the belt at her waist and drew on her own riding boots.

Last, she stuffed everything she might need into Lien's pack: a long, sharp dagger purloined from Ralen's saddle-bags, several lengths of rope to bind any of Cidre's men who could be bested, and bandages and healing powder for wounds.

When she met Ralen in the stable, she ignored his frown over her garb. Then Einalem and Samoht came around the side of the building.

"What are they doing here?" Ardra asked, rounding on Ralen.

He touched his sling. "I am useless to you right now. And it is Einalem who knows where Lien was taken."

"We waste time. If we are to release this nuisance pilgrim, we must be about it now," Samoht said. He eyed Ardra from head to toe before bending close to her ear, his lips hot against her skin. "I will much enjoy stripping these breeches off you and teaching you proper womanly behav-

ior." Samoht grinned before he stalked off, his sister in his wake.

Einalem led them into the woods. Every now and then she consulted a scrap of paper she kept tucked in the bodice of her gown. After a few miles she held up a hand for quiet. They tethered their horses and proceeded the rest of the way on foot. They moved with silent caution until they reached a small clearing. A woodcutter's cottage sat there, smoke writhing from its smoke hole.

"Einalem and I shall distract the guards at the front, while you go in the back window," Samoht said.

Ardra obeyed Samoht's orders, for they must cooperate if they were to save Lien, but she knew they were only on this mission because Einalem wanted Lien for herself. Jealousy spiked through Ardra when Einalem stepped daintily through the undergrowth and around the side of the cottage.

When given the signal, Ardra darted across the clearing to the back window, whose shutter stood half open. With a quick peek over the sill, she took in the room at a glance.

Lien lay on the bed. He was alone.

Heart in her throat, she signaled that only Lien was inside. Einalem and Samoht would handle the guards. She would take care of Lien. In a moment, she had slithered over the windowsill like one of the snakes that had attacked the dragons.

She had her hand over Lien's mouth before he could give away her presence. His face was strangely blank of expression, his eyes wide, but his lips moved in a whisper of a kiss on her palm.

"Who has the key to your shackles?" she whispered.

His eyes went to the door.

"The guards?"

He shook his head, though 'twas more a convulsive shudder. His eyes went to the door again, but then up.

She tiptoed to the door. Samoht's voice could be heard asking the guards if they had seen Cidre.

She ran her fingers along the door's lintel and felt the key. It fit easily into Lien's shackles. Within moments, he was free.

But he couldn't move. She tried in vain to help him rise. Samoht must dispose of the guards and soon. She massaged Lien's wrists and he half gasped as the ugly rash began to fade. Along with it went his pain. She saw the relief on his face. "Oh, Lien," she whispered, and kissed him.

His mouth was hot on hers. She ran her hands over him, his shoulders, chest, hips, thighs. Tears pricked her eyes.

He was found. Ywri had not yet given him the potion.

A commotion at the door made Lien freeze against her. She looked around and saw Lien's clothing in the corner. "Dress," she said, and drew her dagger.

Lien shook his head in wonder over Ardra, who stood with her knife ready to defend him. He quickly pulled on his pants, stuffing the Tree of Valor leaf down the front before lacing them up.

He had his tunic in his hand when the door opened. It was Frick and Frack.

"Out," Frick ordered Ardra. His drawn sword touched her throat. She did as he ordered.

Samoht and Einalem stood outside. There was a wide grin on Samoht's face. "Cidre's men and I have made a bargain, Ardra. You do much enjoy a bargain, do you not? This one may not please you, but"—he touched Einalem on the cheek—"it will please my sister."

"Lien, you are to come with me," Einalem said. "I will see that you are protected from the goddess." She walked to Lien and curtseyed to him as if he were a warrior in truth. "You must be famished."

"And thirsty," Samoht said. "Ardra, you will come with me. I have decided not to take you up on your offer, for you see, I have decided that finding you here in this lonely cottage with a half-naked slave means you are irredeem-

ably wanton, and not worthy of rule. These kind guards will witness that they saw this pilgrim mounted between your thighs." He tossed a purse of coins to each guard. "Would you like to double that?" he asked the men.

"Aye," Frick and Frack said in unison, and Lien felt a sick feeling in the pit of his stomach. He looked around for a weapon.

"Cut that vile serpent off even if it means cutting off his arm," Samoht said and pointed at Lien.

"Nay!" Einalem gasped.

Ardra fought against Samoht, but he held her in an iron grip. "He will be just as useful, dear sister, and less trouble."

"Nay," Einalem cried out. Frack drew his sword. As he turned to Lien, Einalem tore across the clearing.

The guard swept out his blade, and Einalem ran full into it. Blood bloomed in a scarlet line across her middle. She stood still, hands wide, and stared at the soldier.

Samoht moaned and shoved Ardra away. As Einalem crumpled to the ground, he ran to her, but Lien knew Samoht was too late.

Lien felt Einalem's throat for a pulse, but her staring eyes and the flood of blood across her hands told him all he needed to know.

"Go," he ordered Ardra, jerking her to her feet.

Chapter Twenty-six

"Nay," Ardra said. "Not without you."

"I want you out of here. Now," Lien said. "This could get ugly. Now go."

Samoht roared with anger. He tore his sword from its scabbard and turned on the guard. "Murderer."

"Too late." Lien stepped in front of Ardra, unarmed.

"It was an accident," Frick began, but Frack interrupted him.

"It was the goddess's will. She wants these two women dead, and no one stands in her way."

Samoht shook his head. He swung his sword in a terrible arc and with the one powerful stroke sliced the guard from shoulder to waist. The man fell to his knees, then back, dead, his eyes as wide as Einalem's.

"Mercy," Frick said and held his hands out.

Samoht stood before the cowering guard, his sword raised.

Lien took Samoht's arm. "Don't kill him, Samoht. It will gain you nothing."

The councilor stood frozen in place, then sagged and lowered his sword. Lien took it, walked to the guard, and held

out his hand. "I'll feel a whole lot safer if I take yours as well."

To Ardra's complete astonishment, the guard turned over his sword. What was it about Lien that caused strangers to obey him?

Lien strode across the clearing and disappeared for a moment into the trees. When he returned, he was empty-handed.

"I'll help Samoht bring Einalem back," he said. "This guard here will show us the way if he wants to live." Then he leaned close to her ear, his hand on her shoulder. "You have to avoid Cidre. I know she wants you dead. Sneak in through the kitchen and have Inund fetch Nilrem. He may have a calming influence on Samoht. And have him bring my stick. I have a feeling I'm going to need it."

"Something else we need, Lien—the leaf I gave you."

"Would you go?" He cupped her face and gave her a hard kiss. "We may not have much time. Find Nilrem."

"The leaf, Lien—"

"Okay. Now go." He gave her a push.

"I need Einalem's map," she said.

"Get it then, and go." Ardra watched Samoht lift Einalem into his arms. The man appeared as confused as a small child. When he saw Ardra looking at him, he said, "This is my doing, is it not?"

How to answer?

He continued. "I loved her . . ." He broke off. Tears ran down his cheeks, and he buried his face in Einalem's neck.

"It was she who stole the Vial of Seduction, was it not?" Ardra asked.

"She told me it was Tol who took it to barter for a potion to ease his pain."

"She lied," Ardra said. "She wanted someone's love, I imagine, as do we all."

Samoht tipped his head back and stared at the clear purple sky. "How can the sun still shine? How is it possible when she is dead?"

337

Ann Lawrence

"Get your map and go, Ardra," Lien said, pointing to the forest. "He's grieving now, but later he may decide that someone else is to blame."

She touched Lien on the arm, then went to Samoht, who had placed his sister on the bed in the cottage. Ardra made a show of arranging Einalem's gown in a more decorous manner; in the process she plucked the map of the Tangled Wood from her bodice. It was curiously untouched by blood.

Once outside, Ardra showed it to Lien.

"When you've found Nilrem, you're to hide," Lien said. "Hide until I come for you. Do you understand?"

"I will not hide. You might need my help."

"Damn it, I said hide. If something happens to you—"

He jerked her against his body and kissed her hard, so hard she forgot all else save his taste, his strong hands.

"Hide," he ordered, "or I'll take my stick to you when I find you. This isn't about you and me. It's about you being safe to look after your people."

He was right. "I will do as you say. The leaf, Lien. Do not forget." She held him close for one more fleeting moment before darting into the trees, but paused to take a final look back at him.

He stood alone in the clearing. The sunlight painted him bronze and gold. She thought of a statue, every muscle carved in perfect male beauty. He raised his hand to her, and the snake on his arm moved.

Would she see him again?

Ralen tried to get comfortable in his chair, but his arm throbbed in time to the hammer pounding away in his head. Too many people roamed the hall, all speaking too loudly.

"Are you a pilgrim?" a young woman asked. She held a silver goblet in her hand.

Suddenly there were two of her. Twins? Ralen tried to focus on her. He grinned and rubbed his eyes. 'Twas but one small woman . . . a very beautiful one.

"Are you looking for a pilgrim?" he asked. She was bountiful in all the right places.

"I am seeking a pilgrim," the woman said.

"Then I will be one for you." She dipped a moment, but he realized it was he who swayed, not she. Too much wine. Yet his mouth was as dry as the Scorched Plain.

"Would you like a drink?" The lovely woman held out the cup. He took it, looked in, and was disappointed to see water, not wine. But he did not wish to disappoint her. And he would tell her so if she would only stand still a moment.

He raised the cup. Some of the liquid slopped over the rim, across his fingers, as he put the cup to his lips. The water ran cold and sweet down his throat. When he lowered the cup, the woman rose on her tiptoes and kissed his lips.

He lifted the cup again, thirsty for more.

Chapter Twenty-seven

Ardra found Inund in the kitchen. She wasted no time in telling him what had happened. He ran off to get Nilrem, and she looked about the smoky room, where at least a dozen men and women labored.

Where should she hide? It went against her nature to cower somewhere, but she would not disobey Lien.

Ralen. They had forgotten Ralen. Surely Lien would want Ralen to know that Einalem was dead.

Keeping to the shadows, Ardra crept up the steps from the kitchen to the hall. The hall was crowded with warriors and servants.

Where was Ralen?

Then she saw Ywri, a delighted smile on her lovely face. A smile for Ralen. Ralen with his head back. Ralen with a cup to his lips.

"Nay!" Ardra screamed. She flew across the hall and slapped the cup from Ralen's hand.

He staggered at the blow, knocked his injured arm against Ywri's shoulder, then collapsed into his chair, his arm cradled against his chest. Ywri clapped her hands over

her mouth and began to cry. Ardra pushed her aside.

"You must rid yourself of the potion. Now, Ralen," Ardra said, tugging on his arm. He sat as immovable as a statue.

"Potion?" Ralen said.

Ardra dropped to her knees by his side so that she might look him in the eyes. "Please, Ralen. Rid yourself of the potion. 'Tis poison and will kill you."

Ralen leaned back in his chair, a vacant look on his face, a look not unlike Ywri's, who cowered near the chair, weeping.

"Who are you?" he asked.

Inund entered the hall and ran to them.

"What happened?" he asked.

Ardra could say nothing, only point to the goblet on the floor, its seductive contents staining the polished wooden planks.

"Too late, too late," Inund cried. "And Nilrem is off to the forest to find Samoht and Lien. He cannot help us!" He put out a hand as if to touch Ardra, but withdrew it. His eyes, filled with sorrow, must have reflected the torment in her own.

"Can you . . . ?" Ardra nodded her chin toward Ywri.

"I will see to her." Inund took Ywri by the hand and led her away. His cheeks were as wet as the girl's.

Ardra watched a myriad expressions cross Ralen's features while she begged him again to purge himself of the potion.

He shook his head like a great dragon waking from sleep. His fingers, locked on the chair arm, looked like claws.

What was a hard but handsome face took on a malevolent cast. He licked his lips.

She whipped around and impaled the nearest men with her harshest glare. They were Tol's men. "Take him. Purge him. Else he will die! Now!"

Two men rushed forward and tried to snatch Ralen from his seat. He fought them. He held off the two men with just one arm.

His strength was terrible.

Ardra hated what she must do. She reached into the hearth and drew out a length of wood. She doused the stick in a pail of water set nearby in case of fire, then turned and struck a hard blow across the side of Ralen's head.

He wheeled about to face her. For a moment she thought she saw some semblance of recognition in his eyes, but it faded, and he crashed back in his seat, still at last.

As if someone had doused their fears like the flames on the stick, the folk in the hall fell silent.

Ardra ordered them to remain where they were. Even Ralen's and Samoht's men obeyed. She stood over Ralen. If need be, she would hit him again.

A sound drew her attention, but when Ardra turned from the unconscious Ralen, she saw all eyes on the hall entrance.

Lien stood in the doorway. He wore only his buff breeches. His feet were bare. He shuffled forward like an ancient man, his face a stone mask.

Cidre. Ardra looked about. Only Cidre could have such an effect on him.

The goddess stood at the top of the stairs, hands resting on the railing, her face ugly with anger. She stared down at the unconscious Ralen.

Ardra looked back at Lien. His wrists and throat were cuffed in so livid a red, Ardra feared that if she touched him he would bleed. She knew that if he could turn around, his back would bear the knotwork marks, that they would flare from his waist and rise like wings to his shoulders.

Nilrem stood behind Lien with the metal-clad stick. The crowds of slaves and warriors parted to allow the two men to pass.

Ardra knew Cidre must not win. Her evil must not cripple the man she loved. Nor could Ardra allow Ralen to become the fiend Cidre so ardently desired.

Ardra dropped the wood. She met Lien halfway. The pupils of his eyes were so wide, they appeared as solid and

dull a black as the gem around Cidre's neck.

He opened his mouth, but no words came out. A commotion drew her eyes back to the steps.

Cidre was coming. Flanked by two guards, she glided down the stairs. The torches held high by her men gleamed on the gold chains wrapped about her waist, on the Black Eye at her breast. The flames painted streaks of gold in the waterfall of her hair trailing behind her.

Ardra realized that Cidre had garbed herself for some great event. If it was her own mating ceremony, it would not happen, Ardra vowed.

Many in the crowd took a step back from the stairs in fear; Samoht's men placed their hands on their sword hilts.

Finally, the procession stopped at the hearth, with Cidre positioned in front of Lien and beside Ralen. "I am sorry I will not have you, pilgrim. But you had one thing I had not counted on."

When Lien spoke, his voice was low and halting. "Only one?"

"Aye. The help of Venrali's daughter. Did you know she is his child?"

Lien's face did not change, but Ardra felt his questions flow over her like a torrent of water. Why had she not told him? What must he think of her?

"Aye," Ardra said, knowing she must be honest now, before them all. "Venrali is my father. So you see, you already had a consort who had proved himself."

"That is the only reason I allowed him to serve me," Cidre said.

"He ran away from his people, away from retribution. I thought him dead until I saw him here. I had no idea what to do." Although Ardra directed her words to Cidre, they were for Lien.

"And now he is gone again," Cidre said.

"Gone?" The word was a strangled syllable from Lien's lips.

"Gone." Cidre placed a hand on Ralen's shoulder. "He knew he was no longer needed."

Ralen looked like the corpses that turned up in the thawing season from time to time, unfortunate souls who ventured too far upon the ice fields.

Lien took a step toward her, but Cidre lifted her right hand and pointed at him. He swayed in place, one foot forward. "Come no closer, pilgrim. And you"—she swung her arm in Ardra's direction—"stay there or my guards will cut you down."

Lien ignored Cidre. Ardra thought his feet seemed nailed to the floor, but he forced himself forward.

One of Cidre's guards stepped in front of Lien, but the goddess waved the man away with a short laugh. "The pilgrim is harmless. And so is Ardra—as impotent against my will as her father was."

"Ardra." Her name came slowly but clearly from Lien's lips. His hands rose from his sides, fisted, palms up, but so slowly she thought they would never finish their journey toward her.

She knew what he wanted. Nay, *needed*.

"I love you," she said softly, ignoring all the crowds of warriors and slaves who huddled so close, forming an oval much like the arena for the stick fight. She ignored the consequences of telling a pilgrim she loved him. She ignored the consequences of taking sides. "Forgive me that I did not trust you enough to tell you the truth."

Lien's lips trembled; then one corner kicked up in a macabre smile.

She placed her fingertips on his clenched fists, feeling the intense heat, readying herself to absorb the shock that would radiate from the angry lines on his skin.

"No." He spat the word, and she jerked her hands back. "M-my w-waist."

His words drew her eyes to the lacing of his breeches. Not knowing what he wanted, she touched the soft, dark line of hair that disappeared into his breeches. He moaned,

and she knew her touch caused him some physical sensation, whether of pain or healing she knew not.

Silence fell around them. She heard the creak of wood beneath a nearby warrior's boot as he shifted his weight.

"Enough of this nonsense," Cidre said.

Fear of the goddess, her powers, of Ralen's awakening, made Ardra's hand shake, but she kept her eyes on Lien's lips.

He forced out another word. "Lower."

She skimmed her palm down his smooth skin to the lacings on his breeches and lower—and knew what he wanted. She smiled up at him and hurried to jerk the laces open.

"Surprising man," she said, and plucked the small square of white cloth from inside the waist of his breeches.

With her back to Cidre, she opened the cloth and saw the leaf. Glossy. Supple. As fresh as if it had been plucked from the tree that moment. She tucked it into the front of her tunic, and although Lien's whole body urged her to turn and help Ralen, she could not.

Not yet.

She took a huge breath and slapped her hands on Lien's wrists. Hot pain shot through her. It surged up her arms and into her head.

Behind her, Cidre laughed and a murmur rose in the crowd. Ardra hung on, her fingers wrapped around Lien's wrists, her eyes locked on his.

Her knees trembled, her insides churned. The burning sensation flowed from him along her fingers to her arms. A living river of pain. It was fire. It was ice. It traveled straight to her heart.

And beneath it, another current. One as hot as the other, but without pain. His pulse. She felt the running stream of his blood in her fingers, her breasts, her insides.

It aroused her. Here, before them all. Who saw it? Who knew it?

He did.

A flush stained his cheeks—the same flush he wore during lovemaking. A surge as intense as a climax made her cry out and tremble. But she kept her hands in place.

Then his skin began to clear. The stain on his wrists, his throat, faded. With it went the fear, the pain, and the arousal.

"Thank you," was all he said. He turned his hands over, gripped her fingers for a fraction of a moment, then pulled his hands from hers.

She plucked the leaf from the front of her tunic and slit the center vein with her fingernail. "It is the antidote." She handed the leaf back to him.

Their fingertips were stained by a spurt of red fluid that flowed from the opening, but he curled her fingers over the leaf. "I think you should give it to him, Ardra. It probably ought to be someone who is good and brave inside and out."

Ardra took the leaf which dripped its red essence over their fingers like blood.

Cidre laughed when Ardra approached Ralen. "What is this?"

"Step aside," Ardra said.

"There is nothing you can do. 'Tis too late. He has had the potion. And a kiss. He is not the one I wanted, but as Nilrem says, beggars cannot be choosers. It will be soon, very soon. He will awaken. Watch him."

Ardra did. Ralen was no longer unconscious. His eyes watched her with avid curiosity. Before Cidre could stop her, Ardra grasped the thick hair tied at Ralen's nape and jerked his head back.

A gasp ran through the crowd as Ralen stared up at her. His ice-blue eyes looked so cold, she shivered. She raised her hand.

The leaf's blood dripped down the center vein, down the stem, down her fingertips, and onto Ralen's lips. He licked it up as a predator licks the blood of his prey.

Cidre no longer laughed. She raised her hand and cried out, "Enough of this. Take her."

Her guards tore Ardra away from Ralen. Lien growled like a feral animal. He snatched his stick from Nilrem's hand and dealt the closest guard a blow on the wrist.

The man gasped with pain and released her. She used the moment of freedom to smear more of the blood-red fluid across Ralen's lips. Then Cidre ripped the leaf from her hand.

The instant the goddess's fingers touched the leaf, she screamed and dropped it.

The second guard hauled Ardra away from Ralen's side while more of Cidre's men fell on Lien.

He used his stick to hold them off. The swords struck sparks on the metal snake that twined around it. As the crowd formed an oval, coins flew as if it were a simple challenge of warriors, not a fight to the death. And death would come, Ardra knew, her heart in her throat.

She drew her dagger and stabbed her guard's hand. He turned a shocked eye on her as he stared down at his bloody hand. Yet he did not relinquish his grip.

With little thought, she reached across the man's body and pulled the longer, sharper dagger from his belt. As she drew the blade from its sheath, she dragged it along the front of his tunic.

He shrieked and released her. Ardra turned on Cidre— the source of all the evil. "Call them off," she ordered as two more guards surrounded Lien, looking for their chance.

"Never. You will both die here."

Men swamped Ardra from behind. Cidre's men. One struck her a sharp blow on the chin and another hoisted her into his arms.

Lien parried the guards' blows. Small skirmishes broke out all around him as men chose sides. Women fled to the upper levels.

He fought as he never had before, spurred on, by the sight of a guard running from the hall with Ardra in his arms.

With all his strength Lien hurled his stick. It tangled the man's feet, and with Ardra in his arms, the guard could not save himself. He fell, and Ardra scrambled from his grip.

She grinned back at Lien and stomped on the guard's hand when he went for his sword. In moments, Ardra had the guard's sword in one hand and the snake-wrapped stick in the other.

Lien ran to meet her.

"Lace those or you will lose them," she pointed out.

He glanced down and grinned. He quickly laced up his pants and took his stick.

"Cidre!" Nilrem shouted from where he stood atop a table. He pointed, and Lien saw that Cidre had made her way outside and was running across the courtyard.

"Damn. Let's go after her." Together they ran into the courtyard, but they were a moment too late.

Cidre had made it through the entrance, and the huge drawbridge was closing behind her. When they reached the gate, they saw a guard standing there, grinning. Next to him was a severed rope—a rope as thick as a man's thigh, a rope that worked the gears to raise the bridge. There was now no hope of opening it without an army of help.

"We could go up," Ardra said, pointing to a winding staircase against the wall.

"No, you will not," the guard said and raised his sword.

"Yeah, Ardra. We don't have a chance with this guy." Lien pretended to turn away, then swung back and brought his stick down on the man's shoulder. The guard dropped like a stone.

"Well done," she said, and grabbed Lien's hand.

Moments later, they stood on the fortress wall. Behind them, warriors and servants poured into the courtyard. Lien gripped his stick until his hand ached. They were too

late. Cidre would escape into the woods, and who knew what evil she'd cause somewhere else?

"Stop!" he called after the goddess, feeling as ineffectual as an unarmed slave against a warrior.

Cidre did stop, but not in obedience to his command. She turned at the edge of the woods and raised her arms. Her sleeves fell back, and her arms looked very white against the dark backdrop of the trees. She extended her hands to the heavens. Sunlight glinted off the Black Eye on her chest.

Her voice came clearly across the open ground, carried like a voice over water. "By all that is within me, all the sacred charges given me by my mother, I call down the Darkness."

An icy wind rose. It buffeted them where they stood, kicked up white caps on the lake, sent the clouds racing across the angry sky.

A rustle as of thousands of leaves stirring came from the castle walls.

Women and children, warriors and slaves, screamed as the vines shifted, heaved, and raised their flowered heads.

"Lien!" Ardra cried. She gripped his arm as the vines near her feet seethed.

"Sweet heaven," he whispered as all around them vines shimmered and shifted and metamorphosed into thousands of snakes.

Some were as thin as vipers and some as thick as rattlers. They swarmed down the walls toward the hapless slaves and warriors. The vines on the outside walls slithered up and over the ramparts, across Lien's bare feet and Ardra's boots—then into the courtyard. They were like a tide of water over sand. More snakes poured from the hall, and Lien knew they were from the attic.

He felt a surge of anger. It flooded his mouth, rushed through his veins like acid. It filled his ears with such a roar, he no longer heard the screams of the people or the swish of the reptiles pursuing them with icy zeal.

He raised his stick. He pointed to the serpents and shouted, "Stop!"

Silence fell. He felt dizzy. Wasps buzzed inside his head. His arm trembled. His mind reeled at the sight of hundreds, perhaps thousands of snakes poised at his command.

Cidre shrieked and cried out for the Darkness to descend. Lien whipped around and pointed his stick at her.

The snakes stirred. They swarmed in a tide of hissing green back over the walls and across the clearing.

Cidre stood her ground, her hands aloft, her voice raised in appeal to some power which Lien knew had abandoned her. The undulating green wave reached her.

It swept over her in moments. And like the tide, the reptiles receded en masse when their work was done. Not to the fortress, but where he pointed his stick—into the lake.

When the silver surface of the lake was once again as smooth as glass, Lien set the tip of his stick with a thump on the stone wall.

Ardra sagged against him. "You are magic," she said, entwining her fingers with his.

"I don't believe in magic." He squeezed her fingers.

"Neither do I."

Chapter Twenty-eight

Lien sat in a wide wooden tub in the kitchen garden. He bathed as quickly as he could. The air had grown cold, though the water Inund had brought had been almost too hot to sit in.

He laced up a pair of breeches that Ralen had provided. Black leather Tolemac warrior breeches. He did not put on the tunic that went with it. Instead he put on a leather tunic given him by Inund. One donated by the metalsmith who'd made his snake-stick.

It was not pilgrim garb. It left his arms bare. He picked up the other object the metalsmith had made, a two-headed viper earring, a mini-reminder in case anyone missed his tattoo.

Women scurried away from him when he passed through the kitchen. He merely smiled and lifted his stick, as he would if he wore a hat and was greeting the old lady who sold newspapers in the shop next door to his on the board-walk in Ocean City.

Once in the hall, he stood just inside the door. He ignored the murmurs rising around him.

Ann Lawrence

He was not too late. Ardra stood at the fore of the hall. Her hair was braided into a long golden rope down her back, and she looked the perfect warrior woman in her snug breeches and simple tunic. The silver disk pendant lay on her breast.

His whole body ached with a need to go to her and offer his support. But he remained where he was. She didn't need him. She had more than enough guts to take care of herself.

Einalem's body had been laid out on the head table, covered by a turquoise and gold cloth. Samoht sat near his sister, his head down, looking dazed. Ralen flanked Nilrem. The warrior looked weary and far older than he had a day or two before.

Nilrem saw Lien, gave a nod, and then stood up. "For those who have just arrived"—Lien knew the wise man spoke to him—"we were discussing whether it is time for Ardra to take her rightful place. Her eight days of mourning are over, but she failed to secure the vial. It is a small point, but an important one. Should Ardra rule?"

"Never," Samoht said. He roused himself a bit, sat a little straighter in his place. "The Fortress of Ravens needs a warrior. A woman cannot rule such a place. A man must stand beside her at the very least. No one will do so now—not now that her father is known to be alive somewhere."

"Any man would be honored to serve Ardra," Ralen said.

Ardra kept her face serene. She felt a swelling of pride at Ralen's words, but she tamped it down. Pride would be misplaced. She had much to prove before the council would accept her without condition. Any concession from Samoht would be a victory.

"However," Ralen continued, "I agree that Ardra needs a warrior to stand with her."

"Who will that be?" Samoht asked. He waved a hand. "Who would dare?"

"Whoever it is, he must choose the role himself," Nilrem said.

Hope drained from Ardra. There was no one to take the place beside her, and surely no man worthy enough to suit Samoht.

"I will stand with her," a Tolemac warrior called out.

Lien watched the warrior stride confidently to the dais, his hand on the hilt of his sword. It was the man who had challenged Samoht at the feast, and Lien felt a hot surge of jealousy.

"I will," called out another. Soon there was a cacophony of voices all vying to be heard and a line of men behind the first warrior.

Ardra stared at the line of men in consternation. So many? She watched a myriad emotions play over Samoht's face as his men joined the line.

A sound, a rap of metal on wood, caused everyone to fall silent. It was a small sound, but it had the same effect as if the fortress's sonorous bell had tolled.

The crowd opened up, and Lien walked down the hall. He was garbed all in black, his pilgrim robes gone. He was beautiful. Her heart jerked as if a viper had struck her.

She watched him come, his snake-stick in his hand. He did not lean on it. It was now as much a part of him as Ralen's sword was a part of who he was.

"I'll stand with Ardra," Lien said.

Something tightened and coiled within her.

"Never," Samoht said.

"Why not?" Lien asked. He sounded so casual—as if he wanted to know why the meal was not on the table, not whether he could be her champion. "I'm willing, I've proved myself, as has Ardra." Then his voice grew cold and hard. "She's jumped through enough hoops for you."

"You are not a warrior," Samoht said.

"That problem is easily solved," Nilrem said.

"How?" Samoht and Ralen spoke at the same time.

The wiseman slapped his hands on the table. "Come. We all know it takes but two councilors to decree a man a warrior."

Samoht stood up. "And there are two councilors here. Ralen, acting in Tol's place, is one. But the other is *me*."

"It is your place to make this decision," Ralen said to Samoht. "I will stand firmly on Lien's side that he be decreed a warrior, but as head councilor, you must decide."

Samoht walked around the long table. He stood by Einalem's body. He touched the cloth that draped her form and murmured something only she could hear. Then the high councilor turned to the crowded hall. He shifted his shoulders and raised his head. Something of his old manner returned as he looked over the crowd.

"Let it be so," he said. "Lien has earned the right to stand for Ardra."

The ceremony was simple and quick. Samoht asked Lien if he was willing to give his life for the people of the Fortress of Ravens.

Lien answered with a truth that a few weeks ago he'd have laughed aloud to hear. "I will," he said. It felt like a marriage ceremony, solemn, but quickly done, the results to last a lifetime.

Three silver rings were placed around his arm. A common blacksmith placed a strip of leather under them and moments later touched a hot iron to them, sealing them over his tattoo.

When Lien rose from his knees, Samoht sat down and turned toward his sister, everyone else forgotten.

Tears ran down Ardra's cheeks, but no one would see them as a sign of weakness.

She kissed her fingertips, then touched the metal arm rings. Heat swirled along his flesh, along the coiled snake beneath the rings—not a bad heat, but a warmth he imagined was going to be a part of how they were connected from now on.

Nilrem said, "Lien, you have assumed great responsibility today."

"And what of Samoht?" Ralen asked. "There must be more than just a burial today. Resolutions need to be made, penance paid."

Nilrem walked to where Samoht sat, head bowed, his fingers holding the hem of Einalem's drape. The wiseman held out the simple robe that had been Lien's until that morning.

"Put on this robe, Samoht. Return with me to Hart Fell and contemplate your life and future. Take the next conjunction to plan what amends you will make for seeking power at the expense of those who trusted you."

Samoht stood up and stared at the robe in Nilrem's hand. He nodded and took the garment.

"All's well that ends well," Nilrem said.

Everyone broke up into small groups. Lien followed the old man to a table of food laid out for the evening meal. Lien tossed Nilrem an apple. "So, how long have you been coming and going into the game?"

Nilrem took a bite of the fruit. "How did you know?"

"All the little sayings. So, how long?"

The old man glanced around. "I came by accident years ago. A wiseman on Hart Fell took me in. He taught me to love these people and how to help them without—shall we say—interfering in their natural progress. When he died, I took his place."

"Do you miss our world?" Lien asked, one eye on Ardra, who moved about the hall in regal elegance despite her humble garb.

"In truth," Nilrem whispered, "now and then. Once I figured out how to come and go, I sometimes made a trip back to recharge my batteries. The people accept my absences because my mentor used to go on what he called a 'wander' and be gone for days of contemplation in the wilderness."

"And where do you go? Club Med?" Lien quipped.

"Nay!" Nilrem said indignantly. "The Bodleian Library at Oxford."

Ardra found Lien standing on the shore of the lake. The four orbs poured their light onto the glassy surface.

"I'm still marveling that all those snakes are—"

"Gone," she finished. They looked back at the bare walls of the fortress. "There are some around here still, I'm sure. We have them at the fortress. They dwell in the crevasses of the ice."

"Ralen will burn the fortress at dawn. Did you know that? He wants the evilness of Cidre's tree destroyed."

"Aye. He told me. I have offered to take all who wish back to the fortress with us."

"Us," he said.

Ardra licked her lips. They were suddenly dry. "Are you sure you can make my fortress your home?"

He pulled her into his arms. "I'm sure. I think I've learned a simple truth: Home is where the heart is."

She put her arms around his neck. "I thought you would hate me for deceiving you about my father."

He shook his head. "I think you were in an untenable position. You'd grieved for him, mourned who he once was, and then arrived here to find him alive and plotting to use your son. I don't blame you for not knowing whom to trust with the information. I certainly didn't make you feel as if I was here for the long haul."

"Are you? Here for the long haul?"

"If you want me." His voice got a bit husky. "I think you've got my heart all wrapped up."

"Oh, Lien. I cannot imagine my life without you."

"Or I without you. What do you say to a lifemating?"

She found a lump in her throat. "Now? Here?"

"Is that legal?" he asked. He tipped his head and glanced around. His eyes were black in the shining orb-glow, but not the dead black of Cidre's pendant, a sparkling black, alive and rich.

"What do you mean, legal?" she asked. "A lifemating is but a few words, spoken before witnesses."

"Then where do we find the witnesses?"

Ardra shook her head. "That part is easy. We will ask Ralen and Nilrem to stand for us in the morning, if you like. But that is just a formality. We can say the words to each other right here . . . now . . . and it will be so. We will be mated for life. If"—she ducked her head—"if we seal the vows with copulation."

He kissed her forehead. "You don't have to whisper. And I prefer to refer to it as lovemaking." He folded her in a fierce embrace. "What are the words we need to say?"

"Do you wish to be my lifemate? Now and forever?"

He kissed her nose. "I do. I told you so. Now what words do I say?"

She ducked her head and bit her lips. "Those are the words, Lien. 'Do you wish to be my lifemate? Now and forever?' "

He smiled and laughed. "I do." Then he repeated the question for her, and she answered. The words were barely out of her mouth before he snatched her up in his arms.

"It is good to start our time together with laughter." She stroked her fingers along his lips. "Kiss me."

The kiss lasted so long, she thought she might expire of the joy of it. The taste of him was both a promise and a vow. Unbidden, tears ran down her cheeks. Somehow she found herself on her back with her breeches unlaced.

His lips were hungry on her breast, then her belly.

"I want you so," she said, pushing back the leather jerkin from his shoulders. He looked up.

"You are warm. Mine. So strong." She leaned forward and plucked at the laces on his breeches.

"Not now, Ardra," he said, clamping his hand on her wrist.

"Aye. Now. Now." She slid her hand further into the opening.

357

"Not now." He wrenched from her grasp, rolled away, and came up on his knees. He snatched a serpent from the grass, just inches away. "Not now means not now."

The snake was as long as his arm, its red tongue flickering back and forth.

"I still want you," she whispered. "And now would still be nice."

He tossed the serpent on the ground and pointed at it. "Go," he commanded, and when the snake obeyed, he burst into laughter. "I think we'll have to adjust to snakes as part of our life."

She snapped her fingers—twice. And smiled.

The small fire she'd lit inside him flared hot. "So you remembered that, did you? You want me, do you? Right now?"

"Come." She stood up and held out her hand.

"I intend to," he said softly, entwining his fingers with hers.

She led him deep into the orchard, to a spot filled with purple shadows and bright spots of blue-green moonlight. The grass was cool and soft to his feet when he took off his boots.

Ardra jerked her tunic over her head, shoved her breeches down, and tossed them aside. Then she stood still, her hands lightly covering her breasts. She was an ivory column of warm, sweet woman, touched with gold and dusky shadows.

"I think I like watching you take down your pants as much as I liked watching you raise your skirt," he said.

"And I like watching you, too, Lien." She tipped her head.

He found that her intent gaze inflamed him. Instead of ripping off his clothes, he pulled them off slowly, enjoying her quickened breathing. She dropped her hands. Her nipples were tight, dark peaks. The moonlight silvered some marks on the rise of her breasts—marks of motherhood.

"You know," he said, "I was an only child. Until this moment, I'd forgotten how much I used to hope I'd have a home full of kids when I grew up."

She raised her arms and slowly unbraided her hair, her gaze firmly fixed on his groin. "You are very grown-up, Lien."

He combed his fingers through the silk of her long hair. "I love how you smell and taste and think and talk."

"That is a great deal of love, Lien." She captured his hand and placed it on her breast. "I hope to be worthy of it all."

"Let's make some kids." He kissed the edge of her mouth. He thumbed the hard peak of her breast. Then he wanted her so badly, he knew he could not go slowly and gently. He put his arms around her and pulled her to the ground.

She fell back with equal eagerness, wrapped her legs about his hips, and cried out loud when he surged into her.

He gasped and fought for control, felt her nails dig into his back, and knew it was a battle he'd lose.

Ardra held him as tightly as she could. His ear was by her mouth. She took his earlobe between her teeth, gripped the viper earring, and tugged. He moaned and pushed forward—to her heart—to the very center of her being.

Tears filled her eyes. Then his mouth covered hers. She moved her tongue against his, tasted him, reveled in the hard muscles under her hands, the smooth, fluid motion of his body.

A hot coil of need burst open. It shot down her arms and legs. She held on to him, head back, every muscle of her body quivering. He surged deeper when she cried out and held still. She used him as an anchor, battering the tide of her climax against him.

Then she moaned and let out her breath, not realizing she had held it so tightly in her chest. He pushed up on his hands, continued to thrust within her, eyes closed.

Ann Lawrence

She watched his face, her hands on his shoulders, her thighs still quivering against his hips. She stared at the sight of their joining and watched his chain with its impossible glass roses swing back and forth with every move of his hips.

He drew out, then pushed in with a slowness that made her want to scream. Then he groaned, opened his eyes a brief instant, and dropped his head.

His mouth was hot and wet on her throat as he poured forth his essence.

They lay on their backs, fingers entwined, and watched the sky lighten through the trees. They talked of her father. Of Tol. Of her child. And their future children.

Then he wanted her again.

How warm her lips were on his neck, his shoulder, her teeth a counterpoint to the gentle sweeps of her tongue. He lifted her onto his hips, guided himself into the slick, wet heat of her.

"I want to watch your face—every mood, every expression." He shifted his hips.

Her eyes widened. She licked her finger, drew it down her breast, and touched the artwork on his arm. A thunderbolt of ecstasy ran through him, purely visceral, completely unexpected, as strong as any orgasm. He arched involuntarily, bucked against her.

Her hair fell in a glorious tumbling mass of heavy silk that caressed his chest and arms.

He gripped her bottom, raised and lowered her, brought himself to the edge, but held it off for her.

She gasped. Someone moaned—him.

When he reached up to trace her face, she tongued his palm, and a spasm of heat took hold of him and squeezed like a fist.

He would never tire of her golden eyes, her full lips, her nipples tipped with coral. "I love everything about you," he managed before he came.

Then he couldn't talk. He could only bury his face against her and hang on.

She slept in his arms, wrapped in her tunic. Her lips were slightly open, her breath feathering the skin of his arm—an arm with three silver rings. Rings that somehow fit well with the coils of his tattoo.

He stroked her hair and looked up at the night sky. Four strange moons stood like sentinels overhead, completely alien to his world.

"Are you missing your home?" she asked.

"No. Just thinking that one day I'll have to let Gwen know I'm all right."

She sat up and hugged her knees. "I know I will never truly understand how you appeared just when I needed you, but I suspect it was not from across the ice fields."

"I don't think it was—but I don't really know it wasn't, either."

"Will you come back?"

"Come back?"

"Aye, when you go to tell Gwen you are fine. Will you return to me?"

"Yes. Trust me. I'll never leave you." He lifted her chin and forced her to look at him. "I just lifemated myself to you, pledged myself to be a warrior at your side. We probably made a little Ardra just now, I'm not going anywhere."

"It was beautiful, having you inside me, part of me," she whispered. "Was it like . . . a warm, snug glove?"

"Yes. For the first time, the glove was truly a perfect fit."

She rubbed her thumb on his lower lip. "Fit me again."

His hand moved in a languid exploration from her throat to her knee. "With pleasure."

She knew what would happen now when he slid between her thighs. The image of him as he had looked standing on

the ramparts, his stick raised, sent a fireball of sensation through her, like lightning striking her.

But it was her name on his lips as much as his manhood sliding inside her that sent her over the edge.

The abyss was deep, and filled with roiling, hot shards of pleasure. He held her tightly, murmured her name, helped her to ride the pleasure by pushing hard against her.

They lay still again, connected, slick, wet, panting.

"I hope we made a child," she said.

"A daughter who looks just like you. Someone for your son to protect."

"Protect? Nay, stand beside and guide."

He pulled out of her. She rolled to her side and he fitted himself around her, her back against his chest. "Whatever makes you happy."

"Do you mean that?"

"Sure. I'll sit on a wiseman's bench somewhere in the sun while you do whatever it is you do while ruling a fortress."

Ardra smiled at the thought. "You wanted to be a teacher, Lien. You could do that, you know. My people need someone strong to teach them." She folded her arms over his and locked fingers with him. She snuggled her bottom against him and smiled a little when he groaned. "When we slept, it was my first moment of complete peace. It was being here in your arms, loved and wanted, that brought me peace."

Lien whispered against her hair. Just her name. But it was enough.

Inund teased them for missing the morning meal. And Ralen, who along with Nilrem witnessed their vows, snapped that everyone needed to lend a hand if the fortress was to be emptied before dark.

Lien admired everything about Ardra as she organized Ralen right out of a job.

But it was past sunset when they stood on the lakeshore and stared up at the Fortress of Darkness. No torches gleamed from the towers. He imagined he could smell the rotting attic room, though he knew it was just his imagination.

He took Ardra's hand. She was trembling, and he knew that what she was about to do caused her pain. Among the many bundles she had packed, she had placed a small square of paper with a few words from Deleh, words that informed Ardra Deleh was running off with Venrali. They were heading for warmer climes, the note said. Deleh didn't want to be a burden, and Venrali so reminded her of Tol.

Lien figured Venrali would resurface one day.

"We should find out what happened to the two sons your father had," Lien said to distract her. "If they were sold, we should try to buy them back and raise them."

She smiled up at him. Desire flicked him like a sharp whip—or a viper's tail, he thought with an inner smile. How had he ever thought her cold?

"You are constantly surprising me. Once, you would not have wanted such responsibility."

"I seem to keep finding it, though, don't I?"

Nilrem met them in the empty courtyard with a burning torch. "I believe it is an omen that I have counted eight piles of wood at the base of this fortress."

"Why an omen?" Lien asked.

Ardra answered. "When we met on Hart Fell, Lien, I was practicing an ancient ritual. One of beginnings. It is a ritual of the old ways, the old gods, but I was desperate for help from anywhere. It is a practice for each new conjunction. But this one was said to bring special good fortune with it as it was the first time in fifty conjunctions when the sun would remain in the sky as the night orbs lined up."

"It is an ancient augury of good," Nilrem said.

Ann Lawrence

Lien watched Ardra look up at the sky, now deep purple. The scent of the orchard drifted in the light winds. It was a fresh scent. Not rotting or evil.

"I had extinguished my fire as old women might have done in ancient days, sifting dirt on the hearth to end the flames," she said. "Just when the perfect moment arrived, with all the orbs in the sky at once, I was to have lighted eight candles and let them burn down to restart the fire. I never finished."

"The outcasts attacked you," Lien said. He placed his hand on her shoulder and squeezed.

"And you appeared." She kissed his fingers.

"Complete the ritual." Nilrem handed Ardra the flaming torch.

Lien walked at her side as she moved around the base of the fortress walls, stopping eight times to touch her flame to the wood.

Together they walked, hand in hand, back to the people gathered on the lakeshore. The wind kicked up. It tossed her skirt in a sharp snap against her legs and whipped errant strands of her braid against her cheeks. But she didn't look away from the burning building. She watched, her face touched with gold in the setting Tolemac sun, her hand in his.

Epilogue

Gwen Marlowe unlocked the door of Virtual Heaven and wheeled the baby stroller to the service counter. Baby Bob was fast asleep. A rare happening on any day.

She liked to do the bills after church on Sundays. It was a peaceful time. She could have the shop to herself until noon.

"How's it going?" she asked the sleeping infant. "Do you think Natalie and Daddy will save Mommy some pizza?"

Not really expecting an answer, just as she was not really expecting Vad to save her any pizza—nursing and pepperoni did *not* go together, in Vad's opinion—she rolled the stroller with one hand and sorted bills with the other.

A familiar noise penetrated her attention. "Now, how long has that been on?" She walked through the shop to the game booth. When she flipped on the lights, she remembered another time when the game had been on unexpectedly. Her heart began to pound.

The game booth was empty. Then a glitter caught her eye. Hanging from the railing that enclosed the control platform, and looped in the annoying way Neil always

looped his ties on her desk lamp, was a long silver chain with a pendant dangling from the end.

She touched the pendant not believing what she saw.

It was real. It was a silver disk, etched with a pattern she knew was really a map through a labyrinth. But instead of the chunk of amber she knew should be at its center, there was a glass rose—from one of the earrings Neil had said his grandfather made at the Millville glassworks.

She unhooked the pendant and laughed. "God bless you both," she said and turned off the game.

Virtual Desire
Ann Lawrence

His silver-blond hair blows back from his magnificent face. His black leather breeches hug every inch of his well-muscled thighs. He is every woman's fantasy; he is the virtual reality game hero Vad. And Gwen Marlowe finds him snoring away in her video game shop.

She knows he must be a wacky wargamer out to win the Tolemac warrior look-alike contest. But the passion he ignites in her is all too real. Swept into his world of ice fields and formidable fortresses, Gwen realizes Vad is not playing games. On a quest to clear his name and secure peace in his land, he and Gwen must forge a bond strong enough to straddle two worlds. A union built not on virtual desire, but on true love.

___52393-0 $5.99 US/$6.99 CAN

Virtual Heaven
Ann Lawrence

The warrior looms over her. His leather jerkin, open to his waist, reveals a bounty of chest muscles and a corrugation of abdominals. Maggie O'Brien's gaze jumps from his belt buckle to his jewel-encrusted boot knife, avoiding the obvious indications of a man well-endowed. Too bad he is just a poster advertising a virtual reality game. Maggie has always thought such male perfection can exist only in fantasies like *Tolemac Wars*. But then the game takes on a life of its own, and she finds herself face-to-face with her perfect hero. Now it will be up to her to save his life when danger threatens, to gentle his warrior's heart, to forge a new reality they both can share.

___52307-8 $5.99 US/$6.99 CAN

Ann Lawrence
Lord Of The Mist

As he kneels in the darkened chapel by his wife's lifeless body, he knows the babe she has birthed cannot be his. Then the scent of spring—blossoms, wet leaves, damp earth—precedes an alluring woman into the chapel. As she honors his dead wife with garlands, she seems to bring him fresh hope, just as she nourishes the little girl his wife has left behind.

Even though this woman is not his, can it be wrong to reach out for life, for love? He cannot deny his longing for her lush kiss, cannot ignore her urge to turn away from yesterday's sorrows and embrace tomorrow's sweetness.

Those Baby Blues

SHERIDON SMYTHE

Hadleigh Charmaine feels as though she has been cast in a made-for-TV movie. The infant she took home from the hospital is not her biological child, and the man who has been raising her real daughter is Treet Miller, a film star. But when his sizzling baby blues settle on her, the single mother refuses to be hoodwinked—even if he makes her shiver with desire.

Treet knows he's found the role of a lifetime: father to two beautiful daughters and husband to one gorgeous wife. Now he just has to convince Hadleigh that in each other's arms they have the best shot at happiness. He plans to woo her with old-fashioned charm and a lot of pillow talk, until she understands that their story can have a Hollywood ending.

SPIRIT OF THE MIST
JANEEN O'KERRY

An early summer storm rages off the coast of western Ireland, and Muriel watches. From inside the protective walls of Dun Farraige, she can see nothing, yet her water mirror shows all. The moonlight reveals the face of a man—one struggling to overcome the sea.

He is an exile, of course. By clan law, exiles are to be made slaves. Yet something ennobles this man. The stranger's face makes Muriel yearn for both his safety and his freedom. She, who was raised as the daughter of a nobleman, has a terrible secret. And she can't help but believe that this handsome visitor—swaddled in mist and delivered to the rain-swept shores beneath her Dun—will be her salvation.

JANEEN O'KERRY

SISTER
OF THE
MOON

In the sylvan glens of Eire, the Sidhe reign supreme. The fair folk they are: fairies, thieves, changeling-bearers, tricksters. Their feet make no sound as they traipse through ancient forests, their mouths no noise as they weave their moonlight spells. And so Men have learned to fear them. But the Folk are dying. Their hunting grounds are overrun, their bronze swords no match for Man's cold iron. Scahta, their queen, is helpless to act. Her people need a king. And on Samhain Eve, she finds one. Though he is raw and untrained, she sees in Anlon the soul of nobility. Yet he is a Man. He will have to pass many tests to win her love. At the fires of Beltane he must prove himself her husband—and for the salvation of the Sidhe he must make himself a king.

_52466-X $5.50 US/$6.50 CAN

Dorchester Publishing Co., Inc.
P.O. Box 6640
Wayne, PA 19087-8640

Please add $2.50 for shipping and handling for the first book and $.75 for each book thereafter. NY, and PA residents, please add appropriate sales tax. No cash, stamps, or C.O.D.s. All orders shipped within 6 weeks via postal service book rate.
Canadian orders require $2.00 extra postage and must be paid in U.S. dollars through a U.S. banking facility.

Name _____
Address _____
City_____ State_____ Zip_____
I have enclosed $_____ in payment for the checked book(s).
Payment <u>must</u> accompany all orders. ☐ Please send a free catalog.
CHECK OUT OUR WEBSITE! www.dorchesterpub.com

DOMINION
MELANIE JACKSON

When the Great One gifts Domitien with love, it is not simply for a lifetime. Yet in his first incarnation, his wife and unborn child are murdered, and Dom swears never again to feel such pain. When Death comes, he goes willingly. The Creator sends him back to Earth, to learn love in another body. Yet life after life, Dom refuses. Whatever body she wears, he vows to have his true love back. He will explain why her dreams are haunted by glimpses of his face, aching remembrances of his lips. He will protect her from the enemy he failed to destroy so many years before. And he will chase her through the ages to do so. This time, their love will rule.

MORE PRAISE FOR
AWARD-WINNER ANN LAWRENCE!

LORD OF THE MIST
*A *Romantic Times* Top Pick
"A stunning portrait of the dangers of loyalty and the price
of illicit love. . . . You won't sleep until you finish reading!"
—*Romantic Times*

"Passions run high and bedrooms steam with sensual tension.
Lord of the Mist is a superbly written piece of fiction!"
—*Romance Reviews Today*

"Each new twist and turn of this quicksand journey
will surprise and amaze you. Don't miss this story from
an exciting voice in romance."
—*Old Book Barn Gazette*

LORD OF THE KEEP
"Ann Lawrence has penned a thrilling and unusual novel
in *Lord of the Keep*. This well-detailed plot paired with the
excellent historical details and characterizations makes
Lord of the Keep a definite keeper in my opinion."
—*CompuServe Romance Reviews*

"*Lord of the Keep* is a medieval reader's dream that
offers strong lead characters, a memorable romance,
steamy sensuality and enough adventure to keep you
spellbound—a definite keeper."
—*Bell, Book and Candle*

"Ms. Lawrence has created some very beautiful word
pictures that I don't think I will ever forget. I am just
hoping to see more books spin off from this enthralling
story. . . . Ms. Lawrence is definitely an author to watch
as she goes up the spiral staircase to romance heaven."
—*The Belles & Beaux of Romance*